CUTTER (POLICE AND FIRE: OPERATION ALPHA)

BADGES OF THE CAPITAL, BOOK TWO

MISHA BLAKE

Dear Readers,

Welcome to the Police and Fire: Operation Alpha Fan-Fiction world!

If you are new to this amazing world, in a nutshell the author wrote a story using one or more of my characters in it. Sometimes that character has a major role in the story, and other times they are only mentioned briefly. This is perfectly legal and allowable because they are going through Aces Press to publish the story.

This book is entirely the work of the author who wrote it. While I might have assisted with brainstorming and other ideas about which of my characters to use, I didn't have any part in the process or writing or editing the story.

I'm proud and excited that so many authors loved my characters enough that they wanted to write them into their own story. Thank you for supporting them, and me!

READ ON!
   Xoxo
   Susan Stoker

To love that never yields.

"A successful marriage requires falling in love many times, always with the same person."

—Mignon McLaughlin

PART I
THE FIGHT FOR LIFE

ENSLEY

Three months ago

I see it.

In the reflection.

Deep in that image that stares back at us from the mirror nailed to the wall.

There are still echoes of *me*.

Fragments of *him*.

Traces of *us*.

Flecks of the woman I once was.

Pieces of the man he once was.

The reverberations of what we used to be, of what we had. Together. As couple. As marriage. They are there. They have to still be there… Don't they?

My eyes close for a tick just as behind the shut lids an image dances. A memory. A recollection of this same scene. Of us inside this very bathroom. But apart from the similarity of the scenery and the same two people in it, there's no other nexus between the instant playing behind my eyelids and the present one. Absolutely none. Because everything is different. So dissimilar because in front of my closed eyes develops a movie of what we used to be. Of how he used to be. Of how stupidly happy I used to be.

And for a moment I allow myself to let that tick play. Maybe because I'm a glutton for punishment. Or maybe, just maybe, because I crave and miss them so much that I want to live those instances again, even just as a memory.

A cheeky, wide smile tips my lips when I stare in the mirror and I steal a glimpse of the man beside me. Conscious of my gawking, he gives me a sideways glance and a heart-racing, body-melting, lady bits-tingling grin with one of the corners tipped upward in his signature, lopsided smirk that always has the desired effect—turning me into a puddle of lust and molten desire. But it isn't until he steps behind me and envelops me with his thick, bulging arms covered almost entirely in dark ink that I allow myself to become putty in his embrace.

Just as immediately thereafter, my body trembles against his hard one. It shudders with anticipation. A foresight vowed by his lingering gaze while deep, melted dark chocolate eyes roam over my body in the mirror, setting the white tank top I wear on fire with his glance alone. Or so it seems since I suddenly feel so bare before him because the white top can certainly not conceal the pebbled nipples that pierce the cotton fabric as though they're two bullets. It is a reaction that draws a smirk full of satisfaction from the man behind me.

In tandem with his gaze, his hands wander. One glides up my body, his massive palm swathing one of my tender breasts. That touch causes me to throw back my head and lean it against his shoulder while a little mewl tumbles past my lips.

His other hand slides down. It moves past the hem of the white tank top, dusts the inch of exposed skin on my flat stomach, brushes past the waistband of my black panties, and stops at the junction between my legs, cupping my sex as though he has full ownership over it.

Truth be told, he does. There has never been another man who claimed me body and soul, heart and flesh. There will never be another because Mason Carter is the love of my life. My one true love. My one and only.

He might not have been my first kiss—he hasn't even been my second—but he made damn sure to erase even the smallest recollection of the guys who I got kissed by before him. After Mason's lips touched mine for the very first time, experiencing the full potency of his kissing, I have been doomed and forever an addict to Mason Carter's mouth, to his taste and his scent.

Simply put, I am addicted to him.

Something I'm not ashamed to admit because he is just as much of an addict to me.

My twenty-first birthday was the very day when Mason mercilessly fucked me up for any other guy after he lost his—until then—perfectly mastered self-restraint and kissed me for the first time. He kissed me with sheer taking and urgency, and the first instant the tip of his tongue stroked my lips forcing them apart before it thrusted into my mouth, he staked his claim on me unforgivingly.

Granted, that happened because my mother kept pushing his buttons as she—not so discreetly—pledged to take me to a strip club for my birthday and his self-imposed control snapped loose at the thought of me around another man.

Angeline Walker—a through and through romantic and a romance author—said it because she had enough of watching her daughter allow the guy she was madly in love with to slip through her fingers. That as much as she had enough of watching the very same guy deny what he truly felt. In full disclosure, my mother would have really taken me to a strip club and even pair me up with a stripper if that's what it had taken to make Mason pull his head out of his ass.

Honestly, that was the first time I've seen Mason lose his shit and the self-control he had mastered down to a T. The first time he also kissed the living life out of me. But that night we didn't stop at just kissing. That very night I gave myself to him. The very same night when I understood why I didn't go all the way with either of my previous boyfriends. Because Mason was always meant to be my first. Even if that has meant witnessing the panic that settled inside of him in the early hours of the morning when the magic of the moment wore off. After he made love to me and couldn't keep his hands off me the entire night, he told me that what happened had been a mistake.

It had been a lie.

One he told himself for the year that came thereafter. A lie he kept repeating to himself as though that would undo the best night of our lives.

For an entire year, he lived a deception by telling himself that night's events have been a mistake. He pushed me away. He turned down all my blatant advances. He shut down all my flirting. He tried to keep his distance.

Yet, I still pursued him.

I knew what I wanted. I knew who I wanted, so I kept pushing and pushing. I knew it will only be a matter of time until his self-imposed restraint will crack because I knew he wanted me too. Because what had me not give up on him and us throughout that year was what I saw in his eyes when they would meet mine. What had me continue my pursuit of him was the way he'd steal glances at me when he thought nobody saw him. It has all been down to how his chocolate brown eyes would do the talking, begging me not to give up.

Everything changed the day of his graduation from the fire academy, though. During the ceremony, I was asked to go up and pin his badge. Something I was utterly shocked by, not knowing he has chosen me to be the one to pin the badge for him. Once I did it and before everyone who was present, he rested a hand on my back and the other on the nape of my neck. Without an ounce of hesitation, he smashed his mouth against mine, earning laughs, aww, and whistles from all the recruits, academy personnel, and families.

"Miña," he whispers in my ear, bringing me back from the memory while confirming exactly my previous assumption as he calls me his in Galician. "Ensley Carter, you are so fucking mine every inch of your body knows it."

"Always," I breathe out, meeting his captivatingly entrancing dark orbs in the reflection.

They are darker than usual.

It is as though they fade into black. An abyss I'd happily and help-lessly fall into. I'd throw myself without a parachute into that dark depth in his eyes, damned be the consequences of what's waiting for me on the other side.

"Always yours, Mason."

My hand raises and my fingers comb through his dark hair just as my eyes catch on the gold band throning the ring finger of my left hand. All the promises we made to each other are held by the very vow behind the golden bands on our hands.

"Sempre miña, meu ceo. Always fucking mine," he rasps in my ear with arrant covetousness just before his lips suck my lobe, drawing yet another moan from me. "Now, leg up, miña dozura. It's been an awfully long time since I've been inside your sweet cunt."

My heart tumbles in my chest at his chosen endearment terms.

Meu ceo. (My sky.)

Miña dozura. (My sweetness.)

But my heart isn't the only one affected by the sound of him *speaking Galician. The way the words roll off his tongue with the clear accent has my panties dampen more and more.*

Mason might have been born and raised in the US, yet with his mother being originally from A Coruña, Spain, he grew up speaking Galician and English, but he is also fluent in Spanish and Portuguese since Galician is very similar to both languages. So being made love to while being spoken to in different languages is definitely not something I'm unfamiliar with. Besides, I must admit that it also brings the utmost level of pleasure hearing him whisper sweet nothings in my ear in another language.

Thank fuck he's also been teaching me Galician since we were teenagers otherwise I'd have no clue whatever he says means. Although, he taught me basics at first, moving on to dirty vocabulary and filthy promises only when we started dating. But to be absolutely honest, just the sound of his voice gets all my insides tingling. Hence why it is safe to say that even if I didn't know the language, I'd still be soaking wet.

"You had me in the shower not long ago," I counter with a chuckle once I snap out of the little trance his Galician sets me under.

Although my statement might sound like a protest, I assure you I'm not complaining. And the proof is in the action that follows my statement as I grasp hold of the edge of the countertop of the wash basin and haul my leg atop it.

"Just like I said. An awfully long time," he reverts just as I feel his hand skimming the curve of my ass. "Having enough of you is a notion unknown to me because I could never just have enough of tasting you, of making love to you, of ravishing you beyond your own comprehension."

A loud moan escapes me when his fingers push the fabric of my panties to the side and two thick digits pump inside me.

No mercy.

Just taking.

Taking and giving.

Taking my pleasure.

Giving me pleasure.

The action is plain claiming. Because this is what love-making to Mason Carter is like. It is as though every single time is our first time and he stakes his claim on me all over again. As if he wants me to feel him on me and in me every moment of every day.

Early in our relationship, I understood that Mason Carter is the rough between the sheets kinda lover. Because of him, I've learned that love should be lived intently and should be made savagely. No in-between. No half-assed touches.

The proof of that is in the shiver that runs through me from the very roots of my hair to the soles of my feet when his breath fans over my heated skin. The sensation of it is mind-boggling while his bare chest leans over my back and his weight presses me a little more against the counter.

My bottom lip gets sucked into my mouth, biting down onto it to keep myself from moaning my lungs out. However, my attempt is futile. Especially when his lips nibble on my earlobe right before his teeth sink gently into the flesh.

It is on that action that the wantonness inside me gets unleashed and I push my hips into his hand.

"That's it, miña tigresa. Ride my hand," he croaks, his lips removing from my lobe only to dust over the skin of my shoulder where inked is the tigress tattoo.

It is a tattoo I have gotten a couple of years back after Mason kept calling me his tigress every time I'd get angry and ready to charge for someone.

"Rub that pussy on my hand, nena."

I do exactly that. I grind down on his hand as though my own life depends on it. Yet, I lose whatever rhythm I set when the pad of his thumb grazes the crack of my ass. That is when another quake shudders my body.

"You want it, baby?"

Mason's voice is heavy with lust. His deep baritone is smooth and rich. The sound of it dances over my skin as though it is the world's softest fabric dusting over my flesh. One that has my toes curling and my fingers wrapping tightly over the edge of the countertop.

"Want your man to take your ass tonight? Want your pussy to squeeze my fingers while I pump your ass with another? Or is it my cock in your ass you want and my fingers in your sweet cunt? Because either way, I'm claiming them both tonight, nena, and I won't be gentle. I'll go at them so hard and deep you won't know where I begin and where you end."

God, it has been so long since I had him take me that way while he claims every inch of my body he can possibly claim. With his mouth, with his fingers, with his cock, with his whole being.

"Good thing we got a brand-new bottle of lube then," I mutter, *remembering how casually he walked my way and winked as he threw the bottle in our shopping cart yesterday afternoon.*

"With the wicked plans I had for you in mind, it only seemed appropriate to get it."

My chin dips into my chest for a moment as I let out a soft moan when I feel more of him. More of his weight. More of his touch. More of his ministrations. But then, I lean it back against his shoulder when his hand rests on the column of my neck as his thumb grazes my racing pulse spot. His hot, wet tongue flicks softly over the skin just under my earlobe that Mason sucks between his lips again.

Using the hold on my neck, he presses his thumb now against my jawline to turn me toward him. Not a tick later, his mouth finds my lips and his tongue conquers mine the moment they touch. All the while, his thumb lowers until it finds the opening of my sex but only to bring it back to my tight hole, circling it with my own arousal.

"Holy crap."

My mewl gets swallowed by my husband's mouth as he deepens the kiss even more. Every time I think it is impossible for his kisses to get deeper, more fervent and more intense, I'm proved wrong. And this moment is one of them instances when I foolishly think we can't be more connected. Yet, as my mouth capitulates before his own for the feral taking, my body also quells against his. Just like it always does.

As I manage to remove one hand from the counter, I reach behind me to find his hard-as-rock length pushing against my ass cheek through the cotton confinement of his shorts. My hand cups the bulge, squeezing it just the way I know he likes it. Tight and hard.

"Fuck," he breathes out, removing his mouth from mine. "Eyes, meu ceo. Give me your eyes."

Instantly, my gaze darts to the mirror. To our reflections pressed together. To my hand that moves behind me over his hardness. To his chocolate eyes that meet mine and hold me captive just like his touch does.

My head falls back, and I lose his gorgeous, dark stare when his thumb pushes inside my tight hole. The moan that tumbles from deep within my chest and out of my mouth gets more prolonged with each slow push of his fingers inside of me.

"Take me out, meu amor. Take me out and slip me inside you," Mason rasps in my ear and I lose his touch on me. I lose his fingers. "Necesito dentro do teu coño, nena."

("I need inside your pussy, baby.")

Damn! This man of mine will be the death of me one day with his dirty, smut talk. All the more, I can already foresee the cause of death on my certificate being: "her husband killed her with his obscene, lewd mouth and with his expert cock and fingers". Along with that, I can also see a very fitting ruling on the judge's part: "he must be sentenced to life in the porn industry to show them wannabes how it's done".

"*Agora, nena.*"

("*Now, baby.*")

Need takes over my body at his croaked order. Need to be filled by my husband. Need to feel him everywhere. So I do what he tells me. I bring my hand to the waistband of his gray cotton sweat shorts and I lower it just enough for his hard and heavy length to spring free. I don't waste any time. I don't bother even with pushing the fabric down entirely, desperate to have him in me. Desperate to feel him, I bring the head of his cock to my slicked opening and a feral, deep groan resounds from behind me at the touch.

"*Carallo! Brace, nena, this is gonna get rough.*"

One hard thrust and he's inside me to the hilt, causing a loud moan to whirl its way out of my mouth. A second, deep glide in, and my eyes search his in the mirror.

As though he waits until our gazes connect, Mason's control snaps loose. He loses it the very second our eyes meet, and his drives are hard and, oh, so deep. His hot palm traces my spine until he finds my ass. The instant he does, his thumb pushes back in just as his lips dust kisses over the heated skin on the back of my shoulders.

He can say 'carallo' one more time because...

"*Fuck...*"

Whatever other words plan on escaping me get swallowed and replaced by a mewl as he starts thrusting with his cock and his finger deeper and harder. Filling me up to oblivion. Thrusting into me until my legs give way and he catches me in his strong embrace.

I blink.

Reality sinks in on a difficult swallow as my green eyes glance at the man standing next to me. He stepped out of the shower moments ago and he stands beside me. The white towel wrapped around his waist is in contrast with his naturally tanned skin and with the dark ink across his chest and arms. But that same juxtaposition highlights his taut, ripped abdomen all the more as he effortlessly exudes sex appeal, taunting me as though on purpose—though I know otherwise. Even the small silver barbell piercing on his right nipple almost tempts me to turn to him and dart my tongue over it like I've done so many times before.

Mason Carter is a god with his features chiseled nearly to perfection. It is as though the greatest artistic hands of this world have conjured to craft him with sheer precision.

The buzzing of his toothbrush soon fills the air, snapping me out of my discreet—or so I hope—drooling, and I'm glad it does so he won't be able to hear the heavy sigh that crawls its way from deep within me and out past my lips.

At which point did we become strangers? At which point in our fifteen years of relationship did we stop… I don't even know what we stopped exactly. But I know what we started. Arguing. More and more every day, especially in the past few weeks.

It is as though we forgot how to be a couple, how to be married, instead, we choose the arguments over anything else and we choose to push each other away. We stopped fighting for each other every day and we started fighting against one another.

I am all aware that there is trouble in any relationship, in any marriage, which one has to fight to get through. But for the past weeks, it's been feeling like, more and more, with each passing day, we give up on each other.

Ounce by ounce. Fraction by fraction we distance from each other further. He pushes me away more and more, and I begin wondering how can I fight for someone who doesn't want me to fight for them?

Placing the face cream tub in the small basket atop the counter next to the basin, I take a step toward the bathroom door to exit. But it is on the second one that I look over my shoulder at the man inside.

My husband.

Mason Carter.

The very Mason Carter who only a month ago had me bent over this same countertop and drilled inside me as though there was no tomorrow. Took my pussy and my ass at once. Claimed me as his again.

Are there really no traces of us left? No ounces of what we

lived together for fifteen years? Because I still feel every moment on my skin, I have all of them ingrained in my mind and etched onto my flesh.

Is the love we swore no longer there? I know I still feel my love for him down to my bones, but does he? How could have everything changed so drastically in the span of a few weeks?

"I picked up an extra shift this Saturday, so I won't be able to make it to dinner at your parents," he informs me, the buzzing of his toothbrush coming to a halt.

It is what Mason does lately.

He notifies. He doesn't confer. He tells.

"Oh."

It is all I manage to say. Everything that my brain seems capable to muster as I turn to him. As I pivot toward him, my eyes begin a slow perusal of my husband.

No, they take in the stranger my husband turned into. That is what he became. A stranger. But one who I share a bed with. A house with. A life with.

Share without truly *sharing*.

"Mase, what's happening to us, baby?"

I can't stop the question fast enough. Before I get to put a lid on it, the wander is aloud and the heaviness of it lingers in the small master bathroom. My heart shrinks at the sound of my own words as ache and uncertainty settle over me.

It is on that question that for the first time in weeks as his chocolate eyes dart to me and I feel as though he finally sees me. As though he doesn't look through me any longer but allows himself to really see me. To hear the hurt in my voice. To see the pang in my eyes.

There's something that instantly coats his gaze. Yet it is gone before I can indeed pinpoint what it is. Regret maybe? Pain? Is it hurt? I have no clue whatsoever. One thing is certain, though— Mason has become an expert in masking whatever it is he feels. And I mean what he truly, genuinely feels.

At his silence, I shake my head from side to side.

Defeat. It is what I experience taking over my entire body. Plain, ugly defeat.

"I want us to get a divorce, Ensley," he speaks just as my head moves.

The motion has my head spinning... Actually, his words have

my head whirling and my heart squeezing so tightly I'm afraid it will break. It feels as though my heart has been ripped out and my entire body has been trounced. In no particular order but considering I feel the pain in every single fiber of my being, I'd say the ripping out of my heart has been done beforehand. Before my body grew numb from the crush.

It isn't the first time he says that very sentence since only a couple of weeks ago, he *suggested* getting a divorce, giving me no real reason why he wants that just like this time.

Although I've heard him mention the divorce before, it is the first time he says it with utter, unmitigated conviction. As though he made his decision. As though the fifteen years we spent together mean nothing to him.

Cold. Detached. This is how he sounds.

His words resonate in my ears like an echo and tumble inside my mind.

"I want us to get a divorce, Ensley."

Twenty-six letters. Eight words. One sentence. One single sentence that slashes my chest open with each replay. Twenty-six letters that grip my heart. Eight words that tear it right out of my chest.

It is during this moment I realize that I was wrong. Completely, downright wrong. Whatever I thought I saw in the mirror, whatever traces of us I assumed might still be there, they aren't there anymore. Because the man who stands before me isn't the man I love anymore. He isn't the man I married because that man would never give up on us. He's back to being the same Mason Carter who denied me all these years ago. The same coward who'd prefer to live a deception than to admit his true feelings for me.

Over fifteen years ago, I didn't let him give up on me after I only experienced one fleeting night with him. After all these years—when we shared a home, lived together a life with its ups and downs, while our hearts would beat only for one another—how am I expected to let him quit on us? How am I supposed not to fight for our marriage and just take the easy way out? But at the same time, how can I tell him to stay when he wants to walk away?

MASON

Sirens blare atop Squad 2's apparatus as Rhys Thatcher—our driver—skids through the night's traffic toward our latest call— a structure fire.

Right beside him in the front seat, there's our lieutenant, Luke 'Flash' Walker, the man who is also my best friend and brother-in-law.

Or soon-to-be former brother-in-law if you go through with the divorce and I'm sure the term best friend will also be out of the equation, a voice inside my head snarls at me.

I sigh and my thought darts to the image of Ensley... of my wife. My mind instantly floods with memories.

So many fucking memories.

Of her smile. The one that makes my heart thump in my chest with such force I often feel the need to rest a hand over it to make sure it won't just jump out and leave me.

Of her voice. That melodious sound of her talking, and oh, man, my woman can talk someone's ear off. I'll be damned, though, if the sound of her voice isn't honey sweet. Soft and gentle and so goddamn angelical—unless she orders me to pound harder inside her or to give her more that is.

Of her touch. That delicate brush of her hand over my skin that burns me to the bone, and it's etched so deep within me that there isn't anything that will ever erase it. That soothing caress on my cheek when I come home to her after a rough call and she just knows from the instant her gorgeous eyes land on me that something has gone wrong.

Her touch always wakes an overflowing need within me. The need to possess her body and own her mind—a need so feral, so savage and untamed that even though I know I have both, I want to consume her all the more, drain her of everything she has to offer just the same way she does with me. It is as though there's this constant hunger for her that I will never have enough of. The incessant necessity of ravishing her beyond our own comprehension. And the best—at the same time the worst—part is that I know she'd let me do that and more because she already allows me to.

On a blink, the recollection of her green orbs flickers behind my eyelids. The very pair that can bring me down to my knees with the merest of drifts in my direction. The jaded green dyad that makes the wickedest of promises and incites the filthiest of desires. The same gaze that would have me start a war over but would have me surrender to it within seconds of her stare darting my way and become its most loyal servant.

Cristo!

(*Christ!*)

I already am the most loyal servant of her eyes. I have been for fucking forever.

It is on that thought that, almost instantly, right before my very own eyes flashes the image of her in the bathroom this morning.

The pain.

The hurt.

Joder!

(*Fuck!*)

That goddamn image of her has seared itself into my brain and has haunted me throughout the day. So much so that every so often I need to rub at my chest to somehow ease down the ache within. From the very moment she stepped out of the bathroom, to the minutes I rode my motorcycle like a maniac through the morning traffic, and to the here and now, that image of her has tortured me. That very vivid pained look in her eyes agonies me still and breaks me into pieces.

You've never been worthy of her, goddammit! Somebody like you can't even look in her direction without tainting and tarnishing her skin, let alone dare to touch her with filthy hands, but you've been weak, my rational side spits almost venomously.

This is the truth.

The crystal clear, ugly truth.

The dreadful reality.

I've been weak.

Weak to think that *someone like me* would ever deserve somebody like Ensley Walker.

Ensley Carter.

Because this is who she is.

Ensley Juliet Carter.

Fuck!

Fuck!

Fuck!

Heedlessly, my hand slides into the pocket of my bunker pants, and I take out the polaroid photograph I keep inside. A picture I snapped of my gorgeous wife after a romantic dinner we had during our two-year wedding anniversary in Paris last summer. Her plump dark red lips curved into a pulse-racing smile that shines brighter than the Eiffel Tower behind her. Her green eyes accentuated by dark make-up, killing me with their intensity. Her raven dark hair cascaded in waves down her back with the tips reaching the very curve of her magnificent and sinfully delicious ass. Her athletic figure hugged to perfection by a red dress that I graphically remember peeling off her body right before I threw her atop the bed of our hotel room and buried myself inside her to the hilt. Just as vividly I recall the marks of my fingertips and my hands that she wore on her skin the morning after when I watched her mesmerized as she glided out of bed and sensually walked toward the bathroom, her hips swaying left and right, right and left in an invitation to join her in the shower. An invitation that held the promise of another round as though we can just not have enough of each other.

The truth is, we can't… I can't.

The more I have her, the more I crave her. The more I taste her, the hungrier I get. The more I drink her sweetness, the thirstier I become. The more I touch her, the more I want to keep doing it until her skin has every inch of my own memorized just like I have every single inch of her so deeply engrained onto my brain and onto my own flesh.

Carallo!

(*Fuck!*)

How I tainted her...

How I marked her...

How I stained her flawless flesh with my hands...

How I took her in the most obscene, roughest ways possible and how she fucking let me do the filthiest things to her... Over and above, she kept asking for more.

Ensley wanted all my kinks and even shocked me with some of her own, many times whispering to me all the filthy things she wanted me to do to her.

I tied her up. More than once, I tied her up, blindfolded her, and had her star-shaped in our bed, played with her magnificent body until she'd beg me to give her my cock. And much to her dismay, I'd give her all my inches so unhurriedly, taking my sweet time, only to drive her crazy with want.

I had her on her knees, sucking me off.

Xesucristo, that mouth of hers. How she works me with it, how fucking spectacular she looks every time she wraps her lips around my girth, and how she swallows my shaft to the back of her throat.

Early in our relationship, she also let me take her tight ass for the first time because I wanted to claim every part of her body that I could possibly claim. Ever since them, she let me take it every single time I'd crave it. And to think I've never considered myself an anal kinda guy. Well, don't get me wrong because I like a great ass as much as the next guy, but I couldn't say I've got a fetish to claim it because it just seemed too intimate. However, my desire for Ensley, of having her in all the ways possible, has proved me wrong. It has always been all-consuming that it was difficult to just pass on that opportunity, especially when she would more than shake it before my eyes like an invitation every time I had her sit on my face which happens very often. One can't judge me for loving it when I have my woman straddle my face for my merciless feast, for me to bury my tongue in her sweet pussy and play with her clit until I have her shattering with pleasure.

Moreover, I had her spread wide for me while my eyes fed on the sight of her touching herself until she begged me to let her come, but I would still deny her that pleasure. I would let her come so close to the edge and then I'd pin both her arms behind her head just so my twisted self can see her arousal dripping down her inner thighs. I took pleasure in witnessing just how much I turned her on and how much she wanted me. And then I'd have her ride me until we'd almost black out.

I'm a selfish man.

I wanted to reign over all her desires.

I wanted to own her pleasure.

Ensley-fucking-Carter is a woman after my own heart. But a woman I don't deserve.

All my presents must become my pasts because she is too good to be with *somebody like me*. Sooner or later, she will realize that herself. In due course, she'll grasp the fact that she wants all I vehemently refuse to give her, and, ultimately, she'll dump my ass.

I am smart enough to know that a love like Ensley's comes once in a lifetime for a man. It is the kind of love that doesn't only leave traces, it leaves marks. Deep, profound, unfathomable marks because one would walk into life thereafter trying to find her in anyone else around, to get lost between another's legs only to erase the memory of her taste, of her touch, of her love but would never be able to. There's only one Ensley and only one love like hers—innocent, pure, so deep that one would need their heart ripped out not to feel it anymore.

I might have been the luckiest bastard on Earth to have her as mine, to have her love, but now I need to let her go. Not because I don't love her because I do—with every fiber in my being. But because it is easier if she doesn't love me anymore.

Ensley's love is that forbidden fruit that I know I shouldn't want, I shouldn't have, I shouldn't need, but I couldn't resist its pull. Now, however, I need to fight it. For her sake and because I know I'll be that part of her life she'll regret later down the line, I need to battle that pull with all my might. I must fight against Ensley with everything I've got, even if that means I'll rip my heart out in the process.

¡Perdóame, nena! Todo isto fágoo por ti, porque pronto te darás conta de que non te merezo e que realmente queres algo que non che podo dar.

(*Forgive me, baby! I'm doing all this for you because soon you'll realize that I don't deserve you and that you really want something I can't give you.*)

"What do you keep thinking about back there, *Cutter*? I can feel your frown on the back of my head," Luke questions, turning in his seat.

His brows are furrowed, and his blue-grayish eyes lock onto my brown ones as though he's attempting to pierce through me to see what's troubling me.

Only if he knew…

If he knew, he'd charge for the bench and feed you his fist, snarls the very voice that's been throwing snappy comments at me ever since my ride to the firehouse after my mind got tired of constantly replaying this morning's events.

My shoulders lift in a casual shrug to downplay the situation.

"Judging by the picture he keeps drooling over, I don't think you wanna know what he thinks about, Flash. But to give you a hint, it involves your sister," Nolan Santiago warns my best friend.

Immediately, a set of laughs fills the squad's cabin, with the exception of Luke who appears fairly closer to throwing up than to joining the rest of the crew in their jest.

"See why you need to mind your own business, brother?" I quip with a raised brow.

"I'll definitely remember that next time I decide to ask," Luke attests, certainly grossed out about where my trail of thoughts might have taken me.

If he knew he'd shred me into pieces with his bare hands.

Before I get to say anything else—not that I actually planned on adding any more fuel to the fire or to have a heart-to-heart with my best friend about my reasons for wanting to divorce his sister given the situation we're in right now—, the apparatus comes to a halt.

Cocking my head to the side, I glance out the window, and the flames dance before my eyes.

"Let's get going, boys," Luke orders, jumping right out of the squad's truck. "This baby's cooking a little too fast."

With one last glance at the picture I hold, I feel a heavy sigh crawl up my throat before I let the photograph slip through my fingers and fall onto the apparatus floor.

Just as I jump out, the phone inside the pocket of my bunker pants rings and I swiftly take it out to switch it off.

There's an ounce of hesitation in my actions when my wife's smile fills the screen of my phone and my eyes move over her nickname.

Nena.

Sending the call right to voicemail, I suit up and listen carefully to the orders given to us by Luke before we mask up and walk into the building.

The flames roar around us the instant we step in. An inferno that gets stronger by the second and with each step we take further inside.

It is a hell nobody wants to get caught in the midst of. One that will burn everything and anything in its path.

With the fire burning powerfully, the flames nearly manage to bite through the bunker gear.

"We take the basement," Luke informs, eying me for a brief tick.

I only nod, and he turns to lead the way.

The sound of the fire is loud. Its hissing causes a cold chill to crawl up my spine and a weird feeling settles in the pit of my stomach.

Ensley...

Her beautiful face flashes before my eyes, and my gut churns. Yet, I garner all my might and push away the image as I follow Luke down the stairs and into the basement.

We do a quick sweep of the space when the voice of our Captain Owen Tucker—who is our eyes and ears on the outside —resounds in a strong, indisputable order as I am about to move a shelving unit: "Everybody out now."

"Let's go," Luke urges.

I nod and almost immediately, we move to proceed back toward the stairs.

Just as instantly, comes another order from the captain's part: "Walker, Carter, get your asses out of there now." It is his baritone that sets us on alert even more. It is rushed and sterner than the first time and it becomes our clue that this is serious.

I watch how, without delay, Luke rushes up the unstable stairs and I follow.

"Hurry, these stairs won't last for long."

As though on cue, a cracking sound fills my ears and I abruptly stop on the second step from the bottom. It is immediately followed by a nearly deafening hiss that tangles with an even louder roar.

A roar that is all too familiar. One we hear many times when doing the search in infernos like this.

A roar that doesn't foretell good things and the shiver that crawls up my spine only solidifies that belief.

It is a sound that tells me to act now or never.

"*Flash*, watch out," I shout.

With all the force I can garner, I give my best friend a shove that propels him out of the way right before I sense my body flying.

What follows next is a very strong impact.

One that turns everything into darkness.

ENSLEY

My fingers run gently over the clay as the machine twirls the freshly shaped pot.

"I want us to get a divorce, Ensley."

Mason's statement from this morning still resounds in my head. Not only the words, though. His voice. The certitude in it. The assuredness.

I've felt their weight throughout the day. The more I wanted to push them away, the faster they came at me. With more fierceness. And the more they come, hitting with force, the more it hurts. The more my heart shatters.

After spending more than half of my life loving him, how can I suddenly stop? How can I tell my heart to cease beating for him and find a new rhythm? How can I force my mind to forget all the moments we have shared together? How can I stop loving Mason Carter when that's all I've ever known? How can I do that when I loved him even when I didn't know it?

What has happened for him to change this drastically? What happened to us? Am I not enough anymore? Is the love I feel for him down to the very marrow of my bones not enough any longer?

Self-doubt settles as I pass my fingers again over the pot. All the while, I fight off the tears that rim my eyes. But it is an idle effort since a couple of hot tears roll down my cheeks and I snap my eyes shut as memories assail. It is as though a movie plays out before my closed lids. And because I'm seemingly a masochist, I let them slap me right in the face with a time when we used to be happy. When we used to love each other.

"Ámote con todo o meu ser."

He loves me with all his being.

This is what he whispers in my ear while his arms envelop me from behind.

With the plate I just started washing now abandoned back into the sink, I allow myself to relish the warmth of my husband's embrace.

Although feeling his hot breath on my skin sends a multitude of shivers down my body, I focus on the response of my heart at hearing his statement.

Without delay, it sets into a wild gallop, and I feel its beating so intensely against the chest bone.

I can't fight the smile that tips at the corners of my lips even if I try and I nestle further into his arms.

"Ti es toda a miña vida. Non quero un mundo onde non sexas ti."

("You are my whole life. I don't want a world without you.")

As I slowly spin in his embrace, I snake my arms around his neck and tilt my head a little to meet his chocolate eyes. Even though I stand tall at five-foot-nine, Mason still towers over me at six-foot-two.

I chuckle when his hands rest on the curve of my ass, giving the cheeks a simultaneous squeeze. Mason also gives me his signature smirk in return, topped with a wink that would have weakened me in the knees if I hadn't been so focused on his previous sentence that replays in my head.

"There's no need to imagine a world without me. I will always love you and only you," I revert, as my heart melts.

This is possibly the reason I don't manage to acknowledge the wicked, plotting smirk on his face until it is too late. And I say that because, with proficient ease, he twirls us. Not even a moment later, I jump when he turns the sprayer on me. Right on my chest, having the water stream down on my body, soaking my clothes instantly.

My squeal is loud when I jump out of his arms, and he chuckles as he shuts off the water. While my hands wipe the water off my face, I look at him.

No, I glare at him, my eyes narrowed.

"Wanted to get me wet and couldn't find a better way to do it, dear?" I question as I watch his dark gaze move over my drenched

body. The fabric of the white t-shirt that once was loose, now is firm against my skin, making extremely obvious the lack of a bra. The material of my shorts is no exception since it also fell victim to the water attack.

However, the chill that passes through me from the very top of my hair to the bottom of my bare feet definitely has nothing to do with the water, and everything to do with the raw intensity and passion in his eyes as they roam up and down my body. With a smug smile on his face that tells me he likes the reaction of my body to his stare. With the clear predatory look in his brown irises as he advances toward me.

"I can certainly think of many other ways of getting you wet, miña dozura," he proclaims.

His smile widens and gets more arrogant with each step he takes in my direction. Something that has me pinned to the spot as though he sets me under a spell. I can't move even if I want to. Not that I want to, though, becoming a willing captive to his hypnotizing gaze.

With his arms snaking around me when he gets in front of me, one of his massive hands rests low on my back while the other darts a little lower on one of my ass cheeks. I feel his hot touch all over me. Moreover, I sense everywhere on my flesh what his touch does to me.

As my chin tilts and I meet his eyes again, I am taken aback by what I see. By the seriousness that takes over his orbs.

"I'd rather lose myself than ever lose you," he declares, his thumb and index finger capturing my chin to be certain I hold his stare. "Por sempre te amarei e só a ti."

The way he says he'll always love me and only me in Galician is an oath full of emotion. Full of the very love he pledges.

Where's that always he promised now? Where is the forever he made me believe in? Where is the vow of us? Was there something that forced him to make this decision? Otherwise, I can't explain to myself how can that same man who told me he doesn't want a world without me, now pushes me out of that very world himself.

I sigh.

Deeply.

Heavily.

All the while, a feeling of uneasiness settles in the pit of my very stomach. It churns at my gut so fiercely. My heart joins the unsettled feeling and thumps harder in my chest and louder in my ears. It definitely doesn't help as both my heart and my gut complot against whatever peace of mind I have left. They chip away at it with each second that ticks by.

With a quick flick of the button, I bring the machine's spinning to a halt. I stare at the pot that lost its initial shape while I got caught in the whirlwind of thoughts and memories of my relationship, of my marriage, of the man I love. Of the man I fell in love with when I couldn't fully comprehend the meaning of this feeling. Of the first man I gave myself to—heart and body.

Darting my eyes to the clock on the wall in the dark room, I note it just ticks three in the morning. I immediately become aware of how late it is and how tomorrow morning I'm on shift at the firehouse. Yet, tonight's sleep doesn't come easy. Or at all since after tossing and turning in bed for hours, I gave up and decided to distress for a while in the little pottery home studio. A studio that was initially designed as a storage room before Mason and I bought the house we moved into five years ago after we lived in the apartment next to my brother's for a few years.

Inevitably, a small smile tugs at my lips at the fond memory of when we stepped inside this house for the second time—since the first time was during the viewing with the estate agent.

A giggle escapes me as I am guided by Mason. Where? I have no idea because his big palm covers my eyes after he removed the scarf he tied around when we got into the car to prevent me from seeing where we were driving.

"Mind the step, nena," Mason whispers from behind me, keeping me close with the free hand that is snaked around my waist.

With my sight obscured by his hand still, I carefully move down yet another step before reaching an even surface. Immediately after, I'm brought to a halt when Mason's hold around me tightens a fraction as a signal to stop.

From behind me, his breath fans against the skin of my neck, and all small hairs raise as an aftermath of the closeness.

Ten years of relationship and Mason Carter can still awake within me all sorts of feelings. With a glance my way alone, he sweeps me off my feet all over again. With a bare, hot touch, he sets my skin afire.

With a mere wink followed by a lopsided smirk, he makes each part of my body tingle—and I do mean each part because my lady bits are no exception. But my heart is impacted the most by the look on the face of the man behind me. It thumps waywardly in my chest.

When his hand removes from my eyes, I still keep them closed, and the instant his other withdraws from around me, I suppress the small protesting sound that nearly surges from my throat at the loss of his warm touch.

"You can open your eyes now."

His deep baritone is smooth and rich while he speaks the words in my ear. His breath is hot, and it is so close, it feels as though it kisses the skin on the column of my neck. So much so that I don't lift my eyelids for another moment while I relish in the sensation his mere breath creates on my flesh. On how goosebumps dance on my skin as an effect of that simple action.

"Open your eyes, nena."

This time, his voice comes from somewhere in front of me and so close to my face that when I do open my eyes, I nearly liquefy as I meet his brown gaze. A hue so dark as if dark chocolate itself was melted into his eyes that are rimmed by long lashes. Lashes the same tint as the dark brown hair.

Damn, he has beautiful eyes. So easy to get lost in his gaze. So effortless to fall captive to the intensity in them. So cinch to make me fall in love more and more each day when they glance my way.

And god, that hair. So rich when I run my hands through it while his lips claim mine savagely. So smooth when I thread my hands through it as I press his head further between my thighs when he is on his knees, holding me with my back up against the shower wall, my legs over his shoulders, and his hands keeping my body to his mouth for the savage devouring. So silky when I lace my fingers through it while I failingly attempt to get away from his wicked mouth as he throws me over yet another scrumptious edge.

Why is it suddenly so hot in here now?

"Deus, nena! I love it when you look at me like that," Mason rasps, only a breath away from my lips.

"And how is that exactly?" I ask although I'm well aware of the way I look at him and of the heat in my cheeks.

"Like you're imagining all the filthy things I do to you. Everything I'd do to you in this very house."

"Are you a mind reader now?"

26

At my tease, he grins.

"There's no need to be a mind reader to know what my woman thinks about. Because the tinge in your cheeks always gives you away. You don't blush, nena."

He pauses for a brief instance, his hand raising to my face so his thumb can pass over my bottom lip.

"Nothing can make you blush unless I suggestively wink or throw an innuendo at you in the middle of family dinner, when Mom or your parents catch us making out in the corridor, or when we sneak out of their house for a little bit so I can kiss you and cope a feel of that amazing ass of yours" he rants, rather amused at the memory of how red I get when our parents catch us. Something that doesn't stop us from still repeating it every time because being addicted to Mason Carter should be a real medical diagnosis.

His brown eyes bore into my green ones, while his thumb presses on my lip, and I fight the urge of sucking it into my mouth.

"But you blush the hardest when you think of dirty things at the end of which we're both naked, sweating and panting, and you with my cum slipping out of you."

The pad of his digit moves over my bottom lip. With a mind of their own, my lips part a little to make way for a small breath to push its way out. It is heavy. Just as heavy as the clear desire in his gaze.

"Your gorgeous eyes give you away the most," he continues, lowering his large hand to the column of my neck. "The green gets so dark that you can try and hide your lust, but you will never succeed in hiding it from me."

My mouth is slightly agape while I watch him withdraw his hand and take a deep breath as though he fights with all his might to keep himself from jumping me.

"Now, let me give you a tour of our new house before I bend you over the back of the sofa and take you hard."

I blink.

Once.

Twice.

All the while, the first part of his sentence reverberates in my head.

A tour of our new house?

I look at him with a perplexed expression before I let my gaze move from the man before me, to the space around us.

A gasp dances its way out of my mouth.

"Mason," I whisper his name.

"I know we said that this house is above what we called a budget, but I also know you loved it when we first viewed it," he expresses, a smile tipping at the corners of his mouth. "I loved seeing you in this house. I loved how you couldn't hold your excitement. How you already envisioned where everything would be. I loved how you turned an empty house into a home just by looking at it."

"I thought you said you don't like the backyard," I point out as my eyes narrow.

His arms extend just before he rests his hands on my hips. Automatically, my own pair of arms raises and snakes around his neck. Although I'm pretty tall, I still have to tilt my chin up a little to be able to meet his gaze again.

"But I'm ready to tear it apart and do some work," he attests.

My brow quirks with intrigue, and a wide smile appears on my face. "Mason Carter shirtless and with tools in his hands? Yes, please."

His body rocks against mine as he chuckles.

"I feel objectified." His voice is filled with mocked complaint.

Our eyes stay locked and his turn soft as he sees a protest coming from my part. He feels it before I even have a chance to open my mouth.

"I said it before, I know it is above our initial budget, nena. But you know I haven't touched the money from my dad and my grandad, so we can use that to pay off the house or I'll damn well pick extra shifts up at the firehouse and I'll PT at the academy fifty years from now if that means you get to have the house of your dreams with that little pottery home office you've always imagined."

With his degree in Sport, Physical Activity and Health, Mason has been helping out with the PT classes for recruits at the fire academy for five years now. And oh, boy, isn't he just sexy bossing everyone around.

My eyes narrow and my lips tip upward in what wants to be a teasing smile. "Oh, I see your intent. You're doing this for selfish purposes only."

Instantly, Mason grins and his brow arches in a sexy quirk. "Of course. You look so goddamn hot while you get your hands dirty in all that clay and I can't wait for you to give me private lessons," he declares before he pauses for effect as he lowers his head to the crook of my neck. The softness of his lips is gentle against my skin.

"Is this how you plan on making me agree with you, Carter?"

He withdraws his head, and our gazes meet again. His dark brown orbs fake innocence, but he damn well knows what he's doing.

"This how?" He questions, still feigning unawareness.

"By seducing me."

"Oh, don't play coy now because you and I both know you love getting seduced, nena. But I think there's no need to try that since I know just how much you loved this place."

"You're right. I love this house and I want to make it a home with you," I say with a smile.

"You are my home, nena. Wherever you are, that is my home."

Closing my eyes, I let his scent envelop me, then I open them again to find Mason looking at me with the brightest of smiles. A smile that promises. That vows a forever. A lifetime of us.

ENSLEY

The loudness of my phone's ringtone nearly has me jump out of my skin and once again I check the time as though to see if somehow the hours slid past to make it a decent hour for a call.

Still three in the morning.

As my eyes narrow, I get up from my seat at the pottering machine and wipe my hands on the dirty cloth. With steps that appear so heavy, I move toward the desk where my phone keeps ringing.

From the picture on the screen that I set for my father's contact, his smile shines from the screen together with his deep dimples—that have been inherited by my brother and my sister. His blue-grayish eyes stare back at me—eyes that only my brother took after him since he's the younger version of our father while our younger sister and I took more of our mom's features. That much to the dismay of our father who, especially during our teens, has been blaming himself for getting a knock-out, gorgeous wife in the first place and having her pass on the beauty to his daughters too.

I don't get to think too much about the traits we shared, and our family's looks since, all of a sudden, the churning in my gut gets stronger. The pounding of my heart is no exception while its thrumming gets harder and harder. So much so that I nearly feel it leap out of my chest at the galloping pace.

"D-dad?" I ask after I swipe my finger over the screen and

bring the phone to my ear. What I don't expect to hear is the shake in my voice as I answer.

"Enz."

From the way Dad whispers my nickname I can tell something is wrong. Something that has my chest hurting from the fierce pummeling of my own heart. Something that causes my stomach to clench so tightly.

"Did I wake you, honey?"

"N-no, Dad. I'm... I... I couldn't sleep," I admit with a low sigh after stammering for a second or two over my own words since I don't want to worry him. An intention I know is futile since I know he can tell from the sound of my voice that something is going on and that something is keeping me awake.

Nothing goes unnoticed for Derek Walker. Especially when it comes to his three children and his wife. He's like an eagle, remarking and detecting everything and anything that goes on around us.

As I attempt to get into my lungs the very air I let out, the breath occludes in my throat. It gets stuck and it stubbornly remains there no matter what I do.

Dots slowly connect right before my eyes as I avert them toward the clock to see through the blurred vision that it indeed is after three o'clock in the morning.

A cold shiver passes me.

I've been a firefighter for seventeen years. I'm also a third-generation firefighter with my father following in the footsteps of my grandfather—Gordon Walker. I am all aware of what a call at this time at night means for a firefighter's family.

"No," I gasp.

My hand flies to the edge of the desk, holding on to it for dear life as I feel my legs suddenly giving way.

"Please," I beg, my head shaking from side to side. My voice gets weaker and weaker as I repeat the plea. My heart squeezes so tightly and my stomach clenches just as fiercely while hot tears fall down my face.

"Open the door, Enz. I'm outside."

"You're... You're here?"

Without waiting for an answer, my feet carry me toward the front door and within moments, with a shaky hand, I find myself unlocking and opening it. Before I get to see anything through my teary vision, I'm brought into my father's arms.

My body shakes as I hold him tightly.

"Look at me, honey," he speaks gently.

Although at first, I show my rebuttal of doing so by shaking my head, a moment later I lift my cheek off his chest. In the immediate moment, I look into the blue-grayish eyes of my father, and I notice the softness and sympathy. They gleam with sorrow.

In front of me, I have a Derek Walker full of compassion, pained by the hurtful news he bears. Torn by the news he brings to his own daughter.

"Dad, please tell me they're fine," I plead, feeling the tears rolling down my face at the thought of my husband or my brother being hurt. Or worse, both of them. "Please."

"There's been a structure fire in the Fourth Ward... Mason's been taken to the hospital," Dad explains. "We need to go. Mom is already there, and Rennie went to pick up Ary. Luke's been pretty banged up too."

Everything becomes a complete blur for me. I can't seem to be able to perceive anything around me anymore. Not when I rush upstairs with all the might I can garner to put some clothes on. Not when Dad and I get into his car, and although I snap to reality for a second or two when he turns on the sirens, I immediately fall back into the web of haziness. I can somehow hear my dad's voice over the thundering of my heart and my ringing ears, yet I am unable to make out anything he says because of the turbidity that settles over me. So much so that I don't snap out of it until the vehicle comes to a halt in the hospital's parking lot and I jump out, ignoring my father's persistent shouting behind me.

It is the instant everything dawns on me and my feet carry me as fast as they can through the cars parked in the lot, and through the sliding doors of the hospital's entrance. The soles of my shoes hit the hard floor and my run doesn't cease. But regardless of how fast I run, I don't seem to get there fast enough.

I've been in this hospital so many times—visiting victims we pulled out of wrecked cars, out of fires, or when one of my fellow firefighters ended up in the ER with an injury—that I know it like the back of my hand.

Through blurred vision because of the tears, I fight to keep at bay, I make out familiar faces that bring my running to an abrupt stop once I reach the waiting room.

Except for my husband and my brother, the rest of Firehouse 24 is here. The waiting room is filled with the remaining four members of Squad 2, with the firefighters on Engine 24, the two paramedics, and Battalion Chief Jason Sinclair. Some pace up and down, others sit on the chairs, while one or two stand leaning against the wall. They all await news about the state of their team members.

Once I stop, almost simultaneously eyes full of pity and compassion dart in my direction, some even jump to their feet, causing my head to spin because I'm familiar with that look they all share. It is one of commiseration. One I choose to overlook to be able to hold myself together.

My eyes move over the people in the waiting room and my heart pounds. Over a dozen men and women gathered together, praying for the well-being of their fellow firefighters.

The camaraderie and the bond that firefighters share are so powerful. The people in the firehouse become their second family, their brothers, and sisters, and when one is hurting, they all are. A brotherhood, a sisterhood, and a siblinghood that knows no bounds.

"He's going to be fine, Ensley. Cutter's the strongest son of a bitch I've met," announces Rhys Thatcher, one of the other members of Squad 2.

With my head moving in a mindless acknowledgment of his sentence, I go to set myself in motion again to look for a doctor when I note my brother and our mother walking through the doors and into the waiting room.

A gasp leaves my lips when I see the white bandage wrapped around Luke's head and my feet carry me to him as swiftly as they can.

"They made it look worse than it really is," he utters as I throw myself into his arms. He holds me tight, and my eyes sting as I attempt to control my tears. "Mason..."

My husband's name is only a whisper on the lips of his best

friend, and he lets the rest of the sentence hang in the air between us.

"He'll be fine," my brother reassures me.

"He better be," I mutter in return, still holding him.

"I'm so sorry, Enz. It's my fault." Clear ache can be felt in my brother's voice as his arms tighten around me. "I should've..."

"Don't, Luke. Don't do this to yourself. It is not your fault," I argue, not liking it one bit that he blames himself for what happened. Although I don't know the facts, I know it isn't Luke's fault.

Tipping my chin back, I look up at my brother and it is only when his thumb brushes over my cheek that I acknowledge the hot tears rolling down my face. The very tears I fought until now to keep at bay.

"Ensley."

My name is spoken with gravity and I avert my gaze toward where the voice comes from, noting it is Doctor Octavio Reyes —one of the ER doctors I came across many times in this hospital.

His eyes take in the room, not surprised to see the entire firehouse there for support. On the contrary, his gaze conveys pure respect for the men and women present.

"Mason is stable for now and you can go in to see him. He's been asking for you," Octavio relays.

I nod my head and peel myself out of my brother's embrace.

As though the doctor recognizes the look on the face of the people in the firehouse, he continues: "Let's give Ensley a few with her husband and then you can all go and see him, but only for a couple of more minutes because he needs to rest."

There's no word leaving any of them, instead, they all approve the doctor's suggestion with a head signal.

"Follow me, Ensley."

And that I do. I walk in tandem with him through the doors and down a corridor.

My brain becomes a whirlwind of emotions. Even when I go to open my mouth and ask Octavio about Mason's state, to get more from him than what he's told us all, no words are coming out.

I'm brought to complete speechlessness by what's happening,

and I find myself slowing down behind the doctor just as he stops before a door.

The heaviness inside my chest doesn't just persist. Without realizing, it has gotten heavier and heavier with each step that I took toward the room where my husband is in. So much so that now I am rooted to the spot with the weight.

"It's okay, Ensley," Octavio reassures me. "You can walk in. I'll give you two a few moments but bear in mind that he's quite weakened. According to the CT scan, the fall he took caused a pretty bad head injury. His GCS score when he came in was very close to severe."

The newly shared information is a pill hard to swallow. One that stings my eyes and I have to dig my teeth into my bottom lip to keep the hurricane of feelings at bay. Even through blurred vision, I still note the sympathy in his gaze. I also see the debate in his expression as though he weighs if he should tell me more or not.

Eventually, he decides on the former.

"To be extremely honest with you, after the CT scan and the stats, I'm surprised Mason is still conscious at this point. You got your man fighting real hard in there."

Just like earlier when he asked me to follow him to see Mason, all I am capable of doing is nod at his statement because I know if I say anything else, all my strength will crumble. It will hit rock bottom and I will not be able to pick up the pieces.

Carefully, I take a step closer toward the door.

Then another.

And another, until my hand reaches out and touches the cool metal of the knob, pushing the door open slowly. The air occludes in my throat as it opens while my eyes stay glued to the flat surface, following it as it reveals more and more of the room. The smell of sterile fills my nostrils and the beeping sound of machines permeates my ears.

When my eyes take in the room, however, and when they land on the man lying on the bed, a cold shiver passes through me. Emotions overwhelm and take over my body, shaking me to the core as my hand flies over my mouth to muffle the cry that escapes me at the sight of my husband.

Burning hot tears run down my cheeks as my green eyes connect to his brown ones across the room and my feet can't carry me by his side fast enough. I nearly collapse over him as I throw myself to his chest.

Although there's a little groan that surges its way out of his throat, when I draw back a little to gaze into his gorgeous stare, small creases form at the corners of his eyes, sign he's smiling.

"Hey...Hey, no more...of that," he whispers, lifting his arm with a little difficulty until his hand cups my cheek. The gesture has me lean into his touch and I close my eyes for a moment, taking it all in as though only that can calm me. "I don't... deserve your...tears, *nena.*"

Mason's thumb dusts over my cheek, wiping gently at the rolling tears.

"Baby, you scared the shit out of me."

Our eyes stay locked, his chocolate brown ones melting everything inside me. For the first time since my father's call, I can now breathe. I no longer have the lump in my throat, occluding my airways. I can breathe because just the sight of him, just having his eyes connected with mine is all the confirmation I need that he will be alright.

"I don't deserve... you. I've... never did. I just... I just lied by telling myself... that I do."

My eyes narrow.

"I warned you..." There's a little break in his speech. "...I will break you."

A chill runs through my body at the reminder of when he first told me that. The very night I lost my virginity to him over sixteen years ago. That is the first and only time he said to me that he'll break me.

"I'm gonna break you. Whether it is a week, a month or twenty years from now, I know I will break you because somebody like me can't know anything but broken."

Even after all the years that have passed since, I can still remember precisely what he told me then. What I remember most is the clear sureness in his voice as he spoke the words to me. But the assuredness of his words doesn't make it any clearer for me because as confusing as he sounded to me then, just as ambiguous as he does now.

"Mase, baby..."

As my sentence is brought to an interruption when the pad

of his fingers presses on my lips, my frown grows deeper at what I see in his eyes. The seriousness. The regret. The pain.

"I'm not...," he stops, swallowing hard. "...the man you think I am."

"What are you talking about?"

For a moment I lose his eyes while he blinks. A slow blink that has me thinking for a second that he got knocked out by the meds.

"I'm... a... I'm a... I've been... deceiving you."

With each second ticking by, his speech gets more broken and broken and his words slurred.

"Mase?" I whisper his nickname, noting his eyelids close before they slowly reopen, clearly taking a lot of effort for him to lift them again.

The alarming sound of the machines pierces my ears and I feel my own heart thundering in tandem with the loud, frightening beeping.

"Mason," I shout his name.

Slow motion.

This is how everything appears to move around me. In utter slow motion as the doctor and nurses rush through the door. One of the nurses even moves me out of their way, but all I seem to be capable of is to relentlessly mutter his name to myself. I mumble it like a prayer, over and again. Time after time I utter it like everything depends on it.

It feels as though I'm living an out-of-body experience and it's not the good kind. It is an excruciating type of experience. One in which my husband's life can hang on by a thread.

Please, baby! I'm begging you don't do this to me, I plead to myself just as I get pushed out of the room by a nurse whose mouth I see moving, but my brain doesn't want to comprehend her talking.

My left hand rests on my chest, clutching tightly at the leather of my jacket, while my right flies over that same hand, applying a little more pressure as though that would somehow lessen the ache I feel pressing against my heart.

The constraint is so powerful and persistent that all my other organs seem to shrink in size at the tension. So much so that when I go to inhale, I can't. I attempt and attempt, but when even the slightest particle of air enters my lungs, it surges right out. It is as though with each trial, the oxygen in the corridor disperses more and more until non-existent.

As my chest rises and falls with failed attempts, I take a few steps until my back hits the opposite wall since it is the only one that can catch my imminent fall.

"Enz?"

Although the masculine voice that calls out my nickname with concern is familiar, it is as much of a blur as the face that appears in front of me. However, my brother's voice is nothing short of worried after he most likely raced through the doors.

"Enz, take a deep breath," he encourages, his tone soothing. "In and out."

Once he gently instructs, he begins breathing in and out, and I find myself following the action.

"That's it. In and out."

The more I inhale and exhale, the clearer my vision gets and the calmer my tempested mind gets.

My eyes close and reopen to meet my brother's blue-grayish ones. His hands don't delay cupping my face, having me focus on him.

"I don't know... I don't know what happened. He was fine. Then..."

"Enz, let's get you back. The doctors will let you know when they have updates."

Without much effort, I let myself guided by my younger brother—by two years—through the doors.

"He was rambling," I mumble to continue my previous sentence, feeling a set of hot tears rolling down my face as I shake my head from side to side in disbelief. "His speech was slurred. I don't... I don't know what's happening, Luke."

As the words leave my mouth, my body begins shaking more and more, until my brother pulls me into him and holds me close while I let fear take over me.

The fear of what is happening.

The horror of what his state is.

So much so that I forget about the men and women waiting in the room for news.

"My husband..."

Only the two words leave my mouth in more of a whisper than anything else while my body shudders in my brother's embrace. A muttering so hefty it seems to take all the energy out of me and if it weren't for Luke's hold on me, I'd be crushed to my knees.

"It's okay. Mason will be fine. He's a fighter, Enz," Luke utters in my hair, but he doesn't pull away, keeping me steady.

However, moments later, I am the one to withdraw and I take a few steps until my back hits the wall. Letting my body go fluid down the height of the hospital wall, I bring my knees to my chin, refusing to look anywhere else but at the two doors.

Each time they open, my heart leaps out of my chest. Every time I see somebody walk past, my stare follows them in a prayer that maybe one of them would tell me something about my Mason.

For how long I sit on the floor with my knees tight to my chest, I don't know. I merely acknowledge anything happening around me. I barely utter something every time my parents, my brother or my husband's crew ask if I need something. After a while they all eventually give up asking, understanding that balling into a corner is the only coping mechanism that keeps me from screaming my lungs out with utter despair.

It is only when I watch Octavio walk through the doors that I find the energy in me to spring to my feet and nearly run his way.

Hope floods my body.

But only for a brief moment before I meet his gaze and a cold shiver runs through me. My heart beats so heavily in my chest, while my stomach churns.

"We've just finished with another CT scan for Mason. We got him one when he came in to assess the extent of his injuries, there was clear traumatic brain injury which explains the slurring and the loss of consciousness, however…"

My own eyes begin pleading him and Octavio stops briefly.

He delivers the punch, nonetheless.

"I don't come bearing good news, unfortunately," he continues as though expressing his apologies for what he has to say next. "The CT scan shows severe build-up of fluid around the brain that causes intracranial pressure."

Luke's arm snakes immediately around me as if he senses my knees giving way and growing weaker and weaker.

"For Mason to have any chance of survival, we have to

induce a state of coma. Due to the impact, he suffered a head injury that caused cerebral edema. The only option is to induce coma and wait for the swelling to go down, and only then we'll be able to see the damage."

With my hand darting to my mouth to muffle the whimper, I'm brought tighter into my brother's arms. I shake and shake in his embrace while I cry.

Why?

Why does it have to be this way?

My Mason.

No. I can't lose him like this.

"For Mason to have any chance of survival, we have to induce a state of coma." The doctor's words play back in my head over and over again.

And with each replay of that same sentence, I feel everything crumbling inside of me. Shattering into pieces. Breaking into small fragments at the thought of my husband lying in a hospital bed, fighting for his life.

Is the universe that determined to keep us away from each other? First the divorce, now this?!

How can loving somebody down to every fiber of one's being feel like a goddamn curse? Why does loving Mason Carter feel like a blessing, but like a misfortune all the same? Why does it feel as though someone just ripped my heart out?

Only the mere thought of my husband in a coma occludes my airway. The ache makes it so hard to breathe.

Pure torture.

That is what losing Mason would be to me. Pure, utter and complete torture that I can't bear. One that could bring a downfall nobody would be able to prevent. Nobody but my husband himself.

Please, baby, I need you to come back to me. I need you to be able to survive, to breathe again, to carry on living even if that means loving you from afar for the years to come because if a divorce is what you really want, I'll give it to you. I'll quit being your wife if that means I'll still get to see your gorgeous eyes and hear your voice. And even though it will shatter me having you so close and being unable to reach up for you as I did many times before, I'll continue loving you from a distance. Baby, please, I'm begging you, come back to me.

ENSLEY

Two months and three weeks ago

Seven days.

A hundred and sixty-eight hours.

This is how long it's been since Mason has been induced into a coma *to have a chance of survival*. That many days since he's been connected to all sorts of machines and monitored throughout.

A week since the small sofa in his hospital room has become my bed.

Seven days and there's no improvement.

His state is still the same.

The intracranial pressure still persists and, although the doctors are hopeful, same as we all are, fear engrains in my bones with each second that ticks by.

This can't just be it for us.

I know things haven't been the best in our marriage, but losing Mason is something I can't take.

To have a chance of survival...

For me to have a chance of survival, I need Mason to come back to me. I need him like the air I breathe. I need him to be able to breathe.

Heavy raindrops hit the window of the hospital room and

they snap me from my thoughts. Thunder resounds in the distance while a bolt strikes tonight's sky, lighting up the space.

It makes me cower into the backrest of the sofa as my eyes fly toward my husband for a moment before I close them, pulling the blanket over my head.

"Nena, I'm home."

Mason's strong voice echoes around the house and for the first time since the storm started outside, I can allow myself to let out a sigh of relief.

Relief that he is back.

Through the sound of thunder mixed with the rain and occasional lightning, I also hear his hard footsteps as he runs up the stairs.

"Still hiding?"

Although I don't see him because of the comforter I hold over my head, I can sense the amusement in his baritone.

"Not very nice of you to poke fun at someone's fears," I remind him in an as-a-matter-of-fact tone about my astraphobia—an extreme fear of thunder and lightning.

The bed dips behind me under Mason's weight and, soon enough, I feel the hotness of his palm on my stomach as he uses it as leverage to bring me to him. Immediately, my legs tangle with his and I relax between his arms while his warmth envelops me.

It is on the acknowledgment of his bodily warmth that I realize he's already taken off his clothes and kept only his boxer briefs on to be able to provide more of the comfort he knows I need. Which is something that has me snuggling even closer until my body molds into his.

"So, your tactic is to hide under the covers until the storm passes?" Mason asks from behind me, the entertainment of this still clear.

"Exactly."

"And the storm can't get to you if you hide here how?"

I smack his bare thigh without any hesitation.

"Are you done mocking me?"

That's when he lets out a curt laugh.

A yelp pushes its way past my lips when, all of a sudden, I'm on my back and with Mason's heavy weight on me. My hands are brought together and held down above my head by the wrists by one of his much larger hands, while his frame keeps the comforter over the both of us.

Though it is dark, and I can't see him, the sizzling intensity in his gaze can still be felt. As well as the hot air he breathes against my face.

"Nena, you're the most badass and fearless woman I know. You run into buildings on fire without breaking a sweat. Fucking hell, woman, you damn nearly gave me a heart attack when I've seen you jump from the top of a building and into the water without a second thought to save your life. I just don't get it how you're scared shitless of some rumbling noise."

"You could maybe just distract me," I suggest with a sly smile he can't see but can definitely hear in my voice. "I'm fairly sure you're quite good at that."

He chuckles and his hot breath gets nearer and nearer to my neck. "Oh, nena, you wound my ego because I'm fairly certain I'm the best at that."

His tongue swipes over the column of my neck, leaving a burning trail behind right before his lips press against my skin, igniting me.

A wistful sigh escapes me when my eyes snap open and I'm met with the empty darkness from beneath the blanket.

How I wish you'd be able to hold me now...

Just how much I wish you'd be here to hold me through my fear.

* * *

Two months ago

Tears roll down my cheeks as I hold his massive hand between my two much smaller ones. Tears I've been fighting for so long, but that now gained one over me.

"Please, baby, come back to me," I utter before my lips press against his knuckles.

It is the same pleading I've been whispering for the past three weeks that I've spent sitting by his side.

"Don't do this to me, baby. Don't teach me to live without you because I'm telling you right now that I won't be able to. There's no sequel worth living if that life is without you."

My forehead leans against our laced hands and my teeth dig deep into my bottom lip to stop myself from crying.

The love of my life fights for his own life.

"God, don't do this to me," I beg.

The little sniffle that comes from somewhere toward the door has me lift my head a fraction and crane my neck to the side to meet the chocolate eyes of my husband's mother.

Aracely Carter.

A woman almost as tall as I am that she makes one wonder if she's truly from Spain. One with the same pair of dark brown eyes as Mason's. One so beautiful with her long, almost raven hair.

Aracely Carter has always been a stunner. Athletic built with curves in all the right places. She has always left behind a trail of wanting and courting men, witnessing that myself whenever we go out together on a girls' night. Although she dated or entered long-term relationships over the years, she has always been faithful to the memory of one man, Dennis Carter—Mason's father and an agent of the DEA. The two of them met when Dennis was on assignment at the DEA's office in Madrid and Aracely was on a girls' trip to Spain's capital to celebrate a friend's birthday. They fell in love then and there.

No denial.

Only a few months later, Aracely got pregnant with Mason, so Dennis put an end to his assignment and requested a transfer back to the Detroit division—the city where his field office was. Mason was only three years old when he lost his father in an undercover gig gone wrong. That's when they moved to Arlington, Virginia, and where Aracely and Mason started over.

"My son is strong, and he'll fight through it. He'll come back to you, honey," she speaks with conviction as I take in her own glossy eyes. Her Galician accent is unnoticeable in her speech since she was twenty-one when she moved to the US and after over thirty-five years in the States, she has developed a very strong American twang. "He'll come back to us."

On shaky legs, she approaches, and I raise to my full height, letting her arms envelop me.

"I can't breathe without him, Ary."

"And you will never need to learn how to. He has all the

reasons to fight, honey. Mason loves you more than anything else."

"I'm not so sure he does anymore," I utter the words aloud.

Ary pulls back a little and her eyes scan my features just before they narrow at me.

My chin dips, unable to hold her stare.

"He asked me for the divorce."

The confession burns my chest. It is the first time I say the words out loud and the effect they have on me is damn near excruciating. My heart feels the torture of that sentence as though mentioning the divorce aloud, it somehow makes it more real.

Utter shock takes over her look when I lift my gaze to meet hers.

"What are you talking about?"

"Mason wants to get a divorce. He asked me for it just the morning of the incident before he went on shift and before this nightmare started."

"*Que diaños está a planear este meu fillo?*" Aracely blurts out in Galician.

It is a language sometimes she resorts to in order to express indignation, frustration and anger. Actually, any sort of emotion that she feels the need to convey with rather more pathos. And as she wonders aloud—because it is what it truly is, a ponder that is meant more for herself than for me—*what the hell was her son planning*, from what I can gather, the question is a mix of all three.

Aracely lifts her hand, and she caresses my cheek lightly, wiping at the wet trail left behind by the tears I've been shedding. Her eyes are gentle and pleading at the same time.

"*Cariño, volves tolo ao meu fillo. Quérete con todo o seu ser así que che pido por favor, non deixes que renuncia ao máis bonito que lle pasou en toda a súa vida.*"

("*Honey, you drive my son crazy. He loves you with all his being, so I'm asking you, please, don't let him quit on the most beautiful thing that has happened to him in his entire life.*")

My bottom lip trembles as I listen to her. To her pleading voice. To her nearly suppliant words.

"*El pensa que non te merece e que non é digno de ti, pero o seu amor por ti é puro e sen mancha. Por favor, nunca esqueza isto.*"

(*"He thinks he doesn't deserve you and that he's not worthy of you, but his love for you is pure and unstained. Please, never forget this."*)

My brows furrow at her statement. It is as though she knows more than she says. As if she would know of a reason why Mason would want to divorce me.

"Ary, what do you know about it?"

Her head shakes. "Nothing."

"Are you sure?"

"Absolutely. Mason never mentioned to me even the mere thought of divorcing you, but I know my son, he always believed he's not *worthy of you* and waited for you to realize so yourself."

That is not a lie. I can distinctly see it in her eyes, but that doesn't mean she's telling me the whole truth. There is something that made Mason decide so suddenly to get a divorce. Something his mother might have knowledge of.

"*Prométeme!*" Aracely asks, reverting to her earlier words when she asked me not to let Mason quit on me, on us.

"I promise you, Ary. I won't let him give up on us."

* * *

A month ago

My heart hurts.

My head aches.

My body is nearly ready to capitulate.

Another day.

Another week.

One more month slid by.

Two months altogether since Mason has been in an induced coma. As many since I've been by my husband's side, waiting for the swelling to go down, waiting for him to wake up so I can see his beautiful eyes again. Hear his voice again.

Two months filled with life alterations.

But I'd do that and more to have Mason back.

I'd do anything.

I'd sell my soul to the very Devil if that'd mean I'll get Mason back into my life—even if that also would mean he'll ask me for the divorce and put an end to our marriage. That won't put an end to my love for him. In silence or by shouting it from the rooftops, I'll always love Mason Carter.

How can I want anyone else when I've experienced his love? The very feral, fierce, intense and powerful love that he gave to me. The kind that one experiences only once in a lifetime. The type of love that leaves traces.

For fifteen years I drown in him and many more years before that I was surrounded by him. I'm intoxicated by him. I'm addicted to him. Without him, I wouldn't know what true love is, what it feels like and what it looks like.

I've tasted *true love* on his lips.

I've seen the look of *true love* in his eyes.

I've felt *true love* with his touch.

A sigh pushes through my lips as I turn the page of the book that I read to him aloud. Although I read, John Grisham's words don't seem to make sense to me right this moment. My mind is everywhere but on the pages of *'The Reckoning'* which I keep turning, hoping to distract me.

Though I'm more of a romance reader—blame it on mom's romantic influence with her books—, Mason has always been a thriller, mystery kinda reader, so I consider it is only appropriate to read him something to his liking.

During this moment, however, not even Pete Banning's reason for murdering the pastor of the local church doesn't appear to hold on to my attention.

"I'm the worst at reading this kind of stuff," I gently speak, lifting my gaze from the pages to take in my husband. Immediately, tears rim my eyes, their stinging almost unbearable. "God, and just how sexy you always looked when you were reading. Have I ever told you that?"

"I'm pretty sure I've heard more than enough stories about how you jumped his bones every time you'd see him holding a book."

My eyes widen at the accusatory affirmation of my best friend, but when I snap my head to the side, I note the insinuating smile on her face.

Jaylyn Jones or JJ for short, ladies and gentlemen. Captain extraordinaire and the best friend of yours truly.

JJ has been our lieutenant before she got promoted to captain and we were lucky enough that she found an opening for the captain's position right at the station, otherwise we would've lost a great firefighter who always has our backs. I would've also stopped seeing my best friend as often.

"Hey, Enz."

Her gaze softens the moment after they do a quick once-over of me. It might have been brief however her piercing stare saw right into my soul.

"Oh, honey." The utterance is swiftly followed by her approach and by her pulling me into an embrace. I don't know when I'm up to my feet, I only become aware of her arms around me. "Let it out, doll."

And as though it is the encouragement I've been waiting for to shatter through my armor, my body begins shuddering between her arms. It feels as if each piece of the armor that I spent the past couple of months meticulously building around me now falls to the ground with the speed of light. Better said, it doesn't just fall, it downright collapses.

Crashes and burns with no chance of ever getting rebuilt.

Ensley the strong one.

Ensley the powerful one.

Right now, the two are sides of me I'm unfamiliar with because everything hurts.

How can I still be strong when there's a high chance that my world will crumble? How can others say they've been firm and resilient before the hardship that turned their lives into ruin?

"I can't... pretend... I'm strong... when I'm... I'm not, Jay," I whisper into the crook of her neck, my speech broken by the sobbing. "I can't... I can't be... strong for... for a moment... longer when... m...my husband is... in... in a...aaaa... com... coma."

Her hold on me tightens.

"You're the strongest person I know, Ensley Juliet Carter, and your husband is the toughest son of a bitch I came across. He puts up with you, after all, so he ought to be."

She manages to draw a nearly strangled chuckle out of me at the latter affirmation.

"You two will pull through. You always do, doll."

JJ's hand rubs up and down my back soothingly. Her attempt to calm me during my breakdown.

"I can't… watch… hi… him lying… he…re f…f…for…" My sentence dies on my lips as my sobbing gets harder.

"You've got *the fight* in every cell of your body, and you will fight till the end because I know you, Enz. You'll break…" JJ pauses as she draws back, making certain she holds my stare before she speaks again. "Hell, you are allowed to break for once. But let me tell you what you'll do after. You'll pick yourself right up because you're also the most stubborn person I've met in my life. And before you say it, I know you call it *determined*. I and everyone else, on the other hand, call it *goddamn stubborn*. You will do that because you're unyielding, absolute badass and giving up is not in your genes."

Through the tears, JJ manages to get a smile from me. A small, rather faint smile. A smile, nonetheless.

"I'm scared, JJ," I confess.

"And it's okay to be. Honey, the man lying in this bed fighting for his life to get back to you is your husband. So, damn sure it's alright to be scared, what isn't okay is to stop fighting."

Her eyes dart over my shoulder at Mason. They turn serious and firm as she stares at my unconscious husband, though there's a cheeky smirk playing on her lips.

"That applies to you too. Especially to you, handsome, because the only one allowed to break her heart is me when I'll marry a D.J. and live the rest of my life in Ibiza, leaving you two to hump each other like rabbits without having to hear all the filthy deets. That is because I'll be too busy having some hot and heavy sex on the beach of my own at that point and won't need to live vicariously through you both. And I don't mean the cocktail."

I can't hold the chuckle.

Count on Jaylyn Jones to turn every conversation into an R-rated discussion regardless of the place, time and occasion.

"Woman, your sex is unbelievably dirty," she attests as though that serves as her defense. "I've heard you screaming down the walls of your house and there's not enough bleach in this world to erase it. Ergo, it's safe to say that I know just how dirty and loud it gets."

I know her play, though. She's here to put a pause on my pity party of one and she does it the best way she knows how, by joking—JJ's coping mechanism during life and death situations.

"Thank you for being here. I really needed it."

At my admittance, she instantly pulls me into her arms, and we hold each other tight.

For two months I've been strong.

In fact, I've pretended to be strong before everyone else. Before my parents. Especially before my younger brother who keeps blaming himself for what has happened just because he was in the same basement as my husband when the blow-up happened. Besides that, he blames himself because Mason pushed him out of the blast's way before he was thrown across the room with the force of the explosion. But I know Mason did what my brother would've done for him in the blink of an eye had the situation been reversed.

In full honesty, the real truth is that with each day that passes by yet another piece of me breaks. Each moment of pretend takes more and more energy out of me. It subsequently and mercilessly causes every piece to turn into shards that slice my chest open with ache. Ache and fear.

Of what the future will bring us.

For the first time in my life, I'm truly frightened. Many times before, especially in my career of seventeen years as a firefighter, I have been scared. Many times happened that during an incident, there were moments when I've been surrounded by the flames of the inferno, and I have been afraid. Once I even got caught in a building on fire with one of my fellow firefighters and I thought that will be the end for us, which scared me. But never before have I been this terrified. So apprehensive to even close my eyes.

It is a goddamn nightmare.

One that I want to end.

One that I *need* to end.

"I just need this nightmare to be over already."

* * *

A week ago

Improvement.

Hope.

His latest scans show improvement with the swelling going down significantly and all this gives me hope. Confidence that the worst has passed and the turn toward the better has been already taken.

"We'll continue monitoring him, but the inflammation went down, so we'll wake him up," Octavio Reyes informs me.

Besides me, there's my cousin, Jace Walker. He is also a trauma surgeon like Octavio, but the latter has been in charge of Mason's case, although my cousin has followed it closely himself.

A sigh of relief pushes its way past my lips and Jace pulls me to him.

"That's good news," I utter and look up at my cousin with hopeful eyes. "I'm dying to hear him, to talk to him, to tell him that I love him." It is on that continuation that a chortle escapes me as a couple of tears roll down my face. Happy tears. "I'm sorry, neither of you needed to know that."

Octavio smiles sympathetically.

My cousin, on the other hand, shakes his head at me because if there's anyone allergic to even the most remote feeling of love, that person is Jace Walker. Although Jace and I are not blood-related since he was adopted by my uncle Harrison Walker and his wife Willow when he was five years old, we have always been family.

At the age of forty-five, former Navy SEAL medic, Jace Walker has been hardened by war. Before that though, he has been toughened by his own flesh and blood—his father was a notorious alcoholic who would beat him and his mother up. The moment Jace ran into the ER all covered in blood, barefoot and with only jammies on in the middle of a cold January night, it was the instant his life took a different course because that night he met my uncle who was the ER doctor and took care of him.

"It will be a process. We will take him out of the induced coma, but he won't wake up right away. I want you to be aware of that," Octavio explains, reverting me to the here and now.

"We'll gradually decrease the dosage of the sedatives that keep him in this state, but the recovery process and the speed of the recovery only depend on him, Enz," Jace adds. "With the slow reduction of sedatives, he'll slowly begin breathing on his own and we'll be able to extubate him."

"So he can wake up any time thereafter, right?"

Hope can be heard in my voice when I ask the question.

"Yes, it can be between twenty-four to forty-eight hours, or it can take longer than that. The cerebral edema has been present for a long period of time... Three months is a very long time for the swelling to go down which means that the trauma his brain took was very powerful..." Octavio pauses briefly as though looking for the right words. "There's not an easy way of telling you this, Ensley, but I think you should be prepared for secondary effects."

At that, I attempt to swallow.

I try.

And try.

But my throat appears to be clogged.

"We don't know that for sure, but..."

My head might move in an acknowledging signal however it is more of a heedless motion.

"I understand, doc. Thank you!"

Jace rubs at my back soothingly and his lips press against the top of my head, as Octavio excuses himself.

"What could the secondary effects be?" I ask Jace.

His head shakes as he pulls away.

"Let's not think of that now, Enz. I can list you many, but we have to see how he progresses when he wakes up. There's no point to have you worrying and thinking of all the possibilities when each patient is different. Let's just wait for him to wake up and..."

Before he can finish his sentence, the beeping of his pager fills the room.

"I'll come back to check on you both later, okay?"

With a kiss on my forehead, he rushes out of the room and I retrieve my—not so long priorly abandoned—seat by Mason's bed.

Reaching out, I grab hold of his hand into mine and I press my lips against his knuckles.

Finally. After three months, I can breathe slightly easier. I can feel the air entering my lungs. Moreover, I feel it passing through the passage that has only seemed to be clogged for all these months.

"Come back to me, baby! I want…," I stop, shaking my head from side to side gently. "I *need* to see your smile, to hear your voice… I need to see you, baby. I need you to come back to me so I can be able to breathe again because without you I'm suffocating."

What I wouldn't get to know right this moment is that my prayers would eventually be heard. What I also wouldn't get to know until a week from now is that I'll get Mason back, but I wouldn't get back my husband.

What I wouldn't get to know now is that I will experience his denial ten times stronger than I did after my twenty-first birthday. Moreover, I wouldn't get to know that there will be so many challenges before reaching an end. What I also wouldn't know now is that things would get worse before they get better.

MASON

My lungs strain for air.

I breathe in, but not a particle of air gets drawn.

Over and over again, I attempt to take in a gulp. A scintilla of the oxygen that I need so much. I need it to stay alive. I need it to live through another day.

Yet, I can't.

There's something that obstructs my lungs. That clogs my throat and impedes the air from entering my body.

The scorching heat bites at my flesh. It bites so fiercely. It feels so real. Though it also feels so surreal at the same time as if my mind concocts it.

Maybe it is. Maybe this isn't actually real.

Or maybe, just maybe, it is a dream I'll wake up from. So I will my eyes to open. I force my eyelids to lift. At first one by one, then simultaneously.

I will them again.

And again.

And one more time until a brightness hits my irises so strongly that it has me squeeze my eyes shut right away.

"Mason."

That voice.

It's that voice again.

The one I've been hearing.

Am I going crazy?

Why does it sound so real though?

I will my eyes again to open. They flutter to adjust to the blinding light. They slowly close and open over and over again until my eyes become accustomed to the brightness.

Through the blurry vision, I note a shadow hovering over me. So I gently blink until a pair of green orbs connect to mine. Until I manage to make out the long, raven hair.

I groan, acknowledging the pounding in my head as though I've been hit by a fully loaded truck. Or by a fucking train.

"God, where am I?" I ask, more to myself and without actually expecting an answer.

"You're in the hospital. You're okay." Even through my state, I still hear the relief in the voice.

The voice I've heard.

The voice that now is real.

Once again, I attempt to focus my vision to properly see the one whose face hovers over mine.

And I do.

The green eyes and the ink-dark hair get pieced together.

"What are you doing here?"

Her brows knit together. "What do you mean? I'm your—"

"I know who you are, Ensley. You're my best friend's sister," I interrupt, with my eyes narrowed. There's an emotion crossing her green eyes. One that disappears right after I blink.

Christ, I must be dreaming.

There isn't another explanation for the reason why Ensley Walker is here, by my side in a hospital room and although she looks a little tired, that doesn't diminish her beauty even in the slightest. She's the kind of woman who becomes one's fantasy. But also the type of woman who needs to remain a walking fantasy for *someone like me.*

So to confirm to me that I'm dreaming, I blink. However, my eyes still meet her gorgeous green orbs.

My head moves from side to side.

"Water," I whisper feeling the sudden dryness in my throat.

Ensley straightens her back, reaches swiftly for the carafe of water and pours some in a glass. Not a moment later, I feel the cold rim of the glass against my lips, and I let the liquid sate my thirst.

Once I drink enough, she places the glass back onto the bedside table and returns her gaze to me.

"Thank you."

She nods her head and holds my eyes for another second before she looks away.

"How are you feeling?" Her croak is gentle, yet a little frail as if she fights a wave of emotions.

For an instant, I let my gaze move over her features. Over the small freckles peppering her cheeks and nose. Over her jaded eyes. Over her high cheekbones. Over the plump lips. Over the raven hair that has a few strands escaping from her bun. Instantly, I fight the urge to reach up to brush them behind her ear because I know that the merest of touches would collapse everything. It would crumble all the will I garnered over the years to be able to resist Ensley Walker. To be able to keep her at arm's length.

Her eyes nearly pierce through mine as she awaits an answer to her question. They're wide and hopeful while they stare down at me.

They're fucking gut-wrenchingly beautiful.

Don't even dare go there, Carter.

"Like I've been hit by a goddamn train," I eventually reply. "Everything hurts. My head's pounding like a motherfucking bitch."

"I'll get the doctor for you," Ensley rushes to say and before I get a chance to say anything to that, even a mere *'thank you'*, she races out the door.

She rushes out fast.

But not fast enough for me not to see how she lifts her arm and wipes at her cheek.

As I'm left alone and before I get to ponder Ensley's reaction, a strong memory assails. One that begins with my loud shout.

"Flash, watch out!"

And before my very own eyes, I see the image of my hand extending and shoving my best friend before a piercing sound penetrates my ears as though it just happens.

Luke.

Luke was in that basement with me when the explosion occurred. I shoved him out of the way.

"How's Luke?" I ask when I see Ensley walk in.

Distress can be heard in my voice, and she doesn't miss a bit of it. Her beautiful features soften and her hand rests on mine, her fingers wrapping around.

The lack of hesitation makes me aware of just how natural the gesture comes to her. So much so that I resist the impel to drop my eyes just where her warm palm touches me to see just how her hand looks on mine not only how it feels—soft and smooth. Truthfully, I attempt to. Because that is what it is, an attempt. One I miserably fail since, not a tick later, my stare lowers to that exact spot. Her hand is small in comparison to mine and her milky, porcelain-like skin is in contrast with my much tanner one.

Fuck me sideways if it isn't one of the most beautiful things I've seen and felt in my life, though. How smooth her hand feels against my calloused one. How hot her flesh feels against mine, almost burning me. But it is a burn I welcome for another tick, or perhaps for two. I relish in it until Ensley withdraws her hand once my eyes peel off our hands only to lock onto her jaded green eyes.

"Luke is fine, Mason. It's been you who got us all worried."

"I just took a little beauty sleep," I answer with a smirk although the headache turns it immediately into a grimace.

"About three months' worth of it."

It is on her last statement that my eyes narrow.

"Three months?"

Ensley's reply doesn't come as through the doors in walk the doctor and a nurse.

"It's good to finally see you awake, Mason. I'm doctor Octavio Reyes. How are you feeling?"

"Like I've been gone for a minute, but at the same time for years," I explain.

The doctor leans over the bed after he retrieves a penlight and points it toward me.

"Follow the light, please."

With my eyes, I follow the light as he moves it from one side to the other.

"What's the last thing you remember?"

"The fire. We've been called to a structure fire, and I remember shouting for my best friend to watch out. I remember shoving him, but then from there, everything else is pretty much pitch black."

"So you don't remember being awake in the hospital?"

My head shakes and my brows narrow in confusion. "No."

"That's understandable. Your brain suffered quite a trauma. It took three months for the swelling to go down."

"Will there be lasting effects of this? Will I still be a firefighter?"

Firefighting is my life. Since I was a mere kid, I admired the profession. Every time Luke's father, Derek Walker, or Luke's grandfather, Gordon Walker, would take us to the firehouse, that was like Christmas morning for the both of us. For Ensley too who from the age of seven told everyone she was going to become a firefighter when she grows up.

The three of us had a habit of using garden hoses as firefighter hoses, and we'd run around "putting out" fires—nonexistent fires but that didn't stop us from doing all we could to put them out. Once we even damn well near flooded their parents' house in an attempt to put out a "fire".

"I can't say anything for sure right now. We'll have to run all the tests first."

"Stats look great, doc," the nurse attests.

At that, the doctor nods, stopping the penlight and sliding it back into his pocket.

Right away, as though out of reflex, my eyes search Ensley's who gives me a weak smile in return. It is so faint that it barely even reaches her eyes that gleam as tears dance in her gaze.

"We'll need to run a few tests before we will knock you out with something for the headache, okay? We just need to make sure that everything is alright."

"Do your thing, doc."

"I'll go to give a call to the rest of the tribe," Ensley says and walks toward the door.

"Ensley," I whisper her name and she stops, turning toward me. "How's my mom?"

A smile splits her lips. This time, it reaches her gorgeous eyes and they almost sparkle.

I'm a mamma's boy and everyone knows it.

I've always been one.

To me, Aracely Carter is the saintest of all the saints. That woman is an angel I hold to a pedestal.

"She misses her *baby boy*," Ensley replies, her smile wide as the tease is more than clear in the last two words.

So many ways I'd show you just how much of a man that baby boy is, Ensley.

Fucking stop right there!

Ensley Walker is unattainable.

She is off-fucking-limits.

I've touched her one time sixteen years ago. I've taken from her something I didn't deserve—her virginity. Something she gave me without thinking twice. Something I took from her without considering the consequences and my mistake was to think that Ensley Walker was inconsequential. Touching her once is one time too many. Sixteen years later I still feel her skin pressed against mine as though it was yesterday that I touched her.

Hop off that train before it derails, Carter!

I clearly need to get out of this hospital and get laid. Certainly feels like forever since I had some. Especially since I allowed my mind to drift to that night when I felt the smoothness of Ensley's skin beneath mine, when I tasted the sweetness of her lips, when I had her snug, untouched cunt clutching my dick like a vise, when her mouth...

Ooo-kay, that is enough.

"Doc, I think my brain needs a little more than a check-up."

My statement is half in jest, while the other half is meant in the most serious way, knowing I'd probably need a brain reset to be able to push away those memories I have of Ensley. And because the doctor doesn't know what I am going through right this moment, he smiles and, soon enough, I'm wheeled out of the room. They run tests and scans that most of them I haven't heard of in my whole thirty-five years of age.

* * *

Ensley

He is awake.

Mason is awake.

My Mason's beautiful eyes have finally opened. The wicked spark in them—the one I've been used to seeing when he'd look at me—no longer there. Instead, they were cold and detached somehow. The same distant stare I kept seeing in them back when he used to deny his feelings for me. The same one I got a glimpse of the few weeks leading up to his accident.

His eyes were filled with shock when he saw me there, but what I didn't anticipate was the unfamiliarity.

Yes, he recognized me. He knew who I was. I was *Ensley*, but I wasn't *his Ensley*.

"You're my best friend's sister."

His words still resound in my ears.

"I'm your wife" is what I wanted to shout in return, but for some unknown reason, I didn't.

Only to now find out that the cause of it is because he suffers from dissociative amnesia. He remembers most of the things that have happened in his life, many down to a T, what he doesn't have any recollection of is our life together. He forgot the time when I was his girlfriend, when I became his fiancée and when he married me. For some reason, he doesn't have any recollection of all these moments that we've spent together. By a quirk of fate, his mind blocks out all these memories.

"I made him fall in love with me once. I'll make him fall in love with me again."

This is what I told my family after I've made the choice not to tell him that I'm his wife. Call me selfish because he asked me for the divorce right the morning before the accident only to now hide the truth. Call me someone who takes advantage of his lack of memories to make him fall in love with me.

But what I am is determined.

Determined to find out why he, so suddenly, has chosen to opt for the divorce as though he has forgotten all the moments we have lived together and all the words he whispered to me. All the promises he made to me—some maybe induced by the warp passion we many times wrapped ourselves into, but many more vows have come from the love we have for one another.

Judge me for being determined to find out what drove him to make this decision because I call bullshit on it. The man I married wouldn't just give up for no reason and that is what makes me draw the conclusion—there has to be something more to it.

Try me for being determined to fight for my marriage and for what I believe to be true. For what Mason made me believe in—our love. Because I blindly believe in our love for each other to think that it is it for us, that with a signature on a piece of paper we can put an end to us.

And when I decided all this, I didn't know that many things would weigh on this judgment and many others would unfold— in the worst or maybe in the best possible way. I also didn't know that at that particular moment I was choosing between self-preservation and self-destruction.

When I made the choice to hide from him that we are married, what I wouldn't get to know until later is that—one way or the other—Mason Carter would bring me to my downfall.

One more thing I wouldn't get to know until much later is that falling in love and madly loving Mason Carter would be the lethal bullet that would pierce my chest.

ENSLEY

Voices and laughs fill the air inside the bar where we celebrate that my brother's now-fiancée Ella Matthews is back with us safe and unharmed after she was abducted. I couldn't be happier for the two of them because Luke definitely deserves to be happy and to be loved, and Ella is just the perfect woman for him.

As I sit on the stool at the square four-seater high table together with Mom, Dad and Renée, I can't help but let my mind drift.

Choosing to hide the truth from Mason will bring me heartache. I know that. But just because I am aware of it, that doesn't mean I am prepared for it.

As a reality check for that serves the very image before me. Mason sits in his wheelchair—much to his displeasure and after many arguments with me where I'd tell him to his ass back in that chair—and a blonde woman is next to him. She tips her head back and laughs at something he says as she rolls a strand of hair continuously around her finger.

That image right there shoots an arrow into my heart. I feel it breaking into pieces while I look at my husband—who has no idea he is my husband—now charming another woman.

With the fear of losing my husband and the man I love with every fiber of my being, I've taken the decision not to tell him that we're married because that'd mean telling him about the divorce he asked me for.

However, it is a decision I haven't thought through because my fear of losing him, one way or another will transpire into reality.

"Enz, honey," Dad's voice is soft and even gentler is his hand on my shoulder. "Are you sure you wanna do this? You can still tell him the truth."

That is when I realize that Mom and my sister have gone to mingle with the happy couple, and I'm only with Dad who now stands in front of me, leaning against the table. Whether he does it intentionally or not—which I'm inclined to believe is the former—he now blocks my view of Mason with the blondie.

"I want his mind to remember all those memories, I want him to remember me for who I am and how happy we were. With our ups and with our downs. With our arguments and with our reconciliations. With our fights and make-ups."

A comforting smile plays on his lips before they press against my forehead.

"Why did you just have to take your mother's stubbornness?" He jests, somewhat showing demur toward my decision with a head motion. However, his blue-grayish eyes tell me the exact reason why; he doesn't want his daughter to get hurt.

Dad is certainly right about the stubbornness, though. I definitely took that from Mom, something she passed on to Renée too. Though he isn't any less headstrong, what he knows is when to take a step back and decide everything with a clear mind. Whilst we—the Walker women—have a habit of making decisions in the heat of the moment.

"We call it determination, Dad," I correct him with a chuckle.

"Regardless of your decision, if Mason ever hurts you, I'll forget he's like a son to me and use my shooting range training to have him as a target practice."

That is a warning I'm not going to put to the test because it is clear in his voice that it isn't just an empty threat.

"The one where Mom keeps taking you to?"

He smirks, his eyes playful and his features full of youthfulness. "She tells me I look very hot, though I'd go more for badass. But I'll take hot too."

My nose scrunches up.

"Ew! Please do me a favor and keep yours and Mom's kinks to yourselves."

Though I protest at that bit of information I could've lived without knowing, it is impossible not to feel proud of my parents and how the love they feel for each other is just as strong as when they were young, if not stronger. If there is a couple worth of the *'couple goals'* terminology, that is made of Derek and Angeline Walker.

A love so worth of admiration.

A couple worth of the *'through thick and thin'* phrase.

A love and a couple I look up to and idolize not only because they are my parent. I say this also because it has always been my goal to have in my life a love so consuming, so thorough that it gets etched into one's bones. A love so passionate that one can't keep their hands off the other. One so fierce that it defeats all the obstacles thrown its way.

That is exactly what I feel I have with Mason. A love so deep. So absorbing. A love that grips us by the heart and doesn't let go. I know we have that. Regardless of Mason's out-of-the-blue decision to get a divorce, I know that what we have is true, unique, profound and all-consuming. A love that can overcome anything, even our own minds and our own denial. A love that can conquer anything and move mountains if need be.

I only need to make him remember that.

Easier said than done.

"You are a fighter and Mason stands no chance against the hurricane you've got inside you."

Dad's lips kiss my forehead once again and he smiles at me with pride.

"I could never be prouder of the woman you've grown to be, Ensley. Or should I say lieutenant?"

At that, I let a heartful smile play on my lips.

"Chief Hopkins told me you breezed through. Why didn't you tell me you're taking the test?"

My shoulder lifts just a pinch. "I took it when Mason was still… I needed something to keep my mind off everything going on, so studying the materials seemed the only thing that could keep my mind occupied."

"You did great, baby, and I'm proud of you."

"Thank you, Dad."

Over his shoulder, I discreetly search for Mason, only to find him already looking in my direction, our gazes locking across the room. Though, that only happens for the briefest of instances because his conversation partner runs her fingers over the tattoo on his left wrist. Subsequently, that causes him to interrupt our eye contact and revert his attention back to her.

I can't fight the pang of jealousy that builds in the pit of my stomach. It burns and clenches my gut. It squeezes around my heart and doesn't let go.

Mason is a handsome man who always would catch the attention of a willing woman and who'd always get hit on. However, he'd turn them all down saying he's in a happy relationship, happily engaged or happily married.

The heaviness in my heart turns even heftier. Our 'I do's' are not supposed to be this way. Our marriage is not supposed to be tried like this. Or is it? Are we supposed to only have a fraction of happiness then for everything to go up in flames only to see if our love will pass the test? Does our love come with an expiration date? Is that what it is?

"I'm gonna go, Dad."

Though it is clear he wants to counter my announcement and insist that I should stay, once he turns to look over his shoulder, he decides against it.

"Want me to drive you home?"

My head shakes as a negative response. "No, I'll be fine. Maybe you could drive Mason back to the hospital after because I told Jace and Doctor Reyes that I'm taking him out only for a few hours and bring him back for more tests he needs to do in the morning."

"I will do that."

This time, after I slide off the bar stool, I kiss Dad on the cheek. "Say bye to everyone for me, alright?"

Once he nods, I turn and walk toward the exit.

Although I fight and fight, the instant I get to the door, I still throw one last look over my shoulder to where I've last seen Mason. He's still there, displaying a knee-weakening smile that many times had my entire body tingling and my heart thumping in my chest. This time, however, it isn't directed to me, but to another woman.

The sight not only breaks my heart. The sight shatters it, taking me back instantly to a time sixteen years ago when Mason would do anything to push me away, including blatantly flirting with someone else to make me hate him. Are we back to those moments now? Are we back to the times when I'd fight for him and he'd fight against me, denying me with all the power he could garner though his heart would only beat for me?

With a deep breath, I straighten my neck and stare ahead at the hardwood door, feeling as though with each step that I take, I leave behind a piece of me. Pieces I don't know if I'll ever get back, but I for sure hope so.

A cool breeze surrounds me when I get out of the bar. The night air soothes me, though.

"Ensley."

My brother's voice brings my steps to a stop, but I don't turn immediately. It feels as though all the armor I have around me to protect myself against self-capitulation weighs heavily on that brief tick that I take to inhale deeply.

"When I've made that decision, I knew what I was in for," I say after I turn as if that would actually serve as an explanation.

"Why don't you just tell him?"

His question hangs ponderously between the two of us. I know it is something he wanted to ask for a while. A wonder I've seen in his eyes when I've mentioned to all of them at the hospital that I'm not gonna tell Mason we're married. And although I've seen it then, it still doesn't make it a question I know the answer to. It is why I dip my chin.

"Are you willing to watch him take home another woman just because you want him to remember you on his own accord? That's fucked up, Enz."

"Our marriage was struggling, alright? We've been running through the motions for a while and he even talked about getting divorced."

It is a lie.

Yes, we didn't have the perfect marriage, but let the one who does throw the first stone.

Yes, we also had moments when we'd feel like a routine, but it was something we'd come out of quite easily.

And yes, Mason asked me for the divorce, but I know it isn't for these reasons. I know that what we have is way stronger and able to overcome standard and ordinary. It is so strong that it will defeat any kind of hardship that is thrown our way.

His eyes narrow in disbelief at me. "What? He never said anything."

"Because we were trying to work it out before we get to that point."

"What are you going to do if he falls in love with another woman? Christ, what are you gonna do if he falls in love with you again and he still doesn't remember?"

"I don't know. I haven't thought anything through. I'm... I... I don't know." My hand runs through my brunette hair before my head shakes. "I'll see what I'm gonna do."

The truth is, I don't know where to begin.

I don't have a plan yet, which only serves as proof that I make decisions in the heat of the moment.

"Are you absolutely certain? One way or another it is gonna come out that you two haven't only been in a relationship, but you're married too."

I know that is his way of reasoning with me. Of telling me that I'm making a mistake.

Something I don't say anything to. Instead, I make my way to him to give him a strong hug. "Congratulations, little brother. Go to Ella now and stop having a pity party with me."

"So you can have it on your own?"

He knows what a pity party of one looks like. He's been drowning in that since Mason's accident, blaming himself for what happened to him. Self-blame I wanted to punch out of him so many times before.

"Me and a bottle of wine."

My declaration is followed by a forced smile. One that my brother doesn't overlook, his features definitely telling me he believes I'm making a mistake.

However, it is on that last statement that I turn and walk to my car. I know he still stands there, his blue-grayish eyes narrowed at me with what I know to be clear disapproval on his face.

Getting inside my vehicle, I turn on the engine and drive off without even one glance back. But what takes a great amount of effort is to push the image of Mason with the blonde woman. Her touch on his arm, trailing his tattoos with her fingertips. His charming smile clearly affecting her. My heart aches as it is already, yet I still choose to torture myself some more over it.

As I press the breaks when I reach the stop light, something on the backseat of my car catches my attention. I shift in my seat, looking at the bouquet of red roses.

My brows furrow.

"What the hell?"

In my aloud wonder, I reach for the flowers. Almost instantly, a small card slips from between them and falls into my lap.

I pick it up and read.

With each word, my skin crawls. With each reread, a cold shiver runs up and down my spine.

> *"Ensley, Ensley, Ensley.*
> *Such a beautiful name.*
> *So unfortunate that it's preceded by Juliet."*

My eyes dart to the flowers I hold then to the card. Is someone playing a bad joke on me? It must be. Maybe one of my fellow firefighters—who were at the bar tonight playing pool—has decided to pull a prank on me. Firefighters' pranks are known for crossing the line every once in a while.

Lost in that thought, I nearly jump out of my skin when a loud sound pierces my ears. I haven't noticed the lights turned green and the driver of the car behind me honks.

In one motion, I drop the flowers and the card on the passenger seat, and I continue my drive. From time to time though, my eyes would flicker briefly to the two items beside me.

Bad firefighters' joke, I reason.

PART II
THE FIGHT FOR LOVE

ENSLEY

A week later

"Hey, Enz!"

The sweet greet has me snap my head to the side and my gaze from the picture I hold with both hands to meet the bluest pairs of eyes as a blonde head pops atop the rolled-down window of my car.

Penelope Turner.

Known also as Pen.

Or by the press as the Army Princess.

And by her fellow firefighters as Tiger.

She is one of the firefighters of Station 7 in San Antonio, Texas. Because yes, I made a run for it and arrived in Texas after Ella put me in contact with her uncle, Aaron James, who together with his husband, Seth, have more than welcomed me with open arms.

"Hi, Pen," I greet her back, plastering a smile on my face while I reach and slide the picture of my husband and me—our first picture together as husband and wife after we said our 'I dos' in front of our family and friends—into the pocket of the sunshine extender before I swipe the visor up.

"Are you coming in?"

As she asks the question, her neck cranes to the side and her chin cocks toward the bar where I set to meet her, the rest of the crew from Station 7, their spouses and fiancées and some of their other friends.

Her blue eyes dart back to my green ones and I let out a heavy breath. So hefty that I didn't realize just how much it weighs until I let go of it.

I've been spending the last few days in San Antonio. Four days to be precise considering the day after Mason got discharged from the hospital and came home, I simply felt like I couldn't breathe anymore having him so close but so far away. Because Mason not remembering me is excruciating.

Then San Antonio needed volunteer firefighters to help out with a school that has caught fire and nearly burnt to the ground —luckily it happened during the night and nobody got injured. So when Ella mentioned, I put in a request for a few days of furlough and hopped on the first plane. Absolutely not running away. More like taking the time to gather my thoughts.

Pen and her husband Tucker Jacobs—also known as Moose —have been the first people I have met once I've arrived as they were unloading packs of water bottles for volunteers out of Moose's truck.

There was something when Penelope's blue eyes met mine that first moment. Understanding. As though she has done a little running away of her own—which I found out that very evening when all volunteers went to Sloppy Cow bar for a drink that she indeed has run, which implicitly had me explain my own reasons.

Penelope's eyes stay on me for a little while and she sighs, running a hand through her blonde locks.

Over her shoulder, I see Moose waiting in front of the bar's entrance and I give him a curt wave. He smiles and waves back.

The blonde woman's head turns, and I see a wide smile tipping at the corners of her lips when Moose winks at her. When she turns to me, it is impossible not to note the blush creeping at her cheeks.

She rolls her eyes gently as though to brush off her husband's gesture, but the redness in her cheeks does not wane.

"You've got a great bunch here looking out for you and backing you up, Pen. Plus, a husband who's clearly as crazy about you as you are about him," I attest with a smile of my own.

"There was a time when I thought I'd disappointed them all. When I've done them a disservice. When I've let what happened to me in Turkey get the best of me and I've run. I've run away from everything and everyone, including the man I love. I was lost, but they all helped me find myself again, find my way back to the person I used to be, and I understood that running doesn't solve anything because I needed them. It postpones, but never heals because one needs to face their worst fear."

Her chin cocks, her blue eyes darting to the sunshine extender where I hid the picture I stared at only moments ago.

"I can't help but wonder what if he finds someone else, what if he falls in love with another woman," I admit on a hefty exhale.

A frown appears on her forehead.

"And because of that, you are willing to let go of your man without a fight? Besides, staying away from him won't help you with that fear. Keeping away from your husband might actually push him into the arms of another."

It is on her words that my mind begins to ponder.

When I took the first flight to San Antonio it was to help my fellow firefighters and the community, but also because I needed to get away. I needed time. I needed to put distance between Mason and me until my mind clears.

I am aware when I first found out about Mason's diagnosis, I was certain I wanted to make him remember or make him fall in love with me again. Nevertheless, when I've seen him with the woman in the bar, when I saw her flirting with him, caressing his arm, reality hit me straight in the face and along with the jealousy, a feeling of fear settled in the pit of my stomach.

So right now, Penelope's question settles the dust. Settles all that fog that has been clouding me since the day Mason came back from the coma.

As I watch her straighten her posture after she pushes herself off the window, I blink once or twice, allowing her words to still sink in.

For a moment, her blue eyes look at me. I don't miss how she fights the smile once she takes me in as though she recognizes something just like she identified when we first met. She sees a fraction of herself in me.

"Are you coming?"

I let her question hang in the air for several seconds.

"You know, I think I'm gonna take the first flight home and fight for my man."

This time, she doesn't suppress the tipping at the corners of her lips and lets them quirk upwards. But there is no surprise in her peer like she already expected me to answer the way I did. And that only solidifies just how much of herself she saw in me. Just how much I reminded her of herself.

"Go get him, tiger."

"Isn't that your nickname?" I revert with a chuckle.

"I'm fairly sure I used it appropriately."

"Say bye to everyone for me, alright? I'll make sure to come to visit you all some other time."

Her blonde head nods. "Of course. Bring that handsome husband of yours next time as well. And stop being afraid of what might happen. Just fight till the end with everything you got and if he falls in love with someone else, he's a goddamn idiot. But considering I've stared at that picture of the two of you for a whole lot of two minutes, I'm pretty certain he's still just as crazy about you."

I give her a faint smile at the encouraging words.

"Sometimes the mind forgets, but the heart doesn't."

With that, she reaches through the rolled-down window and gives me a tight hug. I hug her back and squeeze my eyes shut.

It is time to stop running.

Now it is time to start fighting.

To gamble on what we can have.

To have a stab at that love that courses through our veins.

It is time to take my husband back—to make him remember me or to make him fall in love with me all over again.

MASON

A little over three weeks later

A light, mid-May breeze surrounds me as I ride my Honda sports touring motorcycle through the late morning traffic.

Done and dusted yet another check-up and one more physical therapy session.

One—or maybe just me—might believe that after waking up from a three-month long coma, doctors and everyone else would leave them alone with their confused minds.

Because that is what my mind feels like.

Confused.

Jumbled.

All over the place.

Although that much is true—confused or not—*post-comatose me* is certainly ready to get back to his life. Especially since I seem to have missed so many things. Among them, I missed my best friend falling in love.

About fucking time, I might say.

Though I thought Luke would forever be hung up on his other best friend—Daphne Spencer or I should say Daphne Levi now—, he took the opportunity of my unfortunate absence to lay eyes on a sweet as pie, but fiery as the very hell redhead, Ella Matthews.

While she has some exceptionably questionable relatives, she's definitely all Luke could have ever asked for and more.

And, oh man, is he punching...

Oh boy, is he robbing the cradle too...

But he is also happy.

Ridiculously happy.

This eventually makes me happy for him because there's nobody else who deserves that more than Luke after he pined over Daphne for so goddamn long.

In full honesty, he isn't settling for Ella because he can't have Daphne. The reality is he's never loved anyone the way he loves Ella. I've never seen him look at someone the way he looks at her and I've known Luke since we were three years old.

It took me only a second—even through my post comatose slumber—to see just how much in love he is with her and she with him.

Ella definitely brings out the best in him and he seems to have realized so himself since not long ago he proposed to her.

I guess post-comatose me is ready for a party and to be the best man. Maybe I'll get lucky with some long-legged maid of honor who'd happily wrap them around me at the end of the night or at the beginning of the night. I'm not fussed as long as she wraps them legs around me.

Downshifting by a gear, I then twist the throttle to accelerate and swerve through a couple of cars to make it in time just before the green light switches. Once I cruise through the intersection, I push the handlebar grip to the right so the motorcycle leans on the side as I take a right turn to enter the street.

After a couple of blocks, I veer another right.

Beneath the visor of my helmet, my eyes narrow and my brows knit together so closely, they nearly become one.

Concomitantly, I shift the gear to bring the bike to a more leisure speed as I get closer to the source of my scowl.

A woman fiercely gesticulates her hands toward the two cars, the back one up into the bumper of the front one. She explains something to a man who stands in front of her. Or I should say shouts at him.

What has me scowling isn't the scene or my hero complex kicking in since she clearly seems more than capable of handling it on her own. It is the familiarity of the brunette woman and the magnetic gray Ford Focus RS.

Raven hair so long I know damn well it nearly reaches the curve of her ass. Eyes so green they look like two jade stones. Athletic body hugged to perfection by a pair of three-quarters length, high-waisted black workout leggings and a white hoodie that's zipped up just below the band of the black sports bra she wears underneath.

Ensley Walker.

Ride past, Carter. She can handle it, I reason.

However, my body doesn't get the message in time. My brain seems to think one thing, while my hand and foot do another, bringing the bike to an abrupt halt right just behind the Ford.

With my foot, I place the side stand down and throw my right leg over the seat, unmounting the bike in one quick, fluid motion. Immediately after I remove my helmet and as I run a hand through my hair to comb it back, her voice pierces my ears.

"You were talking on your goddamn phone," she states, her tone accusatory.

What takes me aback is the fire that seeps through every single pore of her being as she argues her cause. What surprises me even more is how I'd just stand there to watch that feistiness and all that fire that surrounds her.

Fucking beautiful.

She's been back from San Antonio for a little over three weeks now. Those few days she's been gone have been a goddamn nightmare. It made me see that I took her presence in my life for granted because Ensley has always been there. But her time away has also heightened a dreaded, torturous feeling in the pit of my stomach at the thought of what would happen if she met someone there. And I fucking saw red each time that ponder nagged at me.

Hell, I clearly need to get laid before I do something stupid because of that persistent jealousy.

God knows how long has been since. My foggy brain doesn't even seem to recall when the last time I had a woman beneath me was.

The doctors said that after the brain trauma I suffered during the accident and after the three months of coma, feeling confused and disoriented is normal. They also believe I might be suffering from dissociative amnesia since there are certain things I can't remember, place for sure or they just don't fit the circumstances. For instance, the entire day of the accident is pretty much a blur for me and I only remember the last moments before the blow.

In a nutshell, my brain is a jumbled mess.

Certainly not scrambled enough to overlook how beautiful Ensley is.

Joder!

(*Fuck!*)

I need to get a woman under me before I make a mistake I've been avoiding a repeat of for sixteen years.

"You better have insurance, lady, because the cost to fix this car will blow a hole in your pocket," the man counters, crossing his arms over his chest. Or so at least I assume since his back faces me, yet the stance he has—legs apart and arms not at his sides—only suggests a defensive posture.

"Oh, no, you'll be the one to pay for my repairs because you slammed on the breaks without any warning."

Ensley's arms cross just below her breast and her perfectly sculpted brow arches.

Both of them are too engaged in their argument to actually acknowledge my presence.

"Ensley?"

No, a figment of your imagination, idiot. Seriously? Just her name? Is that all you can do?

Of course, it's her.

Truth be told, I don't even know why I said her name in a question. The whole reason I stopped is that I've spotted her from afar.

Surprised green eyes move away from the man and in my direction. They're wide and stunned as they connect with my brown ones.

"Mason," she whispers my name in return.

Sweet.

Angelic.

The best my name has ever sounded on somebody's lips. But they aren't just anyone's lips.

They are Ensley's.

The woman with the sweetest lips I've tasted.

A woman I've denied myself for so long.

One I'll spend just as long denying.

Carallo!

(*Shit!*)

I am aware of what Ensley wakes in me.

That she is the most beautiful woman I have laid eyes on in my whole life.

I have been aware of all this for twenty years. Ever since I was a mere fifteen-year-old who crushed on his best friend's older sister.

Just as aware I am that she has become a heart-haltingly gorgeous woman with the most piercing eyes that just seem to wander into my soul. With the greatest pair of legs that I've ever had wrapped around me. With the most mouth-watering pair of tits—though small, they're round and perky. With the most delicious mouth I've ever had touch mine.

Christ, there might have passed sixteen years since I felt the sweetness of her lips on mine, the smoothness of her tits in my hands, since I've sucked on them last, since her legs have locked at the ankles on the small of my back as I drove inside her snug pussy. But I'll be damned if I don't still feel the softness of her skin.

Caramba!

(*Dammit!*)

I must stop thinking about Ensley Walker as more than my best friend's sister because if I entertain these thoughts any longer, I won't be able to help myself.

And that would be a mistake.

A terrible, unforgiving mistake that will end in a downright mess. In a downfall I've been avoiding for two decades since I've realized that this woman woke in me unwelcomed feelings. Firstly and initially, because she is my best friend's older sister. And after Mom told me the truth, I then suppressed the unwanted feelings because I would never be worthy and deserving of Ensley. She comes from a family who is on the up and up. I, on the other hand, not so much.

While I gently clear my throat and jump out of a nearly derailed train of thoughts, I shift my gaze to the man, pinning him to the spot, before it reverts to Ensley.

I know what she sees in my eyes. Worry.

"Are you okay, baby? Are you hurt?"

Baby?

Fucking *baby* now?

"I'm good, Mason. Thank you."

"But my car isn't," the man argues.

Once again, my eyes dart to him.

He seems to be in his forties. The suit he wears is nicely pressed and not even the slightest crease is on it. His hair is dark, and his figure is tall, muscular. His lips are pressed in a thin line, and he gives the woman at my side a stern stare. One that has me step closer to Ensley and the hands that ball at my sides are the proof that he needs to watch what he'll say before I feed him my fist.

"You slammed your fucking breaks and went ballistic when I tried to check up on you."

"That's what guilty people do, they check the damage."

Ensley's jaw tightens.

Although I expect her to bite her tongue, the brunette gives him a lash instead. "Listen here, ungrateful prick. Without assessing myself first or even making sure I didn't lose a boob during the impact with the steering wheel because you randomly decided to slam on the breaks, I jumped out of the car to make sure your excuse of an ass is fine because I peel idiots like you off lampposts and pull them out of wrecked cars for a living," she rants, the metaphorical flames around her getting higher and more intense.

Xesucristo!

(*Jesus Christ!*)

Such a marvel to watch her all fired-up. To watch those flames lick at her, fueling her annoyance.

And, fucking hell, I'm in love.

The man shakes his head.

"Look, pal, why don't you just call your insurance company and stop wasting our time?" I suggest, my voice severe. "Because from what I'm seeing on the road, the break marks are mostly under your car which suggest how hard the breaks have been slammed on."

He puffs.

"Is she giving you pussy for saying that?"

Rage takes over.

So much so that in the blink of an eye, I slam him against his own car. My left hand is at the collar of his shirt while my right arm draws back, my fist in the air, waiting for one more reason to punch the guy. Because it is only by a miracle my fist is not halfway down this guy's throat right now.

"What did you just say?" I growl in his face.

My jaw clicks in anger while I wait for an answer. One that doesn't come and what I get in return are several blinks of utter shock.

With my body shaking with rage at the man's audacity, it is the instant I feel a hand resting on my shoulder and another getting placed around my left wrist that I feel a calmness running through me. Even through the material of my jacket, I can feel the heat of her touch that spreads a fire within me.

"Mason, he's not worth it," Ensley utters, gathering all her force to pull me back from the man.

She is indeed strong, but I'm stronger and I don't even budge.

"Have the guts to say that one more time, jackass," I dare him as my eyes send daggers. "Say that one more time and give me another reason to kick your sorry ass."

"Mason, baby…"

It is the whisper that takes me aback. So much so that I lose the hold I have on the man and nearly stumble over my own feet as she takes advantage of my very surprise, pulling me off of him.

"Mason, baby…"

My eyes squeeze shut for a tick, or maybe for two. Perhaps even for a little longer. Or so it seems because the two works keep repeating and repeating in my head. Over and again.

It resounds.

And echoes.

It thunders.

And rumbles.

My eyes squeeze tighter as an unfamiliar feeling rushes through me. It feels as though something strikes me to the back of the head without having me fall to the ground. Meanwhile, my head feels like it is spinning. It whirls at miles an hour with the echoes of the two words.

"Mason, baby…"

There is something that settles deep into the pit of my stomach with each repetition.

What the hell is going on with me?

What kind of feeling is this in my gut?

My jaw tightens and my teeth grit right before my head moves from side to side, pushing away the two words that have me disoriented and lightheaded.

Carallo!

"He's not worth it," she repeats.

She is calmer this time.

Her arms never let go of me.

My chest burns.

Now that both her hands are there, keeping me back from behind, their touch scorch my skin more than before.

It is on that realization that I also acknowledge something I'll never let myself admit ever again: I could be in full firefighter gear right now—known for enduring the worst of hells—and I'd still be able to feel the fire of her touch through it. Its feral singe on my flesh. Its sheer burning. Its flames slowly consuming every part of me, of my sanity and of my control.

Because I've always—with the sole exception of sixteen years ago—had control over myself around Ensley. I've forever ignored all the unwanted feelings she's been waking inside of me. I've denied them all even when she tried time and again to make me succumb to them—eventually she gave up. I've kept her at arm's length for so long, she must have given up. But I did it for her own good.

And I won't stop doing it.

I mustn't stop.

Shaking off her touch, she immediately removes her hands from around me and when I turn for a brief tick toward her, I regret my action. Not dodging her touch because I can still feel the burning it left behind, but I regret looking her way. And the reason I regret it is because I don't like one bit what I see in her green orbs. An expression that is pained. What annoys me even more is that I am the one to have caused it because I couldn't shake her touch fast enough. That when in reality all I wanted to do is to relish in that fire that ignites inside of me with her touch. One that shakes me to the bone.

But what I want and what I need to do are two separate

things. Two very distinct things that will never—in this lifetime nor any other thereafter—collide again.

Ensley and I are supposed to walk separate ways into this life. Always.

Our worlds should have never even grazed past each other, let alone strike in the way they did sixteen years ago. When I lost control and became weak. When she let me touch her. When she let me kiss her. When she let me claim her innocence.

That was a mistake I'll never allow happening again. The sweetest and most delicious mistake I've made. The most tempting and most consequential one. A mistake that can never repeat itself because I know I won't be able to live with its consequences.

"Ensley..." I begin, saying her name in what mostly sounds like a whisper.

What do I even want to say?

How do I even begin to tell her that if I've been rejecting her this whole time is not because I don't want her—because she courses through my veins—, but because I want to keep her safe?

Safe from *me*.

Safe from *who I am*.

Safe from the hurt and the pain that can be caused by *being with me*.

ENSLEY

If I thought even for the briefest of instances that it will be easy to make Mason yield to what I know he deep down still feels for me, I've been sorely mistaken.

Given our history, given that whole time he kept me at arm's length, given the many attempts I had before at making him admit to me what he truly felt, I should have known already that he is the most stubborn man I've met.

The truth is, however, when he couldn't get out of my hold fast enough, it hurt. Like a goddamn bitch. As though reality has decided to slap me across the face with some more sense of verity.

To be able to fight for Mason when he fights me with all his might I need all the resilience and determination I can garner. I need to remind myself that it will be worth it in the end. That all the energy and effort I will put into it, it will be worth it. That the time when we were happy, when we were crazily in love with each other and all the memories I have of us, they are the very and only sort of proof that I need to carry on. They are the power that fuels my battle.

I know what we were and what we had.

I know what we can be and what we can have.

And for that, I won't go down without a fight. No matter how hard he tries to fight against me and regardless of how much it hurts.

Mason Carter, you better prepare yourself for the battle of your life because in this fight, there's only one winner and I'm determined to be it.

I can fight clean. It is exactly what I've been trying to ever since I came back from San Antonio, biding my time and giving him time. Nonetheless, I can also fight dirty. What he doesn't know is that I know what makes him tick, how possessive he can get and how jealous he can be. I know how to push his buttons and just how much exactly to get a reaction from him. One that will be the desired reaction.

He might be stubborn, but I'm even more so. I'm determined to find out the truth. I'm determined to find out what happened. Because marriage doesn't go from *"I love you more than life itself"* to *"I want us to get a divorce"* in the span of a few weeks. A love like ours doesn't just come to an end without a reason.

That is exactly what I want, a reason. One good enough. One that would tell me we're indeed over.

If he's fallen out of love with me, I'm willing to accept that and let him go. If he's fallen in love with somebody else, that's again something I will accept and won't have him tied to me if he wants to be with someone else.

They are some of the reasons that run through my head over and over, but then I remember the way he'd love me, how he'd look at me when we made love. How he'd look at me full stop. That isn't the look of somebody out of love with the other or in love with another. That is the exact look of someone who loves deeply and whose love knows no bounds.

And it is this very look I vividly remember that I hold on to most. Because he can be guarded sometimes, but when we make love, that's when all his defenses crumble and all his walls are down, when he's at his most vulnerable, when he loses all the control he has and when he lets me in to see inside his soul.

A reason is all I want. A reason that will tell me to carry on fighting or to quit the fight, but until that happens, until he tells me the truth, I will continue the fight for him.

To be completely honest, dissociative amnesia or not, I know this started long before. The seed of it all is in the past. It is rooted deep in our story because there has always been a part of him he's kept hidden away from me. Something he knew but wouldn't want to share with me.

When I think back, sometimes it feels as though throughout

MISHA BLAKE

the years, I've only gotten glimpses of Mason Carter. Bits and pieces of what he wanted me to see and of what he wanted me to know.

"Ensley..."

My name on his lips sounds like a whisper. The most bitter-sweet whisper I've heard. Sweet because it is him whispering my name in that manner of his that has it brushing against my skin until my flesh gets covered in goosebumps. Bitter because he doesn't know what it does to me, the memories it brings. Memories he doesn't remember.

"It's fine," I reply, not letting him say whatever it is he wants to say.

All the while, I make my way back to my car, stopping next to the driver's door when I feel his hot pursuit.

"I'll handle this myself."

"You actually believe I'll leave you alone with this prick? *Pois non, fermosa, estás tola se pensas isto.*"

("Well no, beautiful, you're crazy if you believe that.")

My brow arches at him. "I can very well take care of myself."

"And who takes care of him? I mean, I'm afraid for the poor guy and what you'll do to him if you eventually find you're missing a boob," he declares, amusement in his baritone. One that is topped with a smirk that nearly has me topple over.

"I truly hoped you didn't catch that," I revert, leaning my back against my car.

"Quite difficult not to."

Mason slides his hands in the pockets of his jeans and leans against the car, facing me. The ink he has across his chest peeks from beneath the white tee he has on after he unzipped his jacket. Even the silver barbell piercing he has stabs through the fabric of his t-shirt when his arm moves, subsequently shifting the right side of his jacket.

Boy, oh boy!

Someone help me with this man because he is a god.

Actually, allow me to revise that thought.

Tattoos, piercing, leather jacket and motorbike. Mason Carter is my very own bad boy fantasy.

He's always been. Ever since he got his first tattoo when he turned eighteen, he slowly started turning into a guy who gave away bad boy vibes.

Truth be told, he's a good guy. He's a great, amazing guy for anyone who gets to see that side of him. However, there's also the other side of him that only one who angers and pisses him off, messing with the ones he cares about gets to see. That fierce and ready for the fight side, who'd shred anyone into pieces with his bare hands.

Goosebumps run over my skin, and I instantly become aware of their source.

Although I don't look his way, I can feel the intensity of his brown gaze on me. It is fleeting to the extent that when I find it in me to look up, his back is now leaned against the car and his head is mid-motion, cocking to the side. Yet, it still has that usual *Mason* effect on me.

"You think he's finally calling his insurance company?" He asks, his chin pointing at the man who's now on the phone, pacing back and forth.

"The asshole," I mumble under my breath.

However, it is loud enough for Mason to hear.

"Ensley Juliet Walker." The way he says my name is admonishing, but the mocking clear. "Angie wouldn't be very pleased to hear her daughter use such language."

Craning my neck to the side, I look at him with narrowed eyes. "How do you think I've learned how to swear? She might be sweet and all, but that woman curses more than a sailor."

"I'm fairly sure she gives that credit to the foul mouths around the firehouse."

I smile. "Of course she does, and everyone believes her up until they pick up her books and realize just how much her characters swear."

A short moment of silence looms in the air between us. A tick that I use to brush back a strand of rebel hair.

"How is it going with the bar?"

A week ago when we found out that the bar we all go to—the same place where my brother has announced after Ella's abduction that she will become Mrs. Walker—Luke and Mason have decided to go into business together and buy the bar. *The Pool Room*—though many thought it could do with a better name—is a place famous among the firefighters in the Fourth Ward as well as the neighboring wards, One, Three and Five, but not only.

"Harder than we thought. Your mom put us in contact with one of the graphic designers who's doing her covers and she did an amazing job with the artwork for the logo." A low, frustrated chuckle follows as he shakes his head. "At least keeps me busy until I get back to the firehouse."

"Any news on that?"

Ever since he's been released from the hospital, Mason has had regular check-ups. Although everything seems to be in order, he has yet to be cleared to return to the fire station.

"I'll have another physical in the upcoming days, but this time with the department's doctors."

"You must be itching to get back."

His head moves in assent.

What he doesn't need to tell me is just how much it means to him to be a firefighter.

Mason is the epitome of an everyday hero and being a firefighter is all he's ever known and wanted. He is dedicated to the job and his drive is admirable. Not to mention, sexy as fuck.

When we were kids, he was the first one to say he'll be a firefighter when he grows up and nobody could get that idea out of his head. Granted, my father and my late grandfather had a lot of influence on that front because they'd always treated Mason as part of the family, as their own flesh and blood and took him under their wings.

"*Beleza*, you've got no idea. I've ridden past so many fire trucks on scenes since I've been discharged from the hospital and there's this fucking itch to jump off my bike and run inside."

"Once a firefighter, always a firefighter."

At my declaration, he nods right before his neck cranes to the side and his eyes drop to meet mine. The intensity in his brown irises nearly has me liquifying down the side of the car I lean against. While I fight near liquefication, I also battle the urge not to bring my hand up to my chest to stop the crazy thumping of my heart.

Dammit!

He always has that effect on me. Whenever he is near and looks at me, he sends my heart in a rebelliously wild gallop and my body becomes my biggest betrayer.

"Like an addiction one just isn't able to quit."

His baritone is low and *oh*, so smooth as he speaks the words to me. So deep and rich that it shakes me to the core. But if the wild shudder that rocks my body is caused by his words or by the implication I hear in them and see in his gaze, that I don't know for certain. However, judging by the way he looks at me, I'm inclined to choose the latter. Because his eyes don't leave mine even for the shortest of blinks. They hold my gaze and even if I try, I can't look away. His stare is so hypnotic. They set me under a spell I can't break because I'm not strong enough to do so. Because they are the only pair of eyes that drives me all sorts of crazy. The only one that has ever driven me crazy and brought out the wildest side of me. The singular pair of eyes that has erased all my inhibitions and obliterated all my cognitive capacities.

Christ!

These chocolate brown eyes better be worth the ache. That pain I can already foresee they'll bring. But what I know with more certainty will be worth it all the more is the happiness they'll bring. That same happiness they brought me thus far.

My mouth opens, but before I get a chance to say a word, the sound of sirens halts my thoughts and my speech.

Running a frustrated hand through my hair, I sigh.

"Let the fun begin with this clown."

"I'll stay with you to make sure you don't make anyone disappear or get yourself arrested," Mason mocks, the left corner of his mouth quirking in a lopsided smirk while his eyes dance with rascality.

Without thinking twice, my hand lifts and I smack his chest —fighting to overlook the raw, taut muscles that I feel beneath, that very hardness I know he hides beneath.

My action causes a chuckle to escape him. A deep sound that makes my heart skip a beat.

* * *

With a discontent sound, I step inside the house and drop the keys atop the entryway table.

Kicking off my sports shoes, I open the door to the shoe storage cabinet and place them back where I took them from before I've left the house for my workout late this morning. That was after I caught up on a couple of hours of sleep once I got home from my shift at the firehouse.

"And here I was thinking that you'll unload all that anger during your workout."

The voice comes from the living room and brings my steps to a halt. My eyes close and I inhale deeply, relishing in the sound of that strong voice.

God, I missed so much hearing it.

To such an extent that my body shudders involuntarily and my heart squeezes so tightly.

It takes a great effort of me not to shout it from the rooftops that I'm his wife, and not only his roommate. It takes an even greater effort to stop that sole tear from slowly rolling down my cheek at hearing his voice again in this house. Something I can't seemingly get used to after spending three months by his side in the hospital, not knowing if I'll hear that smooth baritone again or not. Not knowing, but damn well hoping.

Because the doctor recommended not to make many changes in his environment since being in a familiar space can help trigger memories over time, Mason and I still share the house we lived in before his accident. Although I must admit, my first thought was to pack my things and move out before he got released. But Luke talked me out of my spur-of-the-moment decision by telling me that Mason clearly has memories of being in this house. Although he remembers some, many others are blocked out by his own mind. The ones of us together.

The operation "getting my husband back" is underway with little to no progress during the weeks after my return from Texas. I'm saying that because I've been busy taking in the fact that he's here, that he's doing well and that he's slowly getting back to his usual routine. Also because I wanted to bid my time and do everything at a natural pace.

"I got rid of as much of it as I could, but one of the guys started giving me weird looks because I just kept squatting," I say, ungluing myself from the spot I've been standing in for who knows how long.

Once I drop my gym bag next to the staircase to take it on my way up, I then change direction and saunter toward the open space of the floor that fits the kitchen, living room and dining room. The three are segregated by being on lower or higher levels that are connected by stairs, the design giving the rooms more of an ample space.

After I descend the three stairs, I reach the living room and I fight to suppress the gasp that crawls up my throat. Though I manage to do so just in time, the sight my eyes witness has my heart nearly leaping out of my chest, waving me goodbye while telling me *"see you never"* and *"good riddance".*

My very own heart betrays me at that view.

Mason is on the L-shaped dark gray sofa, leaning against the backrest while his long, muscular legs are stretched across the length of the cushioned couch. In his hands, he holds a book and looks sexy as hell doing it.

Hands down one of the hottest things I've seen in my life and the more I see it, I realize I can't get enough of that view.

Worthy of a candid.

No, what am I even saying? Worthy of getting painted.

If I'm taken aback by that sight, it is on his following action that I'm ready to throw in the towel and beg for him to come back to me, to remember me and just hold me for a little while.

His brown gaze instantly darts to me, and I don't miss just how it moves over the length of my body with sheer interest. The instant fire that glazes his gaze causes a quiver to run through me from the very roots of my hair to the bottom of my feet.

Yet, both the interest and the fire disappear a blink later.

As though it has never been there.

As though it was a fluke of my imagination.

Just like I've been used to seeing sixteen years ago.

He is a master at masking his interest in me. During the year he's refused me, I've become accustomed to that side of him. Despite that, I had fifteen years thereafter to get used to the unmistakable, uncloaked hunger in his gaze, in his actions, in his touch, in the way he claimed me without any mercy. Thus, it is difficult to now be exposed to that same side of him once again. Especially when I'm used to the raw, denuded yearning. To the clear desire and claim that coated his eyes and remained there.

These past weeks since he's been discharged, whenever I see him, I expect him to extend his hand, reach up and pull me to him until I'm in his embrace like he did many times before. I anticipate having his lips on mine without warning. I imagine he'll brush back strands of my hair and then whisper in my ear that he loves me.

And the painful truth is that I know none of these will happen because I always get the heartless reality check. That slap across the face, when he stands there, looking at me, or when he carries on with whatever it is he's doing.

In all honesty, I knew it would be hard when I decided not to tell him about our marriage. I knew it would be even harder to make him surrender to the power of what we feel for each other. But it is hard because how can I have him this close and not be able to reach out to him? How can I have him just within reach and not be able to touch him, caress him, kiss him? How can I simply pretend that I don't know what his touch feels like? What his lips against mine feel like? How his heart beats in tandem with my own? How can I just pretend I don't know any of that when I've got them all memorized?

Most importantly, how can I pretend I don't love him when loving him is all I've known and done? How can I pretend I don't know what his love feels like when his love is the one and only I've ever felt to the marrow of my bones? How can I pretend when he sets and dictates the beating of my heart?

At this moment, I know I'm just his friend and his roommate. Just as I know that the road ahead is not only bumpy, but it is fucking rough. A make or break.

On a hard swallow, I spin toward the kitchen to grab a bottle of water from the fridge. It is only after two or three sips, that I screw the cap back on and place it on the side.

The heat I feel and the small hairs lifting at my nape already tell me that his eyes are on me, so I delay turning around. I stall because I *need* my heart to cease the savage galloping that gives me away. I hold up because I feel the sting behind my eyelids at all the uncertainty that occurs around us. At the unknown.

My heart tells me everything will be worth it in the end. So do all the fibers in my being. They all scream at me to carry on. Yet, for a brief moment, I wonder why haven't I told him the truth in the first place? Why haven't I told him that we're married? Why have I made the decision to hide the truth and lie to him? Is it because of fear that it will mean bringing up the divorce he asked me for? Or is it because I want to fight with all I have for the man I love?

Whatever the wonders are and whatever the true reasons are, in the end, now it is a little too late to back down on that.

Time to face the music, Ensley.

MASON

Pre-comatose me was a fucking idiot.

Living with Ensley is a monumental mistake.

I've reached that conclusion the moment I stepped foot inside the house after I had been discharged, and he hasn't realized that in so many years?

Perhaps he did, but because he's as much of a glutton for punishment as post-comatose me—considering he's decided to stay instead of moving out somewhere else—, he chose to have her close as a reminder that he can't have her. As a daily reminder that regardless of how much he craves her, of how much he wants another taste of her sweet lips, he can't and mustn't because he's no good for her.

Maybe pre-comatose me was also stronger than I am because every time I get even the faintest of hints of her fragrance, all I want to do is grab hold of her. All I want to do is have her against me until I drown myself in that sweet scent with notes of sandalwood and jasmine.

Carallo.

I'm doomed.

So fucking damned even the term becomes an understatement.

Because one way or the other, Ensley Walker will be my eternal damnation.

Sé forte, Carter! Non deas.

(*Be strong, Carter! Don't yield.*)

This seems to be my new motto.

I do need all the motivation in this world to keep myself in check, to restrain my desire, and to put a leash on all that hunger I feel for Ensley.

A hunger that only heightens as I let my gaze roam over that seductive and inviting body of hers—that totally and thoroughly forbidden body of hers—while her back faces me from the kitchen.

One look won't hurt, I justify myself.

And this moment right here is my greatest mistake believing that even the merest of glances at Ensley won't be consequential.

Though everything inside me tells me I shouldn't, my eyes don't get the memo and move along the length of her body. With the long, brunette hair now in a high bun, her bare neck is exposed. Almost immediately I battle the urge to eat the distance between us and run the back of my fingers along that skin to see her tremble and witness the reaction of her body to my touch.

As my gaze continues to lower, it takes in the small of her waist for a tick or two before it drops to her round ass that is an utter tease. One I can only fantasize about caressing with my hand right before I smack it just for the selfish purpose of seeing my mark on her flesh. One I can only dream of spreading while I have her on her stomach to then bury my face in between her cheeks and run my tongue from the slit of her sweet pussy to the crack of her tempting ass. To dive my tongue salaciously into both of them and lick her until she begs me to take pity on her.

The sudden ache I feel in my groin rifts through my wayward thoughts, and I battle the impel to press against my hard-on. Instead, I quickly adjust myself in my shorts.

The last thing I need is a hard-on caused by all the fantasies my mind concocts because of the sheer seductress and temptress that Ensley is.

Merda!

My filthy mind needs to slam the breaks on this kind of thoughts and put them into park otherwise the only thing they'll bring is my perdition and a severe case of blue balls.

Denying Ensley Walker takes far more strength than I assumed and a far stronger man than I am. Hence why I better start praying to all the things holy, to all the saints, to *infinito e o máis aló* to give me all the strength and resilience I need to prevail.

As I run a hand through my hair, I drop the paperback copy of Michael Connelly's *The Night Fire* on the coffee table with a thud louder than intended. One which has Ensley nearly jump out of her skin because the sound just ricochets across the space from one corner of the room to the other.

"Sorry! I didn't mean to," I throw over my shoulder.

Meanwhile, I can't seem able to leave the living room fast enough as though someone set a fire under my ass and exit through the glass sliding doors.

I need air.

I must get some air before I'm going crazy.

Without even realizing it, I find myself opening the door to the shed in the backyard. I also find myself putting the kick-boxing gloves on and then begin punching the bag I've got hanging inside the wooden shed.

Alternating between punching and kicking, I eventually toss my t-shirt on the two-seater sofa-bed, before I resume with a kick of my right foot against the bag.

How long I do it for I don't know because I appear to lose track of time. What I know is that by the time I hear between kicks someone clear their throat behind me, my heart rate is up, and my chest is covered in sweat.

"Hey, man," Luke salutes me as he leans against the door-frame of the shed. "Getting rid of some tension there or what?"

I puff.

"I'd tell you, but you'll kill me, so I choose to live considering not long ago I came back from the dead."

"Okay, someone's got a stick up their ass today," my best friend concludes, his arms crossing over his chest. "What's up with you?"

"I'm eager to get back, man," I confess.

Among my reasons, is your sister. She will drive me so crazy that either I'll end up admitted to a mental facility or doing a goddamn mistake, this last bit continues in my head since what I said just previously is true.

Luke will kill me if I tell him that it is his older sister who has me in knots, and I've shamelessly been fantasizing about her for years. The mere reason I'm still alive is that he doesn't know I slept with Ensley sixteen years ago. If he did, my body would have been already three feet under and would have remained one unsolved disappearance because I'm fairly sure nobody would've found my body.

"And you will. Doctors are positive you'll get back soon enough, aren't they? You've done physio all through the three months you've been in a coma and that helped shit loads with keeping your muscles active. You're on the fast lane to recovery, Mason."

Slipping the gloves off my hands, I throw them on the floor and walk to pick up my discarded tee.

"How's Ella doing?" I ask to change the subject.

It is something that doesn't go unnoticed if Luke narrowing his blue-grayish eyes at me is any indication.

He gives me a pass, though.

And let me tell you that the smile that settles on my best friend's face at the mention of his fiancée isn't just big. It is fucking huge.

So whipped is this friend of mine.

"She's inside with Enz. Going over some wedding stuff," he explains.

I chuckle. "And you're avoiding anything that has to do with the planning, aren't you?"

"If it were up to me, I'd just drag her to the courthouse and marry her right now."

"Did you two pick a date yet? Since I assume I'll be the best man, I'm hoping she'll have a sexy maid of honor."

Luke smirks. "We're still deciding, but it's most likely to be the last weekend of August. And I can't say if she is, but you could certainly tell me."

"Afraid your woman will feed you your balls if you do?" I tease.

However, I would definitely not put it past the redhead to be capable of that. But considering that I know my best friend and just how deeply he loves when he falls for someone, she has nothing to worry about because he'll never look the other way.

"I'm sure she likes my balls where they are, thank you very much," Luke reverts, but considering the grimace that takes over his face, he just pictured that very image.

"So?"

"It's Ensley," he responds, his piercing eyes locking onto mine with curiosity.

"Oh, never mind then."

His brow arches. "What's the matter, *Cutter*? I mean, come on, I'm not an idiot. I know you've been having the hots for her since we were teenagers."

My head shakes from side to side. "I can't go there, brother. I wouldn't deserve her."

Before he gets to say anything else, a set of laughs punctures our ears and redirect our attention to the outside. Ensley and Ella just make their way out of the house and on the rattan garden loungers.

They each hold a glass with a chilled drink that looks like a mojito considering the green leaves inside which I assume they're mint leaves. What's more, they both wear close to nothing as they lay on the loungers.

"Fuck, I'm a lucky bastard," Luke articulates.

Joder, e estou maldito!

(*Fuck, and I'm doomed!*)

"I thought you said they're looking over wedding stuff."

Luke ignores my reproach completely, his eyes not peeling off his fiancée.

I use that time too. The sight of Ensley in nothing but a two-piece bathing suit has my heart thumping in my chest so hard that I sense its reverberations in my ears. At the same time, I feel my cock twitching in my black shorts, the fucker clearly savoring the sight.

And what a view that is.

To the extent that I allow myself another glance. Over her beautiful face that has not even a single bit of make-up, revealing the freckles on her cheeks and nose that I've learned all too well over the years. Over her green eyes that shine in the May sun. Over the slender column of her neck. Over the swell of her breasts covered by two dark-green triangles. Over the trim waist. Over her defined abdomen. Over her hips. Over her muscular thighs. Over her long legs. Over the ink that starts from the side of her right hip and stretches down until mid-thigh. Over the two other tattoos she has that are in my line of vision only when she turns to sit down and her hair swishes, revealing them. One tattoo across her left shoulder blade and another one that begins below the nape of her neck and extends down her spine, reaching mid-back.

Once I take a little fill, and as though it's not enough, I lift my gaze back to hers, connecting our eyes across the garden when she lifts her chin after she lays atop the lounger.

Many times before I've seen her in a bathing suit. I vividly remember all these images of her that have seared themselves into every single cell of my brain.

Although it isn't the first time I see her in just that and, all things considered, not the first hard-on she's caused me, it is the first time I hear a snap in my skillfully mastered self-control.

I really need to get a woman under me. That will glue the crack in my restraint back on.

Yes, that's what I'll do because the best way to keep my urges at bay is to get lost between another woman's legs. To find release in another woman. Even for just a little while.

Someone who'd certainly be inconsequential.

Somebody who'll have me forget about those beautiful green eyes that have been haunting my dreams. The same green gaze I see staring back at me every single blink.

As Luke and I stand in the doorway of the shed, staring at the two women while being completely mesmerized by them, it is something that doesn't go unnoticed since the two of them turn to look our way with wide smiles on their faces. Unremarked doesn't go the wink Ella sends Ensley after she averts her eyes from us to her. Nor does the smirk my best friend sends his fiancée who blushes instantly at what I can assume is a promise I'd rather not know about.

"Don't we have some things to deal with at the bar?" I remind him only to find a reason to get myself out of there.

More because I need to stop looking at the gorgeous brunette with that pair of piercing eyes since my gaze can't appear capable of moving any other way. My eyes just stay glued to her and regardless of how hard I try to look away, I am incapable of doing that. Like I'm under some sort of spell. One that dares me to eat the distance between us, to throw her over my shoulder and only stop once I peel those two pieces of garments off her body. Pieces that barely cover anything. And the only reason I'll stop then is just so I can look at her, take her in and drink in the sight of her until I'm a sated man. Only after I sate my thirst, I'll begin. Begin touching her skin, move my lips over hers. Begin feeling her against my body.

Incoming derailed freight train, my brain warns, the alarm blaring louder and louder.

"Yeah, I think we've got the delivery of the new pool tables coming up, but not until four in the afternoon…"

There's a pause in his speech. Time I think he uses to check on his watch. Yet, that is something I wouldn't really know for sure because peeling my eyes off of Ensley takes the greatest of efforts.

"Which is in two hours."

"I'll shower and we can go already. There's plenty to do around there anyway," I reason.

When I eventually manage to avert my gaze from Ensley to her brother, I note he's already staring at me. His features hard.

"Whatever your reasons are, don't ever lead her on," he asks. "You might be my best friend, but I won't hesitate to bury your ass three feet under if you ever hurt her."

"That's the very reason I stay away because I know I'll hurt her."

Luke furrows his brows at me. "What makes you so sure?"

"Because I would never deserve a love like I know she will give me, Luke," I reply and immediately after I shake my head from side to side. "And you know that and why."

He fucking knows why. With the exception of my mom, he's the only one who knows the truth. He's just stubborn as hell—a trait evidently deeply rooted in the Walkers—and doesn't want to understand that my reasons are well-founded.

My best friend puffs sardonically. "And that's just fucking bullshit. I know it and so do you. One isn't defined by—"

"I'll hit the shower and then we can go," I interrupt Luke's ranting, knowing I won't hear the end of it.

His head shakes in a disapproving motion, but he lets it go for now anyway. "I'll let them enjoy some girls' time and I'll wait for you at the bar," he says, pointing his chin toward the two women.

After I only nod my head, I saunter my way inside the house, fighting every impulse that shouts at me to have one last peek at the brunette who lays on the lounger in nothing but bikini top and bottoms.

So when I get inside the house without having one last look, I give myself a proud mental pat on the back because it takes a fucking great effort not to.

That shower will be an icy-cold one because the sight of Ensley has brought my cock to half-mast, and I need the fucker to go down entirely before he gets any sort of ideas.

The only sort of entertainment you'll get will be with some random chick and not with a certain achingly beautiful brunette with green eyes who also happens to have the sweetest of pussies.

This is just great.

First box on the admission paperwork for the loony bin has just been ticked.

Box number one:
He talks to his wayward cock.

Ticked. At this rate, I'm on the fast track to being the perfect candidate.

ENSLEY

"The way he looked at you?! God, I swear I could see how he mentally undressed and bent you over this lounger with his eyes," my future sister-in-law chirps, fanning herself teasingly with a hand as a wicked smile splits her lips.

My head shakes.

Though that gesture is nonchalant, the pounding in my heart is anything but casual. No, it gallops wildly in my chest, remembering the heat that coated Mason's gaze as his eyes moved over me.

Christ, how will I survive this when—regardless of how many times I told my heart we'll take it slow—it took the plunge on that very instant my eyes locked on to his for the first time since he woke up from the coma.

My own heart goes rogue on me because of his chocolate brown eyes that keep me under a spell.

"How's the seduction plan going?" Ella asks me with curiosity.

Since Mason is inside the house taking a shower before he leaves for the bar he now owns with my brother, and Luke left only a few moments ago after he kissed his fiancée, we can speak rather freely.

Since I've been introduced to Ella at the hospital and over the past months, we became close. While Mason was still in a coma, she'd stop by and because she's a real angel, she'd bring me some nice food, keep me company and I got to know her and her story. I also quickly understood why my brother has fallen deeply in love with her. Not only because she is a downright knockout, but because she also has the kindest of hearts.

It is on the second replay of her question in my head that an involuntary sigh pushes up my throat.

"It's complicated. When I first decided not to tell him anything, I knew it won't be easy. I've experienced his denial before for quite a while and it hasn't just been difficult, it's been painful," I admit, my eyes glued to the shed he came out of only a few ticks ago. "Now I'm extremely aware of the lengths he can go to only to keep me away and that's pure torture."

"He didn't sleep with the woman from the bar," Ella shoots, taking a sip of her drink. "The one he was talking to that night after my abduction. Luke asked him."

I nod heedlessly.

"Well, he had to go back to the hospital."

Ella gives me an unimpressed look. "Let me rephrase that then. He didn't sleep with her that night or any other night. With her or anyone else."

"That doesn't mean he won't. Last time, after we slept together on my birthday, he went on a sex rampage of sorts. He'd just flirt with anyone only to push me away, to prove to me that what he called a mistake really didn't mean anything to him. He'd let them take him home and my heart bled every single time thinking that he'd rather have anyone else but me."

The many memories I have of him flirting with girls are still very graphic in my head.

"I'm sorry to tell you this, but if he decides to sleep with someone else, that's on you because he doesn't know you two are married," Ella mentions.

How aware of that I am…

"Unsolicited advice: you'd spare yourself a lot of heartbreak by telling him he's your husband."

Would I, though?

Would telling him we're married spare me the heartache or would it just heighten it?

"He asked me for the divorce," I confess.

It has become so difficult to hold that thought in. A thought that incites many others. Wonders. Ponders. A battle between my rational and irrational side. One in the left and the other in the right corner of the ring.

Some sow self-doubt. Insecurities about me as a woman, about me as a wife. Have I become not enough for him anymore? Has our marriage become a routine to him, and I haven't seen it? Or perhaps, it turned into a burden for him?

Though these questions tumble in my head ever so often when insecurities assail, all this self-doubt disperses when images of Mason hit. How he looked at me. How his hunger for me would only grow, no matter how much he'd touch me. How I'd found him many times stealing glances at me over the top edge of his books. How much love I'd find in his gaze whenever I'd meet his eyes. How I shudder only remembering the love he gave me, and not only that, the love he made me feel with each caress, kiss, word, touch, whisper, look.

That brings me to the right corner of the ring where my more rational thoughts reside, fiercely and relentlessly fighting the battle. The rational ponders that tell me there's more to the story. They contradict the insecurities through all those memories I have of him. But they also bring more questions. The main question being 'why?'. Why would he ask me for the divorce if he loved me like I graphically remember he did?

"Beautiful, get out of your head," Ella urges. "I can see your wheels spinning and if there's someone who knows how self-doubt looks like, that person is me."

That statement couldn't've been truer. Ella has had it rough. Her legacy brought her hell loads of insecurities. With her father —a former firefighter with the D.C. Fire Department—in prison for arson and with Ella going into the profession of firefighting, it has been tough on her and she allowed self-doubt to reign over her for many years. Until she met my brother who taught her to see herself in a different light. He banished her doubts and vulnerabilities.

"I didn't know Mason then, but I see the Mason of right now, and even one would have to be blind not to see the way that man looks at you. And even blind, they'd feel it."

Once again, I shake my head, not willing to allow her words to give me more hope.

"Mason worships the ground you walk on, Ensley. That man couldn't be any crazier about you. He might not want to admit it, but he is completely smitten with you. We all can see it on his face whenever he looks at you, but you must have patience."

"Sweetie, I'm not sure you're aware of the kind of family you're marrying into. Let me tell you if you don't already. When the patience was given out, the Walkers were either on holiday or it simply skipped us." At that, she chuckles. "Take Luke, for instance. The man won't survive until the wedding and you know it. I'll give him a medal if he doesn't drag you to the court-house to marry you in the next month."

"On our way back from Richmond, he pulled up to the court-house," Ella admits with a wide smile.

"See? Patience is not a Walkers' thing."

"Don't tell me you and *Mr. Tatts* eloped."

Over the rim of my glass, I meet her brown eyes for a second before I avert my gaze. At the same time, I suppress the chuckle at how she chose to address Mason as.

"I wouldn't exactly say elope."

"No way," Ella shrieks with utter surprise.

"We went to the courthouse and got married four months before our wedding. We had a long engagement, though."

"Evidently too long if you couldn't wait four more months to get married," Ella jokes, winking.

The recollection of why that happened is fresh on my mind as I close my eyes for a blink before I reopen them.

"The day before, there has been an all-hands-on-deck situa-tion on the Southwest Waterfront," I begin. "During that call, a fellow firefighter and I got stuck inside the building. We just couldn't find any way out. Squad wasn't allowed to come in for the rescue because the fire was everywhere, spread way too fast, collapsed everything it could, and the windows weren't a go either.

"Mason and Luke were going so out of their minds outside, the chief on the scene asked the police officers to cuff them because he knew they wouldn't stay put. For a second, I thought that was it, but then we managed to get ourselves on the roof through a vent that luckily led there. Before the blast ensued, we made a run for the edge of the building with enough speed and jumped into the water."

My mind takes me back to that night almost instantly, as though it happened just yesterday.

How we made it out of the water, completely soaked and how Mason came running to me with Luke hot on his heels. Utter terror and despair washed over their faces.

Moreover, I vividly remember Mason's hair being a complete mess from raking his hand too many times through it in desperation. And when he pulled me in his embrace, I could feel the relief running through him. It was as though only when he had me against him and between his strong arms that he could believe I'm there and I'm still alive.

"Fuck, that's some serious situation."

"It was right after we got off shift the morning after when Mason came to pick me up and told me then and there that we should get married. He told me he can't wait a moment longer to have me as his wife and can't bear the thought of losing me. So, we turned up at the courthouse to get married right away and after we were done there, we rode to a cabin we managed to rent out last minute in Zapp, Virginia, and spent our days off there," I say with a smile on my lips at the memory. "We only got back in the evening the second day and rode straight to my parents' house where my family and Ary were. We turned up and said nothing, we just showed them the silicone wedding bands. They didn't look surprised at all."

"Eager to consummate that marriage, I see," Ella teases with an insinuating wink just before she takes yet another sip of her mojito.

"And what a consummation that was," I say, my teeth biting into the bottom lip at the memory.

Ella can't hold her chuckle at my reaction. However, soon her brown gaze turns tentative.

"What's that look for?" I question.

"Your mind just went there, didn't it?"

I sigh. "I miss the sex. I'd be cynical to say that I don't. But what I miss the most is that connection I felt with my husband."

My head shakes as I inhale deeply to assure the emotions I feel taking over me won't prevail.

"It's all these memories that I hang on to so I can give myself hope that our love is stronger than all of this. Stronger than his need to deny me. It gives me hope that we will make it through what life throws our way."

"We could give him a little nudge."

It is on Ella's affirmation that I crane my neck to the side to look her way only. I don't miss how her expression turns plotting right before my own eyes.

"Oh, no, I don't think I like what you're planning," I attest with a laugh before I return to my cool drink to take a sip.

Ella abruptly shifts in her lounger, reaching over to place her glass on the rattan table between us before she crosses her legs in a yoga position. Meanwhile, her scheming smile grows wider and wider with each second that slides past, as though she's putting ideas together in her head.

"I don't think my brother knows what kind of woman he's marrying," I jest, already afraid of what her mind concocts.

She puffs, waving me off with a swift gesture of her hand. "Believe me, he knows," the redhead attests with a grin. "Besides, I think all the romance novels I've been reading could be quite useful for tips and ideas on what you could do to give him that little, teeny-weeny jab he needs because I'm awfully sure that's all it will take."

"I love reading romance novels as much as the next girl, but this isn't a romance book," I mention, officially proclaiming myself a buzzkill.

Yet, my future sister-in-law evidently doesn't let my inner killjoy attitude get in the way of whatever her mind is planning.

"First of all, don't be a spoilsport. Second of all, just listen to what I have to say."

Eyeing the redhead suspiciously, I say: "I've got a feeling you're going to make me listen anyway, so…" With a gesture of my hand, I signal for her to go ahead.

"Correct me if I'm wrong. Mason is a through and through Alpha male."

I nod without a fraction of hesitation.

Oh, boy, and what an Alpha male.

"And all these Alpha males, they've got one thing in common. They are possessive and don't like others touching or even dare look at what or who they strongly believe belongs to them. Which means, they get real jealous, real quick," Ella spouts, clearly excited about that if her tone is any indication.

"What if it just comes biting me in the ass?"

"Oh, but I'm fairly sure you'll have your ass bitten all right," the redhead reverts with an implying smile. "Actually, I'm counting on it."

While I chuckle at Ella's words, I can't help but let them dawn on. Each sentence hits home unmitigatedly. Over and over again, as they echo from one cell of my brain to the next and the next and the next.

At the same time, the recollection tumbles in my mind. The one of how he lost his well-mastered control when my mother kept pushing his buttons by saying she'll take me to a strip club. How he kissed me with a claim and a savageness I haven't been kissed with before until him. How jealous he got at the mere thought of another guy touching me. How the night he made me his, he told me he couldn't stand the thought of my lips kissing another guy's lips, of my skin being touched and caressed by another.

His palm rests on my chest just atop my breast to feel the beating of my heart beneath it. And oh, boy, does it beat. It thunders under his hand, pounding so hard that I'm afraid when he'll remove his hand, I'll see my heart pounding in the heel of his palm.

"I can't stand the thought of another man making your heart skip a beat with his words, with his promises. I know I shouldn't want that, and I've told myself so many times that I mustn't, but I cannot think of you with any man who isn't me. I'd rather have my own heart ripped out of my chest, Ley baby."

At that, my heart thumps even harder as my gaze holds his chocolate one. The arrant heat mixes with pure pain onto his chocolate eyes. It is as though it causes him a great deal of agony to admit that. Moreover, what I also see in his eyes is an inner battle. One that ceases when his hand lowers, cupping my breast in his hand, and a moan crawls up my throat. That seems to be the last straw because the pure desire that coats his brown eyes is the only warning I get before his self-control throws in the towel.

In the blink of an eye, Mason's other hand reaches to the nape of my neck. I instantly get drunk in the scent and taste of him when his lips smash over mine without mercy and hesitation. They move over mine for a tick before his tongue thrusts in my mouth, hot and prodding, claiming and dominating.

While his tongue and lips subdue my mouth and all my cognitive capacities, his hands conquer my body, spreading a fire inside of me I have never before experienced. A fire that burns me from inside out, consuming me so completely that all I am left with is capitulation.

"Miña," he growls over my lips, breaking the kiss for a tick before he claims my mouth again with utter passion. He controls everything from the pace of our kiss and the thrusts of his tongue, to the tempo of his hands moving up and down my body, driving me crazy with want.

"Earth to Ensley," Ella's voice breaks through my memory.

I blink several times before I look toward her again. "Mason Carter won't know what hit him," I attest with sheer determination.

"Atta girl!"

With that, we both get our drinks and clink them together.

"To Mason. He shall pull his head out of his ass as soon as possible so my girl can be happy again or we shall pull it out for him," Ella toasts before we take a sip to clinch the deal.

MASON

My eyes take in the space as I retrieve a stool by the bar.

For the past hours, we have helped the delivery guys bring in the new tables, and I've shot a little bit of pool just for fun with Luke. All only to avoid thinking about the woman who monopolizes all my brain cells.

The worst of all is that she doesn't just do it slowly. No, she does it with the force of a hurricane. Taking everything in its path by storm only to leave me weaker and weaker, chipping away at my control.

Fucking bikini...

In fucking bikini...

No doubt it got hot in the afternoon, but did she really have to wear that fucking bikini? She exposed enough of that milky skin for the rays of sun to caress. To caress her as I could never do. Like I must never again do.

Joder!

My cock appears to suffer from a severe case of ignorance toward the opposite sex and flaccidity around all women. All women but Ensley since he's evidently ready to pound nails at how hard he gets at the merest of glances at her. Hence why I was so close to jerking myself off in the shower as my mind replayed the images of her in that dark green two-piece that accentuated her eyes. Not only that, her long, brunette hair, how it cascaded against her frame, it accented her porcelain skin that

I know for sure would look even more so in contrast with my naturally tanned one—blame it on the heritage of a Spaniard.

Joder!

Why did my mind just go there?

Why did I have to imagine my skin against hers?

Why did I just have to go there?

I'm going fucking crazy.

Everything within me turns into a traitor.

My body betrays me.

My mind evidently took the plunge in the same direction and now betrays me too.

Sovereign of the list however—the worst traitors of them all —is my heart. My heart that has beaten solely for Ensley Walker.

For over twenty years it has beaten for her. It hasn't known any other rhythm. I am aware it is time to better make my heart change that cadence, though. I'll force my own heart to stop beating for Ensley fucking Walker even if I have to rip it out of my chest.

I will do everything and anything it takes to forget about her.

I *need* to leave.

I *must* stay away.

Merda!

Why didn't this amnesia just make it easy on me and wipe out all these feelings I have for her? Why didn't it make itself useful and just erase her altogether? Oust the memories I have of her. Cast away all that I'm feeling for her. Banish out of my mind that damned night when I was weak, when I had my mouth on every inch of her body and when she crooned and moaned my name like it was her own as I slid inside her.

Ensley Walker is like the forbidden fruit. The more I tell myself I shouldn't, the more I want her. Yet, I will not. With the exception of that night, I've resisted her, and I must continue. I must garner all the strength I can possibly find within me to make sure it stays that way.

"You seem deep in thought," Luke points out, bending over the pool table before he strikes the white ball with the tip of the cue. He then straightens and places both hands atop the cue's end to lean against it as his eyes fly to me.

My shoulders lift before I reach for the bottle of beer I've been nursing for a while. As I let his words hang in the air for a tick or two, I take a gulp of the bitter liquid.

"I'm gonna leave for some time, Luke," I mention after a few moments of silence. A time I took to weigh my words carefully before he jumps to my throat to kill me right here and now. "After we get the ball rolling with the bar, I'll go away for a bit."

His expression changes right away. It darkens and hardens at the same time. "What? What are you talking about, brother?"

"You were right. I've been having feelings for Ensley for as long as I can remember, and I need space. I need to forget your sister, Luke," I confess.

"Or you can be with her," he suggests without the merest fraction of doubt.

"I can't, brother. It's a risk I can't take. I need to leave because I feel like I'm losing my goddamn mind," I confess. Meanwhile, my fingers rake through my hair, pushing it back even more and I realize I'll soon have all my hair falling out at the number of times I've been running my hand through it lately.

Luke drops the cue on top of the pool table, completely forgetting about his one-man game. "So, you're just gonna take the coward's way out?"

From his voice, I can tell he's angry. Moreover, his heavy steps as he storms my way are the confirmation that he indeed is.

His finger nudges me in the chest.

"I could think anything of you. It never crossed my mind that you'd be such a fucking coward."

Tilting my chin a little, I then hold his furious gaze.

"You know, for the longest time I believed if there has ever been a man who deserves Ensley most, that man was you."

I puff incredulously. "I don't and you fucking know it."

"Your reasons are complete bullshit, but I give you that, you don't deserve her. Not for the reasons you've been giving your-self over the years because you know my opinion on that. You don't deserve her because you'd fight tooth and nail to keep her if you did," he spouts, his irritation reaching limits unknown.

"I can't keep her because I've never had her to begin with," I remind him, my voice turning sharp and drenched in harshness.

Luke scoffs incredulously.

Meanwhile, he holds my own unyielding gaze. So, when his

mouth opens again, I expect him to give me some more hell considering the vehemence coating his blue-grayish eyes. However, he just snaps his eyes close for a brief instant as though he carries an inner battle, only to then swallow his words.

"You know what? You just don't have enough sack to love a woman like her. To screw the consequences and whatever life throws your way. To face whatever there is to be faced, but do it together. Because let me tell you one thing, Ensley is exactly the kind of woman who'd stick around for all the hurdles and all the hardships, who'd be by your side doing the fighting alongside you, who'd… Why do I even bother?"

With a shake of his head, one single motion from the left to the right that only screams disappointment, he gives me one last hard stare. Next, Luke simply turns and his massive figure storms out of the bar with long strides.

"Make sure you lock up," he throws over his shoulder just before the door slams behind him so hard that I'm astounded it is still hinged to the wall.

As my head moves from side to side in frustration, I drink the last dregs of my beer. Before I get back to my feet, I drop the now empty bottle on the bar top with a thud.

Sighing, I comb my fingers through my hair once again.

Joder!

After I carry myself to grab the empty bottle of beer Luke abandoned on the edge of the pool table and after I retrieve mine, I discard them in the trash by the back door. Returning to the front of the bar, I slip my phone into the back pocket of my jeans. I then put on my leather jacket, grab my helmet and keys, and walk out of the bar, locking up behind me.

With one hand deep in the pockets of my jacket, while in the other I hold my matte black helmet, I jog across the road where I parked my motorbike.

Once I mount the bike, I put the helmet on, twist the key to ignite the engine and I ride off.

This is how I begin to ride around aimlessly. No purpose, no direction, but only one thing in mind. To avoid Ensley at all costs. It is enough that I have my mind jumping from one thought of her to the next, from one image of her to the next. It is more than enough that I am so drowned in all that she is as it is. Hence, the avoidance tactic is the best strategy. Also, another strategy is to get another woman under me. And soon.

Maybe I'll just stop at some bar, chat someone up and get them to bed before I make a mistake where there's no turning away from.

Ergo, I continue riding and riding for God knows how long. I drive past bars, clubs, and many streets. Yet, nothing catches my attention.

But instead of finding myself on a busy street with bars and swarming with willing women, I glance around to see myself on the Waterfront. After I parked my bike not too far, my feet carried me to the railing. My hands grasp hold of it and I look down at the water.

For how long I do that, I don't know. What I know is that when I turn, my eyes glue to one of the buildings that overview the Waterfront area.

A sigh crawls up my throat and my hand runs through my hair as a thought crosses me: *I am losing my goddamn mind.* Otherwise, I cannot explain why I'm here.

When I go to walk back to my bike, my head begins to throb and I squeeze my eyes shut. The headache that hits me is merciless and my knees almost give out at the pain.

The groan that gets wrenched out of me is loud while behind my eyelids plays an image. A picture of the flames that engulf the building I've just looked at. But then other image follows. One of me fighting to free myself.

These images repeat themselves over and over in my mind as I try to make sense of them. But nothing does. So I brush them off and I give myself a moment to recover—the piercing headache still ongoing. I then walk back to my motorcycle and ride away, with the same goal in mind as previously. Now needing it more than before.

Imagine the astoundment I feel when, out of all places, I find that my purposelessness brings me into a familiar neighborhood. Arlington Ridge in Arlington, Virginia. The place where I grew up. The place where I've lived since I was three years old. The place where I've begun my friendship with Luke over pushing off the swing and shoving each other. That of course before we dusted off and shook hands, then shared the swing and laughed it off while our mothers were livid at us and apologizing to each other relentlessly. Had it not been for that moment though, perhaps now Luke had not been my best friend nor our mothers would've shared the friendships they do.

Riding until I reach an even more familiar house, I pull into the driveway right beside Mom's car, killing the engine before I push down the side stand. Immediately after I climb off the bike, I look over my shoulder to the house across the road—the Walkers' home.

Before my eyes, flashes an image of three kids—an eleven-year-old girl and two nine-year-old boys—running and laughing while they drag a hose from the back of the house to the front lawn, aiming the water at a nonexistent fire. This is a moment from back in the day when we were young, carefree, and restless. A memory that quirks the corners of my lips upward in a smile. One I let stay there for a tick until I inhale deeply and turn to saunter to the front door, using my spare key to unlock it.

"*Mamá, son eu. O teu fillo favorito,*" I call out as I enter the house announcing myself as her favorite son.

From the kitchen, I can hear a chuckle. "*Autoproclamado o meu fillo favorito,*" she returns with jest, telling me that I'm the self-proclaimed favorite son.

Dropping the helmet and the keys on the table and the jacket on the sofa in the living room on my way to the kitchen, I then continue until I have before me the most amazing, unconditional and incredible woman with the most beautiful of hearts.

My mom.

Aracely Carter.

"*Mira o que trouxo o gato,*" Mom mocks, wiping her hands on a towel. "Finally remembered your own mother?"

"No cat dragged me in, I rode my bike here," I revert with a chuckle before I rush for her and lift her in my arms, spinning her around a couple of times.

"*Ay,* put me down, Mason," she expresses, surprised at my action, but giggling right after.

With a mischievous laugh, I let her feet touch the floor again and she looks up at me with a heartful smile. Her hand lifts, and she caresses my cheek with her soft palm just as her features turn even gentler.

"*Meu fillo querido. Que pasa, amor?*"

(*"My beloved son. What's up, dear?"*)

For the briefest of seconds, I snap my eyes shut, then I open them only to find my mom's softer gaze.

"My handsome boy, I know these beautiful eyes of yours." At that, I hold the air in my lungs, waiting for her to continue. "They have one name and that is Ensley."

A defeated breath pushes up my throat and tumbles out past my lips.

Lifting my hand, I comb my fingers through my hair and my head shakes.

"Mom, you know I can't. I can't put her life at risk for selfish reasons because in the end, I'll never deserve her. I can't put her in danger. I'd rather live a life loving her from afar than do that."

Sudden disappointment washes over her face.

Ah, it seems to be my greatest quality lately. Especially today since I seem to have disappointed two people in the span of a couple of hours.

Furthermore, she lets out a heavy breath.

"Had I known that this is what you'd be doing, that you'd throw away the most beautiful thing that can ever happen to you, I would've never told you the truth," Mom expresses, her brown eyes gleaming with tears. "*Isto é culpa miña.*"

"*Mamá*, you know this is not your fault," I counter her last sentence. "We've never had secrets between us, and you told me a truth I needed to know. *A verdade sobre min.*"

(*"A truth about me."*)

"But that doesn't define you, *cariño.*"

"*Como carallo non?*"

(*"How the hell does it not?"*)

The vehemence in my tone doesn't surprise her because we had this same discussion when I was eighteen and she told me the truth. A pill that was difficult to swallow. One that still is.

Mom takes a few deep breaths as she looks at me. Her chocolate eyes determined.

"Do you know just how many people wander into this life wanting to find the love of their life? Their soulmate. That person who not only sets their soul on fire with one look but ignites their whole being and kindles their hearts with a word, with a caress, with only a mere look their way. That person one can't live without. That person who drives one crazy, but still can't stand the thought of being without. Do you have any idea just how many?"

"This isn't some romance novel or fairytale bullshit, *Mamá*. This is real life and in real life not, everyone gets that happily ever after."

"Dime só unha cousa."

(*"Tell me only one thing."*)

As there's a pause in her speech, both her hands rest on my shoulders. Her stare holds mine and it is in her gaze that I notice she won't take it easy on me. Mom will give me the hell Luke only gave me a piece of earlier. With no mercy. A punch in the face that I can already see coming.

"Are you willing to let another man steal her heart? Are you going to be okay with her falling in love with another man?" Mom questions, and with each one the blood boils in my veins. "Also, let me tell you another thing, son," she continues, even though that's all she's been doing, telling me something. "A woman like Ensley comes around only once in a lifetime and it's up to you if you let her go or if you just grab her and never let go of her."

It is on this ranting that I realize not only that sheer fury builds up inside of me, but that my fists involuntarily ball at my sides at the image of Ensley with another man. It is gut-wrenching. Pure torture squeezes my heart so tightly that I have to garner every ounce of willpower not to rub at my chest.

"Though I know the answer just as well as you do, I'll let you think on it. But make sure you can live with yourself and with the choices you make," Mom says, taking no prisoners or even a scintilla of pity on her own son. "*Eu non criei un covarde, criei un home valente.*"

(*"I didn't raise a coward, I raised a brave man."*)

And that, right there is a punchline only Aracely Carter can deliver with such precision that it feels as though she punched me in the throat.

"Now…" Mom begins, smacking her hands together. "I wouldn't want to seem like I'm kicking you out, but your *mamá* here has a date she needs to get ready for."

My mouth hangs slack.

If Aracely Carter is anything she is absolutely gorgeous. A total babe. A stunner. The fact she goes on a date doesn't surprise me. She went on dates before, and I've witnessed with my own eyes men shamelessly flirting with her. Even my fellow firefighters have been teasing me about her and what a "through and through knockout" and "sexy as hell" she is, their words not mine. Furthermore, they don't miss a chance to blatantly flirt with her every time she stops by the firehouse. Much to my annoyance, obviously.

My arms cross simultaneously over my chest, and a brow quirks. "Oh, so you're dating now? Who is he?"

"Someone I've met at the grocery store," she answers with a casual shrug, but the smile on her face tells me otherwise.

"What's his name?"

"Why? So you can have one of your buddies in the force run a background check on him?"

I admit guilty to that.

I've done it on a couple of her boyfriends with the help of Jesse Lewis, an FBI agent Luke and I became friends with after a fire where he lost his witness. In his defense, Jesse didn't use the bureau's resources to run the checks but the ones of his younger brother—Zaiden Lewis—who owns a private security company. And to my own defense, I've done it because the guys gave me a bad feeling. And I've hit the nail on the head with them. One was some sort of con artist who wanted her to be her next con, while the other was a devoted gambler who would've probably dried her of her money and then leave her hanging.

Call me over-protective. But when the life and well-being of the ones I love are at stake, I'm willing to take all the risks I can possibly take to make sure I keep them safe. I am also willing to sacrifice anything and everything if that means they're safe and sound.

"Is he picking you up?" I fire yet another question without bothering to answer hers.

"Yes, he'll be here in about half an hour," she answers.

"I guess I won't be moving my ass until I see this guy," I inform her.

Something she already knew will come if she mentions her date to me.

Hence, with a kiss on her forehead, I turn and stride to the sofa in the living room, plopping myself atop it.

Again, something she knew I will do.

"Then you're not doing this only to avoid going back home to Ensley?" Mom questions, leaning now against the wall of the living room.

"Of course not," I deny.

However, just on that lie, the image of Ensley in a goddamn bikini flashes right before my eyes as though to prove to me just how much of a flat lie I told.

Long legs bared for my hungry sight. A pair I can only dream of having wrapped around me again.

Trim waist deliciously taut. A waist I can only want to circle with my arm only to bring her flush to me.

And that pair of tits...

That pair of tits is the icing on the cake. An icing I'd lick and suck on for hours on end. Then I'd lick other parts of her body only to return to her tits. To lick at them some more. To play with her perky nipples until they turn so hard it will be pain bordering pleasure.

Joder!

Clearing my throat, I discreetly retrieve a sofa pillow to place it over my aching cock. I hesitate for a tick or two before I lift my eyes. But to my relief, when I do, I note Mom left me alone already, possibly realizing how deep in thought I am.

Thank fuck she did.

MASON

The sound of heels at the contact with the hard floor makes me lift my head from the pillow I have over the arm of the sofa, and I look over the back to my mom.

She looks gorgeous in a blue dress that reaches her knees. A pair of black heels makes her even taller than she already is. Her usual straight hair is now in gentle waves.

A whistle dances in the air and she chuckles, dismissing me with a hand gesture.

"*Non sexas un pallaso*," she utters, clearly blushing.

"I'm not a clown, but you're very beautiful, *Mamá*," I say in return, placing my arms over the top of the sofa.

With a smile on her face, she walks to me and kisses the top of my head. "Don't let your fears rule your heart."

"*Mamá…*"

"No, Mason, listen to me. Life is short. If there's someone who knows just how short it is, it's me."

"Dad was the love of your life, wasn't he?" I ask with a saddened smile. Though I barely have any memories of Dad, Mom has always kept telling me about how great of a man he was, how much he loved me, how much he loved her.

Without the smallest fraction of hesitation, she nods. "I've loved him with all my heart. I still do. Our time together was short, but it hasn't only been memorable, it has been life-changing. It defied all the rules and it etched itself into my heart."

"You look absolutely gorgeous, *Mamá*," I compliment with a

wink. "But that man better keep his hands to himself if he still wants to have them attached to his wrists."

At my warning, she chuckles and shakes her head, but then she sees the seriousness on my face.

Since I was three years old, it has been mainly Grandpa, Mom, and me. Only us three. Pa has always been protective of his family and over the years, as I grew up, my protectiveness has grown too. I became overprotective and vigilant over her. Over everyone I care about, but especially over her because raising me as a single mother hasn't been easy for her. As much as Pa has helped raise me—the reason we moved to DC from Denver in the first place—, Mom still had to do a lot of things on her own. And when Pa passed away when I was twelve, I made him a promise to always protect her.

"*Pallaso*," Mom smacks my arm gently as she calls me a clown with all the love in the world.

A chortle of my own pushes through my throat and past my lips. Yet, before we get to say anything else, the doorbell rings.

Immediately, I push back, looking at Mom blushing. With one hand atop the sofa, I push then forward and throw my legs over the back, leaping to my feet. "I'll open," I offer.

"Don't you dare," she cautions.

"Watch me."

With that, I walk past her, skirting all her failed attempts of stopping me, and I get to the door, opening it the instant my hand touches the handle.

Before me stands a tall man.

He's dressed in a suit. His more salt than pepper hair is slicked back, the silverish color matching the trimmed beard. His eyes are a piercing shade of blue.

There's a look of surprise crossing his face when he sees me in front of him instead of my mom. Well, the truth is anyone would be to see a six-foot-two man opening the door instead of the expected five-foot-nine woman.

Although the surprise is clear, he soon recovers from the shock. "Hi, I'm here to pick up Aracely. You must be Mason," he speaks and extends his hand. "It is a pleasure to finally meet you. I'm Juaquin Vargas."

Normally I'd be more than happy to ignore the names, but I know I'll need them later. Hence why I make a quick mental note before my brow quirks at him for a tick. *Finally* meet me? How long has my mom seen this guy for that he knows about me and got to the point of *finally* meeting me?

Shaking his hand, I look him up and down. "Mason Carter," I introduce myself though the guy clearly knows who I am.

Mom walks around me, her stare telling me to back off. Yet, the look I give her in return is firm and unrelenting. If she believes he'll get off the hook that easily, she's mistaken.

Reaching out and stopping Mom in her steps, I ignore the stare I know she gives me even without looking, and I give the man another glare. "What are your intentions with my mom, Mr. Juaquin Vargas?"

"Mason," Mom says, discouraging my inquisition.

"That's alright, Ary," he reassures her before he averts his eyes toward me. "I only have good intentions with your mother, Mason. She's an incredible woman whom I'd love to get to know better and better."

Too bad I'm not inclined to believe him. Not for now at least. Perhaps not ever.

"For how long have you two been seeing each other?" I fire again.

"For a couple of months," he answers.

My brow shoots up. A couple of months and I haven't heard about him? Poor bastard thinks knowing my mother better and better is in the cards, but the fact that I haven't heard the least about him prior to tonight only tells me just how serious Mom is about this.

"Okay, Mason, stop this. We're late for our dinner reservation," Mom interferes and kisses my cheek. "Lock up after you grab your things."

"Will do that."

I stand in the doorway of my childhood home, watching Mom and her date walk to his car. He rapidly opens the door for her—which makes me give it to him, at least he's a gentleman about it. After I see Mom climb in, he then rounds the vehicle to the driver's side, and soon enough I see them driving away.

My eyes narrow a little.

Juaquin Vargas…

Although I know Mom's MO of date them and dump them, I

slip my phone out of my pocket and shoot a text directly to Zaiden this time. It is a text with just the guy's name.

The tip of my foot kicks the bottom of the doorframe heedlessly just before I go back inside, grab my things, and lock up the house. As I return to my bike, I only get to mount it before my phone pings with a text. I take it out of my pocket and read it.

Your hot mama knows you have me running checks on her dates again?

I growl when I read the "hot mama" part, but knowing that telling him off for this won't stop him anyway, I just run my fingers over the keyboard that pops on my screen.

I'm sure she has her suspicions.

The three dots dance on the screen and his reply doesn't delay.

I'll have Alex look into this old geezer.

I type back quickly, as though doing it any slower would have Zaiden change his mind.

Appreciate it, man.

With that last message sent, I slide the phone back into the pocket of my jacket and turn on the engine.

Maybe another trial to that initial idea of finding a chick who'd make us forget, buddy.

It is on that last thought that crosses my mind that I put my helmet on and ride away. While I do that, I find myself riding the streets past the same bars again, without inciting any interest to stop.

Moreover, I find myself again in a familiar neighborhood and I ride until I pull into an even more familiar driveway and garage.

I think I might need a brain transplant.

What am I even saying?

I need a transplant of every single body part because nothing seems to be functioning as it should. My brain thinks something, my body does another.

And don't even get me started on my dick—because soon enough I'll want a new cock too, one that comes with special functions. Preferably the function to get hard around a woman and the most important function of all—not to even twitch around Ensley Walker, let alone throb and get so rock-hard I can pound nails with it if I want.

Raking a hand through my hair once I remove my helmet, I put the side stand down and climb off the bike.

With a look over my shoulder, I note that the garage door is now closed, and I walk inside the house through the interior door that connects the two.

Silence and darkness cast the first floor of the house as I step inside. My eyes move over the space, and I stride to the front entrance to leave my shoes and hang my jacket. Then, with even longer steps, I walk up the stairs, taking two of them at a time.

I need a shower and plenty of sleep.

Maybe that's the remedy for everything.

By the time I reach the top of the stairs, I already remove my tee, unbuckle my belt, and undo my jeans. When I get near the spare bathroom in the hallway, however, that's when the sound of running water enters my ears and through the open door, I see a cloud of steam dancing in the air.

Although I know that I shouldn't, it is as though I'm spellbound when I lean against the doorframe, peeking inside. The steam must be mixed with some magic dust because I can't walk away even if I try. All I'm capable of doing is standing there, with my t-shirt in hand and with my eyes fused on the glass shower cabin.

The thin layer of mist that covers the cabin is no match for my hungry gaze that seems determined to see all that was hidden earlier by the small two-piece bathing suit.

Só unha pequena mirada, I think to myself.

Only a little glance…

Yeah, of course. Only a little glance my ass.

As my eyes take in the silhouette, I let them lower from the nape of her neck, over her narrow shoulders, the back that is clearly well worked during her training. Then my gaze drops a little more to her trim waist before it follows the rest of her milky skin and zeroes in on that delectable heart-shaped ass.

My stare stays there for a moment or two, picturing the print of my hand on that delicious skin, imagining my fingers digging into that flesh before my hand swats it with less gentleness.

Knocking these concocted images out of my head almost the moment I have them, I then let my gaze lift again. This time, my eyes follow the path of the water that shoots from the head of the shower and rains over her, creating a trail I'd happily follow with my mouth day in and day out.

With my cock throbbing painfully against the zipper of my jeans, I shift a little to ease the ache. But to no avail because the agony of my dick gets more pronounced with each second that ticks by, and my starved stare keeps moving along the length of her body like it hasn't seen another woman before.

The truth is that no matter how many women have been or how many women I've seen naked—since that particular detail is no less fuzzy than it was the day I came out of a coma—, no sight compares to the one before my very own eyes right now and no other compares to the view I already had etched on my brain.

Twenty-one-year-old Ensley was a beauty and a head-turner, my mind clearly recalling the soft curves her slender frame flaunted as she bared herself before my eyes sixteen years ago. However, thirty-seven-year-old Ensley vaunts a full-grown woman's body with appetizing and delectable curves.

The image of her slender body is now replaced with this perfect view of filled-up curves. They're round in all the right places and muscular and taut in all the others.

Joder!

Ensley Walker is a dream.

A naked, wet and tempting dream that I'm not allowed to have. Not even in the wildest of dreams.

Merda!

I know I shouldn't have looked. I know I shouldn't have let my impulses prevail. Still, like an addict, I needed my fill. My fill of Ensley Walker. My drug of choice that I can't quit. The very woman who's been tormenting my days and my nights becoming my forbidden addiction. And now? With this view in mind to hit replay on during the lonely nights in bed, now I'm more doomed than I already was.

The reason I say this is because I hear the metaphorical crack in my restraint. A loud, deafening crack in my self-control. Self-restraint I imposed sixteen years ago after Ensley's birthday. One I meticulously mastered for over a decade and a half. And what I've just done—allowing my perverted eyes to move over

Ensley's naked and wet body—, not only bends my self-control, but it creates a rift through it.

Hurricane Ensley Walker touches down again. In the whirlwind, she takes everything she encounters in her path.

Emotions.

Memories.

Desires.

Feelings.

Yearnings.

Greed.

All of them together create an unmitigated amalgamation. So consuming and enthralling. So tempting and forbidden. So filthy and at the same time so unadulterated.

So fucking good.

It is on the sound of a faint whimper that dances in my ears, that I get wrenched from my thoughts and the back of my head hits the lateral of the door frame. Craning my neck a little more, from the angle I can see her hand passing over her left breast with the soapy shower sponge. The white moose cloaks her flesh from my ravenous gaze for the briefest of seconds until the water stream washes it down her body to expose her tit and pebble nipple before she moves to the other breast.

As I follow the path of the other hand, however, I watch it darting down the trail of her naval, moving past her stomach till I see it disappear between her thighs.

Her eyes snap close at that first contact and the back of her head leans against the glass of the cabin.

Joder!

I *should* move.

I *must* move.

Yet, regardless of how hard I try to peel myself off the doorframe and get my legs to unglue off the floor, it seems an unfeasible demand. The more I order myself to do it and to amass all the strength I need to be able to carry out a seemingly basic command, I'm only met with failure and the sheer defiance of my own body.

What is worse than standing there is that I find my very own hand—which evidently found a brain of its own—lowering past my stomach and slipping beneath the waistband of my black boxer briefs. Not only that, but it wraps around my aching cock, and I pull it out after I lower the fabric of my underwear with my other hand once I drop the t-shirt on the floor.

Another shaky cry escapes her through her slightly parted lips and I nearly come in my hand just from that sound combined with the sight of Ensley rubbing that sweet clit that I'd give a limb to be able to suck on again.

Doce Xesús!

(*Sweet Jesus!*)

What I'd give to have a full view of her. Of her fingers moving over her clit. Of her sweet cunt inviting her to push them in and pleasure herself while she watches me jack off.

And fuck, my hand begins moving up and down my cock, the bid of pre-come slickening my motions. After a couple of glides, I squeeze a little tighter and pump faster, desperate for a release.

Though I can't see her pussy and only her hand moving between her thighs, Ensley looks sexy as hell while she rubs herself. Slowly and deliberately. Purposefully bringing herself toward the verge of orgasm.

Soon enough, I begin thrusting in my own hand and my vision gets blurry with each one of them.

My heart pounds violently in my chest, but I keep pumping the length of my dick relentlessly, chasing the climax as I close my eyes for a moment.

"Carallo," I rasp under my breath.

"Ma...Mason."

The croon of my name on Ensley's lips halts my hand mid-pump, and I snap my eyes open, thinking I got caught. Almost immediately though, I realize her eyes are still squeezed shut while she continues to touch herself. Her chest moves up and down fiercely, her throat clogged with moans and whimpers.

My jaw hits the floor.

Ensley fucking Walker—my sweet delirium, my forbidden desire, my burning warp rapture—touches herself thinking of me. She lets my name roll off her tongue while she rubs her clit, panting with the image of me behind her closed eyes while she dips her fingers inside her cunt.

Joder!

My free hand runs through my hair, and I pull my still-hard dick in my boxer briefs before I race away from there now that I found a much-needed tick of lucidity that allows me to think clearly.

I've just crossed a line I should have never crossed. A line where there's no turning back from. I jacked off to the sight of Ensley in the shower. I let my filthy eyes drown in the image of her touching herself.

To the thought of me…

Rushing away like a criminal from a crime scene, I enter my bedroom and with a thud, I close the door behind me, my back hitting the chill wood.

Fury at myself wells inside. So much so that I spin, and my fist punches the wall.

Merda! Merda! Merda!

ENSLEY

A pounding headache has me pressing my fingers against my temples and rubbing as I walk into the kitchen. After a good night's sleep, but an awful morning with a throbbing headache, now I feel the need for coffee to kick start the day.

Though I know I'll be better with some Advil and hell loads of water, I still saunter for the coffee machine and begin preparing the magic liquid.

Meanwhile, my mind starts wandering. To the drinks I had with Ella when we were mastering our plan. Thought that has my head aching even more.

That is when my mind gets assailed with recollections of the events from last evening. The hot water of the shower streaming down my body. The sponge moving over my breasts turning my nipples into two hard bullets. My hand slipping between my thighs, surrendering to the overflowing need for a release. My other hand that flew over my mouth to muffle the loud moan that tumbled out of my chest. My chest that rose and fell with savageness, straining for every scintilla of air I drew in. My body that shook and quivered, riding the wild waves of the self-induced orgasm.

How my body trembled.

And trembled.

The flashback of how my body crooned along to the melody dictated by the waves of my climax is very graphic in my brain. Sheer surrender shook me to the core last night while behind my eyelids danced images of Mason. Of his mouth seducing mine until I couldn't think for myself. Of his lips on my skin that scorched everything in their path, setting me ablaze. Of his tongue doing wicked things to my body that only he knows how to do. The kind that erases one's inhibitions and incapacitates one's brainpower.

It is on these very recollections that I remember how I circled my clit, imagining that it is his thumb strumming it with masterful precision. I also recall how I pushed two fingers inside me, picturing his much thicker ones pumping in and out, taking me with unmitigated abandon.

Goosebumps dance over my skin at the memory and I fight the medley of thoughts that still strike. However, my ticks of recollections don't stop there because what I vividly remember is the thunder inside my chest. Because what I feel now at the reflection is just a fraction of what I felt last night. Because last night my heart pounded and pummeled, making it even harder to breathe though my lungs stretched to their maximum limit, attempting to catch all the possible fragments of air they could draw in.

There's another thing that's just as clear in my thread of memories. Mason's shirt on the floor by the open door of the bathroom—a door I haven't even realized I left open until I stepped out of the shower.

Ponders of what it was doing there have tumbled in my mind all night long as I laid in bed. But tears soon rimmed my eyes while I breathed in the scent he left behind on his t-shirt. And emotions raided me, especially when I looked around the room.

A room that used to be for guests and now serves as my place to sleep, leaving Mason in our bedroom. Leaving him surrounded by the familiarity of the space, with everything that used to be us—with the exception of pictures of us and anything else which can expose my lie.

A lie I shouldn't have told anyway but the fear of losing my husband has fogged my brain and clouded my judgment. A lie I now have everybody who's close to us tangled in.

One single lie—by omission but no less of a lie—sprung up a whole web of lies told by everyone who knows us.

It is on this thought that a great deal of guilt lashes out at me. For someone who grew up in a family where we'd tell the truth no matter what, I am doing exactly the opposite of that. Not only have I told a lie, but everyone around me tells it and that isn't something easy to bear.

"Morning."

The voice that nearly makes me jump and slams the breaks on my thoughts is strong and smooth, although a little huskier than the normal baritone because of sleep.

And as I spin on my bare feet toward him, I see Mason running a hand through his unruly hair while he still saunters further inside the kitchen. His gray, cotton sweatpants hang low on his hips and the black t-shirt he wears is as though custom-made to fit tightly over his muscles. So much so that I can see the outlines and ridges of the taut abs I know he has. Though after spending three months in a coma, they aren't as well-defined as they used to be—hard as stone and well-marked—they are still evident and getting more pronounced with each day that passes and he hits the gym for his daily workout.

"Morning," I reply to his greeting.

Instantly, my back turns to him, unable to hold his stare. Especially since his t-shirt on the floor in front of the bathroom with the door wide open arises questions.

No. Actually, it arises worries.

Has he just dropped it on his way to his room?

Has he stood there while I showered?

Has he seen me touch myself? And if he did, how much of it has he seen?

"Mason."

The very specific memory of how his name slipped through my parted lips while my hand worked my most sensitive flesh now comes rushing back, resounding like an echo.

Fuck!

What have I done?

"Did you have a good sleep?" I shoot the question to fill in the silence only so he won't sense my sudden awkwardness at the thought of getting caught.

My back still faces him. Although I don't see it, on the nape of my neck I can clearly feel the severity of his gaze. One I'm not sure I want to face.

"Dandy," he replies casually.

Nevertheless, in his baritone, I can hear a twinge of sarcasm.

What I don't get any time to do is ponder too much on it because my body grows a little alert as I sense his approach. It has never happened before that my frame would grow stiff around him. Nevertheless, with the uncertainty of what happened last night still looming over my throbbing mind, it evidently is the only reaction my body is capable of.

Come on, Ensley. Don't be awkward, I encourage myself knowing that playing it cool and ignoring last night's events is the safest bet.

It is on that spur that I snatch the coffee cup from the tray of the coffee machine. It is impossible not to notice that the cup is merely lukewarm now. Note that can only indicate that I've been lost in my thoughts for quite some time before Mason entered the kitchen. Overlooking that little observation, on a deep inhale that is meant to give me the courage I need, I turn to finally face my utmost fantasy.

Instantly, I realize just how close he really is.

A few breaths away, but close enough for the hot air that escapes through his lips to fan against my skin.

"Did you sleep well, *Ley?*"

My eyes widen in surprise at his choice of nickname. A choice that seems accidental, but the way it rolls off his tongue with implication only brings many more ponders. There has been only one time when he called me that. The night he made love to me for the first time. So having him call me that now, only brings memories. Memories I wonder if he remembers or if it's just a coincidence.

Does Mason remember what happened between us that night of December sixteen years ago? Does his mind remember that night but blocks out all the rest?

"Ley," he croaks the nickname with a lot more heaviness now. As though there's some sort of inner battle taking place. "Stop."

The word is a whisper, one that comes on a laborious breath. And just as much of a great effort it appears to take for him to lift his hand, cradling my cheek with his massive palm.

"Stop what?" I hear myself wonder aloud.

All of a sudden, it feels as though my own air leaves my lungs as the tang of his musky scent with spicy hints pierces my straining lungs. The same ones I loved using just so I could be surrounded by his scent whenever he wasn't near. The fragrance of his cologne—a blend of amber, leather, tabacco, and woody notes—has been driving me crazy from the first day I smelt Decadence on him. Yes, that's what it's called and believe me when I say that if decadence ever had a scent, it would smell just exactly like that. Like indulgence, wickedness, and pure sex.

"Stop looking at me like that."

This time, his hot, minty breath is just mere inches away, fanning against my neck. That is when I realize I've gotten so lost in his scent that I didn't notice I lost his burning gaze when his head leaned in, his mouth so close to my ears that an involuntary shudder shakes my body.

"Why don't you make me?" I challenge in return after I crane my neck to the side a little until my lips are only a breath away from the shell of his ear.

In one fluid motion and before I can even blink, I'm spun. The front of my hipbones is against the rigid edge of the countertop while I lose the grip I have on the cup of coffee, causing it to smash on the floor and the liquid to pool at our feet. However, that becomes the least of my concerns because my body is now pinned between the kitchen counter and the hard front of Mason's body, with his bulging arms on either side of me. My own palms rest atop the counter, while his frame presses me a little further over the piece of furniture.

I am astonished for a tick by the zap of electricity that passes our bodies the very instant they press against one another. I feel it fiercely running through me as it simultaneously runs through Mason. It is an unexpected collision that shakes me to the core and judging by the sudden stillness in his body, it has an impact on him too. Taking into account the wild gallop of his heart against my back, it is as though the contact has jolted it into a wayward rhythm. Just the same it did with my own which I'm sure he can feel too.

This marks our first collision since his accident. The first time we touch each other since he lost his memories of me. That jolt of electricity and how it sends our hearts in a frenetic pounding, that perhaps proves something. Something that gets my heart to jounce with a sliver of hope.

The mind might forget. But the heart doesn't and neither does the body. Because in these instances right here—how his heart pummels against my back and how his body responds to my proximity—, it only proves that his body remembers my touch. Or the newly obtained splinter of hope makes me believe that it recalls.

So for a brief tick, I close my eyes to relish in that closeness and I allow myself to ponder briefly.

I wonder if my taste still lingers on his lips. If the caress of my mouth—that once has trailed the inches of his skin—still hovers over his flesh. I wonder if his heart still beats the same rhythm that mine does.

Whether he knows it or not, whether he is aware of it or not, Mason Carter was, is and will always be mine even if his mind doesn't let him fully remember that.

My moments of reflection are brought to a halt when without hesitation, one arm disappears from my side. A surprised gasp rolls out of me when a hand threads into my hair and pulls gently, still hard enough to have my head tip back while my chest pushes outward. My lower body, on the other hand, presses into my husband, my ass against the rigidness of his cock. And oh, boy, he can pound nails with it at how hard he is.

Or he can just pound me, I think to myself.

"Don't tempt me, Ley," he rasps in my ear, his lips grazing my earlobe.

For a moment I don't know if his words are for my previous challenging question or if my silent thought hasn't been as silent as I believed. For just as long I wonder if I tempt him to make me stop or if I tempt him to pound me.

"Why do you fight me, Mason?" I ask almost inaudibly, unable to stop the question from slipping out. "Why would you fight against me when your own body tells you to surrender to what you feel for me?"

At that, my hips gyrate over his rock-hard length. Instantly, it throbs against my cotton shorts as though in spite of him, proving the attestation of my question.

His other hand now lifts off the counter right before I feel it on my throat. He doesn't squeeze, he just holds it there, the pad of his thumb skimming my racing pulse point, drawing a sudden moan from me. It then uprises on the column of my neck until the pad of his thumb darts over my bottom lip, teasing me to suck it between my lips like I've done many times before. It doesn't rest there long enough though because not a second later, it lowers back again to graze my pulse spot.

Mason's heavy body presses more into mine, letting me feel every single part of him. His hard chest against my shoulders. His taut abdomen against my back. His muscular thighs beneath the back of mine. His aching dick pushes against my ass as my hips roll over it mindlessly, forcing a moan from my chest. At the same time, his own growl makes its way into my ears.

Experiencing his touch, his dominance and control, and his hardness after so long cause a pool of desire to amass between my legs. To the extent that only a mere brush of his hand over my skin would have me combust.

"We'll forever be star-crossed, *miña raíña*," he croaks on another groan.

His hand loosens its hold on my hair only to travel to the front of my body and rest on my stomach, halting the gyration of my hips.

"I could be weak and give in. I could slip my hand inside your panties and feel just how wet you are because I *know* you are. I could pull your shorts down and slide my cock inside your cunt right now to see if you're as snug as I remember. I could even take your ass because I know you'd let me do to you all the filthy things I can only fantasize about doing. I could claim your mouth with my own. I could touch your tits and play with your nipples until you beg me to stop. I could do all that, Ley baby. I could and you'd let me."

A gasp pushes up my throat at the sheer certainty in his voice. The tremble of my body betrays me and tells him that he has reasons to be sure about his claims.

"I could do all that to you, but that won't change our fate. We were only meant to collide once and that was a mistake I'm not going to repeat."

"...to see if you're as snug as I remember."

"We were only meant to collide once..."

These two parts of the different sentences replay in my head for a tick or two. Instantly, they serve as the answer I was looking for earlier with my pondering. Mason does remember that night from sixteen years ago. He does remember when he made me his.

"Why?"

Once again, the question slips past my lips before I get a chance to suppress it. This time, however, I'm met with a few instances of silence.

So I crane my neck to be able to look at him over his shoulder, only to find the fiercest of battles known to humankind in his eyes.

The inner battle.

A battle of wills between what he truly feels and what he thinks he should feel. A battle between his body—that recognizes me—and his mind—that still blocks out all recollections of me.

MASON

Her green eyes hold mine expectantly. That very same pair of orbs that pierces through me and shakes me to the bone every single time it connects with my brown one. The very same pair that has been haunting my nights and has been tormenting my days since I was fifteen years old and realized Ensley Walker will be my goddamn perdition because I was in love with her. The very gaze I couldn't get enough of staring into as I made her mine sixteen years ago because I thought that, maybe, just maybe, it will get her out of my system.

Absolutely idiotic of me to think so because it seems the woman with the silkiest brunette hair—that invites me to pull on it as I drive inside her from behind—and the most beautiful eyes—that beg me every single time to get a little closer and a little more until I get utterly lost in her scent and sign my capit- ulation with my mouth on hers and on every inch of her deli- cious body—has embedded herself into me deeper. But that doesn't change anything.

Nineteen-year-old me was nothing but an idiot believing he'll ever be worthy of Ensley Walker. Thirty-five-year-old me knows better than to allow himself to even remotely think of her as anything but his friend and his best friend's sister. Although the same thirty-five-year-old me went exactly the opposite direction, imagining all the filthy things he'd do to her —marking her skin, devouring every single bit of her, drowning her in me until she cannot think straight any longer just the

137

same way I can't when I'm surrounded by her fragrance and her presence.

But then again, now I know better.

"I wanted to deserve you, but the truth is that I never did."

With that last sentence, I let go of my hold on her throat and unpeel my hand from her stomach. Also, with a great amount of effort, I also push back, my body feeling the sudden absence of the heat oozing from her own body. With an even enhanced struggle, I fight the urge of pulling her back to me to feel that sizzling heat for a moment longer. To feel her body molded to mine, fitting so perfectly as though it is its missing piece.

Her frame is still, her hands atop the counter as she takes in deep breaths.

Even from where I stand a few feet away, I can hear the pounding of her heart. That very pummeling I felt beating against her back as I had her pressed to me, finding a familiarity to it that I can't understand.

Carallo!

Everything is going downhill.

Everything is going to the goddamn hell.

"I'll make you another cup of coffee," I say, my voice as casual and neutral as I can bring it like the earlier events haven't even happened.

Except, they really ensued. The very witness to the occurrence is my cock that throbs inside the confinement created by my boxers and my sweatpants. But an even more credible witness makes my heart that still thumps worse than after racing an ultramarathon in full firefighter gear. I still feign they didn't affect me though I know with certainty that Ensley felt all the ways her proximity impacted me.

When she finally turns to me and although I am prepared for anything—I do mean anything—nothing prepares me for what I see in her beautiful green orbs. They don't just ignite. They are like a wildland fire. One that spreads with sheer force with each second that ticks by and burns everything in its path. One that threatens to singe my flesh and scorch me to the bone.

Xesús.

I'm surprised how I'm still standing instead of being turned into ashes at her feet.

But it is only a matter of time. She's a ticking bomb.

"You don't get to fucking toy with me this way, Carter," Ensley bites.

There is utter determination in her eyes as she eats the distance between us and jabs a slender finger into my chest.

"You don't get to act hot to only turn all cold a second later just because you can. Yes, I would let you do all that to me and more. I would let you do to me the filthiest things you can think of because I'm crazy about you. Yes, you heard me because unlike you, I'm not afraid to own up to what I feel for you. I've always been crazy about you. But what I won't let you do is treat me like yesterday's garbage. I'm not a one-night stand. I'm not a toy you play with whenever you see fit and toss away when you get bored. I'm not someone you tell sweet or dirty words to only to then give them a cold shower to cool them off. I know my worth, so if you dare pull this kind of shit on me one more time to only then turn all icy and callous, better be prepared to suffer the consequences. Believe me when I say that I'll tie you to a chair, snatch off your balls and make you eat them, then I'll chop off your dick and shove it down your throat. And I'll do all that with a bolt cutter, so how's that for an irony, *Cutter*?"

Ensley Walker, ladies and gentlemen.

Ensley fucking Walker surrounded by sheer flames that are so fucking mesmerizing to look at, I can't even be mad at her for threatening my jewels and my cock. On the contrary, my balls swell painfully, and my dick gets even harder at how beautiful she looks all angry and fired up.

The woman who submitted to me for the briefest of moments while I had her against my body is now all ablaze with fury. Moreover, she looks ready to rip my head off my shoulders with her bare hands and shove it up my ass. And trust me, at this point, I'm not putting anything past her.

"You've been warned," Ensley sasses, flicking back a long, thick strand of hair.

With that, I watch her speechlessly—but with a grin on my face—as she does a long jump over the puddle of coffee at our feet and the shards of what once was a mug. Then, she struts her fine ass out of the kitchen and through the gliding doors before she plops herself on the sofa on the patio. Her legs cross in a yoga position while she clearly tries to tame the anger that I've ignited inside her.

I shouldn't get so smug about it now. Certainly not when it involves the woman who threatened to have no mercy on my crotch.

Doce Xesús!

I am playing with fire.

No doubt about it.

I am going to pay hell for what I've just done and her heavy, purposeful steps together with her previous rant are only a mere indication of what kind of hell I'll be paying with Ensley.

Her strides tell me it will be painful.

Her earlier words denote that it will be gut-wrenching.

But hell if I won't be there for all of it.

Fai o teu peor, nena!

(*Do your worst, baby!*)

Nena...

That last part of the sentence resonates in my mind. I know I called her *'baby'* just yesterday when I stopped to check on her after that idiot slammed his breaks, but since when do I fucking call her *'nena'*?

I'm losing my goddamn mind.

First of all, I shouldn't've touched Ensley even with a ten-foot pole, much less manhandle her the way I did. Second of all, I should have never let her get to me the way she did. And thirdly but not lastly, I should have never watched her in the shower the way I did last night.

It is as though the more I attempt to stay away, the more the universe is adamant to throw her into my arms. Like a fate one can't escape from.

The truth is that I could pack up my stuff and leave. I could move away somewhere far from Ensley. I could do all that, yet there's something inside me that simply doesn't let me.

Even when I told Luke that I want to go away for some time, I knew deep down I was talking just plain bullshit.

I'm too much of a glutton for self-punishment to leave. I need my daily dose of Ensley Walker too much to quit.

With a sigh and careful not to step on any shards, I clean the mess caused by my momentary lapse in judgment when I've let myself provoked by Ensley. A provocation I know I should have not entertained. But as aware of that as I was, I still let it get the best of me.

Knocking the thoughts out of my head, I finish up cleaning and fill two mugs with coffee, before I take them and saunter my way to where Ensley sits.

A gentle breeze surrounds me when I step outside, and I watch how a couple of strands of brunette hair fly across Ensley's face. She brushes them back quickly and then turns her gorgeous eyes to me.

"Peace offering?"

Following her question, a perfectly sculpted brow arches in an even more defying gesture. As though to up me another one, the challenge in her eyes is as evident as the fire she possessed moments ago when I angered her.

That smart mouth of hers...

And the impulse to just drop the cups, bend her over the sofa and swat that disputing and frustrating ass of hers until she can't sit down is almost unbearable.

Yet, by some means unknown, somewhere within me—very deep within me, I must mention—I find the button to halt my urge and eagerly press on it.

"Could call it that," I return, handing her one of the cups.

"Thanks."

After Ensley takes the cup from me, I take a seat in the armchair opposite her.

Silence glazes between us. At the same time, the air sizzles, the tension of the earlier events still hanging in thick layers over us.

Joder!

How she gasped when I threaded my hands through her hair and pulled. How her body arched more into me as though begging me to take her right then and there. How she moaned when I brought my hand to her throat and grazed her pulse spot. How her lips parted a little more when my thumb brushed over her lower lip. How instead of pushing me away, her hips rolled over my hard cock.

"You didn't flinch," I utter abruptly.

My eyes fly to her green gaze that lifts to mine in that same instant.

"Excuse me?" She asks confused.

"I was rough with you. I pulled your hair. I had my hand around your throat, and you didn't flinch."

Though she avoids my gaze for the longest of ticks, her eyes eventually dart back to me only to narrow.

"I still don't get it. Why would I flinch, Mason?" As though it dawns on her as she says my name in her wonder, her head then shakes before our eyes lock again. "Mase, I know you would never hurt me."

The conviction in her voice as she tells me she knows I won't hurt her aches my heart. Only if she knew the truth. She'd run a mile if she did.

A scoff crawls up my throat and tumbles out in the air while my head shakes in disbelief. "How can you say that, Ensley? How can you say that when all I've been doing is hurting you?"

Without realizing it, I find myself up on my feet and she follows suit. We keep our distance though cautious that one single step in the direction of the other can ignite everything.

"You haven't," she denies, her head moving in a disapproving motion as though to sustain her words.

In a couple of steps, she's right in front of me, her small hand resting on my cheek. Her touch there sends an entire wave of heat inside me. Her eyes as they lock onto mine give nothing but undeniable trust. A trust I haven't earned.

"Mason, baby, you won't hurt me. Is this what you're afraid of, that you'll hurt me?"

Heedlessly, I lean into her touch a little more wanting to feel that soft, gentle palm on my skin for another tick or two before I pull away and step back.

Ensley's lips part slightly in surprise, her green eyes coated in a mix of expectancy and sadness.

"It doesn't matter, Ensley. Someone like me will never be worthy of somebody like you."

Once the words leave my mouth, I turn away from her and storm out.

Better this way.

It's better to leave now before I say something I shouldn't. Or worse, do something I shouldn't. The latter seems more feasible since her lips looked so tempting a moment ago—as they always do. Just out of reach for mine to lean in and take them into a kiss.

However, if I believed for a second that it would be the end of the discussion, I was wrong. And how wrong I was I get to find out when I hear Ensley's heavy steps behind me.

"Why?"

One word.

A single word that halts my steps abruptly.

Only a sole word that holds every meaning.

A question made of a three-letter word that hits the hardest especially because of the hurting in her voice when she asks it.

"Tell me why and I'll stay away. I only need a reason, that's all I've ever needed. A reason why. Why do you push me away?"

Slowly, I turn to face her. Her gorgeous green eyes lock onto mine the second I find them. And it is then that I realize my answer means more to her than she wants to let on. As though she wants closure for something.

"Tell me why so I can understand and move on from you."

Move on…

Fucking move on from me…

"If I were a better man, I would grab hold of you and never let you go. And believe me when I tell you that I'm fighting it with all my might right now. So you'll just have to do it for both of us."

It is all I can muster to say. The ache in my heart tells me I've just made a mistake. The hurt in her eyes says I'm making the worst of mistakes. And when her head shakes before her gaze connects with mine again, that's when I see something glazing her orbs. Something I've never seen in her forever determined stare—a sliver of doubt and defeat.

ENSLEY

My duffle bag falls with a thud on the floor in the firehouse's locker room. My body feels so drained of energy after what happened with Mason yesterday, it takes me a great deal of effort only to lift my hand to press the code on my padlock.

"If I were a better man, I would grab hold of you and never let you go. And believe me when I tell you that I'm fighting it with all my might right now. So you'll just have to do it for both of us."

Mason's prompting resounds for the umpteenth time in my head. On each repeat, it ricochets from one brain cell onto the next and the next and the next.

No reason.

No explanation.

As though it is all it takes to be able to move on from a man like Mason Carter.

With a heavy sigh and a shake of my head to knock the thought out, I put the code in and place my bag inside the locker, before I turn and walk toward JJ's office. On my way, however, I stop to get two coffees and to salute some of the firefighters from the second shift who are in the kitchen waiting for their change.

"Hey," I greet her when I make it to the open door of her office.

JJ's eyes lift from the paperwork she has atop the desk in front of her and she gives me a smile.

"Hey, doll. Come on in."

Entering the office, I hand her a cup of coffee and I keep the other, taking the seat across from her desk.

JJ leans back in her chair and gives me a once-over. "What's wrong, honey?"

That's all the prodding I need to tell my best friend about what happened the past couple of days since we've last seen each other. And I do mean absolutely everything. From my plan concocting with Ella over mojitos, to my little escapade in the shower, to the morning after that when Mason had me pinned between his body and the kitchen counter, one of his hands in my hair and his other on my throat.

"He was surprised I didn't flinch,"

JJ chuckles. "That's because you had fifteen years to get used to that rowdy and rough side of him."

"Which clearly isn't something I can tell him," I explain.

After she takes a sip of her coffee, she sets it back on the desk and lets out a breath. "Why not? I get he doesn't remember, but why don't you tell him?"

"Because he asked me for the divorce just before he went on shift that day," I admit, my heart aching at the words. "Now he keeps pushing me away. I've done this once already. We've danced this dance before and he eventually gave in, but to be completely honest, I'm not so sure if he will this time. He's so vehement that we're star-crossed. You should've seen him, JJ."

"I think Ella's suggestion might make him see that you're what he's always wanted. His mind might block out the memories of you, but it is his heart that will never forget them. All you have to do is give him a jumpstart in that direction."

My finger circles the rim of my coffee cup while I look at the liquid and think about her words.

"Look, I don't think Mason asked you for the divorce because he doesn't love you anymore. That man would lay down his own life for you and there's no doubt in my mind about it," JJ attests and she gives me the kindest of looks. "Doll, I've seen him that day when we all thought we'll lose you and Carson in that fire. Mason was crazy with desperation. One could see the raw torture on his face, and he even punched one of the police officers when they tried to cuff him to the squad car's door. There's nothing in this world that can crumble that man, but do you know what brought him to his knees?" She pauses, gets up from her seat and rounds the desk, taking the seat next to me. "When he heard your voice through the radio, and you told him you love him. That, honey, brought him right onto his knees, holding on to that radio like his life depended on it. What I'm trying to say here is that man loves you and dissociative amnesia or not, blocked out memories of you or not, he'd do anything to protect you."

"Protect me from what?"

Though I ask it aloud, the question is more of a ponder to myself.

"That's a question only Mason can answer, I'm afraid. Maybe he's always been conflicted. Perhaps he's always been torn between what he feels for you and whatever the other thing is that makes him want to keep his distance from you. Only this would make sense considering he kept you at arm's length years ago, to only do this again now.

"Something must have happened and he still unconsciously tries to protect you from it. I know someone, her name is Michaela Rayton and she's a firefighter with the Richmond Fire Department. She's been in a car crash, fell into a coma for a few weeks and then she woke up. Everything was alright after that, but months later she was diagnosed with PCS."

"Post-Concussion Syndrome."

JJ nods. "She loved her husband tremendously, but she thought she'll be a burden to him. So, she made the decision for the both of them and served him with the divorce papers without telling him why. She was trying to protect him, but that man did not give up on her. The more she pushed him away, the harder he fought."

"Are they still married?"

"Happily married and so much in love. With a little girl for a daughter and twins on the way," she answers with a smile before her hand is placed atop mine and gives it a gentle squeeze.

"I'll fight for my man," I declare with my usual determination.

One that makes JJ chuckle.

"That man of yours won't even know what hit him because *Monsoon Ensley* is charging for him."

I chuckle.

"Also, can we please make him jealous? That man's like a

raging bull when he gets jealous. Remember that photographer who was hitting on you when we were doing this year's charity calendar?"

"Oh, no, that was a disaster," I say, suppressing the urge to face palm myself at the memory. "I knew it wasn't a good idea to have Mason there."

"When the photographer kept complimenting you, he was there on the side, and one could see the steam seeping out of him. Truthfully, I don't know how he stopped himself from punching the guy.

"Also, let's be honest for a minute here and admit that Mason being there is one of the reasons why your pictures are so fucking hot. I mean, you're incredibly sexy and an absolute knockout, but that time you were on fire, girl. You seduced the hell out of Mason and considering he threw you over his shoulder and you two disappeared right after you were done, I can only assume what happened thereafter."

"Some hot and heavy sex in the bunker gear room is what happened," I confess with a wicked smile.

Her hand retracts as though mine burnt hers and her nose scrunches up in dismay. "As your commanding officer in charge, I did not need to know about your escapades on the department's property."

"Don't pretend it's the first time you've heard about it anyway or the first time it's happened. Plus, at that time, we were off the clock. And besides, if I'm not mistaken, I've seen Nathan Stone sneaking out of your office more than once." I remind her. "I mean, do you both really think he can just walk past unnoticed? Because I'm sorry to break it to you, but a six-foot-six wall of muscles walking in and out of your office is extremely unmistakable."

Nathan Stone is a firefighter with Firehouse 24 and a member of the same crew Ella is part of. He is also JJ's fuck buddy. Though she prefers to describe it as *"friends with benefits, less of the friends, but more of the benefits"*. I, on the other hand, describe it as *"the situation that comes biting you right in the ass"*. After catching the son of a bitch whom she was supposed to marry in their bed with another woman, JJ swore off dating and relationships altogether. Now she chooses the less complicated —or so she says—side of things.

Plain, no-strings-attached sex.

JJ and Nathan met at the bar that now is owned by Mason and my brother. Nathan made it clear he was interested, however, JJ turned him down. According to her, she decided to pass because of the eight years age gap between them, Nathan being thirty-two and JJ being forty. Something I can only call bullshit on. But at least that got somewhat remedied when about a week later, they bumped into each other again, and ever since they've been in a friends-with-benefits entanglement.

"Don't you have a rig to check?"

A chortle escapes me, and I flick my wrist to check the time on the watch, noting it is getting close to the start of my shift.

"Of course, Captain."

With that, I get up and walk toward the door, my coffee still in hand.

"Oh, and by the way, there's a lieutenant's position opening up soon at the station."

"What do you mean?" I ask, looking over my shoulder. "Don't tell me Turner's retiring."

Marcus Turner is our truck lieutenant. He's a through and through senior firefighter from whom I've learned a lot of things during my own career as a firefighter. He's also one of my dad's oldest and greatest friends of all time.

Though he could have been high up in the department's chain of command by now, Turner has always been more of a boots-on-the-ground kinda man, so incident reports are the only papers he's willing to push. It cost him his marriage because his wife just wouldn't want to understand any longer that he'll be risking his life for others for the whole extent of his career.

"Seemingly so. Apparently, he's been seeing some woman who made him see there's more to life than work and he's ready to trade his boots for a pair of flip-flops."

"He deserves that after his wife left him the way she did."

"Absolutely. Besides, this means we'll have an opening for the lieutenant's spot, and I want you to fill it," JJ states. "That position is yours if you want it. You already passed the test with flying colors."

"Aren't there others who passed the test before me?"

The line for lieutenants waiting for a spot to open is usually rather long, and many of them wait for quite a while to get to step into their new roles, normally with a different firehouse. Among them is Mason, who has passed the test before he went into a coma. Granted, he's still waiting to get reinstated.

"A couple. The number of positions for the lieutenant's tests is pretty much to match the number of spots that the department deems will have available once the retirements are going through that year. Had it not been for Mason's accident, he'd already be with Rescue Squad 3 in Anacostia, but someone from Squad 1 got it instead. HazMat will have one opening in the next couple of months, though."

I nod to that.

"Now, go check that rig before shift starts."

"You got it."

With that, I turn to leave. However, her voice stops me in my tracks again, causing me to turn.

"You'll get your man back, doll. Mason is crazily in love with you and we all can see it. That man has been in love with you his whole life and so have you. For God's sake, Ensley, after what happened to me with that asshole I had for a fiancé, you two actually make me believe in the idea of true love. *Me*, Ensley! *Me*! You can't disappoint me like this because it will crush me."

My lips curl in an askew smile and my eyes take in the gentleness in her hazel ones.

"I'll keep that in mind."

"Oh, yeah, you better because if either of you destroys my goal couple whom I live vicariously through, I'll strangle you both so you can find happily ever after in the after part."

Once my eyes widen at her for a tick, my brows then narrow. "The way you think is disturbing."

"Take that as your warning."

As my head shakes, I spin on the heels of my boots and turn, this time walking away.

* * *

"Someone has a secret admirer."

The strong voice that comes from behind me brings me to a stop. One hand is on the clipboard with the checklist for the truck, while the other halts atop it, the pen between my fingers. I spin to see Carson Morgan walk through the doors and into the apparatus bay, holding a bouquet of roses.

"Evidently said admirer wants to take advantage of Cutter's amnesia," he continues.

My eyebrows furrow as I take in the flowers Carson holds out for me.

A cold chill spreads down my spine at the memory of when I last received a bouquet of roses. Of when I've seen them in the backseat of my car. Of the note attached to them.

However, I knock that flashback out of my head and place the clipboard on the truck's floor through the open door, and I grab the flowers from my fellow firefighter. I look between the flowers for a card, which I find and fish between my fingers.

"Thank you, Carson."

"No problem. Like I said, maybe somebody decided to make a little competition to Cutter," he suggests with a casual shrug. "Though someone should tell them they're wasting their time trying because they don't stand a chance."

"So certain of that," I rebuff.

His brow arches at me in a silent gesture that calls me out on my bullshit. "Gorgeous, I was stuck with you in a building on fire and all you wanted to do was tell your man one last time that you love him," Carson begins. "Not only that, but when you heard his distraught voice and when you heard him tell you that he loves you, that you're the best thing that could have possibly happened to him, I watched you get up and more determined than ever to find a way out. I watched you crawl out and jump off a building only so you could get back to your man. So yeah, I'm certain this secret admirer is only wasting his time because that heart you've got beating in your chest only beats for one man and said man is Mason Carter."

The corners of my lips lift in a smile.

"Thanks, Carson."

"Anytime." With a wink, he leaves.

For the second time, my eyes take in the flowers and once more, my brows knit together.

Over three weeks have passed since I found the bouquet of roses in the backseat of my car. A bouquet that came with a note.

Which brings me to the item in my hand, my eyes moving over the letters.

"I know your secret. I know his too. I wonder which one will come out first."

This is what the note reads, and my eyes narrow in confusion at the words. A cold chill courses through me just like it did that first time. Nevertheless, I don't get a chance to contemplate for too long because the system goes off.

"Truck 6, Ambulance 11, person trapped."

At that, I jog quickly to a table that's in the apparatus' bay and drop the roses atop it. Following that, I shove the note into my pocket and race back to the truck. As I do so, my fellow fire-fighters from Truck 6 rush through the doors, while the two paramedics climb into the ambulance.

We slip inside the bunker gear pants and boots. I then take the driver's seat with Lieutenant Marcus Turner in the passenger's seat and the remaining of our crew in the back.

Driving the truck along the bay's floor toward the exit, my neck cranes a little to the side and my eyes fixate on the flowers. Perhaps this bouquet doesn't have anything to do with the other just because it's made of roses. They are the go-to choice when it comes to flowers.

And perhaps all the books I've been reading and all the series and movies I've watched begin chipping away at the romantic inside of me, only to bring out the distrustful side.

Or maybe there isn't anything and I should stop being so paranoid.

MASON

"Look who the cat dragged in," my fellow firefighter Nolan Santiago shouts when I walk inside the firehouse's common room. It gets everyone to look in my direction before they rush to welcome me with hugs and pats on the back.

My eyes take in each one of them. From Nolan Santiago, Rhys Thatcher and Kellan Monroe who are part of Squad 2, to Captain Owen Tucker, Ian Callahan, Erin Ashford, Daniel Barlow, Emilian Trevino and Cole Dalton from Engine 24.

Except for the two ambulance paramedics who were just driving out to a call when I came in, Luke and Battalion Chief Jason Sinclair are the other two who aren't here. However, I've seen them in the chief's office on my way to the common room.

"I came in to grace you all with my presence and maybe rub off a little of my handsomeness on this ugly bunch that you all turned into in my absence," I revert, patting Rhys on the back.

They nearly roll their eyes at me.

"Never thought we'd miss your arrogance around the fire-house," Captain Owen Tucker speaks this time from behind the stove, a spatula in his hand.

"Things are definitely worse than I thought here if you're doing the cooking, Cap."

He gives me a glare.

"If our designated chef decided to bail on us."

"Seriously, Cutter, if you don't return to firefighting just yet, can you at least come in and cook for us?" Rhys is the one to ask the question.

"Come on, Cap's food must not be all that bad."

"Oh, believe us, it is all that bad," Nolan supports in jest, earning a hard stare from the captain. "No offense, Tucker, but it's the Spaniard in him. You can't compete with that."

Before the captain has a chance to say something to his defense, the alarm goes off. It takes me a tick or maybe two to stop myself from turning and running toward the apparatus floor.

"Squad 2, person trapped."

"Truck 6 is in need of assistance with that rescue," Battalion Chief Jason Sinclair adds, checking his phone.

I watch them rush out of the common room as they hurry to assist Truck 6.

The truck company Ensley works on. She's on a call right now.

She's on shift today and she'll be back home tomorrow. Which reminds me that I might have succeeded in avoiding her for the rest of yesterday after what happened, but I know that won't be for long. Not when in less than twelve hours I'll watch her saunter her way into the house, looking breathtakingly beautiful regardless of how tired she is.

It is a thought that brings me to the reason why I avoided her. Actually, among the many reasons I usually avoid her, now I do it because I should have never manhandled her the way I did. I should have not lost control as I did. But she was so close, her delicious body just out of reach and her sweet fragrance luring me to forget everything about control. A scent that dared me to just give in.

And, *carallo*, I almost did. Especially when I had her against my own body. When I felt her hips rolling over my hard cock. When I had her between my arms. When I breathed in her scent as though it was the sweetest of addictions.

Joder!

I'm so fucking damned is not even funny.

Yet, no matter how much of a temptress she is, I must steer clear of Ensley. I must keep my distance and fight all these urges she wakes inside of me. That insatiable want to possess her in all the ways I can possibly can. To consume her so thoroughly just like she consumes me. To drown her in all that I am until she gets so coated in me. So wrapped in me, in my taste, in my scent, in my touch. To the extent that nothing will ever be able to wash me off her skin, scrub me off her lips. So much so that nothing can ever erase me from her mind just like I can't cast her away from mine.

"It's great seeing you, Carter. How are you feeling?" Chief's voice wrenches me out of my own thoughts, catching my attention before he gives me a welcoming hug.

"All good, Chief. I'm waiting for one last assessment with the department's doctor and get the all-clear after that to come back as a firefighter."

"Finally. Everyone misses having you around here. I think they won't tell you, but they all miss your jokes."

I chuckle.

"I'm aching to get back."

The chief smiles. "Lieutenant Turner's team from Truck 6 and Captain Gunner's team from Truck 22 have got training tomorrow at the academy and Captain Chris Ecker asked if maybe you could swing by. You've got years of training courses experience teaching recruits alongside him. They could use some of your input and guidance."

"If you mean I'm his go-to person when he can't be asked to teach, then yeah, you could say I've taught alongside him," I jest, and the chief lets out a laugh, knowing there's a little bit of truth to that joke. "Anything to keep me busy, so I'd be happy to help."

"Great, they should be there from nine till twelve."

"Thanks, Chief. Appreciate it."

"You got it. There's also something else I wanted to discuss with you."

I nod. "Sure, Chief."

"In a couple of months, there'll be an opening for the lieutenant's spot with one of the HazMat units."

"Edgewood, right?" I ask, knowing that the two HazMat units of Washington, D.C. are part of Ward 5's Firehouse 12, in Edgewood.

"I know you wanted a spot with squad, but Squad 1 just got their new lieutenant a couple of months ago, Squad 2 has Walker and Squad 3 still has Chappelow. Though I must say that there are rumors he might be transferring out of state. If he does, that lieutenant spot is yours. You're the youngest in the department to have made it to squad."

"Come on, Chief, Luke and I both made it at twenty-two, just because he's two weeks older than I am, that doesn't mean I'm the youngest. We're both the youngest," I attest.

"Not on paper, but regardless, if you're willing to wait a little longer than two months, you'll get that spot."

"They've got quite a good team with Squad 3, don't they?"

The chief nods. "Second best in the state. But if you leave for Squad 3 and Luke stays here, I'm pretty sure they'll call it a tie between Rescue Squad 2 and 3."

My brow shoots up at him and my eyes move over him suspiciously. "Is there anything else you need from me, Chief? Because you sure give me lots of compliments."

He smirks. "So good to have you around here, son."

"It sure feels good to be back even just stopping by."

Chief's hand lifts and he pats my back. "You'll be here with the team in no time. Just make sure you take it easy, okay?"

"Copy that, Chief."

With a brief nod of his head, he leaves.

"Now, Tucker, do you need help with that lunch?" I ask turning toward the captain.

"Sure."

Striding toward the counter, I round it and begin helping Tucker with preparing the lunch for the crew. While we do so, the remaining members of Engine 24 begin a game of cards on the large table, soon filling the room with a mixture of laughter, complaining groans, swears and cheerful sounds.

God, I missed being surrounded by these idiots.

And I say that with all the love in the world for this team because they are my family.

* * *

Nine o'clock in the morning finds me leaning against the metal staircase at the academy.

One hand is deep in the pocket of my jeans while in the other I hold the coffee. As I sip on it, my eyes journey the space, taking in the two crews as they lay everything out for the training—

rolled hoses, ladders, breathing apparatus, lines, dummies, jaws, and all other sorts of equipment.

With all the might I can find deep within me, I suppress all that gripping need to look her way. Especially after what happened a couple of mornings ago and the way my control not only cracked but snapped loose. Now more than ever, I need to garner all the will inside me to fight against her further. To push away the memory of how her body fitted against mine. To cast away the recollection of how good she felt against me, how perfectly she fit between my arms like she was always meant to be there. Furthermore, I must alienate the vivid memory of how my heart set off in a wild gallop at that jolt of electricity that zapped through me when our first contact occurred. A contact that seemed so natural when I had her against me as if I've done it thousands of times before.

My head shakes, pushing away the thoughts of Ensley and her body against mine, the thoughts of how much I wanted to claim that mouth of hers once again. Of how the need flew through my body to strip her naked of her clothes and drive deep inside her until I have her sweet cunt sheathing my cock, until it clamps down on my length and clutches it in a vise-like grip. Until my dick and her pussy mourn each time I withdraw but gloat with each thrust back in.

Joder!

I need to get my scrambled brain checked up or maybe enquire with the doctor if the dissociative amnesia comes with a severe case of craving and needing Ensley more than I need to draw my next breath. Especially when everything within me appears to complot against my better judgment and my sanity— or whatever amount of both I got left anyway—and get the upper hand on me, making me a slave of my desire.

"Hey, Mason," Ella greets as she walks past the stairs, rolling out a hose. "It's good to see you though you kinda really pissed off my man the other day."

Her voice is filled with accusation.

"And I supposed your pissed-off man told you the reason why," I revert, taking a gulp of the dark coffee.

"Maybe he did, maybe he didn't," she says with a shrug. "Anyway, I'll be blunt, so I'll come right out and say it."

My brow arches at her, waiting to see whatever she has to say.

"Ensley is a great woman and if you don't see or don't wanna see that, then it's on you. Just don't string her along or your balls will be the ones to end up on a spear."

I look at her impressed. Though I'm fairly certain she'd do exactly what she threatened to do, her words don't scare me. However, it is the vehemency with which she defends Ensley that has me stunned for a moment.

Woman supporting other woman at its finest.

"Oh, and if I were you, I'd hurry to stake a claim because, by the looks of it, that line doesn't lack suitors."

It is the jerk of her chin that has me cock my head to the side and look in the direction Ella indicated. What my eyes lay on is Ensley. She looks absolutely breathtaking with her long brunette hair in a high tail exposing the column of her neck. She doesn't wear even the slightest bit of makeup, her natural beauty nothing short of exquisite and enticing. Her body with curves in all the right places is hugged by the navy-blue cargo pants and the matching-colored t-shirt of her uniform with the District of Columbia Fire Department and EMS crest imprinted on the left side.

My heart leaps out of my chest at the sight of her tipping her head back while she lets out a laugh. However, the blood pumping in my veins reaches its highest boiling point when I move my gaze from the gut-wrenchingly beautiful brunette to the man standing in front of her. The man who has the audacity to draw that beautiful, harmonious sound out of her.

Instantly, my hand balls into a fist at my side and my jaw ticks furiously as I let my stare move between the two of them. My body is ready to charge like a bull as red coats my eyelids.

I see fucking red.

"Aw, they're so cute. Don't you think they're cute, Mason?"

My neck cranes and my eyes dart to Ella right away, drilling her to the wall behind her with my stern gaze. But when I take note of the smirk playing at the corners of her mouth, I figure out her play. That still doesn't stop the words from making their way out of my mouth, though.

"Hey, Gunner, these stairs aren't gonna climb themselves," I shout across the yard, interrupting his conversation with Ensley.

Of course, it had to be Wade-fucking-Gunner.

As his head snaps my way, his brow arches. At the same time, Ensley's neck cocks to the side to glance where Ella and I stand.

"Way to go, Mr. Caveman," the redhead praises beside me, clear amusement in her voice.

"May I remind you it's Captain Gunner, Carter?" the man explains.

My jaw ticks again and I begin moving in their direction.

"And may I remind you that the reason I'm here is to tell you what to do?" I revert, stopping before him. "So if you don't mind leading by example, *Captain...*"

I gesture with my hand toward the stairs and his brow arches a little further. As he looks at me, my eyes same level as his, I see something crossing his gaze. There's something close to understanding. And although he wants to say something, he closes his mouth and puts his gear on. When he leaves toward his team, my gaze meets Ensley's, who looks at me with narrow eyes.

"Should I even ask what's gotten into you this morning?" Her eyes roll at me as she asks the question before she shakes her head and walks away.

You have gotten into me this morning. You have gotten under my goddamn skin.

It is what I want to answer. Instead, I keep my mouth shut.

"Next time you decide to mark your territory, be a little more discreet, will you?" Ella's voice comes from behind me, and I glance back at her with an unimpressed look. The smirk playing on her face pissing me the right off because I am aware the she-devil set me a trap, bating me the way she did, and I fell right in like a blind raging bull.

"Whatever," I revert, containing myself from rolling my eyes at her.

She smiles for a moment at my reply, but then something crosses her features. And I know that look. One I've learned to recognize.

"I'm really sorry, Mason."

Ella doesn't apologize for setting me the trap.

"It wasn't your fault, Rusty."

My hand rests on her shoulder and I give it a reassuring squeeze.

"But it damn well feels like it was my fault."

With my head shaking from side to side in rebuttal, I hold her stare. "We don't get to choose our family, Ella. Just as we're not guilty of the choices they make."

Pushing to her tiptoes, she wraps her arms around my neck and pulls me into a hug.

"I'm really glad you're alright and among the living."

"I'm glad too, Rusty."

The redhead pulls back, keeping her hands on either of my shoulders. "That doesn't get you off the hook, though. Get your act together and pull your head out of your ass before it's too late."

Although she knows I'm already more than aware of who she's referring to, she still cocks her head toward Ensley before she walks toward the other firefighters.

"Okay, everyone. Let's get this training started," I speak loudly. "We'll run through some road traffic collision with multiple vehicles."

And so we begin with the training. The two crews of the truck companies fall instantly into sync with each other, working as a team in no time. Though they don't have to rescue people who are really in danger right now but a few volunteers who gave their time to come and help at the academy with the training, the group doesn't give any less than they'd give during a real car crash.

My stare follows the crews and time their rescue. Through it all, however, my eyes keep darting to Ensley, noting how fluidly she moves and how she prompts ideas to help with the rescue. And much to my annoyance, I'm not the only one who notices just how great she is at her job and how worthy of admiration she is. That if the man who keeps stealing glances at her every so often over the roof of the car as they're executing the extraction serves as any indication.

Wade-fucking-Gunner better look the other way before I gouge his eyeballs out only for staring at her and break his hands before I use them to beat him with for having the mere thought of touching her cross his mind.

Joder!

This is getting out of hand.

ENSLEY

The way Ella smirks at me before she gets into her car as I wave her goodbye has my head shaking from side to side.

We got to the end of our training at the academy after running through a crash drill with multiple cars involved and rope rescues from buildings. After successfully bringing the training to completion, we packed up everything and now it's time for us all to leave, get some rest and enjoy our days off. Or as much as I can enjoy it with a Mason who avoids me half the time, while the other half he seems to have a stick up his ass.

The latter brings me to the reason why my future sister-in-law smiles from ear to ear even as she drives off—Mason's showdown with Wade Gunner, her crew's captain. One I stood and witnessed perplexed because Mason has always been the kind of man to respect the chain of command regardless if it were during a rescue, training or outside of work. Today, however, he decided to screw said chain of command and have a little face-off with a captain.

For some reason, I believe my redheaded friend has plenty to do with Mason's reaction. More than she lets on. And what makes me be even more sure about it is that she offered to give me a ride home in front of Gunner, having me need to explain to him what happened with that asshole the other day and that my car is still in service. Situation that prompted him to offer to drive me since the house is on his way, while the block of flats Ella and Luke live in is in the opposite direction.

It was on Gunner's offer to give me a ride home that I understood Ella's goal and that is all my fault. I should have never told her that Gunner and I used to date when I was nineteen years old and he was twenty-three. It is my fault I gave her the ammunition and her evil mind made use of that particular piece of information.

She-devil that redhead is.

"How are things going with Mason now? How's his recovery going?" Gunner asks as we walk toward his car parked on the opposite side of the road.

"Physically, he's been recovering well. Exceptionally well considering he's spent three months in a coma. The doctors say that all the exercises I've been doing with him throughout helped immensely with keeping his muscles active," I explain before a sigh slips through my lips. "His mind is the problem. He forgot me, Wade. He doesn't remember being with me. His mind blocks out the memories we've lived together during these fifteen years."

"I'm so sorry, Ensley," he utters, pulling me between his arms and pressing his lips against the side of my head. "You and Mason have had it tough from the get-go, with all that dancing around each other, but that has strengthened you both to be able to pull through everything, including this. And coming from a man who knows what jealousy looks like, the way he reacted just because he saw me talking to you, believe me, that man has it bad for you. Whether he remembers all the moments you had together or not, you can make new ones. You can give both of you a fresh start. A second chance."

"It's not that easy, though."

"It isn't. But what is easy in life?"

The sound of a roaring engine has me pull away from his embrace, only to see a familiar motorcycle and a well-known leather jacket. Even more familiarity I find in the man riding it.

Mason.

He stops abruptly next to us and lifts the screen of his helmet. His brown eyes are stoic when they meet mine and there'd be no surprise if his jaw ticks beneath the helmet.

What also doesn't surprise me is the goosebumps that roll on my flesh at the hardness in his gaze and when the tick in his jaw gets revealed as he takes off his helmet.

"Hop on," he speaks, gesturing his head toward his motorbike and extending the spare helmet to me.

What takes me aback a little is his voice; heavy and stern, leaving no room for argument.

"It's fine, man. I'll give her a lift," Wade offers, pointing to his car right behind us.

"Ensley, ass on the seat before I put it there," Mason demands.

Yes, that is right.

He doesn't ask nicely. He doesn't request.

He *demands*.

My brow arches automatically at him in a challenge, defying his bidding. Meanwhile, his arm is still extended with the helmet. One that I don't rush to retrieve from his hand.

"Don't play with me, Ley, because we both know I'll throw you over my shoulder if I have to."

His baritone is full of warning. Clear, downright warning, not only suggesting, but supporting the caution in his words.

"Why would you have to?" I challenge.

Without any hesitation whatsoever and with such speed that I only get to blink once, Mason puts the side stand down to prop the motorcycle and hangs both helmets on each throttle. Then, he climbs off his seat and his knees bend a little before I feel my body in the air, a surprised gasp managing to escape me in the process. The front half of my form dangles over his back while he holds me by the back of my legs like a sack of potatoes over his shoulder.

"Put me down," I complain, straightening my back.

As I do so, my eyes meet Gunner's gaze who appears rather amused by Mason's action. If the grin on his face serves as any suggestion, he clearly doesn't plan on jumping to my rescue. Moreover, he points to his car, then gets into the vehicle and drives off.

Great, Ensley, you're all on your own now with your husband who doesn't remember he's married to you but behaves just like the caveman he's always been.

When I note that Mason won't do my bidding either, I struggle. I kick my legs in the air. Yet my action is brought to a sudden stop as a yelp climbs up my throat and its sound dances in the air when his heavy hand swats my ass. Not one cheek, but both of them as his splayed hand lands right in the middle over the curve of my butt.

"Ow," I breathe.

"There's more where that one came from, Ley. So I'd suggest you stop fighting and willingly stay put in the seat," Mason warns on a deep, guttural rasp. "Or you can carry on fighting me, and I'll smack this tight little ass all day long until you won't be able to sit down without remembering my hand slapping it."

The last sentence is mainly a guttural whisper. A mutter that has an involuntary shudder pass through my body from the tips of my toes to the roots of my hair at the promise in his voice. He dares me to defy him again. Even the way his hand remains splayed out on my derriere at the ready provokes me to challenge him once more.

And, oh, boy, my body begs me to do it so my flesh can feel the sting of his swats one more time.

The traitor is so accustomed to the sweet burn of his palm against the skin. So much so that my ass pushes against his hand as it tips a little more upward in an invitation for him like it just found a mind of its own.

"*Que desvergoñada*," he rasps, his tone heavy as he calls me shameless in Galician, though the smile I sense in it also tells me that he enjoys the reaction of my body. "Such a little vixen pushing your ass into my hand like this. So greedy to get this tight ass spanked, aren't you?"

As though to prove a point, his hand moves and cups one cheek, giving it a squeeze just before he swats it again, completely ignoring the fact that he does it in the street in plain daylight. Following his action, it is not only my moan that fills the air, but also his own groan.

A strangled sound of defeat that makes me realize what Mason has actually done. How he threw me over his shoulder like I weigh nothing. How he slapped my ass for challenging him as though only to prove that he isn't a man to be defied or to be denied a bidding.

If this had happened four or five months ago, I wouldn't've batted an eye since it is quite the norm with us and especially with him. It is something I am well accustomed to when it comes to him, and I know it is in this exact instance that I get a glimpse of *my Mason*. Not the Mason from over sixteen years ago who'd keep a tight hold on his control. But the dominant Mason—my husband—whom I've been introduced to after we began our relationship.

Clear as day becomes the notion that Mason lost his grip on his self-control. He certainly did, otherwise right this moment I wouldn't be dangling over his shoulder or feeling the burn of his thwack against my ass cheeks.

And sweet Jesus, just how beautifully he forfeits that firm hold on his well-mastered restraint to cope a feel of my ass and smack it senseless just because of my feistiness.

"I'm trying to get out of your hold. You're such a caveman," I protest, my legs kicking in the air again as I remember I left his arrogant sentence to hang between us for too long.

The chuckle that slips past Mason's lips is deep and rich, causing another shudder to race through my frame.

"We both know that's a lie, Ley. Your own body gives you away."

With that being said, Mason moves with me still on his shoulder and before I get to process his next move, my legs straddle the seat of his motorcycle. Once I'm where he wanted me all along, he takes half a step back, his dark chocolate eyes locking onto my green ones. They remain connected for a tick, then another. It is on the third tick that Mason's hand lifts and rakes it through his hair. In that same instant, his gaze turns stormy as though he just realized what he's done.

"*Merda*," he curses aloud, his head shaking. "I shouldn't've done that. I don't know what came over me."

As my brow quirks at him once again, my eyes pierce through him with disappointment as I watch how his self-control gets pieced together again and his stare becomes guarded, distant. That before he avoids my gaze altogether.

Long gone is my Mason.

Shaking my head, I sigh and garner all the energy I have in me to collect myself.

"Are we going home or are you just gonna stand there telling me how much of a mistake that was? Because let me tell you there's no need for you to waste your breath telling me that this is what you think. Been there, done that, got the t-shirt."

The sardonic note in my tone doesn't go unnoticed and Mason's eyes snap to meet mine. A couple of creases form on his forehead as it furrows, and in his gaze, I see that he wants to say something. However, right before he opens his mouth to speak, his head moves gently from one side to another as though to shake out of his mind whatever thought he planned to voice.

He strides to round the bike to the left side and at the same time, I climb off to give him room to mount the motorcycle. Once he's on, he leans forward a little to grab the two helmets while I take my seat behind him.

Rotating from his torso a little, our gazes meet again, and he is so close that my own breath gets clogged in my throat. For a tick, his eyes flicker between my own and my lips, making it even harder to breathe without inhaling his scent. The very scent I've been addicted to for so long.

Boy, oh, boy, just how tempted I am right now to lean in and kiss him.

Christ, how much I miss feeling his mouth on mine. Feeling his lips move over mine with their usual dominance that renders me helpless every single time. Tasting the minty flavor of his tongue. Relishing in the feel of his soft lips against mine.

It is on that last thought that I realize my eyes zero in on his mouth already, and when they lift to his gaze again, his chocolate orbs are even darker than they usually are. So cloudy and stormy as though the battle within him threatens to surface.

"*Joder*," Mason cusses on a laborious breath. "You're gonna be the death of me, Ensley Juliet Walker."

His voice is heavy with seriousness. Though the sound of it is still thick and smooth, the gravity and earnestness in his tone are clear.

Mason lifts the helmet over my head then he puts it on, causing me to lose his eyes in the process for a brief instance before our gazes lock once more.

"The death of me," he repeats with utter solemnity, lowering the screen of my helmet.

He turns and I watch him lean forward again to grab his own helmet.

"Hold on tight."

Automatically, my arms circle his waist from behind, my hands resting on his stomach atop his jacket. Even through the fabric, I can sense the way his abdomen tenses at the touch. That is something I don't miss, and I let a smile form on my lips at the effect my I have on him.

One other thing that doesn't go unnoticed for me is how he stops with the helmet mid-air and inhales deeply.

"Jasmine."

The word wants to be a whisper for himself. Yet, it slips past his lips and the sole sound enters my ears. There's recognition in his baritone. Recognition and wonder, all the same.

MASON

Jasmine.

The sweet note that pierces my nostrils at that gentle breeze and gets inhaled into my lungs is jasmine.

A scent that catches me off guard and my hands that hold the helmet remain mid-air for a split second. There's something in that sweet fragrance that stuns me. Something I can't put my finger on, but something that stupefies me for a fraction.

I don't let the ponder hover for too long, nonetheless, and after I shake the thought away, I lift the helmet over my head. Once I slip it on and secure it, I bring the side stand up and twist the key. Immediately, the engine roars and Ensley's hold on me tightens. Just as instantly, the fire that ignited where she touched me, now burns fiercer.

How is it possible that her mere touch creates all these confusing feelings within me? How can she have this hold on me so tightly that I feel like I'm losing my mind whenever I don't have her around? Like I can't breathe without her near me.

Joder!

I'm gonna lose my goddamn mind.

Shaking my head, I push away all the thoughts and twist the throttle. After I pull into the midday traffic, I ride the motorcycle with Ensley holding tightly to me.

Her touch sizzling.

Her body pressed against mine confounding. Sweet and tempting as her form molds against my back, her tits crushed against me. Still, the way it fits so perfectly against my own is disorienting.

Joder!

Joder!

Joder!

My perdition.

My downfall.

My destruction.

Sweet perdition.

Bewitching downfall.

Luscious destruction.

This is what Ensley Walker is to me.

Above all, she's untouchable and off-fucking limits.

Beings worthy of Ensley is something I'm not and if I ever believed otherwise, even for a tick, I lied to myself.

It takes the greatest amount of effort to knock all thoughts out of my head. Eventually, I manage to, so I twist the throttle again and ride the bike till we get home.

Once I pull inside the garage, I put the side stand down and shut off the engine. Meanwhile, Ensley climbs off the bike. I follow suit, removing my helmet. Still, I stand by the motorcycle, leaning against it.

"I'm gonna take a nap. It's been a pretty busy night at the firehouse, and I'm all wiped out," Ensley mentions as she hands me the spare helmet.

My arm extends and I take the item from her hand.

We stand still for a brief instant just looking at each other. Her green eyes expectant. Her lips a little parted as though begging for me to eat the distance between us and smash my mouth over hers. And the effort it takes for me not to do is ungodly.

"I'll be quiet."

It is all I say to her, and she moves her head in understanding. Something takes over her features at the same time. A faint note of disappointment and hurt. One that is gone before I get to properly see it. However, as feeble as it was, it still pierces my heart and I feel it bleed while rage pumps into my body. Anger at my own person for bringing her even that fraction of hurt.

Without hesitation thereafter, Ensley turns and takes the first step to advance further into the garage, heading for the door that leads into the house.

Tremendous amount of energy takes from me not to lift my hand to my chest and rub at the ache that begins to take form within me.

Simultaneously, there's something inside me that screams at me to rush for her, to bring her flush to me and to kiss her. To kiss her with the same passion and insane desire that riot in me. To grab a handful of that long silky hair only to be able to hear that soft moan leave her lips again. To claim her as mine and not let anyone ever again look at her without them knowing she's mine.

It is on that last thought that I picture the way Gunner looked at her today. How he held her against his body. How anger built inside of me every time I caught him looking at her, but how that anger turned into full-on wrath when I saw the way he pulled her to him, and her own arms wrapped around him. I instantly saw red before my eyes and wanted to beat the crap out of Gunner for just touching *my woman*. It angered me so much that I haven't been aware of what I was doing until I set her ass down on the motorcycle. Even then I didn't fully comprehend what happened until I allowed myself to feel the tingle in my palm left by the swats I gave to her delicious ass.

I lost my mind.

So much so that I spanked her ass like she's mine. I threw her over my shoulder like she belongs to me. I treated Ensley like I had some claim over her.

Which I don't.

She is *not my woman*.

"You and Gunner…" Pausing, I lift my hand and scratch the back of my neck. "Are you two rekindling an old flame?"

The question is out before I get the chance to put a lid on it. It gets propelled out of my mouth before I even get to consider what the hell I'm saying.

It is a question that also brings Ensley's steps to a halt just before she makes it to the door. Moreover, her head cocks to the side a little so she can look me in the eyes.

"What if we were?"

My jaw ticks involuntarily at her words. Concurrently, my hands ball into fists at my sides only at the thought of Gunner touching her again. Anger boils in my veins once more. Something that tends to happen very often especially when Gunner is concerned.

Non tes dereitos sobre ela.

The reminder that I have no claim over her has my fists tighten until my knuckles turn white.

"He's a great guy. He might be a player, but that's because he's never gotten over you. I saw the way looks at you and he'd give up his ways for you."

Ungodly is the ache that punctures my chest. An ache that damn well nearly brings me to my knees. Actually, if it weren't for the motorcycle I lean against, I'd be down on my knees because of the excruciating pain that charges through me.

As if that isn't enough, each word that rolls off my tongue leaves a vile bitter taste in my mouth. It is as though I can taste the pain in my heart. The pain induced by pushing the woman I love into the arms of another man.

"Any man in his right mind would worship the ground you walk on, Ensley. Any man would worship you."

Sure, why don't you dig a bigger hole while you're at it, right?

The sarcastic tone of my own thoughts is evident. Even my mind makes fun of me.

"Don't, Mason," she utters, her eyes closing for a brief second before they open again. "I'm not in the mood for your hot and cold attitude. With me it's simple, you want me, or you don't. Do you want to fuck me? Then fuck me. Do you want to make me yours? Then do it. Do you wanna claim me as yours? Fucking do that too. All I'm asking is for you to give me a straight answer and not to play with me."

Her hand lifts and her fingers comb through her long hair, pushing it back.

For a tick or two, we only stand glued to our spots. My brown eyes remain locked onto her green ones, and they stay there even when she eats the distance between us.

Ensley tilts her head back a little to keep our gazes connected and it takes so much effort not to lean in.

"I want you, Mase. I wanna be with you. I wanna be yours," she admits, her green eyes glimmering with hope. "I wanna be loved by you. For me, there's no doubt or hesitation. But I'm not gonna wait for you my whole life to make a decision. To be sure of me. To want me."

With that, she spins on the heels of her shoes and goes to walk away. Before she gets to take a step, my hand wraps around her wrist and I twirl her back to face me. The force of my action propels her right into my arms.

I don't know why I stop her.

I know I shouldn't have.

But before my brain has a chance to catch on, Ensley's already between my arms. Her body flush against my own. Her form molded into mine. Her green orbs piercing into my brown ones. Her lips parted a fraction as a small, surprised gasp escapes her.

Taking a deep breath, the jasmine notes blend into the air once again with her closeness. As I inhale, my eyelids close shut, attempting to grasp hold of my wayward control.

"*Joder,*" I curse under my breath, my forehead leaning against hers. "What are you doing to me, Ley? I'm losing my mind here."

The ponderous rambling is mostly meant for me. Moreover, it leaves my mouth as a mere utterance. Barely loud enough for me to hear, but I don't have a doubt she did too.

"Why does everything in me scream that you're mine? Why does it feel like you belong to me when we both know that you don't?"

My aloud thinking continues just as soft and as much of a whisper as the previous one.

As my eyes open once again and my head draws back enough for our gazes to meet, the mix of emotions in her green irises brings my near undoing.

Hope and expectation.

Desire and anticipation.

Trust and softness.

Faith and conviction.

A blend of emotions that has me barely holding on to the self-imposed restraint.

I need to step back.

I need to put distance between us.

And I must look like I am just a mere fraction away from bolting. Cutting and running from that goddamn tension that licks at the air between us. I am certain I must look that way because before I get a chance to do anything, to skedaddle like a coward, her soft lips brush against mine. A mere dust of her plump mouth over mine. A bare graze of her lips on mine. One that is enough to have me lose whatever grip I got on my control until it sets itself free. Free of my hold. Free to roam wild and create havoc.

Without an ounce of hesitation, my hand lifts and threads into her brunette hair, grabbing a fistful of it at the back of her head, while the other cups her around her jaw with the thumb on one side of her face and the rest of my fingers on the other.

For a moment, I use the hold I have on her to pull her mouth away from mine. To garner even the smallest of fractions of willpower to push Ensley away. But then my brown eyes lock onto her jaded green orbs, expectancy brimming her gaze.

Out the window goes my determination to reject her before it is too late. Because who am I trying to kid? Perhaps I am only trying to fool myself because it is already too fucking late. Sixteen years too late.

I use the hold I have on her. This time around not to push her away, but to bring her to me, and forthwith, my mouth smashes against hers without any other preamble. A gesture that surprises her—if the faint gasp that tumbles up her throat is any indication.

Joder!

My heart nearly leaps out at how hard it begins hammering against my chest when the honey-like taste of her lips seeps into my mouth.

So fucking sweet.

The kiss isn't soft and gentle, though. The way my lips move over hers and how my tongue thrusts into her mouth are plain claiming. It takes and takes, the pace almost bruising.

Without a second thought, I spin us, and I push her against the wall after running the layout of the garage in my head to make sure I don't propel us into the shelves. A moan crawls up Ensley's throat when her back makes contact with the hard surface. Another sweet sound follows right after I press my body into hers and she feels me against her.

My tongue is set to explore the sweetness of her mouth, the kiss deepening. It is so carnal, the savage need inside me to consume and possess her reaches unholy levels. It is as though my addiction to her is finally getting fueled after so long and now I can't get enough. It is as though I didn't know how much I craved this until now. Until I finally had her lips against mine and had our tongues battling for the lustful possession.

The swift capitulation on Ensley's part is sweet and the savageness within me only grows. Her mouth becomes submissive to the dominance of mine, and it is the most beautiful thing I have seen.

Though in the daze of the kiss, I don't miss just how natural her surrender comes and how it feels as if we've done this so many times before. It seems as if, in spite of the sheer dominance I exert over the kiss, she knows that I'll give as much as I take. More so, that I'll give more than I take.

Her capitulation is set in stone even firmer when her hands slide beneath the open jacket and they move past my abdomen, continuing until they're on my back. Any scintilla of a gap that was between us now is nonexistent as she uses her hold to press me into her even more.

My cock is hard and heavy between us, pushing against her stomach and weeping for release. The ingrate fucker is ready to pound nails at how hard he is. It only confirms that the state of flaccidity definitely doesn't apply when it comes to Ensley. My dick is soft and doesn't even bother twitching only around the rest of the female population.

The guttural groan that tumbles out of my chest when Ensley rolls her hips to create some friction is a sound I don't recognize. There's so much feral need and hunger in that sound. An overwhelming urge to claim what's mine for the taking.

The brutality of the kiss is vicious. I can't get enough. Nor can Ensley. We're both the addicts of our own desires. Slaves of our own hearts because despite the many times I told myself to stay away, here we are, devouring each other like there's no tomorrow. Kissing each other with warp, addictive passion. An addiction we can't get enough of. Yet, one we hit pause on when we both withdraw for some much-needed air.

With my eyes still closed as I attempt to calm the erratic breathing, I listen to the sounds of her heavy panting. It is a melody I mentally record and deposit in a drawer of my mind that has Ensley's name on in. It is a sweet harmony, tempting me to find out if her panting will be just as melodious when I slide inside her cunt. When I have her pussy clutching my cock in a vice-like grip, teetering on the edge of orgasm.

Carallo!

My eyes snap open at that thought as if just awaken from the trance her gaze sets me under. They immediately meet her green orbs that gleam.

As I move my eyes over her, my heart drops into the pit of my stomach.

"Did I hurt you?" I whisper the question, my hands moving to cradle her face.

I know the way I kissed her hasn't been gentle. My mouth moved over hers with an ungodly hunger that only Ensley is clearly able to bring out. I wanted to take as much from her as I could, hoping it would be enough to sate me. However, I am aware that it was only a starter and my appetite just got teased.

Her head shakes gently in response to my question.

"No, of course, you didn't."

"Why are you crying then, baby?"

While the wonder hangs in the air for a tick, my thumbs dust over her wet cheeks and all the worry is written over my face. I don't even try to hide it and she can see that. Just as much as she can see the clicking in my jaw at the thought that I hurt her.

Hurting her…

Joder!

That's the reason I keep staying away from her. Because I know that ultimately it is exactly what it will come down to.

Getting Ensley hurt.

I'd rather go my entire life without her, without living all the love I have for her. I'd do that and more to keep her safe, to keep her heart from being broken, but most importantly, to keep her alive.

Nevertheless, what has just happened isn't me staying away from her. It's me giving in to the temptation that Ensley is. It's me losing my once-upon-a-time tight hold on my control. It's me losing my goddamn mind.

"Because for three months I've watched you lying in a hospital bed and I thought…" Ensley's head shakes, her sentence trailing off for a moment. "I thought I'll never get to see you again. Get to look into your eyes again. Get to have you look at me. Get to hear your voice and your laugh. That thought killed me, Mason. It killed me. So don't play with me. Don't treat me like I'm yours unless you really mean it. Don't touch me like I belong to you unless you want me to. Don't kiss me like this only to tell me it was a mistake. And before you tell me that you haven't, let me tell you that you haven't said it *yet*. So don't do any of that unless you want me. I'm right here within reach, heart on my sleeve and with hell loads of love to give you because there hasn't been anyone else but you."

As she withdraws, my hands drop to my sides and her gaze stays connected with mine for another tick before she wipes at her cheeks some more. Without a word thereafter, she turns and walks away toward the door. This time, I don't stop her.

I don't stop her because I don't have a right to.

I don't stop her because I know if I do, I will not be able to bring a stop to it this time. Sixteen years ago, I might have been able to do it, but now I am certain I can't. There's no way I'd be able to stop at just kissing her lips. At just caressing her skin. At thrusting my cock inside her cunt. At having her only once. Because Ensley isn't the kind of woman I can have once and have enough of.

No, Ensley is the type of woman I'd savor over and over again. I'd fuck her six ways to Sunday. I'd taste the sweetness of her. I'd relish her flesh. I'd caress her skin until she becomes so wet and so consumed by my touch that she'd beg me to take her. I'd play with her nipples until she comes just from that. I'd fuck her with my fingers and have her come on my tongue over and over again. And only when she's completely soaked, only then I'd bury my cock inside her. I'd have her so depleted and so spent by the time I'm done with her, only to have her again and again.

To be completely honest, I'd stay *balls in deep* every moment of every day if I could. Because having enough of her isn't possible and if I ever tell myself that once would be enough to get her out of my system, I'm utterly mistaken.

But to take the honesty even further, Ensley is also the kind of woman one would want to spend the rest of their life loving. The type of woman one would love until they draw their last breath. Because I know I will.

ENSLEY

Leaning over Mason's body, I press my lips against his forehead. I hold still for a tick, feeling the hotness of a tear that rolls down my cheeks.

"Hey there, handsome," I whisper just a breath away from his forehead.

After I finished my shift at the firehouse, I drove straight to the hospital. I sped through the traffic like a madwoman to get by my man's side as fast as possible.

My eyes move over my husband's body before they dart to the machines that he's connected to, then to the IV.

Once I take a deep breath in, I climb into bed next to him, laying on my side while making sure I don't unplug any of the apparatus he's connected to.

With my hands holding his much bigger one, my head leans against his shoulder.

"I've brought a Chris Carter novel for you this time. I'll read it to you in a few, I just need a moment here next to you, baby," I mutter.

As I nestle closer, I slip my phone out of the pocket and tap a few times before the first notes of 'Up Where We Belong' by Joe Cocker and Jennifer Warnes fill the room. It is the song we had our first dance on. We danced on it at the cabin we rented out after we got married at the courthouse, but also at our official wedding in front of our family and friends.

"I'm here. I'll always be here, Mase. As your wife. As your friend. As whatever you want me to be, honey."

A sigh slips past my lips as Jennifer Warnes's voice permeates with the first lyrics of the song:

> *"Who knows what tomorrow brings*
> *In a world few hearts survive"*

While I listen further to the words, I close my eyelids for a tick.
One that turns into two.
Two moments turn into three.
Three instances become four.

> *"Love lifts us up where we belong*
> *Where the eagles cry*
> *On a mountain high*
> *Love lifts us up where we belong*
> *Far from the world we know*
> *Where the clear winds blow."*

My breathing begins to level almost immediately after the chorus and before I know it, I doze off. The weight of what's happening together with the heaviness of today's shift at the firehouse take their toll on me.

It feels as though hours tick past, but at the same time, it feels as if just a few minutes pass by. But what snaps me awake is a piercing sound. One that has cold drops of sweat running down my back. It isn't from the song. It is a loud, unremitting noise that has me jump off the bed and to my feet.

"Mason," I shout his name as my eyes lock on his convulsing body. "Help! Somebody, help!"

With fast steps, I race toward the door to get someone to assist.

"I need help in here," I yell across the hallway.

My scream is met by its own echo. Meanwhile, the beeping of the machines gets more alert, more worrisome. Both sounds combined make my skin crawl.

"Help!"

Panic takes over my body when I look down the empty hallway—both behind me and in front of me—and I don't see anyone coming. Furthermore, it all turns into terror the instant I snap my neck to the side and note that my husband's body shakes even more sporadically.

"Mason," I call out his name, rushing to his side. However, when I

am nearly next to the bed, the alerting sound mingles with a more prolonged one. "No, no, Mason. No."

Before I make it to his bed, my knees give way and I drop to the floor. Tears stream down my face as I attempt to bring myself back up. Yet, I can't push myself back to my feet. Regardless of the amount of effort I gather to be able to do so, it becomes impossible.

"Somebody, help."

My own form begins shaking and my vision turns blurry. But even through the fog, when I avert my eyes to the monitor, I can see the straight line moving across the screen.

"Noooo," I yell, my body jerking as an uncontrollable cry takes over me.

"Ensley."

Though the name is a whisper, the familiarity in that coarse, strong voice is what has my form stop shaking.

"Ley, baby, wake up."

At that demand, I will my eyes to open. To no avail.

"*Carallo, nena,* wake up."

My back knifes up and my eyes snap open, connecting right away with a pair of chocolate brown eyes. Worry rims his gaze, and a hard scowl mars his handsome features.

I swallow hard.

The pounding of my heart is so loud that it resonates in my ears. It rings so deafeningly that I need to squeeze my eyes shut for a tick.

"Breathe, *nena.*"

Mason's whisper serves as an encouragement for me to remember to inhale and exhale, leveling my breathing.

Soon enough I become aware of my surroundings. Of the room I'm in and the man sitting on my bed.

"That's it, baby. In and out," he instructs, mimicking the same action. "Keep your eyes on me. Just like that, *nena.*"

His gaze stays locked onto mine and a wave of calmness washes over me almost instantly. Though the memory of the nightmare is still vivid and overwhelming, his eyes and his presence altogether manage to soothe me just like only he can in moments like these.

"I just had a bad dream."

My attempt to downplay it is met by a swift quirk of his brow, telling me that he already knows it hasn't been *just* a bad dream. The possibility that Mason heard me crosses my mind as I take in his hard features.

"*Nena*, you were screaming my name in your dream," he points out exactly what I was afraid he might. "And it wasn't the way I wanted you to be screaming it."

Nena.

Mason called me '*nena*'.

This four-letter word hasn't been part of my dream. He truly called me by that nickname. A four-letter word that has my heart lurch before it squeezes with an instant sliver of hope. Hope that maybe—just maybe—unconsciously his mind puzzles me together.

I am aware that perhaps it is all too farfetched, and he chooses to call me '*nena*' as a Galician term for '*baby*', which is also a moniker he uses for me. However, there's nothing wrong with hoping, is there? Hoping that maybe my husband will remember me. Being hopeful that perhaps his mind allows him slowly to unblock all these memories he has of me, of us. It is a hope I need to grasp on to be able to continue otherwise the uncertainty will tear me apart.

"It was a nightmare. I get them sometimes," I confess.

"Since when?"

As my head shakes gently, Mason's brows knit together, prying for me to tell him only with his unyielding stare alone.

"Since your accident."

"*Joder, nena*, why didn't you say anything?"

Though his voice tries to remain as gentle as possible, the tick in his tight jaw and the hardness in his brown gaze almost contradict the softness.

"And what could you have done, Mase?"

"Go with you to see someone," he suggests, raking a frustrated hand through his dark hair. "*Cono, nena*, I'd sleep by your side and hold you if I have to so I can make sure I'm there with you through it all."

My heart drops at the utter worry and sincerity that I sense in his voice and see in his eyes. When both his hands lift for him to cradle my face to keep my gaze on him, I can't look anywhere else.

"I am the very cause of your nightmares, Ensley."

The bitterness in his voice is as clear as the day is long. A bitterness addressed toward his own person.

"You're going through a trauma and won't be able to get over it unless you talk to someone about it, *nena*."

I don't miss the wild gallop my heart sets into when hearing the sound of that word rolling off his tongue again. At the same time, I know I should choose self-preservation and tell him to stop calling me that. To stop calling me *"nena"* because the memories that sole word brings come in strong, powerful waves. Waves which remind me that perhaps he'll never remember them. I know I should do it, but the survival instinct hits rock bottom at the other possibility that maybe he will remember all these memories we have together.

"Can you hold me?" I ask.

My voice is almost frail.

"Just for a little while."

Without delay, Mason kicks off his shoes and lays his long body on the mattress that dips under his weight.

For a second, I remain in the same position I've been in since I woke up. All I do is crane my neck to the side a little to be able to meet his brown gaze only to find him looking at me expectantly. Right away, he stretches his arm toward me, snakes it around my abdomen and brings me flush to him, turning me in the process so my back is against his front.

My body molds against his, relaxing almost instantly when it feels his. My form is clearly too used to this kind of closeness. Moreover, the speed with which it relaxes tells me it craved Mason's nearness. His presence and his tight hold.

And my body isn't the only one. I missed all of this too. I missed feeling his heartbeat against my back. Sensing all that hardness he's made of against my body. I missed the calmness that always covered me like a mantle when in his arms. I missed the safety I've constantly felt when his strong embrace enveloped me.

"I'd do anything for you, *nena*. If I could, I'd take your night-mares and make them my own so you can be free of them because I don't ever again want to see torment and fright in your gorgeous eyes," Mason speaks from behind me.

His words melt all my insides. My heart squeezes tight and my stomach clenches when he speaks them to me. The meaningfulness is evident in his voice as well as in his action when he uses the arm draped around my stomach to bring me even closer to him, not leaving even the smallest gap between us. Our bodies perfectly forged to fit together.

As his words affect me from the inside, his hot breath against the bareness of my neck—since my hair is up in a bun—impacts me from the outside, causing an involuntary shudder to pass through me.

"Are you cold?"

Mason doesn't wait for me to answer, though. He leans a little over me, pushing me into the mattress just a fraction, and reaches for the comforter that got kicked to the other side of the bed during my nightmare. After he pulls it over us, I expect his hold on me to drop or even for him to withdraw. But none of that happens. On the contrary, the hand he has on my stomach now slips beneath the cotton fabric of the t-shirt that's a few sizes too big and rests splayed on the skin of my abdomen.

A wave of heat runs through my body instantly and I know it isn't because I'm now too hot under the comforter, but because his touch burns. It sizzles my flesh, his hot palm against my skin searing.

In the quietness that dances in the bedroom, the pounding of our own hearts becomes louder, and our breathing turns heavier. Our bodies aren't immune to the closeness. The absolute opposite actually.

"We're better off as just friends, Ley," Mason whispers, his breath laborious as though he's in pain.

As if in spite of him and what he's just said, the hand on my stomach finds a mind of its own and travels a little lower just before it meets the line of my panties. It stops there, drawing little circles that have my skin crackling beneath his touch.

"Tell me about your nightmare."

The voice that encourages me to speak about the most horrendous moments that my subconscious mind concocts is soft. Almost a murmur that I could have easily missed had I not paid attention.

"Every time it starts the same way. With you in hospital, in a coma," I begin after I clear my throat to make sure my voice doesn't give away how badly the nightmare affected me. Though, I'm fairly sure Mason already knows just how bad. "For a little while, everything is good. You're in that bed like you've been for three months. Then everything goes haywire. You're convulsing and the machines make a sound so piercing that the image before me is frightening. What's even more fearful is that there's nobody there. Nobody to help."

Hot tears rim my eyes and I blink several times to keep them at bay.

"I shout for help, but nobody comes. The seizures are getting worse and worse, and fear runs through me because I know it is only a matter of time until you flatline. Because despite all my efforts, you do. You always do."

"I'm right here, *nena*."

As he whispers that to me, his palm flattens against my stomach and his lips press on my shoulder right after. Immediately, I feel the comfort of his touch. It is soothing. Calming.

"I'm not going anywhere. I promise you that I'll always be here for you. Despite everything inside me telling me to stay away from you, I can't. And I ask myself why every single goddamn time. The answer is beyond me, *nena*, but maybe because all that tells me to steer clear of you, also shouts at me that I shouldn't and that you belong to me."

A sigh rolls out of him.

My eyes close for a brief instant and I take a deep breath, letting his words sink in. When they do, I turn in his embrace and meet his eyes, the pad of my index finger resting on his beautiful lips.

"Don't say this, Mase. Until you're ready to come and claim me, you don't get to say things like this," I warn. "But you can still hold me, though."

Turning once again in his arms, I hear his gentle chuckle while I nestle against him. His hand gets placed on my stomach once again and my eyelids close.

"The death of me."

Mason's muttering is soft and nearly inaudible. Moreover, in my drowsed state I almost missed it.

Almost.

MASON

The weight on my chest prevents me from being able to turn my fairly numb body. After three months of lying in that goddamn hospital bed, now my form gets numb relatively fast.

However, my body going numb isn't what has me snap my eyes open. What does instead is the press I feel against my side.

In my state of slumber, my gaze drops to what has my body pinned. A smile tugs at the corners of my lips before I get a chance to impede it when I find Ensley's head on my chest and her body pressed against mine, fitting between the crook of my stretched arm. The involuntary smile that forms on my face is because of the naturalness of this. Of waking up to find Ensley next to me.

The loud crack of thunder that rumbles outside has me lift my stare from the woman who subconsciously nestles closer to take in the space we're in—her bedroom—before it shoots toward the large window. The curtains are drawn back on both sides and past the glass, I note the clouds that now coat the city sky.

Craning my neck a little on the pillow, I take in the numbers displayed on the digital clock set on the bedside table. Just a little after five in the afternoon, but the darkness of the clouds makes it look as if it is later than that.

My eyes travel again to Ensley and, instinctively, the arm I have stretched now encircles her, while the other I have at my side drapes over her. I do it as though I've done it so many times before.

Perhaps I did.

Ensley's astraphobia is something I'm all familiar with. Since we were kids, that's a fear she's been struggling with and fighting against.

I vividly remember her scooting closer and snuggling into me whenever the piercing thunder and the lightning would strike the sky. Just as graphically I recall it was during one of these moments that I realized I'm completely and irrefutably in love with her. I remember how the flash illuminated the living room of her parent's house when we were on the sofa, watching a movie together with Luke. Right away, my arm extended over her shoulders, and I brought her closer, her head resting on my chest. My lips pressed on the side of her forehead, and she relaxed in my arms. That was also the same instant when I swore to myself that I'll never hurt her and always keep her safe. That I'll give my life in the blink of an eye if I have to only to protect her.

Ensley Juliet Walker has been my weakness my entire life and the love I have for her has been my damnation.

"I got you, *nena*," I whisper against the top of her head.

Her hand travels from the place where it's been resting on my abdomen to my chest. The pad of her thumb grazes the piercing I have on my right nipple.

Instantly, a tremble runs through me at the sensation created by that small brush of her finger over the barbell. Just as immediately, my dirty mind slips to an image of her tongue rolling over the silver piercing. Of her lips moving over my skin, darting lower and lower. Of Ensley stopping only after she unbuttons my jeans and lowers the zipper. Of her halting, but just momentarily before she slips me out and swallows my cock to the back of her throat.

Joder.

I'm on a train that's awfully close to derailing. A train that I need to press the breaks on before it is too late.

Heedlessly, my hand flies to her wrist, pausing her action because the rush of all-consuming craving that runs through my body is unendurable and it would take a stronger man than I am to be able to stop once started. Especially when I'm on the brink of diving myself head in first. I teeter on the edge of fucking insanity considering the place I'd dive my head in is between her legs. Relishing on that sweet taste that still lingers on my lips.

Sixteen years and the honey-like taste of her pussy is still in my mouth. So many years have passed since I had her and she lives in me. In every single inch of my body, there's her touch, her fragrance, her taste. Everything that is her is deeply rooted in my bones.

"You're going to kill me one day, *nena*. And that's gonna happen real soon," I declare under my breath.

A sigh crawls up my throat and my eyes squeeze close. Feeling movement beside me, I reopen them and cock my head to the side to find the most beautiful and tantalizing pair of eyes I've ever gazed into. The same pair that haunts my dreams at night and every moment of every day when I'm awake.

Letting go of my hold on her wrist as though it burns me, it drops back on my chest and the skin sizzles beneath the softness of her palm.

As if she knows the effect she has on me, the tip of her index finger begins drawing circles on my chest.

"We fell asleep," she utters.

I find a little amusement in her voice and smile while I take her in. Her features are now calmer and more tranquil than earlier.

It is a realization that, in a blink, prompts the recollection of her tormented gaze. That frightened stare gets pictured behind my eyelids and my heart aches. The thought of what she's been going through all these months because of me pains me. All that anguish. All that torture.

If there has ever been a concise moment when I didn't deserve Ensley that is right now. She cares about me more than I deserve. Something I remember she's been forward about is wanting to be with me. She's been blunt about how she feels toward me. I, on the other hand, all I've done is deny her.

Un dia, vai perdela.

(One day, you're gonna lose her.)

The swift reminder doesn't delay resounding inside my head like an echo. A bitter cue that one of these days, I'll watch her let another man in. A man who'd deserve her like I never did. A man who can love her without having to look over his shoulder every step of the way. A man who'd give her everything and anything. And that man won't be me.

It is only a matter of time.

Sixteen years.

Has she waited for me this whole time?

"My mind is a goddamn mess," I begin, my eyes glued to the ceiling. "There are some things that are hazy."

The finger that's been drawing on my chest now stops midmotion. It is as if it almost freezes on my skin until I feel her touch no longer.

"You're one of them. Despite all my efforts, I seem not to remember a lot of things about you, Ley. There are bits and pieces, but they are a jumbled mess that I'm trying to puzzle together."

Silence coats the room. Even the thunder appears to have paused momentarily as though to bear witness to us.

"And I believe that whatever that puzzle will amount to, that's the reason behind all the contradiction I feel that's driving me crazy. The one behind my heart telling me one thing while my better judgment completely disagrees."

In spite of everything inside me telling me not to, I crane my neck to the side and my eyes connect to hers. What I find is something I can't decipher. It is as if an entire aggregation of emotions garners in her gaze and amasses to something that I can't work out.

"I'm losing my mind here, *nena*."

My admittance is full of sincerity. There's also torment. That is because for the past few weeks, I've been a tortured man. Tortured because there are memories my mind blocks out for one reason or another. Memories I know involve Ensley to some extent since she's the only one in my life that my own mind can't properly place. Despite me being aware of that, they're recollections I'm afraid to unlock. Afraid of what might be hiding beneath that fog that blocks them.

"Lying here with you in my arms feels so natural and so normal that it makes me crazy trying to figure out why. Sleeping and waking up beside you feels like the most familiar thing I've done since I got back from the hospital."

A hand rakes frustratingly through my dark locks at the same time as I let out a hefty breath.

"And kissing you? The way you surrendered to me in that kiss, that didn't only feel natural. That felt like you've done it a million times before."

The heavy breath that crawls up my throat pushes my chest upward. Ensley's head remains there as she lets out her own slow breath, her green gaze still locked onto mine.

"It's easy to submit to you, Mason. It is because I know you will give to me as much as you take from me," she asserts, utter conviction in her timbre. "I've known you for over thirty years. We grew up together and it's easy to notice you haven't grown into just any kind of man. You've grown into a man who dominates. One whose presence alone exudes control and domineeringness."

A lopsided smirk shapes at the left corner of my lips at her description of me. She's definitely not wrong about that. I enjoy the dominance of the sexual act. A dominance I've exerted with Ensley on that first night we spent together. But it hasn't been the dominance of the act itself because nineteen-year-old me was definitely as far from a Dom as possible and so is thirty-five-year-old me. Because for me has been and is more about the possession. More about how she willingly gave up her control. More about how I had the power to obliterate all her abilities to think with my touch alone. It was a power I used for her own pleasure.

No wonder all these moments have played over and over in every single fantasy my mind subconsciously developed. Especially when I've dreamed about fucking the woman who's now in my arms—and that has happened more often than I'm comfortable to admit—, I've possessed her body and her mind. I played with her tits until she begged me to have mercy. I strummed her clit with my fingers like it was my very own musical instrument and, *carallo*, the sounds erupting from her chest were the sweetest of melodies.

I'm in a hell of my own making.

No fucking doubt about that.

Instead of claiming the woman in my arms, I punish myself, crafting a hell even the devil himself can't match.

The piercing rumble of the thunder fills the room and if it weren't for my hold on her, Ensley would be already jumping out of bed. Considering the way she jolts in my embrace, nuzzling her head into my chest and throwing her leg over my thighs, she tries to grasp a hold of me as tight as possible.

"Holy shit," she gripes, her breathing hitched.

I let out a small chuckle and she smacks my chest before absolute darkness surrounds us when Ensley pulls the comforter over our heads.

Beneath the *protective mantle*—like Ensley sees it—, she stays quiet and keeps snuggling into me with every rolling thunder. Although it seems like there's no inch of her body that isn't pressed to mine, she proves me wrong each time because she appears to find a tiny fraction that doesn't touch.

Okay, time to take her mind off it now, I urge myself.

"If you were my woman, I'd have so many ways to distract you right now," I speak, the words slipping out before my brain has a chance to catch on my mouth.

I almost facepalm myself at the idiocy that just rolled off my tongue.

Almost because she doesn't give me a chance to.

"Like what?"

Ensley's challenge has a frown forming on my forehead. Although I know she can't see it, she can certainly feel the warning in my gaze.

"Ley."

The nickname is cautionary, using my tone to warn her to tread carefully.

"Humor me."

That fucking dare.

Because that is what the two words are filled with when she utters them to me. Clear, downright dare.

"Nena, xogas co lume e te queimarás."

Once again, the warning is clear in that sentence as I tell her she's playing with fire and will get burned.

"I'll take the risk," Ensley reverts.

A griping sound pushes up my throat.

All kinds of alarms blast in my head. Some command me not to do it. Others tell me it's a trap. There are a few that scream at me that it'd be a mistake.

However, being the sucker for self-punishment that I am, I wave them off. I ignore them against my better judgment, especially when I sense her expecting gaze on me.

There's still time to back off, an inner voice warns.

"I'd begin by getting you on your back so you can focus on the weight of my body when I'd get on top of you instead of what's going on outside these walls," I commence, her form shuddering against mine.

As though the words aren't enough, and the hell I'm already living isn't enough of a purgatory, in the blink of an eye, I have her exactly where I said—on her back. Just as immediately, I prop myself on my elbows above her body. I give her only some of my weight, but enough for her to feel me.

The faint moan that tumbles out of her chest and echoes into my ears only spurs me on when she spreads her legs to fit me in between her thighs. The hold on the sole fraction of self-control I have left doesn't only loosen. That fragment slips up through my fingers, crashes and burns.

Keeping my weight on one arm, I bring the other to her face, cupping her cheek. Instantaneously, she leans into my palm, and I hear her gentle inhale.

"Will you just stop there?"

Ensley's voice is soft when she asks the question. A sound so sweet that I know there's no turning back.

"If you want me to, I will."

My affirmation is quickly met by her head moving from side to side in refusal, her cheek grazing against my palm every time it shifts to the left side.

"In that case, absolutely not because I'd want you to relax. To forget about what's going on outside and focus on me only. Though I'm pretty sure I can make you block out the sounds with just being here on top of you."

She lets out a little chuckle at my arrogance, her tits pressing against my chest every time her body rocks upward.

My cock pushes against the zipper of my jeans. Although when I woke up it was already at half-mast after having her pressed against me, now my dick is hard between her open legs.

"Very confident, aren't we?" Ensley teases.

"Tremendously confident because the thunder struck twice since I've gotten you on your back and you didn't even flinch," I point out.

"You may continue."

The pad of my thumb dusts over her bottom lip and her

breathing hitches on a deep draw of air at the unexpectedness of my action.

"I'd press my mouth against yours," I whisper, so close to her lips that I can feel the hotness of her breath over my face. "I'd kiss you like you've never been kissed before by anyone. I'd kiss you until I'm all you feel, and all your mind can think about."

As my lips brush discreetly over the left corner of hers, I listen to the sound of her sharp inhale and pause. I am still for a tick or two, without pulling from her or leaning in further. I only keep my weight on my elbows above her and take in her sweet fragrance.

"Tell me to stop," I plead, and I barely recognize my own voice. It sounds as though strangled by the need for her that overwhelms me. A need that runs into my veins and aches every part of me.

"Stop."

Ensley breathes still just an inch away from my lips, her own voice filled with the same desire that overpowers me.

Though want flows heavily in the air between us, I'm ready to respect her and step away, thanking all things holy she is more rational than I am by putting a halt to this. However, when I go to draw back, her legs wrap around me, bringing me closer between her thighs. So much so that I can feel her heat over my groin.

Even in the darkness beneath the comforter, I see it when my eyes lock on hers. I see the plea in her gaze as her hands lift, her warm palms cradling my face as though to make sure I look at her. Honestly, she doesn't need to because I wouldn't be able to look away from her anyway since everything within me simply knows when she enters a room, my eyes always on her. Not that I don't enjoy her touch, though, because I do. I fucking do.

"Stop overthinking and just feel me. Let my body show you just how much I want you to never stop, Mason."

"*Nena*, we shouldn't," I try to reason, though I make no effort to escape her hold and withdraw.

"Yes, baby, we should," she whispers, one hand removing from my face to travel to the back of my neck. The other travels down between our bodies, dusting over my abdomen that strains at the touch, for it to stop only when it cups my hard bulge. "Don't think. Just feel."

It is on that last muttering that she uses the hold on my neck to bring my mouth down onto hers while her other hand caresses my cock over the jeans.

Oh, I feel all right.

All too fast, she pulls her beautiful lips away from mine, but the closeness and heat of the air she gently lets out tell me she's just a breath away.

"Cast away all the thoughts and reasons why this shouldn't happen. Let our bodies do the talking, baby. Let our hearts dictate the rhythm of what comes next."

"Why can't I fight you? Why every single time I try to fight you is a battle already lost?"

The ponder that should have been an inner wonder now dances between us after I'm unable to stop the words from slipping out of my mouth. Something I should be accustomed to by now considering that my brain seems to fry each time I have Ensley near me.

"Then stop fighting."

Her slightly parted lips brush against mine and a groan makes its way out of my chest at the softness that touches me. A brush so delicate and feeble that I could've easily sworn it was a figment of my imagination.

With both arms now back on the mattress, I keep myself rooted there still as if that would hold me from making a mistake. But when her hot palms rest on my shoulder blades and the skin burns at the touch, I know that my efforts are in vain. That because the way my blood pumps in my veins and how my flesh sizzle beneath her soft caress prove that I'm nothing more than a doomed man at her mercy.

"Show me what else you'd be doing if I were your woman," Ensley pries, her hands moving slowly down my back.

Even in pitch-black darkness, I can feel the anticipation and tease in her green orbs. Just as well as I can sense her tremble against my body when I lower myself a little more on her, giving her more of my weight.

My erection prods at the junction between her legs. Through the confinement created by my boxers and jeans, I feel the heat that's welcoming me and beckoning me to sink deeper between her thighs. I can almost hear the gripe of my dick at the layers

191

that separate him from that sweet cunt he's weeping to thrust into.

"You don't want me to."

Once again there's caution in my tone as I shift my weight on my left elbow, and my right hand rests on her hip for a second before it travels up her body. My fingertips graze over her oblique muscles that tense up beneath my touch. But when they dust over the side of her breast, her body shudders exquisitely against mine.

Fucking beautiful.

Count on Ensley Walker to make this damned man feel like the king of the fucking world with how marvelously she responds to my caresses.

But that isn't the only thought that crosses my mind. Simultaneously, another strikes. More of a realization, actually. I'm past the point of no return. I'm past the line I told myself I won't cross. A line that got so blurred by the denied temptation that Ensley represents for me and by the emotions I harbored within me over the years, that now I didn't even become aware that I crossed it until I found myself on the other side.

"Please," she breathes out.

"Please what, *nena?*" I question in return, my palm cupping her cheek. "Ask me and I'll give you anything. I'm gone beyond any rationality right now. You can ask me for the goddamn world, and I'll find a way to give it to you."

My own words echo over and over again in my head while I patiently wait for her to tell me what she wants. Though alarms still blare over the same words, I can't seem able to amass any ounce of energy to grab hold of my rioting restraint.

ENSLEY

My heart squeezes, and my stomach tightens as my mind replays Mason's words. With each repeat, there's a strong sting behind my eyes because the instant he spoke was when I got a glimpse of my husband and of the Mason he was fifteen years ago when he kissed the life out of me at his graduation.

The promise in his voice brings up vivid memories I have of my husband.

The defeat in that strong, deep baritone of his makes me remember when I pinned his badge on his uniform and he whispered to me:

"Miña."

("Mine.")

No doubt, but plain surrender in the sound of his voice.

"You can ask me for the goddamn world, and I'll find a way to give it to you."

"Kiss me," I whisper just a breath away from his lips. "Kiss me like I'm yours."

As if that's all he's been waiting for this whole time, his mouth presses against mine unhesitatingly. And if I believed the way he kissed me in the garage was pure claiming, he takes this kiss up a notch. This one is full of passion, dominance, and ferocity.

His tongue thrusts into my mouth without preamble. He doesn't probe, he downright prods. He doesn't take my own tongue into a slow tango, he conquers it. But his mouth is not the only one that has gone on a conquest. His whole body is set to obliterate every single capacity I have and to stir every stimulus in my form.

When Mason drops his hand from my cheek, it slowly begins to travel down. His palm rests on my throat for a short beat for his thumb to graze my racing pulse point. He does it as if to verify the extent of his effect on me. Judging by the smile that I feel in our kiss, he's extremely pleased with what he finds. Of course he is considering it races a million miles an hour.

His fragrance, his touch, his kiss. Together they make me crazy with desire. And the way his heart thumps against my chest while my very own seems to follow the same rhythm is life-altering.

My mind splits into focal points and the whirlwind it gets caught into nearly makes me lightheaded.

First thing that my mind focuses on is the way his mouth moves over mine with sheer claiming. How Mason withdraws lightly only to catch my bottom lip between his teeth, pulling gently before his lips press back onto mine and his tongue thrusts again.

The second thing my foggy mind rivets on is his hot palm against my skin. Every inch of my flesh burns beneath his touch. Even when he moves his hand further down, igniting yet another millimeter of my body in the process, the fire left behind is still as fierce as when he first touched me. It is as though a wildfire takes over my body. It burns me from the inside just as savagely as it does from the outside.

Which brings me to the third point of focus—his cock between my thighs. It is as hard as a steel rod while it presses at my center. With him fitted firmly in the junction of my legs, the wetness that pools at my core seeps through the fabric of my panties.

The heat emanating from our bodies only contributes to the high temperature beneath the covers. But that level skyrockets when Mason's lips lower to my neck while at the same time his hand moves to my breast, cupping it. For a brief instant, I lose his touch, but his mouth stays on my neck, nipping at it lightly. He eradicates every cognitive power to the extent that I am so focused on him that I don't realize he pushed the covers off us until I inhale deeply, the cool air in the room entering my lungs.

"Oh, God," I breathe out when his teeth graze the skin on my neck before his tongue darts over that same spot soothingly.

"Absolutely breathtaking," he whispers on my skin.

I throw back my head with a moan as his lips travel lower and lower. His hand moves to the hem of the t-shirt and slips underneath. My muscles tighten beneath his fleeting caress, but when he cups my breast, my back arches.

"Too many clothes," I mumble when I eventually find my voice.

At the same time, I garner all the energy I need to slip my palms further down his back until I grab the hem of his t-shirt.

"Too many goddamn clothes indeed."

After his agreement, Mason pushes to his knees.

Panting from the intensity of the kiss and from the ardor of his touch, I attempt to catch my breath while I look at him through half-hooded eyes.

His chest rises and falls as his gaze locks onto mine, his hands resting on either of my calves. That until they unhurriedly begin to move back and forth on my skin, from the calf and up past my knees till he reaches my quads that stress under his touch.

The instant his fingers only brush over my inner thighs, my teeth dig into my bottom lip and Mason mirrors my action, shaking his head leisurely as though with incredulity.

"Look at this body of yours," he roars, his chocolate stare unlocking from mine only to move up and down my body, causing my skin to inflame.

Without an ounce of hesitation, Mason draws his arm covered in ink back, catching a handful of his t-shirt then he pulls it over his head. His tanned skin is on display for my roving eyes. It is muscular and taut in all the right places, his abdomen so defined that it invites me to touch.

So that is exactly what I do as my hands lift, my fingertips tracing and caressing the mounds and the valleys of his abdomen.

"Look at this body of yours," I repeat his own words to him, my eyes telling him just how much I enjoy what I see.

His gaze follows my hands for a beat, then he locks it onto mine, letting me know that I might like what I see, but he loves what I do.

"Take that off, Ley," he commands, his eyes catching fire. "I wanna see those tits."

Straightening my back once I push upward, I do his bidding without delay and my chin tilts upward to be able to look at Mason just as he lets out a strangled groan. His stare roams my body like it is the most beautiful thing he's ever seen. And when his gaze comes back to mine, the flame that ignited in his eyes now is a wildfire.

The tip of his index finger dusts over my skin. It travels from the galloping pulse point on my neck, to the valley between my breasts, my body shuddering at the touch. His gaze trails each move he makes, blazing my skin alit before they lift to meet my anticipation-filled eyes.

His chocolate orbs roam over my face like he's trying to look for something that would tell him I want him to stop. I make sure he sees no shred of doubt.

"You're so fucking beautiful, Ley. So fucking sexy and tempting, it aches that you're not mine," he rasps, his head leaning in closer and closer. "I want you. I fucking crave you every moment of every day, but I know I can't keep you."

"Why not?" I pry, the pounding of my heart ringing loudly in my ears.

"Because I don't deserve you, Ley."

When he draws back and our gazes connect, I see the conviction in his orbs together with the aching defeat.

"There are things about me you don't know. Things that in the long run will prove to you that I indeed was not worthy of you."

"Things like what?"

The attempt I have to get more details out of him is met with silence. A bitter quietness that aches my heart because it is in that moment that whatever Mason keeps to himself, he's been keeping it all along. All through our relationship and marriage, he's kept it from me.

"I'm not the man you think I am."

The memory of what he told me at the hospital almost four months ago before he was induced into a coma now reverberates in my mind like an echo. An echo so resilient that it takes great effort to push it away, but one that triggers the need to finally contemplate on what he told me that day.

Only occasionally I let my thoughts slip to that moment and to what he said, but I didn't allow myself to pay much mind to it, ascribing it to the trauma he suffered, especially after he had to be induced. Now, on the other hand, I can't seem to be able to halt the onslaught of my own ponder.

Has he really kept something from me for so many years? And if he has, have I really not known the man I married? Am I fighting for a man I don't know?

All these thoughts now attack me from one part of my mind to another. The mercilessness of the assail making me dizzy.

Hence why I knock the thoughts away with a shake of my head and I roll out of bed right under his sharp stare. I don't care I'm pretty much naked. All I want is to put a much-needed distance between us so I can think clearly.

"I'm not playing this game with you, Mason. I'm not going to fight for you if you just keep pushing me away."

The anger is clear in my voice. An infuriation also evident in my eyes that flare with ungodly amounts of it as I look at him.

"I fought for you. Since that night, that's all I've done and now I'm tired. If you want me, Mason, earn me."

With that, I saunter toward the bedroom door not caring that my ass cheeks are on display for him because of the thong I wear. On the contrary, I add a little sway to my hips as I walk out, heading for the bathroom across the hallway.

Something else I don't appear to care very much about is the thunderstorm outside. The thunder rumbling in my chest overpowers the force of the nature and subdues my fear—at least for a little while as I'm too concentrated on my aching heart.

Easy I knew it won't be. But does it make it hurt any less when he is hot for a moment to then turn cold? No, it doesn't. Especially when he tells me sweet words and then gives me a cold shower because he believes he doesn't deserve me for a reason only known by him.

I'm not willing to play any games anymore. Screw the seduction plan. What I'm not going to screw with are my feelings. My love for the man in the other room. Because at the end of the day, it will be me who's gonna end up suffering most.

Perhaps Mason was right to ask for the divorce in the first place. Maybe we lived our love to maximum capacity already.

Perhaps there's no more road for us to walk together. Maybe...
Maybe this is it.

Taking a deep breath, I then let it out and reach inside the
shower to turn the water on. Immediately, the sound of the
stream fills the bathroom and I take off the only garment that
still covers my body. I don't miss the wetness dripping down my
inner thigh after I remove the sole piece of fabric that main-
tained caged the proof of all that desire Mason awoke inside of
me. The evidence of his effect on me—of his touch, of his kiss, of
his words— doesn't only stare me dead in the face from the
dampness of the fabric in my hand, it also trickles down my
skin.

With a frustrated breath, I throw the thong into the laundry
basket and step inside the shower and under the water. Though I
wash away the aftermath of our moment from between my legs,
what I am unable to rinse off is his scorching touch. His heated
caress dusting over my flesh. His fingers tracing my bottom lip
or how he gently bit into it and pulled at it, driving me crazy
with need. The tips of his digits barely brushing against the side
of my breast, causing goosebumps all over my body and turning
my nipples pebbled.

As my body fights off the recollection of his touch, my mind
battles the image of the unbridled look in his eyes. An image that
is now seared into every single one of my brain cells. The way
his roving gaze blazed my body. How my skin hissed under the
intensity of his chocolate eyes as they roamed. How the unre-
straint desire I found in his stare made me combust with my
own need for him.

The all-consuming hunger and the bone-deep love aren't
enough. If I ever thought they were, now I know they aren't. If
he can't be honest with me, then what's the point of us?

Lifting my hand, I wipe some of the mist that covers the
glass. My chin dips while I let out a heavy breath, then I reach
for the shower faucet and switch the water off.

Once I squeeze some of the water from my hair, I step out.
After I wrap a towel around my body and use another for my
hair, I exit the bathroom and pad barefoot across the hall into
my bedroom.

I don't know I hold my breath until I let out a relieved sigh
when I note that Mason isn't there anymore. But although he's

not in the room physically, the fragrance of his cologne—that scent that invites you to indulge in the wickedest of pleasures— dances in the air.

My gaze darts right away to the bed. The sheets are no longer tangled and messy. The comforter isn't kicked to the side anymore. Mason took the time to make the bed. My bed after I stormed out.

For the briefest of moments, I contemplate whether to rip the bedding off the mattress, the cases off the pillows and the cover off the comforter or not. And I weight that thought knowing that same smell that teases the air inside the room is also etched onto the fabric.

Shaking my head, I open the bottle of body lotion I fished from the bathroom on my way out and I apply it, letting it soak into my skin before I put on a pair of leggings and a t-shirt.

Heedlessly, I crawl into bed and take the pillow his head rested on, bringing it to my chest. My eyes close while I inhale that scent that is embedded into it right before I let out a heavy sigh.

"I want you. I fucking crave you every moment of every day, but I know I can't keep you."

Mason's words from earlier resound, my heart lurching right into the pit of my stomach. Although they hurt, I still find myself breathing in that fragrance of his cologne that I missed.

MASON

A week later

My eyes roam.

They rove in the mirror over the reflection of the woman I stand behind, my hands on her hips. My fingers dig into her flesh, my thumbs playing with the white lace band of her thong.

As my eyes zoom out for a moment to take in the full view of the woman between my arms, Ensley's bright smile sends my heart into a wild pace. Her long brunette hair cascades down her back and a few thick strands of hair fall down the front of her body, on the sides of her breasts. Her milky skin and the two white lacy pieces of garment she wears are in utter contrast with her inky-dark hair. But what the dark and light set an antithesis further on is her gorgeous green eyes that strike into my soul when they meet my chocolate ones in the mirror.

She continues smiling wildly at me and I kiss her cheek lightly before I home back on her lower body.

Following the path upward from where my hands are, my hungry stare journeys on the bare skin of her abdomen, the definitions of her oblique muscles clear in the reflection. But my gaze doesn't stop just there. It travels further up her body until they land on that pair of delicious tits that now are covered by a thin layer of white lace.

Her pebbled nipples pierce through the fabric and I can't fight the urge any longer. I can't fight that ungodly desire that runs through me with an electrical intensity. I can't win against that depraved need I have to consume the woman between my arms. What I can't also battle is that wicked hunger that burns me down to every fiber and atom in my being.

While my gaze runs up and down that deliciously exquisite body, over the milky skin, the filled-out curves, my hands remove from her hips, the urge to touch her too strong to be fought. And my right hand doesn't delay drifting more to her center, dusting over the lace that hides her pussy, only to have her tremble in my arms. My left hand travels up on the length of her body, though, not coming to a stop until it cups a small tit in its heel.

The black rubber band I note throning my left hand sets my heart into a wild gallop while a grin tips at the corner of my lips at the sight of it—the meaning behind that very band settling an even more possessive feeling within me.

After another instant, I avert my attention to the woman between my arms, Ensley's body molding into mine as though it is my missing piece.

Truth be told, it is.

She's always been that piece that always fit so perfectly. The piece I didn't need to question or doubt because I know she is mine.

As though to prove that thought exactly, my left hand kneads the small breast, and the middle finger of my right hand gently traces circles on her skin through the fabric.

One more melodious moan crawls up her slender throat and I can't help but cock my head to the side a little. My lips move over the skin right before my tongue swipes the same place my mouth kissed.

The hands she has draped at her sides now dart and rest on my bare ass cheeks, the fingertips and the nails digging into my flesh. At the same time, the action presses me further into her, my achingly hard cock pushing between her mouth-watering butt cheeks.

"Mason, baby..."

Her sentence drifts away when my hand slips inside the thin lace, cupping her sex while my left hand slides to her other breast, kneading it and tweaking its hard-as-a-bullet nipple.

"Joder! Can't believe you're all mine now," I breathe against her skin.

My finger teases between her folds, smirking when I find her absolutely soaked.

Just like I knew she'll be.

"I've always been yours," Ensley croons, her core moving further into my hand, seeking the pleasure she knows it's to come. "Only yours, baby."

"Only fucking mine."

The pad of my finger finds her clit, giving her proof of my words. I barely graze her bundle of nerves and her body shakes against mine.

My very own loud groan fills my ears and my eyes snap open, gluing to the ceiling for a tick. The sound of my heavy panting fills the air while my heart riots at such speed in my chest that it feels as though I've run an ultramarathon.

As with one hand I wipe at the sheen of sweat covering my chest, my mind tries to make sense of what I've just dreamed of. Not that there is any sense to make considering my mind is usually set on concocting the filthiest of images of Ensley and me. But this time it was different, though.

The ache in my groin hits, however, and my right hand travels to my dick. I don't find it just hard, it is like a fucking steel rod, ready to pound masonry nails into concrete without trouble.

Joder!

My own fucking mind is playing tricks on me with all these dreams.

They have mercilessly assailed me stronger and harder, time and again since a week ago after what happened with Ensley in her room. The day I lost control and threw her over my shoulder, smacking her sweet ass. The very day my self-restraint snapped loose and my unfulfilled and well-suppressed desire for Ensley have rioted against me and the wellbeing of my goddamn mind. The day my heart highjacked my mind and I've allowed myself a moment of weakness with her in my arms, with her lips against mine, with her body molded to mine.

It was so fucking wrong.

Yet, at the same time, it felt like the rightest of things that I remember to have ever happened to me.

What felt even more wrong thereafter was how she avoided me. How every time I'd enter the kitchen, the living room, or any room of this house and she was there, she'd look at me for a moment with those gut-wrenchingly beautiful green eyes of hers, and then she'd walk out of the room.

She also has barely said a word to me. Even if I tried, she'd give me a monosyllabic answer, then she'd strut her stubborn ass away.

Well, to be honest, out of the two of us I don't know who is more stubborn. Her for standing her ground with me and setting my ass straight? Or me for punishingly pushing away the woman I've been absolutely crazy about for twenty years but do not deserve to have because worthy of her I am not?

Many times during our brief encounters this week I wanted to stop her. I wanted to reach out and grab her, bring her to me and hold her. Keep her between my arms for a while before I capture that sweet mouth of hers with my own. Kiss her while she gives me that enthralling submission that I didn't know I've been craving until she first gave me a glimpse of in the kitchen during the incident with the coffee cup. That riveting submissiveness she gave me when I kissed her in the garage after she brushed her lips against mine.

I'd be damned if I don't want that again.

But what I want more is to hear her sweet-as-honey voice when she speaks to me. To have her look at me with anything else apart from disappointment and resignation because what I've been seeing this week in her beautiful eyes has been pure torture.

The fight I remember witnessing in her orbs when I pushed her away sixteen years ago is still seared on my mind. How she fought and fought for me to stop denying her, to make me claim her as mine. That resilience is still as clear now as it was when I first saw it. The same resilience I've seen after I came to and saw her in the hospital. However, it has now been replaced with the waiver and defeat I am not familiar with when it comes to Ensley Walker.

She's doing exactly what I wanted her to do. Stay away from me so I can be able to steer clear of her.

Yet, why does it feel so damn wrong?

Why does it feel as though I allow her to give up on something that is beyond my comprehension?

As my own defeated sigh pushes up my throat, I toss the covers to the side and throw my legs over the edge of the bed, my heart thundering in my chest as hard as earlier.

"Cono, nena, que me fas?"

(*"Fuck, baby, what are you doing to me?"*)

My hand lifts and I rake its fingers through my damp hair before I push to my feet, fish a pair of sweatpants to cover my naked body and walk out of the room.

Voume tolo.

(*I'm going crazy.*)

I am definitely going crazy.

Sauntering down the hallway barefoot, I let the chillness of it calm my raging cock. Or at least I pray it does before I suffer from an acute case of blue balls.

To be completely honest, I do my best to try and ignore it, but the ache in my groin is torturous as I pad down the stairs and into the kitchen for some water.

Once I grab a glass from the cupboard, I then retrieve the water jug from the fridge and pour myself some. I quickly take a few gulps of the cold liquid while I put the jug back and close the door.

After I down the water, my stare toward the garden through the floor-to-ceiling sliding glass doors.

My heart skips and lurches into the pit of my stomach when my eyes land on the breathtakingly gorgeous brunette who keeps haunting my dreams at night and torments my day, causing me to lose goddamn sanity—or whatever scintilla of it there is still left.

Ensley sits on the ratan sofa on the patio. Both of her bare feet are up on the cushion, her knees up to her chin while her arms hug her shins, a blanket covering her.

The darkness of the night surrounds her with only the gentle light coming from the solar string garden light overhead.

While my gaze is on her, I note she looks deep in thought as she stares in the distance. Instantly, I can't help the empty feeling in my gut or the tightness in my chest. It fucking hurts and it is so goddamn hard to breathe with her this close. Yet, I know I'll stop breathing altogether without her near.

Heedlessly, my hand lifts and I rub at my chest.

I rub at it as though that would disperse somehow the ache I feel there. That maybe it would, in some way, fill that voidness I feel making its home in the pit of my stomach because I can't have the woman I crave and love. Because what we have is damned by my own legacy. By who I am.

Instantly, I acknowledge how the pain in my crotch lessens tick by tick and I stand rooted to the spot for a moment or two.

"Can't sleep?"

The words slip out of my mouth as I slide the door open and step into the patio, the cool night air enveloping me. The coolness of it hits me right in the chest, reminding me that I only put on sweatpants.

Her green orbs dart my way when she cocks her head to the side and they pierce my heart.

So fucking beautiful it hurts.

So damn gorgeous my heart aches.

But what aches even more is how her beautiful eyes move from mine to roam over my bare chest before they lower past the waistband of my sweatpants and over the cock I barely just managed to bring to half-mast. The motherfucker within me enjoys it and I fight to suppress the smirk playing at my lips that she can't battle the attraction she feels toward me.

"I needed a little bit of air," she answers, averting her gaze as though unimpressed.

As much as she tries to hide it, I hear the little vibration in her voice, how it hitches, how it trembles, giving her away.

Advancing further into the patio, I stride toward the sofa. Her eyes follow my steps and when I get near, she averts her stare.

"Don't you wanna put a t-shirt on or something?"

My brow arches as I stop before her.

"Is this distracting you?" I ask, pointing to my abs cockily.

Ensley puffs sardonically and rolls her eyes.

"You wish."

"Liar."

While I call her out on her bullshit with a grin, I take a seat next to her. Her eyes remain focused on something in front of us, but I can easily bet she does it so she won't look at me.

And for a while, I let her.

What I also let is for the silence to wrap around us. At least I do it for a moment or two while my mind drifts to the dream I had. How real it felt. How good it felt to have her between my arms without any worry. How fucking surreal it felt to have her mine like that—like she'll never be outside my own fantasy.

"I'm sorry," I whisper and let the words dangle in the air for a second. "I'm sorry, Ensley. I'm sorry I don't know how to deserve you, how to keep you. I'm sorry I keep fighting against you, but I can't fight for you."

Another puff crawls its way through her lips. This time it is filled with incredulity as she shakes her head before she jumps to her feet as though the seat beneath her catches fire.

But what catches fire are her eyes when she aims her green stare my way.

"Every single time you look at me, it feels like a dagger pierces my heart. Every time you turn me down and deny me, it feels like a bullet goes right through my chest. Do you know how it is like to have your heart constantly bleeding because the wound keeps reopening right when you thought it healed?" Her head shakes from side to side again. "I don't want your sorry, I don't want whatever excuse you keep telling yourself. I want you to free me of you."

Joder!

That pain in her voice.

Fucking fuck!

That tortured look in her green gaze.

I caused all that.

I am the cause of that pain.

Of that torture.

For a woman who has never been mine in the first place, it feels an awful lot like she's slipping through my fingers. As if I am a very close step away from losing *my woman.*

Without thinking twice of the repercussions of my actions, I leap to my feet and extend my arm, reaching for her wrist just as she goes to turn and walk away.

"*Nena,*" I whisper, bringing her to my chest.

My hand lifts and I cup her cheek, while my other tightens its hold around her waist, keeping her flush to me. Her hands rest on my bare chest, feeling its burn right where she touches me. A mere press of her palms on my skin and it scorches me.

"Every time my eyes land on you, my heart thunders in my chest. Every time you touch me, it feels as if you ignite a fire within me, a fire that only burns fiercer and wilder, and all I can... All I must do is pretend it doesn't blaze inside me because if I acknowledge it, it only chips away at my sanity."

Her eyes stay locked onto mine, her lips sealed shut as she lets each word synch in.

"If only we could rewrite the stars, I'd write them for a world where I am not who I am. Where my legacy isn't tainted and where I am a man who deserves you. A man who is worthy of you and who can give you a life without putting you in harm's way just because you're the woman I am madly in love with."

"Mason, what are you talking about?"

My head shakes, avoiding her gaze.

She knows I'm now backpedaling from whatever I had in mind when I reached for her.

"I want you not to be afraid to fight by my side, to fight with me for what we can have. I put my life on the line every day I am on shift. I put it on the line for a stranger and you believe I'm not going to risk everything to be with you?" Ensley questions, plain vehemency in her voice. "I'd take any risk for you. I just want you to let me and fight with me. By my side."

Keeping my hold on her, my forehead leans against hers and I let out a heavy breath, sensing every bit of control trickle through the cracks that have been made in its defense and it slips through my fingers.

"Just let me in, Mase," she pleads, her hand lifting off my chest to my cheek, caressing it gently. "Let me in for real, baby. Fight with me for what we can have together because that will be something beautiful. Something worth fighting for. Something worth taking a risk for."

With a gentle smile, Ensley raises to her tiptoes and gives me a peck on the lips, pulling away too fast. Too damn fast for my liking.

Hence, the hand on her cheek moves to the back of her head, grabbing a handful of her hair to angle her just how I want her as I smash my mouth against hers hungrily. It is as though I made peace with the thought that I am utterly helpless when it comes to her.

My tongue thrusts into her hot mouth, caressing and teasing hers. She tries to push against it until I give her hair a gentle tug, cocking it at a little more of an angle to give me even further control of her mouth. That instantly has her sign her sweet capitulation with one last stroke of her tongue against mine. Then she gives me her full submission.

Her body molds into mine.

They fit together just as perfectly as they did in my dream.

I'm so fucked.

I can't stand away.

I am so fucking doomed is not even funny.

"*Joder, nena,*" I breathe out against her lips before I claim them again, my hold on her tightening.

Ensley moans into our kiss, the sound of it vibrating into me, while my own groan resonates into her.

And if before there was any fraction of self-control, after seeing how she kisses me back, with as much fervor and passion, that mere scrap is now gone.

Poofed.

Evaporated.

Fucked off.

When her lips remove from mine, I let a complaining groan crawl up my throat. My eyes lock onto hers and she smirks playfully then the pad of her thumb swipes over her bottom lip.

"Want more of that, earn it."

As a proud smile tugs at the corners of her mouth, she pulls out of my hold and twirls on her feet, making sure to drop the blanket.

Ensley looks over her shoulder for a moment, the playful glance not ebbing even the smallest of fragments. She takes the first step back inside the house right after, her hips swaying left and right sensually, causing me to fight the urge to race after her and continue what we've started.

She is a through and through seductress.

And I am fucking gone.

MASON

Sweet Ensley.

My bitter-sweet damnation.

The unmistakable hurt in her eyes still haunts me. And it's been aching my chest so atrociously ever since that I find myself rubbing at it each time I think about that pain in her gorgeous green orbs.

What also still torments me is the seductive look she gave me and how her hips enchanted me as they moved. To the extent that I had to jack off. It was already as painful as it was after I woke up with a hard-on I didn't take care of. But after that, with the look she gave me, I couldn't take it anymore and I had to fist my cock. Fist it while thinking of her. Thinking that it is her hand instead of my own. Thinking about how it would be like to have her swallow me down that pretty throat.

That sweet juxtaposition between wanting to keep away and seducing the hell out of me. That contradiction which makes me lose my ever-loving mind moment after moment.

My mind is an utter contradiction. I say this because when I don't think about the unbridled hurt in her eyes when I pushed her away and denied her, how it pained me to witness it and how my heart dropped into the pit of my stomach, I think about how beautiful she looked beneath me. How good her skin felt under my palm. How soft and sweet her mouth felt against mine. How I almost died to touch her some more. To drive her crazy with my fingers and my mouth.

And oh, *meu Dios*, that sweet, heart-shaped ass. When she walked away from the bedroom a week ago and swayed her bare hips. It took the greatest of efforts for me not to rush after her and throw her on that bed to finish what we've started. The same as it did yesterday morning when she dropped the blanket and strutted her ass away with the most seductive sways in her hips only to drive me crazy with desire for her and test my restraint. A restraint that is awfully close to hitting rock bottom.

So damn close that I am now pacing in front of the bathroom door ready to walk in and take off my clothes to join Ensley in the shower. To step under the water stream and kiss her. To allow myself to touch her and finally claim her. To tell her that she's mine and the past doesn't matter. To say to her that I will take the risk if that means I will have her. To promise her that I will protect her. To vow to her that I will love her so thoroughly and she won't remember a time when I denied her and pushed her away. Because if I allow myself to love her, there won't be a moment when I will not.

I bring my pacing to a halt and squeeze my eyes shut for a tick before I reopen them and wrap my hand around the doorknob. I am just a fraction away from twisting it when the sound of the doorbell fills my ears and I let out a breath.

Is it a relieved one or is it a cranky, protesting one?

Considering the disappointment that settles in my stomach and the protest of my cock that jerks in my black jeans, I would be inclined to opt for the latter.

After I'd just gotten home from the bar where Luke and I had to meet with a couple of suppliers, I only had the chance to come upstairs, and the running shower halted my steps. For several instances I have paced back and forth, weighing my options—walking away and keeping hold of whatever restraint I have left, praying it won't snap—, or giving in and claiming the woman I love. Now, when the decision is made, I get interrupted.

So yeah, I am certainly inclined to say that the breath I let out was a complaining one.

Maybe just as complaining as the cuss I let out under my breath while I make my way back downstairs and open the front door. But I swallow all my words when I see who stands in front of me, greeting my mother with a smile.

She lifts two paper bags from the market.

Joder!

I completely forgot she is coming over for dinner.

"Am I interrupting anything? Did I get the day wrong?" Mom asks, her eyes moving over me.

"No, you didn't interrupt anything," I quickly reassure her, maybe too quickly.

Although Mom and I have a close relationship, I'm not gonna tell her she just stopped me from walking in on Ensley while she was in the bathroom to make her mine.

"Also, no, you didn't get it wrong. It was tonight. I just... I just forgot."

"Not missing your *Mamá* as much as you claim to," she jokes. "Hungry?"

"Starving," I reply, leaning in to drop a kiss on her cheek before I take the bags from her. "*Ola, Mamá!*"

"*Ola, meu fillo!*"

"Come on in."

Once I say that, Mom enters inside the house and I follow, kicking the door close.

"How's Ensley?"

My chin lifts, pointing toward the stairs.

"She's taking a shower. She shouldn't be long."

"We can get started on dinner then."

And that we do, placing the vegetables in a large bowl with water to rinse them while Mom places the meat on a plate.

Retrieving a cutting board, I set up at the island in the middle of the kitchen and begin rinsing the vegetables.

"*Ola, miña nena fermosa!*"

("*Hi, my beautiful girl!*")

It is that greeting that has me cock my head to the side and see Ensley walking inside the kitchen. Her hair is still damp, and she looks breathtaking, wearing a t-shirt and a pair of leggings.

"Hi, Ary!"

"How's my beautiful girl doing? Handled okay the storm last week?"

It is on Mom's question that her green eyes dart to the floor-to-ceiling windows that separate the kitchen from the outside and I follow her gaze to see the clear evening sky, before I revert it back to her.

"Mason made sure I'll get through it just fine," she replies.

I note she doesn't look at me, instead she avoids my gaze by keeping her eyes on Mom.

"Oh, you did, didn't you now, *meu fillo?*"

The insinuation in Mom's voice has Ensley's cheeks tint pink and when she eventually finds it in her to dart her gaze toward me as I continue to casually chop a zucchini, I know she can see the twitch in the corner of my lips. I fight off the smirk and almost succeed until I drop my eyes for a moment then look back at her, connecting our eyes across the room.

"Sorry to have intruded on your evening," Mom apologizes. "Since my own son forgot we set dinner for tonight, I doubt he's told you."

"Nonsense, Ary. You know you're always welcome

here," she speaks in return, placing her hands on Mom's shoulders to give her a side-hug. "Anyway, I'll go and dry my hair, then I'll help you both with dinner."

"Of course, *cariño.*"

Ensley spins and my eyes can't help from zeroing in on the globes of her ass as she walks away.

It sways in the same alluring way it did when she walked out of the bedroom a week ago and back inside the house late last night. Though it is covered by the fabric of her black leggings, it is nothing short of enticing.

"Okay, can you please stop?" Mom's voice pulls me from my thoughts.

"Stop what?"

My eyes narrow at her before I lower my gaze to make sure I don't chop my finger while cutting zucchini.

"Stop looking at her like your *Mamá* isn't here. Have some respect," she speaks with a teasing smile.

I sigh, resting both hands on the countertop after I place the knife on the cutting board. My shoulders lift with that heavy breath and my chest expands as my chin dips.

"I kissed her," I admit. "I got carried away and kissed her."

"Apparently you didn't get carried away enough," she reproaches with sass. "Get your skates on already, Mason. Kissing and holding hands doesn't give me any grandbabies. I know that's a once-upon-a-time story I told you, but I'm sure you've figured out by now that they aren't made that way."

I can't control the chuckle that pushes up my throat at my mother's ranting.

"Thank you for the reproduction crash course, *Mamá*," I revert with sarcasm. "I know I shouldn't have kissed her."

"Por que diaños non?"

(*"Why the hell not?"*)

The vehemence in my mother's voice as she asks the question is evident and as if that isn't enough, her hands rest on her hips.

"Because it won't end well for her and I. I'll hurt her or worse…," I let the sentence trail off, all courant she knows what I'm referring to. "I not going to risk the life of the woman I love because I can't keep my feelings under control or my hands to myself."

"You don't have to do any of that, Mason. You don't have to hold yourself back from loving Ensley. You shouldn't hold yourself back from truly giving yourself to her."

The meaning behind her last two affirmations rumbles thunderously in my head.

"I should because once she finds out who I am…"

"You are *my* son."

The sheer ferociousness in her voice surprises me for a tick when she interrupts me. She's like a lioness defending her cub. This is who Aracely Carter has always been, a mother who'd stop at nothing to protect her child.

"If you ever believed otherwise, it means I failed you as a mother."

"Mamá…"

"On the assumption that you tell Ensley the truth, what makes you believe she won't understand? What makes you think she'll kick you to the curb and won't fight tooth and nail for the man she *knows* you are?"

My mouth opens for me to speak, but Mom lifts her hand in an '*I'm still not done saying my piece*' kinda gesture that halts the words I intend to speak. It is also when I realize that Aracely Carter is on a roll and there's nothing stopping her.

"And if she doesn't see past it—though I'm certain she will—, then she's not the woman for you or deserves your love. Think about that while you let the love of your life slip between your fingers."

That renders my speech capability unserviceable. No words come out, the previous thought I wanted to voice still clogging my throat.

"You have one of two choices: you let her go completely or you stake your claim on what's yours."

"I think you and I know the choice," I speak. "*Mamá*, you and I spent our lives looking over our shoulder. It would be selfish of me to have Ensley do the same."

"But…"

"No, *Mamá*," I interrupt her. "And you know what would be even more selfish? To refuse Ensley the family she wants, the kids she wants because I don't wanna have kids. Yes, I'd want to be with the woman I love, but I can't and that's exactly why I need to stay away. Because I don't want them to spend their entire lives looking over their shoulder."

"What if she's willing to take that risk for you?"

"What we have is impossible, *Mamá*."

Her dark brown-haired head moves in disagreement. "The only time when love is impossible is when the significant other is gone."

Mom's chocolate eyes gleam with pure emotion. An emotion I know is attributed to the impossible love she's been living half of her life after Dad's passing.

"That is the one and only time," she continues, her voice although gentle, still filled with emphasis.

On this occasion, however, I don't get to say anything because Ensley makes her way inside the kitchen. Her long hair is brushed back. The t-shirt she wears isn't too tight or too loose, but enough to see she doesn't wear a bra if one would look close enough—which I do look more than attentively.

Her beautiful, long legs are covered by black leggings. Yet, my mind extracts from the drawer of exclusive content with Ensley the image of her bare legs. Smooth beneath my palm. Her quads tensing when my hands traveled from her calves and up her legs.

The way she responds to my touch is simply breathtaking. She quivers, her own body betraying her and how much she wants me.

Her green eyes move between Mom and me, making me

wonder if she heard our conversation or how much of it she heard if she did.

"Would you like a glass of wine, Ary?" Ensley asks Mom, clearly knowing that wine is my mother's drink of choice.

"I'm having the tea Mason made me. But I might have a glass at dinner," Mom answers, moving a little so she can gesture toward the cup of tea behind her.

"Don't mind me if I have one now then."

The little chuckle that erupts from her chest is a melodic sound that nearly has me trip over my own feet. There isn't much in this world that can have me weak in the knees. Actually, there's barely anything to have that effect on me. Only Ensley Juliet Walker can make my knees grow weak with her presence, with the sounds that come out of her mouth, with everything that she is.

"I'll get it for you," I offer, moving away from the island throning the middle of the kitchen.

With long strides, I am beside her by the countertop where the circular wine holder is. As one hand reaches for the under-the-cabinet goblet holder, I crane my neck to the side a little. When I meet the jaded gaze that has me all in knots, a small smile forms on my lips, realizing she is already looking.

For a moment, everything seems to fade around us while we hold each other's stare. Something that happens every time Ensley enters a room, and we search each other's gaze.

My hands tingle to touch her. To continue what we've started in her room last week. To not stop until we're both sated and depleted of all the energy, panting for air.

I'd have her in so many ways if I allowed myself the chance. I'd make even the author of *Kama Sutra* blush with the ways I'd have her. Hell, I'd be able to write my own book and it would be a very thick book given all the explicit and graphic details. A book written for our eyes only because I'd never share even the briefest of details with anyone else who isn't Ensley.

"Joder," I curse under my breath.

The sound of someone clearing their throat snaps us both out of the enchantment our eyes set the other under. Right away, I clear my own throat to make sure that next time I speak, the effect of our little moment isn't evident any longer.

Grabbing the bottle of red wine from the holder, I place on

the countertop the glass I didn't realize I still held and reach for the corkscrew. Once I pop open the bottle, I pour some into the glass until it's half full, and hand it to Ensley.

"Thank you," she utters with a smile, taking the goblet from me.

"No worries."

It is on the sound of the two words that come out of me that I am thankful I took a moment to speak because if there are still remains of the effect Ensley's green orbs had on me, I can only imagine what it would've sounded like had I spoken earlier.

"Am I the only one who's starving?" Ley asks, turning to avoid my gaze.

"Roasted vegetables and steak sound good to you?"

It is on Mom's question that the automatic protest of Ensley's stomach enters my ears, causing her to place both her hands over her abdomen.

"I guess we know just how hungry you are."

The jest in my voice is clear and she gives me a sharp stare. That piercing jaded gaze isn't cutting, it is soul-slashing. But something tells me it isn't because of my joke as much as it is because I act like everything that happened between us last week didn't occur.

How can I be sure of that?

Simple. Ensley's eyes are an open book. It is as though they open a window into her soul and allow me to see within.

If you want me, Mason, earn me.

With the recollection of that gut-wrenching sentence now roaming my mind and with the image of her hurt gaze stabbing at my chest, I bring my hand to my chest and rub discreetly at the ache that suddenly hits me.

"I'll give you a hand with the rest of the vegetables," Ensley offers, placing her glass of wine on the island's worktop.

Smoothly after she grabs another knife and cutting board, she sets them next to my *chopping station*.

In order to get to my spot, I need to go around her. Which I do, making sure to be close enough so I can take a deep inhale of that sweet jasmine fragrance of her shower gel. Action that has her body tense a little, drawing a smirk from me.

Gilipolla.

I know I am an asshole grinning like an idiot and reveling in the effect my closeness has on her.

What I am also aware of is that I am playing with goddamn fire because coordination between my mind and body seems to exist no longer—to be absolutely honest, I don't believe it ever existed, at least not where Ensley is concerned. It goes up in fucking flames when I'm around Ensley and I am a damned contradiction who always says one thing, but then goes and does the complete opposite.

Therefore, once I retrieve my spot by my own board, I will my brain and body to fucking synchronize before I am losing my mind completely.

As I resume the chopping, with the corner of my eye I watch the breathtakingly gorgeous brunette beside me dip her hand into the bowl with washed vegetables. And out of all the picks in the world, her hand has to come out holding an eggplant.

"Interesting choice," I whisper, leaning my head more toward her to make sure it's just her who hears not only what I say but also the innuendo in my voice.

The sucker-for-punishment me expects anything from Ensley. Particularly because she's been a little tamed and collected. The calm before the storm. A volcano about to erupt, setting off blazing warning bells in my head. What I don't expect her to do is dive the knife into the eggplant in one fluid move-ment, cutting it in two halves while she holds my stare.

I swallow hard, the smile that was once on my face fading in a matter of nanoseconds by the time the blade gets to the other side of the eggplant.

"How's that for interesting?" She challenges on an utterance, keeping the little exchange only between us.

"Like you pictured cutting something else."

"Ding, ding. We've got a winner."

The defiance in her voice is such a fucking turn-on that I ignore she just imagined having my dick on that chopping board instead of an eggplant. And to think that for a second I believed it will make the fucker shrink and hide under my balls for a change. Hell no, he's happy to come out and play if the stirring in my jeans is any suggestion.

"I could always resort to tongue and fingers," I revert, my timber deep and daring. "Though believe me you'd miss…"

Letting the sentence trail off, I note her chest rising and falling with more rapidity than normal. She definitely tries to appear indifferent, however, the biggest betrayer is her body just like mine is the worst of traitors.

"I wouldn't know."

It is all she says before she reaches for the glass of wine to take a gulp.

"Liar."

A sardonic puff crawls up her delicate throat and even in that sound I can sense her defiance. A rebellion that only snaps loose something inside of me. I wouldn't say with confidence that I know what that *something* is, but it is categorically of importance considering the way she spurs me on.

"You know, I'd bend you over my knees and smack your ass senseless for that lie," I prompt.

"Promises, promises."

Two words.

Two words still kept on murmur just like the rest of our conversation. The lack of loudness doesn't affect its delivery or intent. Quite the opposite, to be honest, taking into consideration that the insolence possessed by her mouth is goddamn torturous. Yet, it is nothing short of beautiful when she sasses, considering the way my cock pushes against the zipper of my jeans and jerks in its cage like it is on steroids, and how my pulse jumps into high gear.

It is like my memories sell short the version of the woman Ensley Walker turned into. Don't get me wrong because she has never been a push-over and more than once she has actually punched some dirtbags at school for being assholes—ultimately getting herself in trouble. But what I remember of her is nowhere near this fierce and daredevil version she became.

Do I dig it, though?

Hell, yes, I do. Who wouldn't?

What person in their right mind would not be completely enchanted by a woman like her?

I don't miss the strain on my heart when I glance at the brunette while my mind gets crossed by the thought that I somehow seem to rediscover Ensley. Though I know her, there are things that are anew. Or maybe just things that my mind has blocked out for one reason or another.

Joder!

I am indeed a glutton for punishment.

Clearing my throat to hide the aftermath of our exchange, I lift my chin to look at Mom who seasons the stakes, her back facing us.

"Ary, I meant to ask, but I wanted to see you in person for it. How was your date last week?"

Ensley's question has me crane my neck to look at her with a deep frown, before my gaze darts to my mother's chocolate one when I note Ley ignores my sharp stare.

"You knew about the existence of this guy and didn't tell me anything?" I rebuke, my scolding eyes now traveling back to the woman beside me.

After she drops the utensil on the worktop, her arms fold over her chest, pushing her small tits up. Yeah, my hungry stare zeroes in right there the second she thrusts them upward. But when it travels back to her gorgeous face, I don't miss the twinge of crimson on her cheeks.

Non o fagas, I order myself.

Against my better judgment and the command my brain gives my body to not do it, I find my gaze dropping back to that pair of luscious tits she hides beneath her t-shirt.

Merda!

Hell is a downright understatement to express what I'm going through right now. A purgatory filled with so much torture that I garner all my energy to suppress the words from slipping out of my mouth. Words that'd tell my mother to leave so I can throw this woman over my shoulder like the caveman I am and take her upstairs.

ENSLEY

Mason's piercing chocolate gaze has been on me throughout the time that it took for us to prepare the food as well as all through dinner.

From the instant his intense stare homed in on my boobs and my nipples saluted him from beneath my t-shirt, I was in complete agony. The two bullets they turned into caused me so much pain that occasionally I'd found myself wincing.

Even excusing myself to race upstairs and put on a bra didn't help. It might have hidden some of the effects of his unmitigated gaze, but the ache was still there. More intense. Fiercer. More vicious. Especially when my pebbled nipples brushed against the inside of the bra's cups.

The newly added piece of garment certainly didn't thrill Mason who looked quite disappointed after I came back down. However, the unholy grin that took over his handsome features might have told me that he was not pleased with what I did, but what it also told me was that he was undoubtedly satisfied with my body's reaction.

Moreover, my action only egged him on. A few times he'd brushed past me close enough that his hand would graze my skin so softly that hadn't I been so hyperaware of him, I could've missed it. On several other occasions, he'd come close enough to whisper something in my ear that didn't make sense at all. It took me a repeat or two of that for me to understand that his intention is to simply bring me to the brink of sheer insanity.

Which he successfully manages to.

Not that before he didn't drive me crazy. Because he indubitably did. Now, though, he seems like he is on a mission and does so at an utmost level, inebriating me with his touch, with his fragrance, with his closeness.

I know I shouldn't get my hopes up. I am aware of that and it is something I keep repeating in my head like a mantra. Over and over again it echoes in my head. Nonetheless, my traitorous heart can't help but skip a beat more often than not.

There's no doubt that I should know better. That I should will my heart to halt its gallop because if we get the hot side of him now, soon we'll also get the cold one. That cold-as-fucking-ice shower that serves as my reality check. A bitter actuality and a reminder that I should choose self-preservation.

"Thank you so much for lending me that dress. I've had it ready to take it with me tonight to return it, but I've rushed out," Aracely says as I hand her a plate to put it in the cupboard after I take it from Mason who's in charge of washing up and I dry it.

"I'd like you to keep it, actually. You looked amazing in it," I compliment with a smile. "Besides, it's been hanged in my dresser for so long and I never wore it."

"Are you sure?"

The kind smile on her face only broadens my own.

"Of course."

"Why do I feel so left out? You not only knew about my mother's date, but you also gave her one of your dresses."

As the reproach in Mason's voice pierces my ears, I turn my head to the side to look at him with sharp eyes.

"This is the exact reason why you've been left out," I explain, arching a brow at him.

He scoffs.

"You should be happy your mother found a stand-up man she can spend time with." At my continuation, he lifts his own brow while our eyes lock, the war between our stares evident. "Just because you want to deny yourself the happiness life can bring to you, that doesn't mean all of us should."

The tick in his jaw tells me he didn't miss the double meaning of my revert. What it also tells me is that he doesn't like it even in the slightest that I'm pushing his buttons.

We finish washing the rest of the dishes in silence.

"I'll leave you two to enjoy the rest of your night."

"Are you sure you don't want to sleep here tonight, *Mamá*?" Mason offers once again, first being extended during dinner.

"Don't worry about me, *meu fermoso bebé*. I told you, I brought my car and I'm good to drive."

Her hand rests on her son's cheek as she looks up at him with so much love in her eyes. A love that is reciprocated by Mason down to the last scintilla of it.

"I can drive you."

At her son's insistence, she shakes her head.

"It's fine, Mason."

With that, she turns to me and pulls me into her arms after she presses a kiss on my cheek.

"*Miña nena fermosa*, don't stop fighting for him," she whispers in my ear, soft enough for just me to hear. "He's as stubborn as his *Mamá*."

A gentle chuckle crawls up my throat.

"Drive safe and make sure you message when you get home."

"I'm the mother here, young lady," she reverts with a laugh, drawing back from our hug.

She doesn't get far as Mason pulls her into his chest, kissing the top of her head. "And you, young lady, should listen to Ensley. Drop us a message when you get home, okay?"

"I will. I promise."

After she kisses us both on the cheeks, we walk her to the door. She gives me one more hug while Mason walks to her car and opens the driver's door. Aracely pulls back from our hug and walks to her vehicle. Her hand lifts and rests on her son's cheek, telling him something inaudible to me from the distance. He nods and kisses her on the forehead before she slips inside her car, turning on the engine. I give her a curt wave as she drives off, Mason doing the same.

His back still faces me for another moment. After he turns on the heel of his shoes, he walks back toward the house. While he does so, my eyes can't peel off him. They take in his movements that are full of natural swagger. And when they lift to his handsome face, I don't miss the way his gaze journeys my form.

A lopsided smirk tips the left corner of his lips as he approaches, stopping just before me for a tick. This has me tip my head back a little to look at him and I can see something crossing his stare as he peers down at me. He doesn't say anything and nor do I. We only stand there quietly for a moment or two just gazing into each other's eyes as though they're the ones having a conversation.

Unable to hold it any longer without the risk of throwing myself at him, I turn and enter back inside the house with Mason following suit after he closes the door.

"Want another drink?"

He asks the question looking over his shoulder on his way to the kitchen straight from the foyer while I descend the level to the living room.

"I'll have another glass of wine, thank you," I reply, grabbing the empty glass from the coffee table where I've abandoned it.

As I saunter toward the kitchen with the glass in hand, I let my eyes move over Mason's back while he grabs the bottle of bourbon to pour himself a drink. He smoothly shifts to retrieve a tumbler and I follow his moves, realizing that even the most mundane thing he does, he makes it look incredibly hot and utterly magnetic, full of confidence and charisma.

To be truthful, I already knew that, but somehow this moment reminded me of it. Which is why I let my gaze linger until it shamelessly zeroes in on his ass.

Mason has great everything.

But his butt?

Oh my stars and garters, he has a spectacular ass. Muscular with tight cheeks that I always loved grabbing onto, digging my nails into while he drove his cock into me mercilessly.

Why is it suddenly so hot in here?

In a blink, I gather all my might to push away that image from my mind.

"Here you go," Mason speaks, his deep timber causing goosebumps to break on my skin.

Perhaps because it is the first time when I don't dash out of a room that he's in like I've been doing the past week. I know that last week's events have shifted things between us. I can feel it between us. I can see it in his eyes.

Since then, a lot has happened, but not much at the same time. The feeling of confusion and turmoil weighing heavily. Concomitantly, the tension now crackles in the air between us.

Thick and hefty, it surrounds us with layers and layers of unmitigated attraction and savage impulses.

"Thank you."

My utterance when I take the glass from his hand clearly betrays the effect Mason's presence has on me, especially when his chocolate eyes remain on me. To break that visual contact that has butterflies rioting in my stomach, without delay, I take a sip of the wine. However, that plan fails since I keep holding his stare over the rim of my glass as I swallow the deep dark red liquid.

"Still sober?"

His question draws my eyebrows together and I watch him lean against the kitchen counter. His left arm drapes to his side before his hand rests on the counter, his fingers wrapping over the edge of it. In his right hand he holds the tumbler, swirling the two fingers of bourbon while his right leg bends from the knee, his foot pointing downward as he places it over the left one.

"I only had that half glass of wine," I mention.

With his intense gaze still on me, he takes a gulp of his drink and places the glass on the countertop behind him. His stare isn't just ardent, blistering my skin. It is predatory. It is as though I'm the prey and he's the predator, ready for the takedown.

Just one step in retreat is enough to have the edge of the kitchen island dig into my lower back. It is on that action that I note it. The smirk playing on his lips tells me he has me exactly where he wants. Before I even blink, he eats the distance between us with complete dominance.

I know now there's no escape.

Not that I'd look for one.

Without delay, Mason places his hands on either side of my hips, caging me between the island and his body. At that, I tilt my chin up to meet his eyes again only to find the flames I know he sees in mine, mirroring now in his orbs too.

On the first draw of air I take, his musky fragrance mixed with the gentle, yet strong twang of bourbon, I become unequivocally intoxicated by his presence altogether.

"I believe you extended a dare," he rasps, his mouth close to my ear once he leans in. "*Promises, promises.*"

A sound I almost am unable to recognize dances through my parted lips when Mason sucks on my earlobe. It is half-moan and half-gasp. A sound that seems to spur him on judging by the arm that circles my waist, bringing me flush to his strong body.

For a brief tick when he draws his head back, leaning it against my forehead, I listen to his own erratic breathing whilst he attempts to calm it down. This is the instant when I believe this is it, and that he'll pull back completely. That is when the cold side overcomes the hot and I'd be left craving just like before.

I close my eyes, unwilling to watch him reject me one more time. As I keep them close for a beat and then another, I begin feeling the lack of his body pressed against mine. His weight isn't firm against my form any longer.

Between the pounding of my heart and the ringing in my ear, I find myself unable to hear any other sounds around me. So when I will my eyelids to lift, what I expect to see is an empty spot. Much to my surprise, though, my gaze connects immediately with that dark chocolate pair of orbs which has me in a constant turmoil.

"Strip."

It is an order.

Clear and concise on even more of a demanding timber. An order that has my mouth fall slack for a tick.

"What?" I ask, making sure I heard him right and my mind is not playing tricks on me.

"Your defying mouth lost its tongue now?"

Although he is two or three feet away from me, not even his breath reaching me, it feels as if he touches me everywhere, waking every cell and fiber in my body.

"My tongue is exactly where it should be, thank you very much for your worry."

With the sass of my revert dancing in the air between us, Mason's lips twitch while he fights off a smile.

"There's another place where I'd like it to be. But I guess that's a talk we can have some other day. Now, take off your clothes, *nena*, so I can swat this impertinent ass of yours until you won't be able to sit down. Until each time you look at yourself in the mirror, you see my mark on you for days."

A thrilling shiver runs across my body at the promise in his voice.

Fuck. Me.

If this isn't Mason's restraint snaping loose, then I don't know what it is. His control is firm, though. Not the control over his own person, but over me and what is about to happen.

The shock of his words combined with the fire in his stare still me. All that I am capable of is looking at him and tremble to the core as the vow in his timber resounds.

Right now, my body betrays me more than it has done before. Not only does it shudders under his unbridled gaze, but it also amalgamates between my thighs the undiluted tension and incontestable attraction that hover over us.

"You've got about five seconds to decide if you're gonna take off your clothes or if you want me to walk away, *nena*."

His voice is heavy and hoarse, and when I let my eyes roam over his body, it is impossible to miss the bulge tenting his jeans.

"Five," he begins the countdown.

On that, I blink.

Is he serious?

"Four…"

My heart skips a beat.

"Three…"

With my breath hitching in my throat, I will my body to act. I will myself to do his bidding. A command that he can do himself just by eliminating the distance between us.

"Two…"

That is when it downs on me what he wants. Because indeed he could easily come close and remove all my clothes without hearing the faintest of protests on my part. Yet, he wants *me* to do it. He wants *me* to take off my clothes because he wants my submission. He wants my surrender so he can finally wave the white flag of his own capitulation.

Just as his mouth opens for the last second of the countdown, my hands find a mind of their own, grasping vigorously at the hem of the t-shirt. In a blink of an eye, the first piece of garment touches the floor.

Mason follows every single move with his prodding gaze, the uncloaked fire in his stare intensifying with each passing second. It scorches my skin to the bone.

"Keep going," he urges.

In view of his tense form and how his fists ball at his sides, he fights the impulse to get closer. To wipe out the few feet between us and rip my clothes off, his control chipping away with each piece of garment that hits the floor.

Resting my hands on the waistband of my leggings, I lean forward ever so lightly and shim the fabric off slowly. Oh, so slowly, that the sound of an impatient growl ricochets across the room, from one corner of it to the other, proving my point that his control erodes. It threatens to snap loose just like his self-restraint did.

"Everything off."

The effect in his voice is unmitigated. Even if he wants to deny it, he cannot because everything in his body betrays him too. Because behind that fire in his gaze, I note the inner torment when I tilt my chin just a fraction and lock our eyes.

Indubitably, there are still traces of his repression and of his will to deny me, but his desire and hunger for me have reign for now.

Consequently, I don't give him a chance to back off and once my leggings are down on the kitchen floor, I move for my bra.

It is impossible to ignore the scream of my nipples to free them. To set them free so they can fall willing victims to Mason's piercing eyes. Though the thin pad that covers them is no worthy opponent against how hard they are, I'm convinced he can see them poking through the material.

"We offer ourselves as tribute" is what I imagine they must say as the ache becomes unbearable. To the extent that when I bring both hands to the front of the bra, unhook the sole fastening mechanism and let it join the heap of clothes forming at my feet, my breasts feel so heavy as though they grew a cup-size or two in the last few minutes.

The erect buds salute him again and I fight the urge to bring my hands up. Not to cover myself, but to touch my pained nipples that get impossibly harder when I watch Mason's tongue slide out and dart over his lips like he pictures all the ways he'd play with them.

And boy, oh, boy, just how bad I want him to do that. To feel his hot tongue circling them, driving me insane with need. To have his fingers tweak and pull at them. To have his mouth suck on the hardened nipples. Even to have him order me to push them together so he can drive his cock between them like he's done before.

"Once your panties are down, there's no turning back," he warns, his voice a deep, heavy rumble while his roving eyes move up and down my body. "If you want to stop this, it's all in your hands. Just say the word and I'll walk away."

A bulging arm lifts, and he rakes it through his hair, his chest rising and falling.

"Decide for me, Ley. Decide because I'm so wrapped up in you, *nena*, and so lost in you that I can't think clearly."

Without a ounce of hesitation, I dig my fingers into the thin band of my thong and push it down, making my decision crystal clear.

"*Joder,*" he breaths out on a hard swallow. "This fucking body of yours is a masterpiece. So fucking beautiful."

My heart sets into a wild gallop. So much so that I fight the urge to lift my hand and rest it on my chest to cease the rebelliousness of it.

"Turn around and bend over," he demands, taking one singular step in my direction.

Once again, my breath gets obstructed in my airway, turning into a gasp.

"Turn around and bend over," Mason repeats himself. "Ass in the air and tits to the counter."

The shaking in my legs almost has me topple over, but I grasp hold of the edge of the island before my butt hits the floor. Much so that it takes me a blink or two to execute his order.

But when I do, and my stomach touches the chilled countertop of the island with my breasts crushed against it and my palms flat atop it, a quake shudders my body. It draws a small moan out of me at the same time as the sound of a sharp breath dances into my ears from behind me.

My eyes squeeze shut momentarily. My form trembles again at that affected sound. It grows so acutely aware of his presence that even the smallest of steps he takes closer to me, and the most silent of noises manages to puncture my ears.

As I feel the nearness of his body, my eyes reopen and my teeth dig into the lower lip, anticipation taking over my body. When his finger lazily traces from the nape of my neck to the lower of my spine, my back arches, my breasts push further into the counter.

His hot breath fans against the side of my face when his form presses against mine and another shudder bolts through me.

"Better hold tight, *nena*," he croaks.

The instant his fingers comb through the length of my hair, he fists a handful of it, using the hold to tilt my chin up.

"Tell me, Ley, do you want me to spank this sweet ass of yours?"

"Yyy-yes," I breathe out, the need clogging my throat for a beat before I successfully let the word out.

"You do, don't you?!"

Without any preamble whatsoever or any warning, his hand lands on my bare ass cheek, drawing a whimper out of me. However, when his palm begins rubbing at the sizzling flesh soon after his smack, it turns into a clear mewl.

"Fuck…"

The stinging of his swat burns my skin. But it burns in such a delicious way that I push my butt more into him, earning me yet another one.

MASON

Doce Xesús!

(*Sweet Jesus!*)

I have lost my fucking mind. I am past the brink of insanity. I have crossed that line with flying colors like I sprinted for it as if my life depended on it.

Doce Xesús, the sounds that surge out of her throat when my palm lands on her. How she pushes her ass further into my hand. And the imprints of my palm on her flesh? Marvelous.

My cock aggressively pushes against the zipper of my jeans, weeping to be left out of the cage. It is so hard that it aches and if I continue spanking her ass, I'll fucking come in my boxers.

"I fucking love this sweet ass," I rasp, giving it a tight squeeze. "It gets me so hard when I see you stubbornly strutting away."

"Is it just my ass that gets you hard?"

The tease in her question is heavy and as clear as the day is long.

"This sassy mouth of yours is another thing that gets me hard." As though to prove it, I push my erection into the side of her ass cheek and a groan crawls up my throat. "Though—side note—I'm dying to see how sassy you are with your mouth full of my cock."

"Fuck, Mase. I'm going crazy here," she gripes, drawing her hips back against my dick.

"You and me both, *nena*. You and me both."

Following my agreement, the palm that kept caressing her

butt cheek after I swatted it, now lifts and collides a second later with her other cheek, only to land on it immediately after.

Thwack.

Thwack.

Not even a small ounce of finesse or gentleness present in my action.

"Better start counting, *miña dozura*, because I believe you dared me that I don't have the nerve to smack this tight ass until you can't sit down without remembering just how your ass burned under my palm."

"And I believe you told me you'll have me bent over your knees," she reminds in a sultry voice, her neck craning so she can look at me over her shoulder.

With a grin on my face, I place the pad of my thumb on the middle of her back, savoring the anticipation that quivers her body. But it has nothing on the shudder that runs through her exquisite form when I lower my thumb down her spine and pause when I reach the cleft of her cheeks, rimming her tight hole lightly.

Interesting, I wickedly think to myself.

"Oh, fuck," she croaks, her head snapping back as the melodious sound enters my ears.

Slowly, I lower it between her legs, finding her opening.

"*Joder, nena!* You're so fucking wet. Is this all because of me?"

"You know it is."

The pad of my finger draws circles around her opening, gathering some of her excitement before they drop a fraction lower until her clit is under my thumb. I immediately begin rolling the pad over the bundle of nerves. In response, her red ass cheeks tremble, her legs shake and I grin to myself, relishing that I've been the one to do that.

"Holy hell, Mase!"

One more circle around her clit has her close to the brink, and I draw my hand back, taking a couple of steps in retreat.

A complaining moan pushes up her throat, and she spins around, her small tits giving a little bounce. They only distract me for a tick though before I lift my gaze to her face. My heart drops when my eyes connect to her green orbs, realizing what must go through her mind at my sudden withdrawal.

"I want you over my knees," I rush to clarify, my chin lifting to point at the sofa in the living room.

Once Ensley registers my words, her chest deflates, letting out a heavy breath.

"I thought you're gonna..."

"Too far gone."

At that revert, I bring my hand up and suck on the arousal that coats my thumb. Her excitement.

"So fucking sweet," I groan, my eyes closing to revel in her taste, my mind a mess. "Bend over. I'm gonna eat out your cunt before I continue smacking your ass."

There's no holding back. My mouth runs on the filthiest of functions, the uncloaked desire for Ensley pumping in my veins. My body wants to touch as much of her as it can as though it wants to collect all the memories possible of her because we are a ticking timebomb.

"Do you want my mouth on your pussy, Ley?"

Her head nods eagerly.

Yet, that's not a good enough answer for me.

"Words, *nena*. I want words."

"Yes," she chokes out.

A grin plays at the corners of my lips when she spins back around and displays her ass as she bends over the island's counter. She looks absolutely breathtaking bent in half for my roving gaze.

Ensley's at my mercy and she enjoys every second of it. So why disappoint?

In the blink of an eye, I eat the distance between us and stop when my body leans forward, hovering over hers, while my cock pushes against her splendid ass.

My lips drop to her shoulder before my eyes follow the ink on her left shoulder. They rest on the tattoo for a few moments, unable to unglue from it for some reason.

"Tiger or tigress?" I hear myself asking when I make out the design.

"Tigress."

After she gives me her answer in the form of a whisper, my fingers trace around the ink, something about it inciting some sort of molten hot feeling within me. A possessiveness I can't wrap my head around, especially not when my heart pounds a million miles a minute in my chest as though already knowing the meaning behind it and waiting for my mind to catch on.

Instead of pondering on it, though, I shake my head and my fingers dust down her spine again, savoring the effect my caress has on her.

"Legs farther apart," I murmur in her ear. "Let me see how wet you are."

With one last kiss on her right shoulder this time, I take another step back, watching her.

"Get on top. I want you on your hands and knees."

At my instruction, my eyes follow her reaction. And like the few times before, her body doesn't disappoint, and my gaze burns her.

With one hand lowering to unbuckle my belt, then to unbutton and undo the zipper of my jeans, I pull the denim down enough to slip that very hand inside my boxers and grab my aching cock. Because there's no doubt that my entire body hurts with all that consuming need.

Her back straightens and her head cocks to the side so she can look over her shoulder. When she does and she holds my eyes for a beat, before they travel down my body to where my palm wraps around my heavy dick, tugging at it, her stare catches fire. The unmitigated yearning I find in her gaze and the way she slicks her lips by darting her tongue over them is my fucking undoing.

When she turns to face me—her naked body on full display—and she strolls toward me with a wicked grin on her face, that is the instant I'm ready to sign my goddamn capitulation. Her bare hips move left and right, right and left, and for once I don't know where to look first because my eyes go into overdrive as they travel up and down her form.

However, what unhinges me is when she drops to her knees in front of me, taking my jeans and boxers down with her, while my hand lets go of my length.

During the first moment of freedom, my heavy cock springs free, a bead of pre-come coating the tip. The ache in my dick is torturous as it is so hard that I can easily use it to pound nails around the house.

"Ley," I caution, clenching my jaw tightly.

"Just a taste," she replies.

MISHA BLAKE

Her hand wraps around me without the smallest fraction of hesitation. Simultaneously, her mouth lowers to the tip of my cock, her tongue darting over the crown, licking at the pre-come.

"*Joder*," I curse aloud, my head throwing back at that soft action.

"How's my sassy mouth doing?"

The quip in her sultry voice draws a guttural groan from deep within my chest. And when her lips part, they cover the mushroom head of my cock before the length begins disappearing inside her mouth inch by inch. At that sight, my mouth falls open with a savage grumble surging out of me.

"*Merda*, Ley, stop!"

She doesn't listen, though.

Her splendid mouth takes me deeper and deeper until the tip of my cock reaches the back of her throat. On that action, my hands ball into fists at my sides, attempting to fight the pleasure.

Yet, when she withdraws and then takes me to the back of her throat again, holding there still for a blink or two, everything in me snaps. My hand hastens with the speed of lightning to the nape of her neck, grabbing a handful of her long hair.

"*Carallo, nena*. You take my cock so good," I groan, tightening my fingers around her hair. "Relax that throat a little more for me."

She's swift to listen to my instruction and, on the next swallow, my length is taken so deep that my knees nearly give way, and my hips buck lightly. There's no need for the hand in her hair to keep her down on my length because she does it herself, but I still tighten my fingers around her hair. Her hands bolt to my ass cheeks and her nails dig into my skin, while she holds herself still again with my cock lodged down her throat. Not only does she do that, she does it while she keeps her eyes linked to mine like she doesn't want to miss the smallest of reactions.

"Mmm…"

She *mmm*'s.

Ensley fucking *mmm*'s.

She doesn't only suck my cock, she savors it.

My balls ache and my length throbs in her mouth.

"*Fódeme!*"

("*Fuck me!*")

I am unable to recognize my own voice as I groan the words aloud. Sound that blends with Ensley's moan. That together with what her mouth does to me have me so fucking gone, with the pleasure amalgamating in my balls.

When Ensley pulls back from my cock, her gasp for air pierces my ears. The proud smile plays on her lips when my brow quirks in a silent gesture that tells her how impressed I am. However, when she goes to wrap her mouth around me again, my hand tightens in her hair, preventing her from advancing.

"You had your taste. Now it's my turn," I rasp in a guttural voice, not bothering any longer to hide the effect she has on me.

Letting go on the hold I have on her hair, both hands now hook under her armpit, and I bring her to her feet. Though, I know that won't be for long because after I stare into her hungry green gaze for a second, I have all the answers I need.

Nothing will stop us this time because all better judgments are out the window, getting swallowed by the night's wind.

After I kick to the side the denim around my ankles, in one fluid motion, I spin Ensley around and bring her back flush to my front.

My throbbing length pushes into her ass, and she rolls her hips over it shamelessly.

"You want my cock inside your cunt, don't you, Ley?" I whisper before my teeth dig lightly into the shell of her ear.

Her answer is a nod.

"That'll have to wait."

Once these four words leave my mouth, one arm goes over her chest while the other goes between her legs from behind, picking her up and carrying her to the island. I set her down on the worktop, her sweet ass in my face while she's on her hands and knees.

The beast inside me has been unleashed.

No more messing around.

Not until I have her shaking and quivering beneath my touch, coming on my fingers and tongue over and over again.

I'm a man on a mission now.

My mission: to take as much from Ensley as I possibly can.

No holding back.

No backpedaling.

MISHA BLAKE

Allowing myself to be weak for the second time in my thirty-five years of age. Permitting myself another moment of debility with the woman who reigns over my heart and thoughts as much as I hope I do over hers—or at least just now.

"Elbows and tits to the counter, Ley," I demand, swatting her tight butt cheeks, one and promptly after its pair, no proem or warning.

The crimson tint on her skin brings me a twisted feeling of satisfaction. Twisted because I shouldn't be relishing the fact that I thwacked her flesh. However, the pleasure-filled sounds she let out then—same as now—play at my elation. Moreover, knowing that it is my fucking mark on her body, only skyrockets my level of satisfaction.

"Lean forward and give me your ass."

Although she goes to do my bidding on that second instruction, my level of patience hits rock bottom. So I press a hand in the middle of her back, pulling a surprised yelp out of her while I prompt her to drop to her elbows while her luscious ass is in the air.

"Spread your legs farther apart."

This time around, she's swift to comply, parting her legs wider. All the while, my hands are on her butt cheeks, kneading and squeezing, wrenching moan after moan from her chest.

And she isn't quiet.

No, Ensley is fucking loud. She holds back nothing or cares that she might wake up tomorrow with no voice, or that the screams the walls of the house down and that perhaps our neighbors hear her.

Nope, nothing matters to her.

"Fucking beautiful," I compliment, taking in the sight before me while I make sure to snap a mental picture of this.

"Mase."

The way she whispers my nickname on a lust-filled suspire is a plea. A goddamn supplication. One that spurs me on. My head leans forward and dives in between her cheeks after I spread them open using the hold I already had on her ass. My tongue swirls over her sleeked entrance, her arousal teasing my taste buds.

So goddamn sweet.

She tastes like heaven.

I must have died and made it there.

"Holy fuck," she cusses, trying to pull away.

I keep her still, digging my fingers into her flesh some more while I fuck her with my tongue. No mercy whatsoever, but plain, utter claim in my actions.

"Mase... Oh, God!"

Her knees buck at the leisure attack. But when my hand lowers just beneath her left butt cheek and my thumb zeroes in on her clit, pressing tenderly against it before it begins moving in circles, she shamelessly pushes more into my touch.

My other hand swats her ass.

The need to consume her so completely and work her up so thoroughly takes over me, clouding my brain and stopping everything around me.

Right here and now, there's only Ensley and me, and our need for each other.

"So fucking sweet. This cunt is pure addiction, Ley," I whisper against her core, blowing air on her clit.

Another series of moans roll out of her and her body quivers vehemently.

"I've been dreaming of this moment for so fucking long, *nena*. I want to taste every inch of you."

Flattening my tongue, I lap at her arousal in an attempt to take my fill of her. Though, I know that won't happen. So I continue taking and taking, lapping and swirling my tongue at her center. Meanwhile, my thumb doesn't let up either, teasing her bundle of nerves while Ensley shakes and trembles.

My mouth travels upward and my tongue circles her back entrance, the erotic sounds that escape Ensley only serving as my encouragement to keep pleasuring her—not that I plan to stop anytime soon. Simultaneously, I twist my hand at the wrist to be able to still play with her clit and push a finger inside her.

Leisurely, I lick at her tight hole that puckers under my touch, and one single digit inside of her cunt turns into two. They move in and out of her with no hurry, wanting to drag this moment out for as long as I can.

"Mas...Mason!"

My name has never sounded better than now. Sultry and lude while it rolls off her tongue.

"Your pussy feels so good, *nena*. It clutches my fingers so tight."

While my mouth moves along the curve of her left ass cheek, kissing her skin before it moves to its pair, I remove my thumb from her clit. I do that only to then line a third digit at her entrance right by the other two, continuing to finger-fuck her. Suddenly I feel so desperate to have her come. Probably just as desperate as she is for a release since her hips keep pushing against my touch, chasing the orgasm on her own.

"Give it to me, Ley. Come for me," I urge, throwing my other arm around her, circling her waist tightly until I home in on her clit that I tweak between my thumb and index.

That does it.

Her body catches fire and begins riding the waves of the orgasm that hits powerfully, her forehead hitting the palm she has splayed on the countertop.

With my fingers still inside her, moving in and out, slower this time, her inner muscles clenching and releasing around them, I watch with marvel just how beautiful she is when she breaks apart at the seams.

More than that, I memorize all the sounds she makes while she comes. How she pants. How she moans. How she curses. How she screams my name.

"You're gonna be the death of me, Ley. But I'll be damned if I won't die a happy man just because I bore witness to this moment."

As I speak the words, my index and thumb let go of her sensitive clit and the three fingers of my other hand pull out of her. They glisten with the proof of her climax, and I can't help the urge to bring them to my mouth.

Just as my tongue darts over the fingers coated in her arousal, Ensley turns her head a little to the side, her hazy green gaze watching me through half-hooded eyes.

I relish her excitement, licking my digits clean, and a groan crawls up my throat at the same time as Ensley's own moan fills the air.

Once I savor her taste, I wrap my arms around her form, pick her up and bring her to my chest. I carry her through the kitchen and down the three steps that descend into the living room.

My cock throbs heavily between my legs as I walk. I also begin praying to all things holy that I'll make it to the sofa without tripping over my own two feet since all my blood drained from every vein in my body and conglomerated in my groin. It is so fucking painful and watching Ensley come apart has me aching even more because nothing can compare to that sight.

Like a man on a mission, I don't stop until I sit down on the sofa with her naked body straddling my lap, pressed against my half-naked one.

"Can you take off your t-shirt?" She mumbles against my chest, her voice feeble from the force of the orgasm.

"Wanna feel me, *nena*? Wanna feel my skin against this beautiful skin of yours?"

I don't wait for an answer, wanting to feel her with no layer between us as much as she wants. So bringing a hand back, I grab a handful of my t-shirt and pull it over my head. When my ink-covered flesh touches hers, I swear I can hear a hiss. My pulse pumps into my body with a speed I don't think I've ever experienced.

As I wrap my arms around her naked back, destroying any fraction of a gap between us, my heart thrums wildly. It stubbornly thunders in my chest, meeting each one of Ensley's beats.

And with her in my arms is the instant when everything ceases to exit. If I thought when I had her pussy on my tongue that it all stopped, I was wrong because it just hit a pause. But now, it stops. Nothing else matters but the woman between my arms. Nothing else apart from how right she feels in my arms as though she belonged there all along.

"*Cristo*, Ley. What are you doing to me, baby? Why can't I stay away from you?" I wonder aloud, kissing her shoulder while her head leans on mine.

Ensley's heart thunders against my chest, reverberating in my own body with its intensity. Or maybe it is mine that rages against her at the closeness and it is mine that hers echoes.

Gently, my hand moves up and down her spine, while the other keeps brushing her long, brunette hair away from her back.

My lips press against her shoulder again.

"You didn't…"

"It's okay, baby," I interrupt, angling my head to press my lips against the column of her neck this time. "Tonight, it was all about you."

"Aren't you aching?"

Ensley draws back a little, her gaze locking onto mine. Her shift in my lap snatches a grumble out of me. What has my dick twitching even more is the fire burning in her green eyes.

ENSLEY

My stare holds Mason's chocolate one. The intensity and lust I find there darken his eyes so much that they turn into a wicked inky color. A dark depth that has my heart skip a beat and my body tremble.

"I'm in fucking purgatory, *nena*, but I'll take care of it later."

His confession is filled with pure honesty. One that is clear in his features too, not only in his voice. The ache is also evident on his face.

"Will you think of me?"

"*Joder*, Ley! You're killing me right now," he complains in a guttural groan. "To answer your question, I always think of you. I've jerked off so many times at the thought of you. Imagining you in so many positions, taking my cock in your sweet cunt, and sucking me off. But *fódeme*, *nena*, nothing compares to the way you swallowed me down your pretty, tight throat."

A sound that is half-gasp and half-moan crawls up my throat at his words, and his cock jerks between our pressed bodies.

"I thought of you while I jacked off, just like you thought of me when you were touching that sweet clit of yours."

The breath I take clogs my throat and I nearly choke, while I blink several times at him in disbelief. Meanwhile, a smirk breaks on his lips and the wickedness in his gaze doesn't ebb.

"I saw you, *nena*," he begins. "The other day in the shower when you were touching yourself. I saw you and heard you moaning my name."

My mouth falls slack, and my gaze widens in shock.

"*Mason, oh, Mason,*" he mocks on a really bad impression of me, voice more high-pitched than deemed necessary.

I smack his tattooed chest.

At the same time, though, a giggle still tumbles out of me and Mason smiles. Not a grin, but a genuine smile that reaches his eyes.

"I don't sound that way."

"You're right. You're way louder than this."

His teasing tone brings heat to my cheeks and my palms raise to cover my face. However, as though he knows what I'll do, his hands wrap around my wrists, halting me.

After my gaze drops to where his hands touch me, it then travels back to the only pair of eyes that has always brought me calm and tranquility, and a lot of love.

It is on that thought that a feeling of guilt assails, and I avoid his gaze because I'm lying to the man before me. Though with the best of intentions at heart, it is still a lie.

Nevertheless, the ponders don't stay for long in my mind because the softness of his lips presses against my forehead and my eyes close.

"Where did you go, *nena?*"

His thumb dusts over my lower lip and I reopen my eyes, meeting his once again. We silently hold each other's gaze, only the sounds of our heartbeats and our breaths filling the air. There's a little duel between our stares, mine daring his while his challenges mine.

But not a tick later, Mason's hand goes to the back of my head, grasping a handful of my hair. His other hand cradles my cheek, and he keeps my gaze for a moment, before he curses under his breath and uses the hold to lean me forward, bringing my lips to his.

Even if I tried to fight him and push him away—not saying that I'd want to do that—, I know it is impossible to do so because I fall victim to the sheerness of his lips. The kiss is as bruising as he's used me to. Just as consuming. Just as vicious as he thrusts his tongue through my lips, and I can't amass any ounce of energy to withdraw even if I tried.

As I fall prey to the kiss and let him in control of my mouth, I will my hand to act. After a try or two, it travels down the hardness of his abdomen muscles and in between our bodies. It wraps around his rock-hard cock and a groan crawls up his throat and joins our kiss, prompting my next action.

Withdrawing for a moment, I watch Mason's eyes drop to where I touch him. That is when I let go, earning a complaining growl out of him. One that turns into a full-on groan when I run my fingers through my wetness, before I wrap it back around his steel rod length, moving slowly up and down, using my own arousal to sleek my pumping.

"*Joder*, that was fucking hot."

His voice is a throaty sound as he speaks. So husky that I almost don't recognize it.

But I'd be damned if I don't love every second of my effect on him. How he twitches in my hand with each glide down.

"Harder. Squeeze a little harder, *nena*."

That is all the encouragement I need to tighten my hold and slide my hand up and down faster. And that is all it takes for Mason to put his mouth back onto mine as we both let out a groan.

My spine tingles when his hand drops from my cheek between us, zeroing in on my clit. There is no delay in his action as he pinches it between his fingers or circles it with his thumb. He has no mercy on me as he works me up toward another orgasm while I continue pumping him.

Our pants begin dancing in the air.

My loud moan soon ricochets across the room.

His deep, rough grumble joins in too, the sound of it shuddering my form.

Unmitigated rapture is what we experience when my body reaches its peak and Mason's hot come spurts on our stomachs.

"*Carallo*," he curses aloud, his forehead touching mine while we attempt to catch our breath.

"You've made quite a mess," I reproach in jest.

"That's because you jacked me off too good."

At his revert, his fingers run through my folds.

I close my eyes at the sensation and when they open again, I find him licking at the fingers that he just pulled out of me.

"You know, for an adult, you spend an awful amount of time with your fingers in your mouth."

A grin pulls at the corners of his lips.

"Only when I've got the taste of your sweet pussy on them, Ley," he quips with a wink.

With a smirk of my own, I twirl my finger over the come on his stomach and bring it to my lips. All the while, Mason's dark stare follows every single one of my movements. Hence why I add as much seductiveness to the way I slide my index coated in his come into my mouth.

"You're fucking killing me here, *nena*."

"Not my intention."

"Absolutely your intention," he rebuts.

I nod at that with eagerness.

Before any of us get to say anything else, the loud sound of a ringtone fills the air from somewhere behind me and Mason looks over my shoulder.

His hand gently taps my bare ass, and he drops me to the cushioned sofa.

"That should be Mom," he speaks and gets up.

Reaching for the blanket atop the sofa, I cover my body with it while I don't miss a step that Mason takes toward the kitchen. My eyes follow his broad shoulders and muscular back, his taut, fine ass, his thick thighs and long legs. I shamelessly check out the man sauntering away from me butt naked, the confidence and dominance in his strides breathtaking.

He picks up his phone from the kitchen counter, his eyes moving over the screen.

"It's Luke," he tells me. "Do you think your bother has some sixth sense that tells him his best friend just smacked his sister's ass red and she jacked him off?"

The implication in his voice and the wink he sends me across the room have my cheeks turn pink.

"I think his best friend did more than smack his sister's ass," I quip.

Shaking his head at my tease with a smirk playing on his lips, he stretches his arm to grab a tea towel. The ringtone quiets and Mason brings the phone to his ear. He wipes at the come on his abdomen and winks, while he listens to what my brother says on the other end of the call.

My gut churns when I take in the hardness of his features. Right before my eyes, I see the snap in him. How his gaze turns glacial. How his lips press into a thin, angry line. How the glimpse I had of my husband—the jester, easy-going man I fell in love with—vanishes and gets replaced by that controlled, guarded and cautious version of him that he keeps portraying.

From where I sit, I note the color leaving his face as his chest rises and falls rapidly. The towel he used to wipe at his release now drops to the floor and that very hand balls in a fist at his side. As his body becomes taut and tense, it downs on me.

Something must be wrong.

Something must be very wrong because otherwise I can't give myself an explanation as to why his stare turns icy-cold and he's like a volcano getting ready to erupt.

It is on this realization that, without thinking twice, I get up and rush across the living room, up the three steps and into the kitchen.

My hand holds the blanket tightly around my body as I look at him. I am all aware of what he sees in my eyes—worry.

"Which hospital?"

His gaze is ice-cold, but the desperation and red-hot anger in his voice hiss in the air. My visual and decerning faculties overheat at the view of the man before me and the possibility of what it all means.

With the phone still at his ear caught between his cheek and shoulder, he fishes his boxer briefs and puts them on, launching rapidly after his jeans once the cotton material covers his groin and wraps around his thick thighs.

"Mase, what's going on?"

His stare lifts to me and his jaw ticks. A sight that breaks my skin in a multitude of goosebumps making me believe it is so cold in the room all of a sudden. Though I know he is the one who causes that chillness.

The phone drops on the island's top with such a loud thud that I would be surprised if the screen is still intact.

It is not the only thing that drops, though. Because my heart lurches to the pit of my stomach at the image before me. Especially when he holds my gaze for more than I am able to hold.

"There's been an accident," he says, his baritone almost broken.

That's all he tells me while he buttons and zips up his jeans, buckling up his belt, before he begins striding rapidly across the kitchen.

However, that sentence causes cold chills to run down my spine.

"There's been an accident."

The four words I started to hate the most since I opened the door for my father to tell me that my husband is in the hospital. Those dreaded words I've learned to loathe during the three months I've stayed by my husband's side, waiting and praying for him to wake up. But with all the energy I can garner, I push that thought away.

"Acc...Accident?"

"Yes, Ensley, an accident," he spits abruptly, turning to face me for a beat. "My Mom is in the hospital now. It rained a little on that side of town... She might have lost control of the car and went off the road."

Anguish can't only be heard in his voice, but it can be felt. It can also be seen in his hardened features as he runs a hand through his hair in distress.

When he turns away and rushes to the sofa, picking up the abandoned t-shirt, I hear the mumbling and angry cursing in Galician, though I can't make out what he says.

My eyes sting while I stand glued to the spot and I know that if I make the slightest of moves, I'll keel over.

His words roll in my mind as memories assail me.

The same flashbacks and thoughts that began spiraling in my head just moments ago. Only now they attack with a fiercer power, not letting up that easily. The feeling of despair and helplessness. The consuming wretchedness and agony. The images that have seared themselves into my head after watching my husband lay in a hospital bed for three months.

"I should have never let her drive home by herself."

His timber ebbs the wave of memories and wrenches me to the reality of here and now.

Breathing in and out, however, I collect myself and bend over to grab my clothes.

"How is she?"

"I don't fucking know, Ley. At the moment she's getting checked up by the doctors."

My head moves in a gentle assent before I fix my bra on and slide the thong up my legs.

"I'm coming with you."

There's no room for argument in my voice. Considering the small ounce of relief that crosses his handsome face for a brief tick, he wants me there with him.

"I'm gonna put on a pair of jeans and get my jacket. I'll be right down."

Without delay, I rush out of the kitchen and up the stair. Heavy steps are right behind me and I look over my shoulder to see Mason coming up too.

"I need to get a pair of socks and my jacket too."

Again, I nod and stop in the middle of the staircase, turning to face him. My eyes lock onto his when I look down at him since he's a step below and I cup his face.

"She will be okay, Mase. She's a fighter just like her son is."

"Thank you, Ley. I didn't know how much I needed you to say you'll be there with me until I heard you say it," he mutters, giving me a small smile.

"Always, baby. Whatever you need, I'm here for you. Now and always."

With that said, we both continue our ascent and I go to my room, while he goes to his.

Remaining still in the doorway, I watch him enter what used to be our bedroom and a heavy sigh surges past my lips at all the lies that have been told.

That is a thought I don't ponder on for too long nonetheless, and I enter my room, hurrying to the dresser. Once I slip on the pair of jeans, socks and a pair of trainers, I put on my jacket and speed down the stairs, and into the garage.

Mason waits for me already on his bike, the leather jacket stretching nicely over his back muscles while his feet are propped to the floor, the seat caught in between his thick thighs. He has his helmet on with the visor up and his gaze follows me as he presses the button on the small remote control for the garage door to lift up.

By the time I make it to him, the motor roars to life and I stop by the motorcycle, letting Mason slip the spear helmet on.

"Hold on tight, alright?"

I nod and put the visor down just as he does so too, and I climb behind him, my arms wrapping around his waist tightly.

It will be a way over-the-speed-limit kinda ride.

And Mason doesn't hesitate to prove to me that my belief is true when the garage door is barely all the way up and he rides away. He presses the button once again for them to close back up and we wait for a moment or two until they are low enough.

The instant they are, he pulls into the light evening traffic, swerving past any car with speed, but great control also.

As a mere kid he used to watch a lot of motorcycle racing, so it is safe to say that Mason has always been a fan of them. So much so that when he turned eighteen, he replaced his car with one. He's learned everything there is to know about them. Hence why when something happens and it needs a repair, he's the one to do it. Which, by the way, he looks extremely hot doing it.

Surely this is why I can say with confidence that I trust Mason will bring us to the hospital in one piece, in spite of the maniacal way he rides it through traffic, grazing a couple of the red lights.

A street fogs into another and into the next and the next one after that. All throughout, I hold hope. Hope that Aracely is not hurt and that it is just a scare for all of us. Hope that subdues the whirlwind of thoughts threatening to take over my mind.

It is a feeling of hope that I grasp tightly onto, especially when we climb off his bike and run toward the entrance of the hospital.

My heart beats a thousand miles per hour.

It thunders in my chest as loudly and powerfully as a storm. Simultaneously, my gut churns and tightens, and my breath gets clogged in my throat.

Unimaginable is what Mason must go through. Although the distress and uneasiness are noticeable on his face, for the moment, he keeps himself cool and collected.

Aware I am that it is just a matter of time until he will explode. He is a ticking time-bomb, and the question isn't if he'll blow up, but more like when.

Heedlessly, my hand reaches for his and I squeeze it lightly. A way to tell him that I'm here for him. That I'm not going anywhere.

When he gives me a gentle squeeze in return, I know it is his way of saying that he knows and appreciates I am there. What surprises me, however, is that when I go to withdraw my hand, his clasps around mine a fraction stronger, before he laces our fingers together.

MASON

In the typhoon that takes over my brain, her touch is my only solace. From the second her slender fingers wrap around my hand in our rushed stride inside the hospital, I sense the calmness the contact brings. To the extent that when she attempts to pull her hand away, I hold on tight, intertwining our fingers.

My entire being clearly needs all that tranquility that she gives to me, and my body doesn't hesitate to take it. Even as we race for the emergency room, I still keep my hold on her hand.

When we walk through the ER doors, my eyes search for my best friend and his fiancée who were already on their way when they called after Jace Walker—Luke's and Ensley's cousin—phoned him to let him know that my mom was being taken to the hospital because there has been an accident. Jace is the one who drove by on his way from his parents' place and saw the car on the side of the road. He also called the emergency services and hasn't left her side.

I don't ponder for too long on the reason why he didn't call me directly, I'm just glad he drove by when he did.

For crying out loud, it seems like we're cursed. The Carters are fucking damned with these hospitals. After I spent three months in one, having my mother here, it's pushing the limits of my tolerance.

Seconds click by before my eyes land on a familiar face after they travel from one corner of the room to the next and to the next. Ticks that feel like hours as my heart thrums in my chest a million miles an hour. At the same time, my mind doesn't ease off on the monsoon that has my thoughts whirled and the ringing in my ears doesn't ebb.

"There's Jace," I hear myself speak and the scintilla of relief is evident in my voice that represses the continuous ringing.

Tugging at Ensley's hand, I lead us up to Jace and when we round the reception desk to where he is, I note Luke and Ella are there too, sitting down in the chairs.

"How's my mom? What do the doctors say?"

With the questions firing out of me filled with distress, the three pairs of eyes move over us. They dart between Ensley and me, jaws almost touching the floor. However, when they look at one another before reverting their attention to us, they can't fight the grins that play at the corners of their lips.

"*Non fodes conmigo,*" I curse aloud. "One of you fucking tell me how my mother is doing."

The anguish in my tone is replaced with anger aimed at the three of them who stare at us like idiots.

It takes Ensley trying to pull her hand away once again for me to realize the reason they look at us like we've grown two heads each right before their eyes is exactly because I hold her hand.

"*Polo amor de Deus, meu fillo.* I didn't know I raised a son with such a filthy mouth."

Ensley's touch brought me a great deal of calmness and I would've climbed the walls had it not been for her. However, in this situation with the anguish being caused by my mother's state, hearing her voice from behind me annihilates any ounce of worry.

The woman next to me chokes on thin air and my head snaps toward her for a second, noting the redness of her cheeks and I know what my mother's words made her think about. Just how filthy my mouth got with her today.

Giving her a wink, I let go of Ensley's hand and turn rapidly to take in my mom.

At the sight of her, my eyes move swiftly up and down her to check if she's alright and if she isn't, why is she standing in front of me instead of being in bed.

"I'm fine," she speaks, her kind brown eyes gentle as they lock onto mine while her lips tip in an even softer smile.

With an unyielding gaze, I continue looking at her. First, I take in her face, noticing that there are a couple of scrapes on her forehead. Then I zero in on the sling on her left arm. Apart from that, there's no other injury visible to the naked eye.

"*Mamá*."

The inflection of my voice is an evident manner in which I call her out on her bullshit.

"So the sling is just a new fashion statement?" I counter with jest, pointing with my chin at her arm.

As my hand drops Ensley's, in a couple of steps I'm in front of my mom and I give her a tight hug, making sure not to hurt her.

There's a little wince that comes out of her and I draw back right away, giving her a stern glare.

"I'm fine, Mason. I promise I am."

"She is."

Those two words have me look beside her and it is when I notice the woman standing next to my mother dressed in uniform and with a doctor's coat on. A woman I haven't acknowledged until she spoke, busy with my perusal of my mom.

"I'm Doctor Adams, I've consulted your mom," she introduces herself. "Don't worry, Aracely is well. Her left arm suffered most of the impact, but the brace will keep it steady. Just stop her from making too much effort."

"Absolutely certain? She didn't bribe you with one of her delicious dinners so you can convince me that she's fine, did she?"

"Is it so hard to believe your mother is a badass?" My mother asks with a frown on her face, her hand on her hip.

"Adams, if she didn't bribe you, I'm willing to take the bribe if it includes a side of that smart mouth besides the presence of a lovely woman."

My neck cranes and I look over my shoulder.

No, I glare over my shoulder.

Jace fucking Walker smirking at my mother while his eyes move over her, up and down.

"What the hell did you just say?"

"Relax, Carter!"

"Get anywhere near my mother and you'll know the taste of your own balls, Walker," I warn.

My best friend lets out a laugh while Ensley and Ella share a chuckle. Jace, on the other hand, doesn't find it all that amusing since I have just threatened to shove his balls down his throat. Moreover, he cringes.

To be completely honest, I would too. Just like any other man does when his dick and balls are threatened or when graphic images are pictured in his mind.

Protectively, my arm goes over Mom's narrow shoulders and my lips press to the top of her head.

"And to answer your question, I know for a fact just how much of a badass you are. I only want to make sure you're okay, *Mamá.*"

"I am, baby. I am."

Though her words are calm, there's something in my gut that tells me it isn't all alright. Not the way she makes it seem.

"I'm even better after what I've just seen."

At the teasing whisper and gentle jab of her elbow into my ribs, my gaze travels to meet Ensley's green one.

Damn if my breath isn't taken away by her.

Goddamn if my heart doesn't thunder in my chest.

Fuck if I'm not the slave of this woman.

Since I've realized that I love Ensley more than just my friend, there has been an inner battle between my heart and my mind. All that because I fell in love with someone out of my league. With somebody I didn't want to love me back because I didn't deserve her. I still don't, but goddammit, I want to.

"Life is short. If there's someone who knows just how short it is, it's me."

Mom's words from a few nights ago resound in my head. They echo sharper and louder at this moment than they did before. Perhaps because I've had enough of staying away—though what happened between us less than an hour ago is the exact opposite of me staying away. Or maybe it is because tonight's events and Mom's accident put everything into perspective.

Life is indeed short.

"I'm done being a coward," I mutter, my eyes staying locked onto that jaded hue that has me at its mercy.

There's a sweet, gentle smile forming at the corners of her lips and the breath I take leaves my lungs almost instantly. Because Ensley has been, is and will be the only woman able to do it with the smallest of actions. Just as much as she always gets my cock twitching with the faintest of moves.

"Can I take my mom home now, doc?" I ask her, garnering all my strength and power to will myself to break the eye contact with Ensley.

"We advised that Aracely should stay overnight for observations, which she refused. There doesn't appear to be any concussion or any internal bleeding. With the exception of her arm, all of the injuries sustained are superficial scrapes, so she can go home. But please get her to rest."

"We'll do that, doc. Thank you."

"I've recommended her a drug to take in case of pain. Doctor Walker already administered her one in the ambulance on their way here, so she shouldn't feel a lot of pain for a few good hours."

With that said and a nod, the doctor walks away.

"Gave us quite the scare, Ary," my best friend speaks, coming to us and pulling Mom into a hug. "Don't ever do that again."

Mom chuckles. "I'll try."

After Luke pulls away and Ella gives her a hug too, Ensley rushes for her. Mom's face softens as she brings her arm around her, and I can't fight the smile from forming on my face at the sight of the two women.

"*Miña querida rapaza.*"

("*My sweet girl.*")

"You're staying with us at least until you get well."

It isn't a question. The words that leave my mouth form a definite sentence that leaves no room for argument.

Although knowing my mother, I expect one just for the sake of it, it doesn't come. Instead, there's a curt nod of her head over Ensley's shoulder as the two hold each other.

Her agreement only strengthens the belief that everything isn't as right as she makes it seem. Not by a long shot. Which only causes my mind to whirl a thousand miles an hour in an attempt to find out what it is and why doesn't she just come outright and say it.

After all, we've never kept secrets from each other. Or at least not after I was old enough to be aware of certain things.

I let it go for now, though.

I do because it's been a long night and she needs the rest before I begin my inquisition.

"Call me if Ary doesn't feel well, a'right?"

"Will do. Thanks, Jace."

"No problem." He smiles and nods his head, turning to walk away.

My hand shoots and I grab his shoulder. It stops him from advancing and he cocks his head to the side to look at me.

"No, seriously, Jace. Thank you!"

He acknowledges my gratitude with yet another nod. "Nothing you wouldn't have done for me, brother." And then strides toward the exit.

"Thank you for being here. Both of you."

Luke comes next to me and pats my shoulder while his fiancée gives me a smile. "Come on, we'll give you a ride home."

"Take Mom and Ley with you, I'll be right behind you on my bike."

"You got it, brother."

With that, we all begin to walk toward the exit of the hospital while I pray to all things holy that I won't step foot in one ever again, especially for the people I love.

* * *

Less than half-hour later, Mom, Ensley and I enter the spare bedroom at the end of the hallway after I hit the light on the wall.

"Can we get you anything, *Mamá*?" I ask, eyeing her from head to toe, just to make sure that she's well.

"I'll bring you a pair of clothes to change into," Ensley offers.

Mom nods appreciatively. "Thank you, honey."

"Would you like me to bring you a tea as well?"

"Don't worry, Enz. Just the clothes are fine."

With that, Ensley leaves the room and I stand put. Meanwhile, Mom takes a seat on the bed and when her chin tilts so she can look up at me, there is something in her gaze I can't quite figure out. That before a smile splits her lips and her eyes gleam.

"So you and Ensley?"

"I don't know, *Ma*." A sigh crawls up my throat as I sit down next to her. "Ever since I woke up from a coma, all the feelings I remember having for Ensley aren't the same. They have heightened so much that I can't control them. I can't fight them like I used to, and the dissociative amnesia doesn't help in the slightest since I feel that, one way or another, they are memories of Ensley I keep blocking out."

Her right arm lifts and rests on my back while she pulls me to her. The softness of her lips presses on the side of my forehead.

"Always choose with your heart, Mason. Don't make a choice using your head because you'll wind up losing. Your head will try to find the rationality of things, but there's nothing rational and logical about love. Otherwise, we'd be able to choose who we fall in love with." She pauses for a beat as she draws back. "We don't get to choose that, our hearts do."

With a prolonged exhale, I lean forward and rest my elbows on the top of my thighs, my gaze aimed at the door Ensley walked through.

"But what if my choice will put her in danger?"

The question hangs in the air for a moment or maybe two, silence taking over the bedroom.

"Honey, he's out of our lives now," Mom states with vehemency. "He's been out of our lives for so long. We ran as far away as we could, and he won't be able to find us."

Her hand retreats from my back, but an instant later, it squeezes my much bigger one.

"Don't let Ensley slip through your fingers because of a *what if*."

But *what if* that said '*what if*' is the difference between life and death? What if it is the ounce that decides which way the balance slants toward—the thriving *forever* or the tragic *cessation*?

Footsteps quiet whatever ponder and thought that tumbles in my mind and a blink later, the woman my heart belongs to walks in my line of sight, my eyes traveling up and down the length of her body.

Heedlessly, my tongue slides out and darts over my lips, relishing the taste I still find soaked into them. Her taste. That sweet-as-honey tang that I'm addicted to.

While I savor her off my lips, my eyes follow her, and they don't miss the way she subtly rubs her thighs together. She is discreet when she does it, however, it is no match for my hungry, prodding gaze. There are a couple more things I don't miss. For instance, how her chest rises and falls. Or how her delicate throat bobs on a swallow.

I blink a couple of times and when I look beside me, I'm met with the empty spot where my mom sat. She must have gone to get changed whilst I was entrapped by the gorgeous brunette before me.

The sound of the running shower that travels from the hallway is my confirmation that Mom went to get ready for bed.

A smirk pulls at the corners of my lips, and I bring myself to my feet. Ensley takes instinctively a step back and my grin grows.

"Mason," she breaths out, my name a seductive melody on her lips.

"Ensley," I rasp back, holding her green gaze.

It is on a replay of my name that all my better judgment wooshes out the window, and realization settles within me. If I were a better man, I'd stay the hell away from her. But I am not.

Under the spell casted on me by her eyes, only one step in her direction has my control snap loose. All common sense and any fraction of restraint I have left now unchain. One singular step that brings me closer to her is enough to unleash the beast within me. Just like a beast held in a cage for too long, once it unshackles, I am aware I am an unhinged man.

It is only when I have Ensley only a breath away that one arm wraps around her waist and my other hand goes to the nape of her neck. Using the hold as leverage, I immediately bring her flush to me and only a low gasp manages to escape her before my mouth is on hers.

I don't kiss her like she's mine.

I don't move my mouth over hers as though she belongs to me.

I kiss her *because* she *is mine* and she *belongs to me.*

Because together or not, Ensley has always been mine and

belonged to me. Pushing her away or not, my heart has always been hers from the moment it learned how to beat for someone. Denying her or not, her heart has been mine. I know that now.

I know because there's no fighting this pull between us. Not anymore. Not ever.

As I draw back, my eyes search hers and I grasp hold of her hand, resting it on the left side of my chest for her to feel the erratic beating beneath her palm.

Lifting my hand, I place it atop her chest, the hammering I sense under my palm matching my own.

We are two imperfect hearts that only beat a perfect rhythm when they beat for each other.

ENSLEY

Warmth surrounds my lower body and I squirm on top of the mattress, looking to pull off the comforter. In my slumbered attempt to find the fabric covering me, my eyes snap open when my fingers thread through something soft. But it isn't the comforter.

My back lifts a little until I'm able to prop myself on the elbows, the coolish air in the room hissing at the contact with my hot, bare skin.

As my eyes meet a pair of chocolate ones in the dimly lit room, my heart skips at the wicked smirk playing on his lips. My thighs are apart and he's between them, his head hovering just above my stomach as he blows air over my flesh.

Last night, after we made sure Aracely has everything she needs and she went to sleep, Mason and I walked out of her room and stayed quietly in the faintly lit hallway with only the sound of our breathing and our heartbeats filling the air. That of course, until Mason lost all his patience and pushed me against the door of my bedroom, kissing the life out of me before he whispered just a breath away from my lips: *"I need you, nena. Let me hold you tonight"*.

But when I moved to open my bedroom door, he stopped me and tugged me into his instead—our bedroom. We showered quickly then slipped into bed and under the covers fully naked because we wanted to feel each other completely. After we only shared a few kisses and spooned, we fell asleep.

"Waking you took less time than I thought it will," Mason greets, his mouth pressing gently against my abdomen before his heated gaze rides along the length of my body. "Now, mind me not, *nena,*"

What time is it even?

It is a question that crosses my mind for a brief tick when I note the light darkness that still covers us.

Do I even care? Hell no, no I don't.

Especially not when my husband's mouth is between my legs.

"Think you can be quiet?"

And it is on this question that I realize exactly the main reason why the wonder about the time only exists in my mind for about a second. Not only because it is absurd to ask myself that while his lips are so close to my core that I can feel tehem. But exceptionally because the wickedness I note garnered in his eyes when he asks the question is a pledge for what's to come next.

"Judging by that dirty look on your face, I can't make any promises."

My body shudders at that unholy stare he gives me, his brown eyes darkening so much that the color of his irises blends into the same hue as his pupils.

"Oh, that's because I'm planning on doing very dirty things to you, Ley."

The promise in his voice weighs in the air and hovers over my body right before it plunges into me, shaking my form with the anticipation that skyrockets to a whole new level.

"Try and be quiet, and after I'm done with tasting this sweet cunt, I might give you my cock."

Mason doesn't allow me the smallest of chances to process his words because not a moment later, his head drops right at the junction between my legs. His mouth assails my core with no mercy, my head throwing back while a moan slips out of me. My back arches in response and my fingers grasp tightly onto the sheets. His lips are soft against my sensitive skin. His tongue hot as it circles my clit. His stubble grazing my flesh, a sweet contradiction to the gentleness of his mouth.

What he does with his mouth—how he nips, how he sucks on the bundle of nerves, how he licks me from the opening to the clit, how he flattens his tongue and laps at me, how he eats me out like I'm his last supper—should classify as illegal. And everything becomes a blur of pleasure when he slides his hands beneath my ass cheeks to bring me closer to his mouth. But said pleasure magnifies when his thumb finds my tight hole and presses against it lightly, circling while his tongue finds my entrance and thrusts inside me.

My hand flies to cover my mouth to muffle my moans while he fucks me with his tongue and the pad of his thumb teases my back entrance.

"I *need* you to suck me off while I eat out this pussy of yours and finger-fuck your ass," he rasps, pulling away from my center ever so lightly, his hot breath scorching my already blazing skin.

He *needs* me to suck him off.

Not *want*.

But *need*.

He *needs* my mouth on him.

An involuntary, complaining moan surges out of me when I lose the heat of his body. My frame, on the other hand, shudders when he smacks my ass cheek before he pats it lightly in a silent urge.

While Mason lays on his back, I push up and turn toward him. My roving eyes take him in. They move from his handsome face, down to his broad tattooed chest and thick, ink-covered arms that fold beneath his head, then over the six-packs of his abdomen.

Slowly, oh so agonizingly slow, it travels further down, following the well-defined "V", before it homes in on his thick, long, throbbing cock, a white bead of pre-cum on the swollen head.

There is no denying that Mason is a very well-endowed man, and I don't need to see any other dicks to know that mother nature has been very gifting with him. He hasn't only been gifted with panty-drenching looks and natural charm, capturing the attention of people wherever he goes because oblivious to the looks he gets from others I am not.

Mother nature's gift for him also extended to the thick and large member between his legs that is now straight and hard as a steel rod—for me. With all the foreplay, with how wet he gets me and although his thrusts are sleeked with my arousal, the walls of my pussy still stress to accommodate him.

Oh, man, I miss feeling the stretch of my inner muscles every time he slid inside me, filling me with all that thickness of his girth and thrusting so deep within me.

"Nena, get that cunt on my face and your mouth on my cock in the next two seconds before I lose all my patience and ever-loving mind. Do it before I play with you until you're so close that it feels like you're losing your mind just like I am right now. And before you get too excited, let me warn you that I won't let you come even if you beg me to."

With a smirk when I feel the burn of his swat on my skin, I push to my hands and knees, swinging my leg over him. Once I reach for his cock, I wrap my hand around his girth, my fingers unable to touch as I move them down, then back up.

"*Merda*," he breaths out.

His strong hands grasp hold of my ass, and he lowers me to his open mouth. The stubble peppering his cheeks scratches lightly against my skin. The sensation created by his mouth and that three-day-old beard makes it close to impossible to focus on the task at hand.

"Holy hell," I croak, my mouth so close to his cock.

Once my tongue darts over the pre-cum and the slightly salted tang seeps into my taste buds, I wrap my lips around his length and take him down my throat. Simultaneously, Mason's thick fingers push inside me without any preamble, and I moan around him. It is a sound that has him twitch in my mouth as he continues to play with me.

His fingers coax.

His mouth takes.

Together, they give.

And he drives me in a fast car to insanity with need.

Just like he always did, relishing in toying with me until I'm brought to the brink of losing my mind.

Mason strokes two fingers inside of me with his usual proficiency and curls them, working me up with wicked mastery.

Jesus, I missed feeling him. Not only the sexual element, the warp abandon, the possession, the touch. But I missed everything he makes me feel. All the emotions he awakes within me with his presence alone; emotions that run out of control. I miss how easy it is to laugh around him when his walls aren't miles high or his control with a tight lock on. I miss how easy it is for us to get lost and so wrapped in one another like the world outside doesn't exist.

In all truth and honesty, I miss us. I miss my husband and everything that we shared during our relationship, during our marriage. So much that I need to garner an ungodly amount of effort not to turn around and tell him the truth right here and now. Not to pull away and storm into the attic to bring down all the photo albums we have and splay them all out for him, begging him to remember me. Begging him to take a look at all the pictures and try to remember. *Me. Us.*

Knocking away all the thoughts, I focus on the present moment before all the guilt I hold assails stronger. I rivet my attention to what he makes me feel. To what he does to me and how he works me up so well. To the cock in my hand that throbs, pleading for release.

And who am I to deny that?

Without any drop of hesitation, I take him to the back of my throat and then pull back. But when I lower my mouth again, I relax my throat some more to wedge him deep. I hold still and flick my tongue over his length, moaning, before I draw back for air.

"Joder, nena. This sinful mouth of yours is made to swallow my cock."

The groan that ricochets out of him and across the room is a gruff, sexy noise, and I don't know what shakes my body to the core most. His voice. His breath against my skin. His fingers inside me. His words. Or maybe just a little—or hell of a lot more than a little—of all of the previously mentioned options. Whether it is one, the other or all of them together, I can't give a damn about solving that puzzle. Definitely not when I've got his dick jerking in my mouth and his fingers inside of me.

A moan tumbles past my lips and my body shakes, my inner walls clutching his fingers. On each drawback, the muscles tighten to hold him deep within me, and when he plunges them back in, they strain even harder.

I'm so close. So goddamn close that I can taste it.

"Suck and jack me off, *nena,*" he commands, his fingers pumping faster.

I follow the demand immediately, my hand moves in tempo with my mouth, using my saliva to smooth the pumping. My cheeks hollow, and I add extra suction to my lips while my small fist slides up and down his shaft with a tad more pressure, earning me a deep, guttural groan from him. A sound so erotic and lewd that has me smile around his length at the thought that it's me who causes him to lose control, to draw those carnal, bawdy euphonies out of his chest and past his lips.

While I let the sounds Mason makes guide and egg on my motions, he smacks my ass gently with his free hand, compelling a mewl to surge past my lips and around his girth. The vibrations from my throat convey to the thickness of him that throbs in my mouth.

"Fucking hell, Ley. I'm gonna come if you carry on like this."

As though the target of his mission shifts on that very acknowledgment, his fingers pull out of me. Before I get a chance to complain, he drags my arousal to my tight hole and rims it gently with his index finger. This time around, he doesn't stop at just circling it, instead he pushes in slowly.

"My woman always gets to come first." His tone is matter-of-factly. What he doesn't know—remember, actually—is that I am all au courant with that axiom.

"Holy... Fuck. Shit. Fuck, Mason," I cry out when he inserts two fingers inside me and begins to move them both simultaneously with the one in my ass, while his mouth latches for my clit.

Fucking hell!

Making love to Mason Carter has always been intense and dirty and fueled by wicked desire. Bondage, paddles, nipple and clit clamps, butt plugs and anal. During our relationship, we've done and tried them all.

Right here and right now, however, it is more passionate and ardent than ever. Each touch, caress, kiss and stroke are magnified a hundredfold. Just like the fire that burns within me, fiercely and violently, searing me to the bone.

Arching my back and pushing my ass further into his touch, I take his fingers deeper. Mason doesn't let up, working me faster with his mouth and digits, having me unable to focus on anything else apart from what he does.

"Mase...Mas...on," I moan, rolling his name off my tongue, closer to the brink.

"Now come for me, Ley."

And just like his permission to come serves as my encouragement, my orgasm doesn't delay. It surges through me right from my core and my body explodes, trembling and shuddering. So hard that my knees buck, and I almost fall forward. If it hadn't been for that tight hold he has on me and how his free arm circles my waist, I know I would've planted my face in the mattress.

Still shaking, his fingers pull out, but his tongue moves to my opening and follows me all the way through each ripple and wave of the orgasm that assails my body, licking me and lapping at my core.

"I *need* to be inside you, *nena*."

There is that *need* again.

That very need that pumps into our veins and flows into our hearts, fuels our bodies and overpowers our minds. That need that can't be denied or fought against.

Once I amass the energy that's been taken from me by the strong climax, I turn and straddle his lap. The hunger in his gaze is consuming and I don't hesitate to move over him, his length sliding through my folds. The thick mushroom head rubs against my clit as my orgasm sleeks the back and then forth movement of my hips.

"*Pidoche por favor, nena*, put me out of my misery and slip me inside you." The plea in his voice quakes my form and only consolidates the need he expressed before. That same need I see in his chocolate eyes that hold me captive while my hips roll.

"I need you inside me too. I need to feel you. Your skin against mine. Your lips on mine. Your—"

Without allowing me to finish my rant and in the blink of an eye, I'm with my back on the mattress and his body atop mine. There's no uncertainty in his gaze but pure determination as he props his body on one elbow by my head, his other arm traveling over my skin, setting it on fire. He finds my thigh and his scorching palm caresses lower. Eager to feel him closer, I let him hoist my leg over his waist.

All the while, his gaze stays locked onto mine as though seeking something. And that is something he doesn't hesitate to voice aloud.

"You've got a second to tell me to stop, *nena*. You've got a second before my cock is inside your cunt and I have you crying out my name. One second before all bets are off and I'll make you mine again."

In response to that, my hand slips between us and I wrap it around his heavy, hard length, nudging it at my entrance. Meantime, my other arm snakes around him. Beneath my palm, I feel the muscle of his back stress and atop me, his body shakes lightly with the last ounce of self-control he holds. One that doesn't delay ebbing when I throw my other leg over his waist and lock my feet at the ankles, bringing him closer to where I ache for him.

"Are you on the pill, *nena*? I'm clean." His voice a deep rasp as he speaks this time. It is coarse with need and coated with desire. One that I reciprocate in spades.

"Yes. Please, Mase, I need you inside of me. I need—"

My words turn into a moan when he roots himself inside me to the hilt in one deep thrust. My mouth is agape, and my eyes squeeze shut at the sweet sting as my inner walls strain to accommodate his thick girth.

"*Doce Xesús, nena*," he utters on a groan, his voice a beckoning for me to open my eyes. When I do, I meet his dark stare and hold it for a tick before it skirts to his lips that are just a breath away from mine. "You feel so fucking good. Your pussy around my cock… *Joder…*"

His words trail off and his mouth captures mine. He kisses me with savage, unbridled need, his tongue thrusting between my lips.

Mason deepens the kiss so intensely and it obliterates all my capacities. There is only the ability to feel—his mouth on mine, the touch of his palm on my hip before it advances farther up my body, his bare cock sheathed inside of me. That is all I am left with as Mason takes from me everything I have to offer and all that I didn't know was up for the taking.

With my back arching when his hand kneads my breast, my head throws back into the pillow, and I lose his lips.

I am ready to complain, but when his mouth drops to the column of my neck and his lips press against my skin, nibbling before his tongue caresses the heated flesh, only pleasure-filled moans escape me.

Moving a little lower to suck my pebbled nipple in his mouth while his hand continues to play with its pair, his cock draws back, and a quiver shakes my body.

For four months I haven't felt the sweet stretch of my pussy. Nor did I have inside me anything apart from my fingers. Something that truthfully happened only once—the very same time he saw me touching myself in the shower and heard me moaning his name with wicked abandon.

Right now, that deliciously slow withdrawal of his length until only the head of his cock remains inside of me before he fills me up just as unhurriedly, that motion feels utterly surreal. Dreamlike also feels the weight of his body on mine, the thrumming inside his chest that I can feel reverberating through my own. Unreal because not long ago and for three whole months I lived with the fear that I'll lose him, that I won't get to hear the sound of his voice, the sound of his breath in my ear, his sweet caress. I was terrified I will have to learn to leave without him.

"More," I plead in a moaned whisper, needing to feel even more of him to assure myself this is real.

His head lifts off my chest, and he lets go of my hard nipple with a low pop, his dark chocolate eyes filled with warp need as they lock onto mine.

The fire I find in his beautiful gaze is mirrored by mine. The flames behind the brownness of his irises dance in tandem with the ones I am aware he can see behind the greenness of mine.

With his mouth hovering just a centimeter away from mine, he shifts and props both of his elbows on either side of my head, his cock sliding in at the movement.

"*Joder*," he curses aloud. "This sweet pussy of yours is heaven."

On a gentle glide out, he pushes back in, my pleasure-filled moan and his unrestrained groan crackling in the morning air. Mason doesn't only fill me up with all the inches of his length. He possesses me. Me, my heart, my body, and my mind.

"This cunt is mine."

As though to prove his own statement, he thrusts hard inside of me. Swiftly, my pussy welcomes his deep slides in and glides out, while my body croons at the fullness I feel, at being filled by him to the brim once again.

"You were made to take this cock," Mason croaks, pushing in hard and deep, his thrusts measured and controlled. "*My* cock. *Only* my cock."

My chest heaves with straining breaths while my body takes every single one of his punishing drives. With proficient thrusts he coaxes me to the edge, only to decelerate to a crazily low rhythm. It is as though he can't decide if he wants to propel us right over the edge with fast, hard thrusts, or if he wants to drag this moment out for as long as he possibly can.

My heart lurches to the pit of my stomach. Fear settles right there. Fear that it will come to an end once the high of the orgasm wears off.

"Please," I beg, the close taste of the orgasm just within reach as his hips pump inside me, but I fight it.

"Please what, *nena*?"

After the question is out, he pushes up on his arms. Although I lose the heat of his upper body on mine and the hammering of his chest against mine, the angle only seems to take him deeper, his glides slow. On each glide in, his hips roll, pushing me to the brink of insanity.

"I can't come, Mason."

MASON

My brows narrow and my thrusts slow even further.

"*Nena*, I feel you right there. I feel how your pussy squeezes my cock."

"Because I am close, but I don't wanna come. I don't want to because I'm afraid when it will finish, when the daze of the sex wears off, everything else is going to end."

The vulnerability of her admittance weighs heavily in the air between us and my heart thunders in my chest because I know I'm the cause of her insecurity.

Frailty is not the only thing that coats her voice, though. It is also filled with an incessant need that contradicts her earlier statement. Especially when she lifts her hips to get closer to mine, meeting me halfway while driving me deep inside of her.

Lowering myself on her again, my forehead leans against hers. My breathing is labored and when her hands travel over my back, I know she can feel my muscles tremble beneath her palms, my need for her just as unceasing and rampant as hers for me. But before we move further with this, I am aware there are certain things that need clarifying. Even if these certain things will have to be clarified while I'm balls deep inside her of.

"I know I've denied you for so long, *nena*, but this won't end at just this." Honesty glazes my tone and my gaze while I hold her green one. A green so deep and rich that I need to fight with all I've got not to get sidetracked. "From the moment my cock slipped inside your tight pussy, you became so mine nobody will ever be able to wash me off your skin, not even you. You're so fucking mine now just like you should have been all along."

My stomach clenches.

My heart hammers.

All that because it is true. Ensley should have been mine. I have denied and postponed the inevitable. Because that's all I've been doing since there is no such thing as moving on after falling in love with her and being with her.

Yes, I tried and fooled myself.

To no fucking avail because here I am, ready to worship the very ground this woman beneath me walks on. And not only the ground, but her. Worship her and her body. Be her most loyal servant. Be the man she deserves to have by her side.

Fearing the past no longer.

I'm a coward no more.

I know there will be hell to pay, but I'll fight anyone and anything to keep her. I'll take a fucking bullet for her. I'd lay my life down for her. What I won't do any longer is fight against her. Fight that pull and hold she has on me and on my heart.

"Baby, this won't end. We will do it again and again and again because your pussy belongs to me." There's no doubt in my voice as I speak. "Your ass is mine. Your mouth is mine. Your body belongs to me. But most important of it all, your heart is mine, *nena*. Because *you* belong to me and with me. You belong to me just like I belong to you because you've owned me and my heart for twenty goddamn years, if not longer."

"No more pushing me away?"

My head moves from side to side, pure sincerity in my stare as I peer down at her through half-hooded eyes.

"No more pushing you away."

"Then, please, make me come," she pleads. "And fast otherwise I might die."

Oh, man, that plea is the sweetest of melodies.

A smirk plays at the corner of my lips and the wickedness she clearly sees in my eyes causes her body to shudder with anticipation.

When I push to my knees, her lock around my waist loosens to give me room so I can reach the position I want. My quads beneath the back of her thighs, keeping my cock inside her all through my shift, moving slowly within her as she moans.

The way her sweet pussy clamps down on my length is pure exhilaration and torture wrapped into one.

"Ass up."

The demand is filled with dominance, and she rushes to do my bidding, lifting that glorious ass off the mattress. That prompts my length deeper inside her tightness, but I am a man on a mission, and I need to stay focused.

So I stretch my arm to grab the pillow by her head and I don't hesitate to place it under her butt, keeping her at an angle.

"You wanna come, *nena*? Wanna come on my cock?" I ask with just as much urgency in my voice that I see overflowing in her eyes.

"Yes," she breathes out.

That is enough to spur me on.

Grasping hold of her hips, I draw then thrust my hips and drive inside her. The angle given by the pillow under her ass has her taking me deeper and deeper inside of her.

A groan surges out of me when I feel her tightly wrapped around my cock and when I watch Ensley's widen eyes as she lets out a moaned gasp, her lips beautifully shaped in an "O".

Fuck, I died and made it to heaven.

This is what it feels like.

Not only because I'm inside her tight body, but because I finally have her. I'm allowing myself to have her. To have the woman I've forever loved and craved. The only woman who has brought me to the brink of insanity just with how much I wanted her. And, in a way, I believe she has, otherwise right now I wouldn't be filling her pussy with my cock. Nor would we be moaning each other's name as we move together, giving her my length inch by inch so slowly that it is pure purgatory for the both of us.

"Mas…Ah, Mason."

"*Doce Xesús*, Ensley," I rasp under my breath, the pace of my thrusts quickening.

When my gaze lowers from her gorgeous face filled with elation, I follow the length of her body. Her chest rises and falls as she takes shallow breaths each time I draw back. Her boobs bounce with every hard thrust inside her. Her defined abdomen tightens. And when my eyes land on the junction between her legs where we are connected, I watch with warp marvel my cock sliding out of her—drenched in her arousal—, before it glides back in, touching that sweet spot inside of her that has her thrashing and going wild, crooning a melody so honeyed.

"I need to feel you… My skin…on yours."

It is on the last statement that leaves her mouth that I remove a hand from her waist and yank the pillow from under her ass. While I do it, the red marks of my fingertips don't go unnoticed and at that sight, an overflowing feeling of possession pumps into my veins.

Ensley lets out a surprised gasp, but I don't give her much time for anything else. My body hovers over hers and, in an instant, one of my hands grabs both her wrists and pins them to the mattress while my other finds her ass cheek. My fingers dig into her skin when I thrust in, and my head knocks back at the feeling of her clutching around me.

Fucking perfect.

Ensley taking my cock is goddamn perfection.

The first time I slid inside her, filling her to the brim, my vision turned blurry, and I saw stars.

I fucking saw stars.

Now, it is no different.

She is so tight and wet, and her inner walls wrap around my girth with a vice-like grip as she arches her back some more, her chest pressing against mine.

On a glide out and a slide back in, Ensley lets out a mewl, her heat welcoming and taking every single one of my thrusts.

As I look down at her, I am mesmerized by how beautiful she looks. The dim light coating the room is only from the lamp-posts outside, but it is enough to give me a glimpse of how absolutely divine she looks beneath me. Frankly, just as I'm sure she'll look on top of me, in front of me on her knees sucking my cock or with my length ramming deep inside of her from behind.

It is on the third stroke back in that my mouth smashes over hers, and everything else disappears for me the same way it does for her.

I feel it in the pliancy of her body that I'm all she's able to focus on. What I make her feel with my smooth, claiming drives, with my dominating mouth on hers, with my fingertips that dig into her flesh on each thrust in. Just the same way that all I'm able to concentrate on is her. How her sleek walls clutch around me. How she takes every single glide in and moans complainingly when I draw back, but only to let out a cry full of pleasure when I slide in again. How she submits to the kiss and to the love-making. How she obliterates everything around us with just a mere rake of her hands over my back after I let go of her wrists.

We are connected down to the marrow of our bones.

So tangled up in each other and our pleasure.

So wrapped up into our love-making that only the sounds of our panting and our bare skin slapping together fill the room, the passion of it burning us so deep.

"*Joder*," I curse aloud over her lips. "You feel so goddamn good, *nena*. So mine."

"Yours, Mason. Only yours."

I lose control at that confirmation. Not only does my mouth drop back onto hers, my tongue thrusts against hers before she sweetly capitulates. But I also drive harder and deeper inside of her. My thrusts punishing and all-consuming.

Her pussy squeezes my cock, my balls tightening.

"Come for me, Ley," I egg on, my hand slipping between our bodies to find her clit. I thrust in while the thumb of my finger presses against her bundle of nerves, toying with it. "Let it go, *nena*."

My encouragements and my ministrations are all she needs for her body to begin shaking and for her pussy to clamp down on my cock so tightly.

"Mas…Oh, God, Mason," she moans, her palm flying over her face to muffle her pleasure-filled screams. "I'm com…coming."

The rippling of her body is bewitching as she falls over the edge. Ensley doesn't just come. She detonates beneath me, prompting me closer to the edge too, and I slow my thrusts within her.

With her form shaking under mine and her inner muscles squeezing me tight, I drive in a couple of more times before I root myself deep. My balls draw and I come inside her, my body tensing and shuddering atop hers, while my head drops in the crook of her neck.

"*Joder*, Ensely," I rasp, my breath heaving.

We hold each other with all the energy we have left after the orgasm bulldozes through us.

"Mason."

The way she whispers my name, sounding spent and sated, has me smiling against her skin while she peppers light kisses across my shoulder.

She chuckles and I follow, our bodies rocking together.

"*Merda*, Ley. This was…"

The sentence trails off as I still try to catch my breath.

"Yes, it was."

Her slender arms wrap around my neck and Ensley holds me pressed to her, the muscles of her thighs tightening around my waist like she doesn't want this moment to end. Justly, nor do I.

Drawing back my head from the crook of her neck, I press a light kiss on her lips and lock my eyes onto hers.

"Thank fuck I jacked off since I got back from the hospital, otherwise I'd have come the second I slid inside you. Embarrassingly fast," I confess with a chortle and her body rocks beneath mine as she lets out her own giggle. "How I've been able to stay away from this snug pussy of yours for so long is beyond me."

"Oh, so it's just my pussy you're after then."

The teasing revert earns her a low, deep chuckle from me. One that turns into a groan when I feel my cock jerk and the wickedness in her gaze only grows.

"Your tight ass too," I mention with a wink, lowering my hand to the part of her body just mentioned before I give her a swat. "*Nena*, you caught fire when I lodged my finger in your ass, and I want to claim it with my cock too."

A shudder quakes her body and mine shakes also at the thought of claiming everything and anything Ensley is willing to give me.

However, a moment later, there's something that crosses her expression. Something I can't put my finger on. An emotion I can't quite define because of the dim light, but also because it disappears faster than it appeared and instead, she gives me a smile.

"Most of all, I'm after you and your heart, Ensley."

"What made you change your mind?"

The curiosity of her question hisses in the air between us and hangs there for a little while before I answer her. "Because it is impossible to fight against one's fate and you are mine."

Her expression softens and her hand moves to my cheek, caressing it gently. So much so that I barely feel it, but at the same time, it gets all my blood boiling and burns my skin.

"You already have me. My heart is *yours* and I am *yours*."

Her voice almost a whisper. Or maybe it is what it sounds like because the wild galloping of my heart doesn't allow me to hear her louder.

"But I'm warning you, push me away one single time and I'm out, Mason," Ensley warns, and I swallow hard, realizing that one wrong step will have her out of my life for good. And this time, she means it. "I'm completely in love with you and I love you down to every fiber of my being, but I'm not going to take the push and pull any longer. You have me or you don't. Love me or leave me. Take me or push me away. I'm willing to move mountains for you and fight anything and anyone, but I won't take you pushing me away anymore."

Though I force myself to listen to everything she says— which takes the greatest amount of effort to do so, yet I manage to—, my mind still gets fixated on one particular part.

"I'm completely in love with you and I love you down to every fiber of my being."

If my heart was in overdrive before, now it overheats and almost sub-circuits at how fast it thunders in my chest.

For a moment or two, my eyes stay connected to hers while my mind replays the words. Her confession.

After it echoes so many times that I know I've learned every single word of it, I bring a hand to her wrist and lower her palm from my cheek to my chest, right above the wild beating of my heart, but also atop the ink.

"You are like these tattoos, Ensley. I have you etched on every part of me. I carry you on me every goddamn moment of every goddamn day."

A soft smile plays at the corners of her lips.

"You on my heart is the very first tattoo I got."

Ensley's delicate fingers trace the ink across my chest. All the while and without missing a beat, her green gaze follows the path trailed by her fingertips. And so do I.

I do because right here and now seems so surreal that I want to have every single instant of it memorized and stored safely in that drawer of my mind especially designed for Ensley.

The moment her palm returns from its wander across my chest and rests completely atop my thrumming heart, her eyes lift and lock onto mine. That is when I know it is real. As real as it gets.

"I love you too, Ley. I've loved you all my life to the marrow of my bones and I could never unlove you even if I wanted to. And believe me, I wanted to because I'd be lying if I say I didn't."

Out are the words now.

The confirmation that it can't get any more real.

Ensley is mine.

Because after tonight, no other man can even stare at her without the risk of losing an eye—if I'm generous enough to leave them with one—or maybe two—which is the more likely scenario.

Ensley Walker is mine.

My woman.

My woman to keep.

Mine to love until I draw my last goddamn breath.

My woman to make love to in the dirtiest, filthiest, and most obscene ways possible. Mine to make sweet, gentle love to.

She is mine to protect.

Mine to keep safe.

Mine to shelter from harm even if that means using my body as a shield to do it.

Because from this moment forth, there's no more denying and pushing away.

From here on out, we fight. Not *against* each other, but *for* each other.

All this because now I know. Now, after pushing and pulling for so long only to come down to this, to the here and to the now with her beneath me after I made her mine, there is no doubt in my mind.

We are two imperfect hearts that only beat a perfect rhythm when they beat for each other.

MASON

My arm stretches on the mattress and pats the spot only to be met by emptiness. Immediately my eyes snap open and land on a naked back with nicely defined muscles, trim waist, and a magnificent heart-shaped ass.

Turning on my side to face her better and propping my head on my palm, I watch Ensley slip out of bed while I get a full view of her.

And what a sight that is.

My cock instantly hardens beneath the thin comforter, unable to resist the vision that the woman before my eyes is. Especially when there are still faint red marks of my fingertips on her skin.

Because Ensley and I didn't stop at just once. We couldn't get enough of each other, so three in the morning—the time when I couldn't help myself any longer and teased her awake—and two orgasms became four orgasms. I ate her out again, unrushed, ravishing her until she turned into a moaning, babbling mess—that was number three. Orgasm number four happened with her sliding up and down my cock. She rode me so hard, driving is both crazy with never-ending need while I finger-fucked her tight ass.

And, oh, man, did she go wild.

Carallo, did she ride me.

Had Ensley not been a firefighter, she'd have made a goddamn fine cowgirl.

MISHA BLAKE

Oh, *Doce Xesús*, she just knows how to ride a man to oblivion... Scratch that actually because she knows how to ride *me* to oblivion.

Just me.

Only me.

From here on out my cock will be the only one she'll ride. The only one that will be gliding in and out of that honey-sweet pussy.

"Slipping out on me already, *nena?*" I tease.

A groan instantly surges out of me and tumbles past my lips when she bends over to pick up something, that enticing ass of hers up in the air.

Joder!

Throw a leash on those thoughts, Carter.

Although I attempt to knock the idea out of my head as soon as I have it, that is a failed try because I can't help but picture how she'd take my cock up her sweet as sin ass.

With Ensley, only the filthiest of thoughts tumble in my head. Maybe because I want to claim her in ways she's never been claimed before or if she has, to obliterate whoever has touched her that way and replace it with my touch, my caress, my mouth and my cock. To annihilate any sort of remains from whatever boyfriend she had before and consume her with my own until she is unable to scrub me off her skin. Until I'm so deeply embedded in her body and in her soul that nothing and nobody will ever erase me.

"As much as I enjoy the view of you all bent over, if you want my cock up your ass, all you have to do is say so."

When Ensley turns to face me after she slips my t-shirt over her head and through the sleeves, the wickedness in her smile— one that gleams in her green eyes too—tells me I am in trouble. Something I knew already, but the last twenty-four hours have only solidified that awareness.

Ensley is intoxication personified. A lethal mix of sensuality, defiance, sexiness, and sultriness wrapped in a heart-thundering, knee-weakening mien with the most beautiful pair of green eyes and the silkiest hair.

"Well, say so and throw me a bottle of lube, *nena*" I add, my lips tipping in a lopsided smirk.

Ensley rolls her eyes at me.

"And what if I want your cock in my mouth?"

Santo inferno!

(*Holy hell!*)

I nearly choke on my own saliva.

My heart skips at that wicked question, but I give her my own suggestive grin while my hand extends. My fingers wrap around the edge of the comforter, and I pull at the fabric, my dick rock-hard.

"It will only be fair after you had me coming twice last night on your mouth," she states, her eyes glistening with pure mischief.

At that, I drag my feet over the edge of the bed and push to my full length, looking down at Ensley who tips his head a little to be able to meet my gaze.

"You wrap your lips around my cock because you want to. Because you want to have me hit the back of that tight throat when I fuck your mouth. Because you want to taste me on your tongue." Her eyes narrow at my declarations, but they widen when my hand travels between her thighs for me to cup her sex, a moan slipping out of her. "Only because I had you coming on my mouth and I love eating out this sweet cunt, that doesn't mean I'll ask or expect you to suck my cock if you don't want to just so we can even the score. No, *nena*, there's no score to even out because as far as I'm concerned, I enjoy having my head between your legs as much as you are."

"But I want to suck you off."

This time it is my strangled groan that pushes from deep within my chest, crawls up my throat and flows through my lips.

"*Cristo, nena*, you're gonna kill me."

And there's that mischievousness glowing in her green gaze. It only intensifies as her palms rest on my bare chest before they begin to travel lower.

With that rascality in her stare, I need to gather all my might to be able to gain a hold over my impulses.

I try.

I really try and even remove my hand from the heat pulsating between her legs.

To no avail, though, because one more second of staring into her eyes, plus another tick of her palms descending past my abdomen, and the savage beast inside me gets unleashed. A beast that gets fueled only by Ensley's sounds and my unremitting need for her.

"On your fucking knees right now. Get on the floor, *nena*."

The command slips past my lips before I get a chance to stop it. I wouldn't generally be so crass with a woman—especially with Ensley—, ordering her to her knees, but everything goes out the window when it comes to the one before me.

Fuck if I can be gentle with her as though I want to tattoo myself so deep into her mind, her skin, her heart.

The woman in front of me doesn't seem to mind my lack of finesse, though. Instead, she looks like she enjoys it, and judging by the way she stares up at me with her eyes gleaming and lips quirked in a smirk, she enjoys the effect she has on me more. My inability to control myself around her since it seems to snap loose whenever she's in my proximity.

"Knees," I order again.

Without any hesitation whatsoever, she continues smirking and happily obliges. She lowers before me until her knees touch the hardwood floor, my heart remaining still for a split instant.

As she's on her knees and her soft hand wraps around my cock, her eyes journey from where she touches me and up the length of my body until she finds my gaze.

Her hand slides up my shaft and another rumbled groan pushes its way out of my chest.

"*Joder*," I rasp when she runs her tongue on the underside of my cock.

The wickedness in her eyes doesn't ebb even a little. On the contrary, it increases. Especially after she reaches the swollen crown of my cock and wraps her seductive lips around my girth, taking me deep in her mouth.

My breath hitches and my eyes widen while my jaw falls slack at the goddamn pleasure that I feel surging through my body as she works her mouth and hand up and down my length.

Who would've thought?!

Ensley-fucking-Walker on her knees and with her beautiful lips wrapped around my cock. Only in my fantasies I've seen this moment possible—and there have been plenty of them.

I don't let my mind trail too far, though—not that it would be possible to focus on something that isn't her eyes or her mouth. Specifically when her hand glides up my girth, and her eyes flick from mine down to my cock as it slides out of her mouth. Her lips remain wrapped around the crown of my shaft and her gaze zeroes in on it before it roams back over the length of my body until they connect to mine once again. As my gaze pierces into hers with a fire so intense it consumes both of us and at the same time fuels us, her mouth lowers on me and as my shaft disappears inside her mouth, while her other hand moves to cup my balls, toying with me, her eyes never leaving mine.

And she works me. With her mouth and hands, she works me until I lose it. Until I lose control over my own body and thread my fingers through her hair before I grab hold of it.

My gaze searches hers for any scintilla of doubt, but when I don't find any, I thrust my hips, Ensley taking me to the back of her throat.

Almost instantly, her hands move to my ass cheeks and her nails dig into my skin while I push a little deeper into her throat and hold there.

Ensley's gorgeous green eyes widen, and I withdraw my entire length from her mouth. The sound of her gasping for air fills my ears and I hold her stare, hunting once again for a fraction of hesitation.

When she sticks out her tongue and opens her mouth a little wider, I use the hold on her hair to tilt her chin a little and rest the swollen head on her tongue, then I thrust my hips again and push my shaft inside her hot mouth.

I fuck her mouth.

No holding back as all sorts of carnal urges run through my body and they savagely take over. They control the speed of each thrust inside her mouth. They rule every second that I hold still in the back of her throat and govern over every second that I have her choke on my cock.

Ensley moans and *mmm*'s, egging me on further and further. Her sounds beckon me over the edge, my own groan signaling just how close I am.

"*Merda, nena,*" I rasp on a deep, rumbled breath, trying to keep my voice as low as possible, just like the noises that billow out of my chest every single time my cock slides in and out of her mouth.

Each thrust of my hips pushes her limits. But she takes each one of them. She lets me fuck her mouth without protest, her fingers digging into the flesh of my ass cheeks occasionally for me to hold still for a moment down the back of her throat.

Santo inferno!

A pleasure so intense builds at the very bottom of my spine and my knees almost give way at the ripple that shakes my body.

"*Carallo, nena*, you're gonna make me come."

It is on this sentence that my hips falter, and Ensley takes over, moving her lips up and down my shaft. Her fingertips don't even touch when she wraps her hand around my thick girth, but she still pumps me hard.

"Mmm..."

There's that fucking "*mmm*" again.

That goddamn sound she makes when she moans with me lodged deep into the back of her throat.

Joder!

Right from the bottom of my spine, that surge of pleasure shoots into my balls that tighten.

Ensley lowers her mouth on my cock once more and withdraws until her lips are only wrapped around the swollen crown, her hand moving up and down my shaft a couple of times. It is on the sight of my cock disappearing into her mouth again that the carnal pleasure unleashes.

"*Merda*, Ley. I'm... coming," I rasp warningly, my chest rising and falling, my vision turning blurry.

That caution is her last chance to back off my cock before I come. A caution she ignores, halting the movement of her mouth when I'm down her throat, her hand still pumping.

She fucking wants me to come in her mouth. Moreover, her hand works me voraciously and I plunge over the goddamn edge. Her eyes close when the first spurt of cum touches her throat and she swallows with another "*mmm*". The sound greedy and sultry, spurring me on further with a second and a third and a fourth rush, until I empty myself in her hot, avaricious mouth.

"*Joder!*" The croak is on a heavy breath and on a voice I barely recognize as my own.

Ensley's thumb wipes at the corner of her mouth where a drip of my come remained as the very proof of what just happened, and oh, man, I lose it. Bending my knees a little, I slide my hands beneath her armpits and lift her to her back on her feet, bringing her flush to me and my lips capture hers.

"*Nena, a túa boca vólveme tolo.*"

("*Baby, your mouth drives me crazy.*")

Cradling her cheek with my hand, my thumb moves over her bottom lip, tracing it. My eyes stay locked onto hers as she moves her head a little, parting her lips until they wrap around my finger.

A groan leaves my chest.

"I think we should shower and get a start on this morning before you throw me on the bed and not leave this room."

At Ensley's words, my brow quirks and the left corner of my lips quirks upward. "So what you're saying is that you plan on taking advantage of me."

She laughs at my statement.

"You didn't seem to complain five seconds ago when I had your cock in my mouth," Ensley reverts with a defying tone.

"Such a dirty mouth you've got on you, Ley." Her arms wrap around my neck, her tits pushing into my chest.

"I'd say I'm just trying to match your own filthy one. Which let me tell you, it is extremely obscene."

"And you love every dirty word and promise that comes out of this mouth, *nena.*"

Her head moves from side to side. "Let's just shower," she urges, untangling her arms from around my neck before she grasps hold of my hand and leads us to the en-suite bathroom.

As we walk, my eyes begin to rove.

They wander from her back to her small waist and home in on her delectable ass. The way her hips move left and right, right and left, it beckons me to touch. And I don't delay halting her steps, my naked body pressing against hers, and grab a palmful of her ass with my free hand.

"Just as a side note, pretty soon I'll take this ass of yours," I whisper in her ear and her body trembles against mine. "I want to claim you in every imaginable way, in any way you'll let me. Will you let me take your ass, *nena?*"

"Y-yes," she breathes out, the back of her head leaning against my shoulder.

"Good."

It is all I say before I smack her naked ass cheek and walk us to the bathroom.

ENSLEY

With a giggle, I try to remove Mason's hands from around my waist so I can get the coffee started. To no avail, though, because he just loosens his hold on me enough for me to move. His hands remain wrapped around me and his lips press on my shoulder, neck and cheek.

After we stepped into the shower together, I warned him multiple times to keep his hands to himself—which evidently didn't happen. While he kissed me with gentleness and unhurried passion, his fingers pumped in and out of me so slowly, driving me crazy with incessant need until I was pushed right over the edge.

We can't get enough of each other. We touch and touch, caress and nibble at each other's skin every chance we get. Hence why right now Mason stays glued to me.

As I reach to press the button on the coffee machine, his lips drop to the column of my neck and I giggle again, twisting in his embrace, his touch tickling me.

"Mason," I complain in a whisper, trying to swat his caress away. "We're gonna wake up your mom."

It is just after half seven o'clock in the morning and Aracely didn't come down from her room. After yesterday's evens and her accident, they wore her off and took their toll on her.

Thank God she is well, and nothing happened to her.

"She needs to rest, and you need to settle down before we

wake her, okay?" I caution again and he nods, resting his chin on my shoulder.

"I'll behave," he promises, drawing his arms from around me. "I'll make us some breakfast."

With that, I lose the heat of his body against my back and cock my head to the side to watch him saunter full of swagger and charm to the fridge before he returns to the hob.

"Checking me out, Ley?"

The teasing in his voice shivers my skin.

"Not my fault you've got a great ass," I retort with a casual shrug, yet the smile playing on my lips is anything but nonchalant. It is taunting and insinuating. "Besides, at how much you seem to be liking my ass, making indecent propositions to it, it is only fair to like yours too."

"Just so you know and before you get any ideas of making any indecent propositions to mine, I'm quite frowning upon having things shoved up my ass," Mason jokes, his chuckle is rich and deep from within his stomach. A sound so soothing. A sound that I missed so much.

In two long steps, he's right behind me again, pressing my front to the edge of the counter, while his pushes into my back.

With his head leaning over my shoulder. His hot breath fans against my face. His arms encircle me.

"But I quite figured out last night how much you like my ass when my cock was inside you and this morning when you had it in your mouth and your fingers dug into my ass."

His hands rest on my hips and he pulls me further into his body while he catches my earlobe between his lips and nibbles on it gently.

I chuckle in his embrace, trying to wiggle out of his arms, but he only tightens his hold.

"Polo amor de Deus, meus amores."

("For the love of God, my dears.")

Almost immediately we jump away from each other and turn toward Aracely who stands leaning against the wall. While she looks at us with a broad smile on her face, we both look like two deer in headlights at getting caught.

Honestly, after we turned up at the hospital hand in hand, Aracely must have suspected something. She didn't pry, though she threw a couple of hints. But after seeing us the way she just did, there mustn't be any doubt in her mind of what's happening here. And by the wide smile, the three of us know exactly what that conclusion is.

"As much as I love this sight of you two, spare your *Mamá* of an instant need to bleach her eyes, *vale?*"

Mason lets out a chortle, while I, on the other hand, feel my cheeks on fire at getting caught by my mother-in-law. It isn't like it is the first time, especially when her son has a knack for getting inappropriate in the worst of moments that end up with us getting busted.

"Sorry, Ary," I rush to apologize.

Aracely waves me off with her hand, the smile on her face not ebbing even a fraction. "Don't be silly."

"How are you feeling, *Mamá?*"

As he asks the question, he strides to her side and presses a kiss on her forehead.

My heart skips a beat at the image before me just like it has done million times before at the same sight of the two of them. A sight that had me hope I'll be at least half of the mother she is if I ever have children.

If I'll ever have children...

That thought has me still in my spot.

It has me tense as Mason's words assail me.

"I'll give you anything you want, nena. Beautiful memories, scorching hot sex, a good life by my side. A happy life. I'll give you all of me and anything you want because you own me, but there is something I'll never give you." He pauses, taking a deep breath. *"I'll never give you kids. So if you want to kick me to the curb, I'll understand, but please do it now."*

My form turns to stone as his hands cradle my face to keep my eyes on him.

"I'm sorry, nena. I don't want to take away from you the possibility of having a family. But I'm telling you now that if this is what you want, you won't have that with me."

A lump forms in my throat, my heart squeezes so tightly and my lungs constrict to the extent that it becomes impossible to breathe.

"I won't be the one to give you a family, Ensley. I'll give you anything but that."

"Why?"

As the question tumbles past my lips, I feel the heaviness of that single word. I feel it weigh heftily on my shoulder. I can also taste its sheer bitterness in my mouth.

"Because this is how it is. I don't want kids and as much as I want to be selfish, I can't. I can't lead you on and promise you a happy family with three-point-five kids and a house with white picket fence when that will never happen. I will give you the house you want, I'll give you all that you want, nena, but not the family you want."

"I want to be with—"

His finger rests on my lips, interrupting me.

"Don't make that choice now. I'm refusing you the family I know you want and that's not a decision you take so easily."

That day, I knew what I was giving up. I was more than aware of what that meant, and I gave up on the idea of being a mother only so I can be with the man I love. And although from time to time my mind slips to that *"what if"*, I always manage to press the breaks on the thought.

Just like I did before, I knock that *"what if"* away from my head. Though, this time around, it takes a lot more of me to push it away. A lot more than I am willing to accept and it would've taken so much more if it weren't for the gentle voice that pierces through my ponder.

"Nena."

I blink and my green eyes fly across the room to meet a pair of chocolate eyes. What I find in his gaze are worry and confusion.

"I'm...Erm... Sorry, I got distracted," I speak and turn to the coffee machine.

Reaching for the cup of coffee, I spin.

"Would you like one, Ary?"

She nods and I hand her the cup. "Thank you, dear."

Mason returns to the hob and begins preparing breakfast while Aracely and I take a seat at the island.

"What time do you have the appointment for your checkup with the department's doc?" I ask Mason after I take a small sip of the dark liquid.

"At ten. I'll leave right after breakfast and I'll get back in the evening. I'm meeting Luke at the bar to see one of the guys who applied for the bartender position," he explains, turning to face us while he holds the spatula.

"Didn't you already have a bartender?" Aracely asks.

"Yeah, we did until we didn't. He pulled out of the job last minute to attend to some family emergency out of state."

"And you can't pour a pint?" I tease.

His brow quirks and so does the corner of his lips as they turn into a smile. "I'll have you know my bar-tendering skills are on point, *nena*. But we need a full-time bartender for when Luke and I aren't there."

"Ella and I can help too. We already talked about it and we can tend at the bar too."

He smirks at me and opens his mouth to say something. However, after his gaze darts to his mom, he closes it.

"Oh, please, don't stop on my account, *meu filho*."

"Believe me, *Mamá*, you want me to keep my mouth shut, otherwise you won't only need bleach for your eyes, but for your ears too."

"Appreciate the warning," Aracely speaks, scrunching her nose.

"How are you feeling, Ary?"

This time, I am the one who asks the question, realizing I fell deep in thoughts and didn't catch her answer.

"I'm good. The painkillers they gave me at the hospital knocked me right out and I slept all through the night. Now, the arm bothers me a little, but it's bearable."

"How did it happen, *Mamá*?"

Mason's voice is filled with worry. Concern that is evident in his brown gaze as it reverts to his mom.

A moment of silence later, his stare turns piercing and I can see the wheels spinning in his head. And they spin. And spin. And spin, until Aracely's voice fills the quiet kitchen after she avoided her son's eyes for a few ticks.

"I just lost control of the wheel. I wasn't speeding or anything, I…" Her head shakes from side to side. "It happened so fast. One second I was driving on the road and the next I was trying to get control of the car."

While she explains the events, my eyes remain on Mason, taking in all his reactions. Mainly the stoic expression that takes over his features as his lips press into a straight line.

Instantly, my gaze moves between Mason and his mother, not missing the qualm in my husband's look as he continues to stare at Aracely.

Am I missing something?

The wonder tumbles in my head before I get a chance to suppress it. But by the silent argument their stares appear to have, I certainly am missing something.

What is going on here?

"Mason, the road was wet, and it happened really fast. Now, can we please just not have an argument about it?"

"*Mamá*, you scared the living life out of me," he confesses, letting out a heavy sigh.

And right here and now, before my eyes, there is a version of Mason Carter I don't get to see too often. The vulnerable Mason Carter. A side of him most times he keeps locked away. A side of him that perhaps I've only seen one more time before apart from last night. That was three years ago, the night when I got stuck in that building on fire. The night when I thought it will be the end of it all.

"It is why I agreed without any dispute to come and stay with you two for the next couple of days, so you can see with your own eyes that I'm fine and get the idea that something is wrong out of your head," Aracely states with a small smile aimed at her son.

"Young lady, if you believe you're out of this house in the next day or so, I'd suggest you think again. At least until they take that sling off your arm, you're staying with us," Mason argues, returning his attention to the pan with scrambled eggs.

"I don't want to impose. Especially not now."

Aracely's words catch me with the cup of coffee mid-air and I refrain from bringing it to my lips while my eyes narrow and my head cocks to the side to look at her.

"Not now?" I ask, needing clarification.

Her smile widens. "Now that you two are... You know, you need your own space so you can make me grandbabies."

I choke.

On my own goddamn saliva.

To be honest, I've never been so grateful for not sipping on coffee, otherwise, I'd be doing more than just choking.

As I calm my cough, my gaze flies to Mason who doesn't seem surprised at all to hear this.

Truth be told, Aracely has always been forward about wanting grandchildren in the first few years of relationship. Nevertheless, ever since we've been honest with her and have told her we don't plan on having kids, she refrained from asking about it. Until the recent months when the "grandmother" within her gets very persistent.

"Sorry, darling, but this body of mine is still good to chase after toddlers for a few more years," she argues, shrugging as though she said the most natural thing in the world.

And for a moment, I let her words get to me. I allow my thought to stray, my heart shrinks and my stomach twists. But even then, I still indulge in the images that seep into my mind. An image of a swollen belly. Another of a baby in my arms, close to my chest. Then another with a little girl with long dark hair and chocolate brown eyes running and laughing in the back garden. And yet one more; this time with a little boy, kicking a soccer ball to Mason who kicks it back to him as they both have the widest of grins.

"I'll never give you kids."

That sentence resounds in my head, and I try to wrench myself back to reality before my thoughts have a chance to run even wilder. Yet, that's a failed attempt because my traitor mind races right for the gut.

With my knees up and my arms around my legs, my chin tilts and my eyes unglue from the carpet in the living room. The same carpet I kept staring at for what seems like forever, before it now darts to the man I hear walking down the stairs.

I don't know if he'll come to the living room before he leaves for his shift. What I also don't know is if I want him to do so or if I want him to just ride off to work. Not after what he just asked me for in the bathroom less than twenty minutes ago—to get a divorce.

But before I even get the smallest of chances to consider the options, the sound made by the sole of his boots at the contact with the hardwood floor fills the air and my breath gets obstructed in my throat as I wait for him to show up before me.

He wears a pair of black jeans and a white top over which he has a black leather jacket with brown Sherpa lining.

My heart skips at the sight.

Simultaneously, it also squeezes tightly. Especially when his gaze meets mine across the room.

"I'll get the lawyer to start on the paperwork tomorrow after shift," he speaks, hands dug deep in the pockets of his jacket.

I nod.

That is all I am able to do.

Just nod at his words.

I am aware if I do more than just nod, I'll shatter into pieces. Because the words already clog my throat, making it impossible to say anything else. Making it impossible to fight when he's giving up.

He's already made his decision. To divorce me. To put an end to us. To give up on what we have. He's already decided all that. For him. For me. For us.

And while his words are still hefty between us, we keep each other's stare.

For a tick.

Two.

Perhaps for three until he simply and absentmindedly nods and turns, ready to walk away. Yet, before he gets to take the first step, the question skids through my lips: "Is it because of the pregnancy test?"

Mason's feet root to the spot and his form tenses. Not only that, it turns into stone.

"The pregnancy test you saw in the bathroom a few days ago?"

I am more than aware that there isn't any need for clarification. With the exception of a pregnancy scare we had a few months into our relationship right after we got carried away and had sex without a condom while I was on the pill, there has not been another pregnancy test. Up until about three days ago when I took one because my period was late—still is.

Mason walked into the bathroom just as the timer went off and his eyes homed in on the test atop the side of the washing basin. His features have never been as dark as they were when his gaze darted to meet mine.

"It's negative," I told him with nonchalance then, but my heart thrummed in my chest while a sentiment of disappointment settled in the pit of my stomach for a blink or two.

A disappointment I only kept to myself. Not because I was

purposely trying to get pregnant because I wasn't, but if that were to ever happen—birth control pill or not—I'd be lying if I said I wouldn't be happy.

"I told you that I don't want kids, Ensley."

His deep, dark rumble has me blink only to realize that he faces me now, his jawline ticking, his features matching his timber.

"And I told you I was late and that's why I took the test," *I revert, pushing to my feet.* "I wanted to get the possibility of a pregnancy out of the way before considering anything else."

"There's more to it than just that, Ensley. I've been lying to myself and so have you because you taking that test means that deep down, you still hold some hope."

"Hope?"

"Yes, Ensley. Hope," *he repeats, running a hand through his hair as his brown, stoic gaze stays on mine.* "Hope that you'll have the kid I've been denying you for so many years."

"My period was late and that could've been a possibility, Mason. We've been having sex without a condom for years and although I'm on the pill, there's still a chance to get pregnant."

Silence falls over us once again, but this time is only for mere seconds until his heavy breath fills the air.

"The divorce papers will be ready as soon as possible. I'll make sure to put a rush on them."

A sting brims at my eyes, but I fight it and clear my throat.

"So this is it?"

He lifts his shoulders in what wants to be a casual shrug. Although his deadpan nonchalance is almost on point, there's something in his gaze that contradicts him. For the briefest of ticks, something awfully close to ache can be seen in his eyes. So brief that I could've missed it had I not paid such close attention.

"You know damn well I don't want kids. You've known that from the start. So if your plan is to trap me..."

Anger builds in my body as I storm his way and I don't stop until I have him right in front of me. "Trap you? Fucking trap you? How can I trap you? Mason, we're married."

"It's not the same thing. We're married and I've told you already that this is all I'll ever be able to give you. Love, a marriage and great sex, and you fucking agreed to it. This is who I am, Ensley. This is all I'm capable of and all I'll ever be capable of," *he spits out bitterly.* "I can't care for a child and when I've seen that pregnancy* *test, I've realized I'm not giving you what you want, what you deserve, because just the fact that you took that pregnancy test means you hope and I'm stealing away from you the possibility of bringing a child into this world because I'm a selfish bastard." Momentarily, he pauses as though considering his next words. "So yes, Ensley, I want us to get divorced because I can't give you what you need and what you want. This, what you see, is all I'll ever be able to give you."*

"And that is enough for me. Don't you think that's my decision to make?" I argue, pushing at his chest.

"It is, but I also know what you'll choose. Who you will choose and you'll choose me, nena. That's why I prefer to press the breaks on everything now. I'd rather have you hate me now and thank me later when you'll get to hold your baby boy or baby girl, when you'll have by your side the man who's able to give you the family you wish for. I'd rather have that than have you broken, alone and hating me years down the line."

"Is this what you want? Is this what you actually want, Mason? Another man touching me like you do? Another man giving me the love you give me? For me to wake up next to a man who isn't you? To be held, to be kissed, to be made love to by another man?"

With each question that leaves my lips, I shove at his chest. He is rooted to the spot though, and regardless of how hard I try, he barely moves.

"Tell me your blood doesn't boil in your veins at the thought of it alone!" Shove. "Tell me your own mind doesn't hate you just for picturing that!" Push. "Tell me your heart doesn't bleed thinking of me with another man!" Shove. Shove. "Tell me! Fucking tell me anything but that you want me in another man's arms."

His hands wrap around my wrist, halting me. His chocolate gaze stays locked onto mine, anger brimming his gaze while his jaw ticks.

I struck a nerve.

I know that.

"I want..."

Mason's chest rises and falls rapidly, then his hands drop and his fists ball at his sides, as though trying to keep himself in control. To maintain that restraint I saw in his eyes sixteen years ago right before he pushed me against the wall.

And when my back touches the wall, his body pressed against mine, it now feels as though I'm living a déjà vu. His hard body pressed on mine. *His heart thrumming in his chest while mine gallops wildly. His mind caught in a whirlwind of thoughts—of maybes and what ifs.*

Though my mind is all over the place, my eyes hold his stare. It is unyielding and daring. Challenging my husband to tell me exactly what I asked him to.

His face is a mere breath of air away from mine, the hot, minty air that escapes him blowing gently against my face, casting a spell on me that I'm unable to break. Not until I lose his gaze when his forehead leans against mine and his eyes close.

"Tell me you're mine."

The ache and plea in his voice break my heart. There is surrender in it, but also a fraction of finality. It is as though he asks me to tell him I'm his one last time.

"I'm yours," I whisper back without delay.

That is when I feel his breath against my face again. When I feel his lips brushing over mine fleetingly. So cursorily that I could have easily imagined it.

"Carallo!"

With that curse under his breath, he spins on the heel of his boots. I am left there, against the wall, watching him rush away like someone set fire to his ass. Like he can't get away fast enough. My heart sinks. And it only drops further into the pit of my stomach when he stops near the shoe storage cabinet and places something atop it. Something I don't need to actually see to acknowledge the distinctive sound made by the golden wedding band at the contact with the wood.

And here is the finality I heard in his voice. Right here and now is the conclusion of us. Our cessation.

Blinking several times, I knock away the flashback. The memory of the last thing that's been said between my husband and me before he went on shift that morning. The memory that has been haunting me every day for the months I've spent by Mason's side at the hospital while he was in a coma, afraid that it could be the last thing we said to each other.

I need to tell him the truth.

I have to tell him the truth about us, so he can make his own decision.

I must tell him the truth before he finds it any other way because we all know lies only last for so long...

MASON

Taking a deep breath on the doctor's instruction, I feel the cool metal of the stethoscope on my back and hold the air in for a moment before I let it all out.

After an hour or even more in the room with a doctor who takes pleasure in putting me through the wringer, I am more than ready to get back into action and race into buildings. I am ready to feel the adrenaline pumping in my veins from the very instant the alarm system goes off in the firehouse. I am ready to climb into squad's truck and let my eyes take in the blurry surroundings as we speed past.

"Everything looks and sounds good to me, Mason," the doctor says, rounding the exam bed until he stands in front of me. "I've got all your test results in already and after what I've seen today, I believe you're ready to be back on duty."

A relieved breath pushes its way past my lips.

"Thanks, doc. It feels like I've been waiting for so long to hear you say that."

"Your recovery was speedy, and you should really thank Ensley for doing all that daily physical therapy with you while you were in a coma because it helped massively. It kept the muscles active and stopped them from atrophying."

My brows furrow together for a short moment. Short enough for the department's doctor not to notice it at least.

Daily physical therapy?
Ensley?

My mind begins to wander because I know Ensley was there every now and then as they used to take turns in staying by my side in the hospital.

What I didn't know is that she used to come every day to do physical therapy with me.

Did she?

Why would she sacrifice so much for me?

"You're one lucky man. Certainly won the lottery with your w—"

Before he gets a chance to finish his sentence, the door to the room opens and his assistant walks in with a stack of papers in hand, placing them on the desk.

"Anyway, Mason, I'm glad to tell you that you can go back to the firehouse."

"Appreciate it, doc."

Grabbing my t-shirt, I pull the fabric over my head and drop to my feet.

"So when can I get back?"

"Next shift," he states, no doubt in his voice.

A white smile spreads on my face at his reply.

"I still want you to come and see me next month, but if in the meantime you experience any changes; dizziness, blurred vision, lapses in memory, anything at all, you come here, alright?"

"Will do that."

After I already had my review with the board of chiefs to make sure that the dissociative amnesia doesn't affect my capacities as a firefighter, passing the last check-up with the department's doctor is the final step to be able to return to the firehouse.

With it out of the way now too, I am now about to get back to the only thing I've wanted to do my entire life.

Well, the only thing apart from Ensley.

Because, *Cristo*, I want to do her. Over and over and over again I wanna do her. In all positions and on top of all the surfaces in our house.

After I had a taste of her last evening, I became more than aware of the many ways I'm screwed. Screwed because there is no turning back.

Without a doubt, there will only be hell to pay for that taste. I know that. Just as cognizant I am that I would worship the Devil himself for another taste. Another touch of her lips on mine. One more press of her hot, bare skin against mine. Another instant of feeling her heartbeat thrum the same frenzied cadence as mine. One more thrust inside of her that dictates the tempo of our breathing. Yet another moment in which our pleasure-filled moans and our skin slapping together mingle into the only soundtrack that caroms from one corner of the room to the other. And one more tick of feeling that goddamn zap of electricity running from my body into hers and in reverse.

However, I want all these "another" and "one more" to go on and on, and repeat one time after the other and the next because I can't satiate my constant and all-consuming need for Ensley.

She is my weakness.

She is my kryptonite.

And she will be my downfall.

Yet, that's a perdition I am willing to risk because everything that I knew I've felt for Ensley is a billion times stronger, more heightened, more intense and more savage. Every single feeling she wakes in me has been magnified to a point that fighting against it is a battle I stand no chance to win.

Now.

Or ever.

Perhaps it is all as a result of the time I've spent in a coma. Maybe everything was put into perspective and served as a wake-up call for how frail life is.

There are still questions and ponders. Questions I'm afraid to ask. Ponders I'm terrified to contemplate on. All because they all might lead to an answer I don't want to hear. An answer I'm not ready to find.

"Thanks again, doc," I speak, my own voice pulling me out of my thoughts.

He nods and extends his hand, which I shake with and head out of the exam room.

There is a weight that's been lifted off my shoulders knowing that come next shift, I'll be back at the station. Riding with the guys.

"So?"

Pairs of eyes fixate on me.

Mom's brown eyes.

Luke's blue-grayish ones.

Ella's brown gaze.

Derek's blue-grayish eyes—the older version of my best friend—and Angie's green ones.

Right next to her is her daughter. The younger version of Angeline, from the hair, to the natural, exquisite beauty.

When I first exited the room, my stare instantly searched Ensley's gorgeous eyes, before they moved to the others. But now, her absolutely tantalizing green orbs beckon me to return to them, and I do. I lock my brown ones with that jaded gaze that pierces right into my soul. That pair that has been haunting my days and nights—blessed and cursed them all at once.

I hold her eyes for a moment, or maybe two. Perhaps even three, because I don't know exactly for how long I stand there under her hypnotic stare. All I know is that, once again, time stops.

It does until someone clears their throat, prompting me to dart my eyes to the rest, noting mine and Luke's teammates—Rhys Thatcher and Nolan Santiago. But as I move along from the two, I see that there are six more pairs of eyes aimed in my direction. They belong to Ian Callahan, Erin Ashford, Daniel Barlow, Emilian Trevino, Cole Dalton and Captain Owen Tucker.

They all stand before me, gazes filled with expectancy. They all came without my knowing and waited outside all through my check-up.

If this isn't a family, then I don't know what is.

My features are hard as I let my eyes travel between them all and it is only when they revert back to Ensley's green gaze that my façade falls.

"I'm back, baby," I call out and do a couple of bachata steps—my Latin roots definitely responsible for my dance moves and abilities as I smash it with the moves.

My fellow firefighters rush and give me a tight group hug before they pull away.

"Had time to practice them moves, hadn't you, Cutter? Those hips of yours ain't lying, brother."

Nolan's tease triggers a set of laughs from everyone and it is at that moment that I realize just how much I missed the banter with my fellow firefighters.

Right away, I search for Ensley's eyes once again after I

momentarily averted my stare to Nolan. The instant they lock, I send her an insinuating grin and an even more playful wink, completely disregarding her parents and her brother's presence. "They certainly don't lie."

I don't care if or who catches the innuendo in my voice or if or who sees the implying smirk on my lips. I don't concern myself even with who notices the little twinge of pink in her cheeks when she blushes. What I do concern myself with is the fact that her mind clearly went to how my hips moved last night when I was driving in and out of her.

Just as much as I don't care that in a long stride I'm right in front of Ensley and not a second later my hand is at the back of her neck and my lips are on hers, kissing my woman in front of everyone.

My woman.

Fuck if I don't like the sound and the thought of that.

If there's a moment of complete silence while I kiss Ensley or if the sweetness of her mouth blots out all my other senses, that I don't know for sure. What I am certain of is that there is a tick or two of quietness and when I withdraw—fighting to keep a complaining groan from surging up my throat at the loss of her soft lips—, I feel multiple sets of eyes on us. And the first one I meet is Derek's. There's a wide, proud grin that takes over his features.

"Couldn't wait to plant one on my daughter now, could you?"

"I definitely couldn't."

While I respond, my eyes move to Angie who beams with joy. Her green eyes are glossy as she wraps both arms around her husband's arm, her smile as wide as a kid's on Christmas morning. It is as though she's been waiting for so long to see this. At the same time, there's that emotion that I cannot pinpoint.

As I then take in the rest of the team, I can attest with utter certainty that there is not an ounce of surprise on their faces. Not even a scintilla of it as if they all have seen it coming. And maybe they have.

"So I guess it is that time when we'll keep telling you two to get a room."

It is the captain's voice that fills the air with jest, and I don't miss the plotting grins. Furthermore, I swear I can hear Rhys at the back telling Nolan that he owes him twenty bucks.

Do I want to know what that wager is about?

I don't believe so.

These two idiots bet even on the air they breathe, so I'd rather not even entertain the thought of what that bet might entail this time. However, there's little to no doubt in my mind that their little wager involved Ensley and me, considering the timing of the events.

Once I take one more step back from the woman I'm close to throwing over my shoulder and taking home—even if that means doing so in front of her father—, I aim my gaze on the second woman in my life who is my weakness—Mom.

With glossy eyes, she pulls me into a single-arm embrace, and I hold her against my chest between my own. Her body shakes and a small whimper fills my ears.

"It's okay, *Mamá*. It's all good now."

Against my form, I continue to feel her shudder as she grips my t-shirt, still fighting to keep her cry at bay. When she pulls away a few fractions to look up at me and caress my face with her palm, I note that the attempt is to no avail because a couple of tears roll down her cheeks.

"When you told me you wanna be a firefighter, I knew there were all kinds of risks. I knew it was dangerous, but I wanted you to be whatever you want to be in life because you were meant for incredible things." Momentarily, she pauses. "What I also know is that you can't make this promise, but please don't give me this scare ever again in your life because I will kill you with my own two hands and bury your body where nobody will find it."

I chuckle.

"And I'll gladly help with that because I'm willing to get behind the "dig-up-holes-to-get-rid-of-your-body" part of the program if you ever make me lose my mind the way you did," Ensley adds and, with the corner of my eye, I see my best friend also nodding.

"Glad to have you back, brother," Luke speaks, patting my shoulder. "Though these are words I know we'll all regret the instant you step foot in the firehouse."

My fellow firefighters share a laugh and an approving nod.

"At least we'll have great food. That ought to make up for

putting up with your cocky ass all day," Ian Callahan argues, shrugging casually.

"Callahan, if you want to be on mopping duties for the rest of your days in the firehouse, all you have to do is ask. No need to throw shade at my cooking skills," Captain Tucker reverts, folding his arms over his chest in a defensive mode.

"Mama Carter, you raised a fine chef," Rhys declares, winking at my Mom.

The bastard just winked at her.

To piss me the right off.

"Do you have something in your eye, Thatcher? Because I don't believe you just winked at my mom unless you want to wear a patch for an eye for the rest of your life."

His hands lift in surrender.

"Of course not, Carter. I wouldn't dare."

My head shakes.

"Thank you for being here. All of you."

"We're family," the guys say simultaneously.

"Always," Luke adds, patting my back.

Truth be told, they are exactly that. My family. We've been there for one another in the worst and in the best of situations. We were all there when Daniel Barlow got married to his high school sweetheart and when his wife had a miscarriage before they had their little girl. When Erin Ashford had her first kid and we were there for her when she went through a nasty divorce, or when she fought tooth and nail to get custody of her daughter. When Ian Callahan pissed off the wrong chief—a bully who made use of his position and title to mistreat and harass firefighters—and kept being bounced from firehouse to firehouse for a couple of weeks until we all did our own digging into said chief and got everyone who he's ever bullied to file an official complaint which eventually had him out of the service and Callahan back with us.

Also, we have been there for Emiliano Trevino when he found out his wife is pregnant with their fourth child and the man nearly had a meltdown. Luckily we were all training at the academy at the time and he took out his anger on a wrecked car that we used for a road traffic collision drill as he swore he'll never touch his wife again until he gets a vasectomy. Now, he's the happiest father of them all after he finally got the baby girl he wished for.

We were there when our youngest firefighter, Cole Dalton, finally came out of the closet and when he proposed to his boyfriend three years later, or when they got married and later decided to adopt.

Furthermore, we were there for our captain, Owen Tucker, when he lost his wife in a car crash. To this day, the image of how the color left his face when his engine got to the scene and he recognized her vehicle. I vividly remember how terror took over him and he tried to run to the car. I was the one who stopped him, though, after we checked for vitals just before they arrived, concluding it was too late and she was already gone. That happened eight years ago, and we all know he still hasn't recovered even the bare minimum.

If most of the engine firefighters have families or had been married at a certain point, the squad firefighters have been single and dating around—at least Luke, Rhys and Nolan have been because my memory is still fuzzy and, for the life of me, I cannot vouch hundred percent for what I've been doing. Have I been a man-whore? Can't say that for sure. Have I been loyal to one woman? Can't say either since the only woman who's claimed me as her man is Ensley.

As I sense the thought tumbling into the forefront of my brain, I knock it away, changing the trajectory to my best friend considering that now Luke is the most faithful of them all. He put a ring on his girlfriend's finger and looks ready to get hitched any moment now. He is the first of all of us on squad to take the plunge, while Rhys and Nolan appear to be just as far away and repugnant to the idea of a relationship and marriage as they were before.

Even though I am not too far behind them with the marriage —despite just saying that I'm not repellent to that idea—, I am ready to take my chances with Ensley. I am willing to set my cowardice and all my fears aside and give us a real try. I don't wanna hide away from my feelings for her, and I wanna do everything in my power to keep her safe, be worthy of her. Because for years I believed there is no way in hell I can ever deserve Ensley Walker and although I thought that, she still gave me all of her anyway. She gave me her virginity and I took it.

She gave me her heart the very night I gave mine to her in return.

Moreover, she still gives me. She gives me her love because only someone who loves somebody is willing to wait this long or fight for them as fiercely and unceasingly as she has.

Ensley Walker gives me an all-consuming passion and a love that leaves marks. A love that claws its way into each atom and fiber of my being. A love worth taking risks for. One I will fight for.

"Also, just letting you know that your return could not have been better timed," Ella speaks, pulling me from my thoughts.

My brow quirks at her. "What do you mean by that?"

She grins.

Oh, I don't like that grin.

"There's an auction I'm helping organize and the guys signed you up for it too."

My eyes go wide, and my lips press in a thin line, my look deadpan as I take in my team.

Shit.

I knew why I didn't like it.

"You're kidding me, right?"

"It's a charity auction," she adds, batting her eyes at me, faking an innocence I know she does not possess. "It's for the school in San Antonio that caught fire and the firefighters there are trying to gather money for the repairs. The same one Ensley went and volunteered for."

A defeated sigh slips past my lips.

"You had me at 'charity' already. As long as I don't need to get naked for someone who isn't my woman, I'm good."

With my head automatically turning and my eyes beckoned by Ensley's green ones, I wink at her and her cheeks catch fire. At that, my arm reaches out over her shoulder, pulling her into my chest while I press my lips on top of her head.

"Afraid the ladies will turn you down after your physique had a three-month break?" Rhys jabs, his smirk daring. "Or is it because you're scared they might not like a resurrected man?"

"Wouldn't you like to believe that, Thatcher?" I revert. "I'm more afraid if Ensley doesn't win me at the auction, she will feed me my balls as she so kindly threatened before. Of course, she did that for completely different reasons."

A playful smile tips on my lips as I drop my eyes to the woman in my arms.

"And she'll so kindly see it through," Ensley returns, the guys laughing among themselves at her words.

"Sounds to me like we've raised our daughter right," Angie points out, looking at her husband as she chuckles.

Derek's eyes drop to his wife in return, his features filled with the kind of love that some of us would only dream to experience in this lifetime.

"Make sure you do that after you two give us grandbabies."

"Mom."

The complaint in my voice is clear.

"I'm sure she had her reasons to make such a threat."

Mom and Ensley have definitely allied, otherwise, I don't see why my own mother would side with her on this. Especially when it concerns the well-being of my balls.

Hell, the whole team seems to be plotting something.

"If you don't want that to happen, give Ensley all the big bucks and you'll get to keep your balls right where they are."

Santo inferno.

I did say Ella is no innocent, didn't I?

"You know, for a minute I actually liked you," I tell her, and she shrugs off casually before I avert my attention to Luke. "Brother, you still have time to back down."

My best friend laughs at the seriousness on my face—although the jest in my baritone gives away my true feelings—and wraps his arm around his fiancée's waist.

"I told you that you two will get along just fine," he mutters to Ella with an amused expression.

To be completely honest, I do like Ella. She takes no bullshit, and she has no brain-to-mouth filter, which is exactly what Luke needs. Someone to give him hell. In the best possible way.

"We should go," Luke says to me.

I nod.

My head turns to take in Mom and then Ensley. But before I get a chance to say anything, Ella comes next to us.

"I'll give them a ride home, Mason."

"Appreciate it."

Reverting my attention to the two women beside me, I give them a smile.

"I'll see you when I get back."

I give Mom and Angie a kiss on the cheek and a short hug each, and Derek a handshake before he pulls me in for a hug as he pats me on the back.

"Take care of my little girl, Mason. She's been through hell these past few months," he utters.

"I love her, Derek, and I promise you that I'll make her happy."

"I have no doubt about it, son."

With one last pat on the back, they walk away with Ella after she kisses Luke, while my eyes drop again to Ensley.

"I love you," I whisper to her.

There's a little surprise on her face. One I know I feel also because the words just left me without giving them a second thought. They rolled off my tongue so naturally and with a degree of familiarity.

"I love you too," she mouths in return just before she presses her lips against mine.

It is just a curt peck on my lips. Too brief as it only has me want more. More than just an abrupt taste. More than just a terse brush of her lips against mine.

Cristo, I don't know how I survived without this, how I tamed this addiction for the past sixteen years after I had Ensley on her twenty-first birthday. Tasted. Caressed. Liked. Kissed. Coaxed. Claimed. Owned.

Looking over my shoulder and seeing the guys chatting between themselves, I grab Ensley by the hand and lead us just around the corner. Her green eyes are wide in a mix of astonishment and confusion, but they don't last long because my palms cup her face, and my lips are on hers in no time.

Ensley moans into the kiss as I concurrently let my own groan tumble out of my chest. This time around, it isn't just a peck. It isn't just a brush of her lips on mine. With this kiss, I thrust my tongue between her parted lips and explore her hot mouth.

Although we're out of the guys' sight, we still keep the kiss PG, but enough to temporarily quench our hunger for each other.

Drawing back a little, I then lean in again and place a gentle peck on her lips.

"Don't stop loving me," I whisper just a breath away. "I know I don't deserve it but, *nena*, I promise I'll do anything to be worthy of you."

A deep frown mars her gorgeous features.

"That is just nonsense, Mase. You are—"

The pad of my index finger rests on her enticing mouth, interrupting the trail of her sentence.

"You told me if I want you, I gotta earn you, and that's exactly what I'll be doing. Let's start that by allowing me to take you out for dinner tonight." My thumb traces her bottom lip. My gaze filled with promise and intensity as I keep it locked onto hers. "So then I can take you home and peel off every piece of clothing you'll wear until I have you completely bare and at my mercy."

Her arms wrap around my neck, her eyes playful.

"At your mercy?" In her voice, curiosity blends with taunt and a fraction of challenge. Nothing short of sexy and sultry, inviting me to do to her all the dirtiest things I can think of.

Ensley Walker is a walking and talking sin.

A sin I plan to feast on. To spread on my bed and feast on till she feels my mouth on her skin days from now.

"Yes, Ley," I rasp, almost unable to recognize my own voice at how affected I am by just the thought of what I will do to her. "You'll be at my mercy and will enjoy every moment of it."

The corners of her mouth twitch, but she fights the smile begging to form. "Tryin' to seduce me, Carter?"

Unlike Ensley, I don't suppress the grin that quirks my lips. "And wait until I put my mouth on you, *nena*. Seduction at its finest."

"If it will be just like it was when I woke up with your head between my legs, consider me seduced already, baby."

My head leans in further, closer to her ear.

"Wouldn't you wish to know the plans I have for you?" I whisper. "Better said, the plans I have with you."

Pulling away, I wink.

"Such a tease," she gripes, smacking my chest lightly with the back of her hand.

My retreat is well-timed as sets of steps approach and the crew turns the corner, giving us an insinuating grin.

"I'll definitely not come to your house unannounced," Rhys speaks out.

"You're not supposed to come over unannounced anyway."

He almost rolls his eyes at my revert.

"I'll see you at home, baby," Ensley mutters and I cock my neck to the side, nodding at her before I give her a quick peck. "Bye, guys!"

"I'm gonna walk out with you, Ensley, before these fools take out their dicks and measure them," Erin adds with a chuckle and Ensley shakes her head at us, knowing from her experience as a firefighter and being surrounded by men, that it is only a matter of time until we'd start busting each other's chops.

They all say their goodbyes to Ensley and Erin, and for a few seconds, I watch my woman walk away. Just for as many instances, I remain still and mesmerized by the way she moves. How her hips sway from side to side, elegantly and temptingly at the same time. Left and right, right and left, bewitching me with every step that she takes, beckoning me to chase after her. Inviting me to screw the interview with the bartender and just take her on that date already so then I can take her home, have my wicked way with her exactly as I promised her I will. Because I'll be damned if I won't.

"You're so fucked, brother. Your woman has you by the dick and the balls." Ian's voice causes my attention to snap from Ensley to him. "Well, to be honest, they've been in her possession for—"

"Okay, can we please not talk about my sister holding his balls? As much as I like the fact that they are together, there's only so much I can take before I get a sudden urge to throw up my breakfast," Luke interferes, his nose scrunching up in revolt.

The guys laugh at his complaint, and I join in, my eyes taking in the repugnance on his face.

"It's time for us all to leave. You two need to get that bar ready so I can finally patronize it for free drinks," Nolan states, patting my back.

Luke's blue-grayish eyes fly to mine before they dart to our teammate simultaneously and we share a laugh, dismissing the idea of free drinks.

ENSLEY

"So, you and Mr. Tatts."

Ella's patience didn't last long.

I'd say it lasted for about three seconds from the moment I climbed in the passenger seat while Aracely went into the backseat.

With that amount of patience—or lack thereof—Ella definitely fits in with the Walkers who are known for their deficit of patience.

The smile is wide on her face as she cranes her neck toward me for a tick before she returns her eyes to the road.

A wistful sigh escapes me as I lean further into my seat, my eyelids shutting for a tick. They reopen and I aim my gaze out the window.

"I was sure it won't take long," Ary speaks, and I can sense the smile in her voice. "My son's always been crazy about you and there was never a question of *'if'*, but more of *'when'*. One can't fight the pull of true love, no matter how hard they try."

Over my shoulder, I look at Mason's mom and the corners of my lips lift.

"He's taking me on a date tonight."

As I say the words out loud, my heart skips a beat and I feel as though I'm a beaming teenager who just got asked to go to prom with their crush.

"No wonder you're all lit up more than this city during

winter holidays," Ella adds, tease filling the redhead's voice. "This calls for an emergency lingerie shopping."

"Who says I'm planning on wearing any?"

The words roll off my lips before I have a chance to think about them and now what I wear is a mortified look on my face because I didn't blurt them out in front of my friend only, but also in front of my mother-in-law.

Oh, the shame.

It burns my cheeks.

Especially when she chuckles.

"Don't mind me. Nothing to be ashamed of, *cariño*. Less things to take off means more time to make me grandbabies," Ary reverts with a nonchalant shrug.

"Ary—"

"I know. I know. You and Mason don't want to have any kids," she repeats our usual lecture with displease and incredulity. "But one can still hope, right?"

As the car comes to a halt at a stop light, Ella's eyes journey to me again and I feel the confusion in her gaze.

"I'm too old for kids now. I'll turn thirty-eight in a few months."

Although I do my best to mask the unwanted sadness in my voice, I know there are still traces of it.

"I'm no fool, Enz. I know how my son feels about having kids. I've heard it many times before, he loves them, but he doesn't want to have any of his own, blah, blah. You, on the other hand, do. So I am more than aware you made the compromise." Aracely's right hand rests on my shoulder and she gives me a light squeeze in a reassuring gesture.

My eyes lower, avoiding her brown ones. Did she know all along that Mason is the one who doesn't want kids?

"I'm beyond happy that you two are together. I am happy because you both are. You love each other so much that nothing has ever stood in your way, not even my son's stubbornness and his denial or him losing his memories of you." She gives me yet another gentle squeeze. "I'm sure you two will find a way for whatever it is you both choose to do."

"Thank you, Ary."

"Always, *cariño*."

"To be completely honest with you, Enz, I'm surprised you

didn't pop any babies by just looking at him or how he didn't just get you pregnant with those scorching stares he gives you," Ella chips in, giving me a plotting smile.

"Because even his stares are on birth control," I quip and the redhead giggles, shaking her head at me.

"Apparently I educated my son a tad too well on using protection," Ary grumbles under her breath, but loud enough for us to hear her.

Ella and I share a laugh at the complaint we hear in her voice.

"You know, I love Angie to bits and she's the best mother-in-law I could have ever hoped for, and the fact that she's one of my favorite authors is more than a bonus. But, girl, with this gem on the backseat of my car, you won the lottery," the redhead declares.

Automatically, my head cocks to the side and I look at Aracely who gives me one of her soft and kind smiles, which I return immediately.

Truthfully, I did win the lottery with Aracely as my mother-in-law. She hasn't been that, though. She has been and is a mother to me. From the moment she and Mom met, she became family and ever since, I've always said I have two moms. Even more so when Mason and I started our relationship.

My family was incredibly happy when Mason and I finally got together after we danced around each other for as long as we could remember. But Aracely? She was ecstatic and eagerly reminded both of us how when I was eight years old and Mason was six, we used to say we'll get married when we grow up. When we got to our teens, we used to joke about it. Yet the joke was on us because we indeed got married. Twenty-six years later we vowed to love each other, although we unknowingly swore it the very first night we spent together.

"Wanna come in for a coffee?" I ask Ella when the car comes to a halt in front of the house.

"Thanks, girl, but I'm meeting Dad for lunch. Ever since he moved out of the apartment next door and works at the academy, I barely get to see him."

"Or better say that my brother keeps you occupied."

At my tease, the redhead grins.

Her eyes shine with a mix of wickedness and happiness. "Well, that is partially true."

"Okay, that's something I'd rather not get the confirmation of."

I chuckle and so does Aracely.

"We should organize a ladies-only night," my mother-in-law suggests, resting her hands atop the backrest of our seats. "The three of us, Angie and Renée."

"That would be so much fun," I say excitedly. "Ella, you haven't experienced a full-on night out with Mom and Ary just yet, but you're in for a treat. These ladies are wild."

"Oh, are they?" Ella's neck cranes to the side to look at Aracely over her shoulder with a gaze filled with suspicion.

My mother-in-law casually shrugs as though she and Mom didn't cause Renée and me major hangovers on each one of our outings.

"Where is Renée, by the way? I haven't seen her in a while." Ella's eyes narrow.

I sigh. "She's been traveling with work. If not, she's been with her boyfriend."

"She's got a boyfriend?" Surprise is clear in the redhead's voice. "I mean, Luke's never mentioned him before. Nobody has actually."

"They've been together more off than on for about two years I think, but the guy's a dirtbag and doesn't deserve her. It is clear she doesn't love him and isn't happy with him. You might not believe it, but she used to smile and knew how to have fun, but something happened that changed my little sister. Something she doesn't want to talk about..." I let my dislike for my sister's boyfriend trail off as I shake my head. "She turned into the Ice Queen of the Walker family, and I don't think it's just because of her job. Partially, maybe, but not entirely. She's more guarded and... I don't know... But I miss how she used to be, you know?"

Ella smiles gently at what I say last, her brown eyes understanding.

"Okay, you really don't like the guy," Ella concludes. "But we should definitely get her to come with us too."

"I'll wait for you inside, *fermosa*. Thank you for the ride, Ella," Aracely says and gives the redhead a kiss on her cheek.

"See you soon, Ary."

Mason's mom slides from the middle of the backseat to the

side and opens the door. She waves at Ella, then turns and walks toward the house.

"How is she doing?"

Worry can be heard in Ella's voice.

I let out a breath in return. "She says she's fine. Well, even the doctor says she is, but I don't know. There's something weird about how things happened."

"How do you mean?"

Ella's brows furrow as she looks at me.

"I don't know, I just feel like there might be more to this accident than she lets on." My head shakes. "Don't mind me, maybe I'm just imagining things."

My friend's hand rests on my shoulder, and she gives it a light squeeze. "She's alright and it is all that counts."

I nod. "You're right. Maybe after what happened with Mason, then us and now his mom, I just feel like I need to question each moment of tranquility and happiness."

"But you deserve all that and more. Everything will settle down for the three of you. Don't let the fear of what happened these past few months be the judge of how you continue living your lives."

Once again, my head moves in assent.

"I'll see you in the next couple of days."

"That if Mr. Tatts lets you out of the house," Ella taunts in return and I chuckle. "Maybe he wants to make up for the lost time."

"It hasn't been that long," I argue.

Her brow shoots up challengingly. "Not what he believes which has its advantages. Rabbits will have nothing on you two. Maybe you should slip some notes in your neighbors' post-box to let them know you're screaming out your pleasure."

"Get out of here."

I still laugh at her revert though.

"Gladly because I'm starving."

"You're always hungry. Had I not known that about you, I'd have thought you have a bun cooking in that oven."

"Oh, God, no. Nothing cooking in this oven," she declares, pointing at her flat abdomen. "Not yet, at least."

A low sigh rolls through my lips. It is involuntary. So much so that by the time I realize it slips out, it is already too late.

Moreover, when I meet Ella's brown gaze, I also understand the bad timing of it.

"You and Mason… Have you two really never wanted kids?"

My neck cranes to the side and I look through the window at our house. The very house I thought we'll raise our kids in. That, of course, until Mason came out and told me he doesn't want to have kids. Ever. But I loved him, and I wanted him to be my family, with or without children.

"I always did, but I understood that if I wanted to be with the man I love, something's gotta give." I pause briefly, turning my head back to look at Ella. "And I made my peace with it. I'll never be a mother, but I get to be with the man I'm completely in love with."

Ella's eyes gleam as she stares back at me.

"Before Mason's accident… I was late and I thought…"

"That you were pregnant?"

My head moves in assent.

"Were you?"

This time around, my head shakes. "No, but Mason saw the pregnancy test and a few days later, he asked me for the divorce, saying that he holds me back from something I want. From becoming a mother."

"He wanted to divorce you so you can be a mom?" Ella's gaze widens in shock. "That's kinda fucked up."

"Mason believed I still held hope to get pregnant and have a kid. I do want to be a mom, but not if that means losing him."

"So, you're sacrificing something you want…"

"Only so I can be with the man I love, yes." Another sigh slips out of me. "Anyway, now go and enjoy lunch with your dad."

"I'm here for you, okay, Enz?"

The genuineness in her voice gets a smile from me.

Ella and I might not know each other for long, but we've definitely created a bond and a friendship. It doesn't matter I'm about twelve years her senior, she's mature and a lot of fun to be around, especially because she has no mouth-to-brain filter. She speaks her mind and there's no stopping it.

"Thanks, El."

With that, I open the passenger door and step out of the car, waving Ella goodbye as she drives off. Once her vehicle is out of sight, I turn and walk on the pavement toward the house.

313

"Any idea where my son's taking you tonight?" Aracely asks after I saunter right for the kitchen.

"He didn't exactly share that with me," I respond, meeting her curious gaze.

"We can still choose a couple of outfits for you."

We smile complicitly at each other.

"A couple that might not necessarily require lingerie," she teases.

My cheeks are aflame at my mother-in-law's tease. She certainly is a one-of-a-kind type of woman and mother-in-law goals.

Although my face is on fire, with the same conspirative, sneaky grins on our faces, we head upstairs, and she moves to rummage through my closet. I, on the other hand, just before I get to follow her, my phone rings.

Extending my arm, I grab it from the nightstand where I've placed it when I walked inside the bedroom.

A smile plasters on my face automatically as I note it is Mason, and without delay I swipe my finger over the screen, answering the call.

"Missing me already, handsome?"

The taunt in my voice is crystal clear, the smile on my face matching while I run a hand through my hair. With the corner of my eye, I see Aracely pulling dresses out of my closet, the little grin on her lips unmissable.

"Listen to you, shamelessly teasing me."

His deep, guttural timber has a shiver run through my body. Or better said, a goddamn zap of electricity that courses through me, quivering my form.

"But to answer your question, yes, I do miss you already. I was actually planning something for us for tonight and I thought I should ring you to tell you that you can wear whatever you want," he casually declares.

"Anything I want?" I question teasingly and I don't miss how the smile on Aracely's face grows at the little taunting exchange she witnesses. "What if there is no underwear?"

This last bit I whisper under my breath just enough for him to hear. But the guttural groan coming through the phone's speaker in my ear is loud. And not only loud. It is also extremely clear. So clear that my words affected him in the exact manner I wanted, and I can't help but grin cheekily at that.

"*Nena*, do you want to fucking kill me?" Mason asks with a groan.

"Do you like that idea?"

Another grumble fills my ear.

"I love the idea of you wearing nothing beneath."

There's a pause as he lets out a low whistle.

"Actually, I've changed my mind. You can wear a dress so I can slip my fingers under the fabric and find you bare and dripping wet for me. But I gotta warn you though. Because of this little game of yours, I won't touch your pussy. I will touch your inner thighs. I will caress you close enough until you're on the brink of losing your mind just like you have me losing mine right this second. And only when we're home, that's when I'll finally touch you where you ache for me. I want to find you drenched, *nena*."

The giddy smile I had playing on my lips when Mason first called now gets wider and naughtier.

Christ, the mouth this man of mine has on him.

It is as though it was made to torment me, to test the willpower of my body.

On one hand, there's the teenage girl within me who gets ecstatic. She giddily does a backflip, followed by a triple-flip roll with a double leap. He can take me on a date to the ice-cream parlor around the corner for all I care, and I'll be just as excited.

Hell, he can take me on a date at the back of our garden and I'd still be thrilled. Thrilled because I miss Mason taking me on little dates. Which happened quite often, I might say. He'd argue he does it for selfish purposes only so that I am fueled enough for a whole night of love-making. Though, I am au courant he loved every moment of our date because it seemed like we are courting each other all over again. Also, we loved showing each other off.

On the other hand, there's the woman within me who knows what her man is capable of. How crazy with need he can make me by only looking at me. How close to the brink he can bring me with the merest of touches.

Mason is sex personified. He exudes confidence and sex appeal from every single atom in his body.

With the risk of sounding narcissistic, I'm not too shabby myself and the way Mason can't seem to keep his hands to himself only solidifies that belief. How his hands roam all over my body whenever he gets the chance—which when he doesn't get it, he creates that chance.

"I'll come back home for a shower once I'm done here with Luke and then I'll take you on that date."

My mouth opens, ready to give it another try and ask him where we're going. However, he seems to know what's coming next.

"Don't even try to have that extremely seductive mouth of yours convince me to tell you where I'm taking you because my very wicked mouth will give nothing away."

The little warning in his voice is playful and sexy as hell.

If he wants to play, this is a game we both can play, the thought crosses my mind as a grin tips the corners of my lips.

MASON

I know there will be hell to pay.

And that because I unleashed the hellcat within Ensley. But I'd be damned if I can't wait to bear witness to that—though I'm fairly sure I'll regret it the instant I have her right in front of me.

In all honesty, I already do. Especially after that tease of hers with the lack of underwear. Taunt that had my cock jerk in my jeans, the confinement created by the cotton boxer briefs and by the denim becoming almost skin-tight.

This is what I get for playing with fire.

For playing with that fierce fire that burns within me. The one ignited by Ensley and all that she wakes in me.

My soulmate. That notion every single one of us has heard of, has wondered about and only few of us are able to find, to recognize, to grab and hold on to. This is what Ensley is to me. The love of my life. My soulmate. My everything.

She is also my walking and talking fantasy, getting me as hard as a steel rod with only the mere wonder if her lips are just as soft as they were when I kissed her years ago, if her milky skin is just as sweet beneath my mouth and just as hot on my tongue.

Oh, man, the number of times I jacked off with the thought of Ensley on my mind. I've done it almost every single goddamn night since I came home from the hospital and each attempt of mine to stop myself has been futile. Just like I couldn't help myself any longer after her soft lips touched mine.

A fucking addiction.

"Appreciate you coming in, Evan."

Luke's voice breaks through my thoughts.

Right.

Back to the interview.

Evan Prescott.

"Appreciate the chance."

It is the first time since halfway through the interview that his words register.

Luke must have noticed my lack of concentration and took charge of the interview. Not that it was very long anyway, but the thought of Ensley had me distracted. Especially after the conversation we had just before Luke and I got started with Evan.

"You can start on the soft launch night," Luke continues, and I simply nod, supporting the decision.

"Thank you."

My eyes take in the man across from the bar as I sit on the barstool next to my best friend. While doing the interview, we had him demonstrate his skills. We knew already what kind of person we are looking for—someone we can trust with taking good care of the bar while Luke and I are on shift and someone who can entertain by talking to patrons and pouring good drinks.

Evan Prescott has served. After being honorably discharged from the Navy, three months into his civilian life, he was arrested and sentenced to two years in prison because while on a night out with a couple of his Navy brothers, he went up to defend a woman who was being harassed by a drunken man. The man got aggressive, punching Evan when he interfered and when he punched the man back, he stumbled and hit his head on a nearby. He died in the hospital a day later. The District Attorney's office offered him a deal, manslaughter charges with two years in jail with possibility of parole after six months. He was released after those six months after his lawyer—the very woman who he's defended in the bar that night—fought to get him out.

Although Evan served time, he did an honorable thing defending that woman. He was just unlucky. But that could have easily happened to Luke or to me or to anyone else.

"Honestly, thank you both for this. It's been very difficult to find my footing after prison and you two have been pretty much the only ones who have listened to my side of the story, without jumping the gun on the rap sheet that I've got."

"We would have all done what you've done, Evan," I speak with absolute certainty in my voice.

"You're a great man, Evan."

Cocking my head to the side, Luke and I share a knowing look. It will be only a matter of time until Jesse's brother will take him away from us.

Zaiden Lewis can sniff a great soldier and an even greater man from miles away, and in no time, he'll walk through the doors of this bar and offer Evan a job with *Hellhound Corps* that we can't match even if Luke and I put all our investments on the table.

Over the years, we've met Zaiden a few good numbers of times, but from the first meeting, I understood he's not an easy person to sway. When he wants something, he goes for it. That man breathes and moves military style—if there is such a thing as that.

Once Evan shakes our hands, he turns around and walks toward the exit. Not a moment later, Luke's eyes snap my way.

"Damn, you're whipped."

A smirk plays on his lips.

The corners of my mouth lift almost automatically at that. Because, damn, I am. Ensley has me by the heart, by the balls and dick. She's the reason my heart still beats. The motive my dick is always rock hard around her and useless around any other woman.

"Go home already and take my sister on that date," my best friend urges. "But make sure you're not late tomorrow."

"Got it, Lieutenant," I state, lifting my hand to my temple and saluted him mockingly.

"I'm serious, you're a minute late and your ass is on scrubbing duties."

I shrug. "It'd be worth every second of scrubbing if that gets me an extra minute or two with my woman."

Luke's brow lifts daringly. "Your woman, heh?"

"My woman," I repeat, not even the smallest fraction of doubt in my voice.

"What made you change your mind?"

"I'm done being a coward, man. I'll protect her with my life if ever comes to it, but I'm done pushing away the woman I love because of a *what if* that might never come."

"I'm glad you reached this conclusion, brother. I was worried you'd settle for watching my sister move on with someone else."

My head instantly shakes with vehemence.

There's no way in fucking hell I'll let another man love her. Allow another man to conquer her heart. Another man to touch her body.

"Tell me your heart doesn't bleed thinking of me with another man!"

The words ring in my head with such velocity it takes yet another repeat or two for me to actually understand them.

I don't know where they come from.

The voice shouting them is distorted.

Although I don't recognize the voice, there's something in the way that sentence hits me. It is like someone punched me right in the throat and knocked the air out of my lungs.

My eyes squeeze shut and my palm flies over my forehead, applying pressure as a throbbing headache strikes, my ears ringing.

"Fucking fuck," I curse aloud and my teeth grit, while my body bends in half and my hands now rest just above my knees.

"Mason."

My best friend's voice cuts through the ringing in my ears and my eyes snap back open, meeting Luke's worried gaze when I tip back my chin.

"Are you alright?"

He places his hand on my shoulder.

"I am," I groan the answer. "Just got a little headache."

Luke's brows knit together. "That didn't seem little," he calls me out. "So don't try to shit me now."

"There's a random sentence that..." My head shakes. "It doesn't make any sense."

"What kind of sentence?"

"Never mind, Luke."

"Did you have this kind of episode before?"

Instantly, my mind darts to the first time it happened. Just not long ago.

"Mason, baby..."

"Only once," I admit. "I don't actually know what triggers them for sure or what they mean."

"You should consult your doctor. Maybe your memories get triggered by random sentences or situations, but your mind fights to block them back out."

"I'm not too sure. I'll check in with the doctor in the coming days. Now, I need to see my woman."

"Sure thing. I'll see you tomorrow morning at the firehouse, brother."

"See you tomorrow, bro."

Luke spins on the sole of his shoes, heading towards the door. However, not two steps later, he stops and looks at me over his shoulder.

"And please keep whatever happens tonight to yourself. As much as I like that my best friend is getting laid because that means you're less of a pain in the ass, since it is my sister the deed involves, I'd rather not know."

I grin devilishly.

Oh, man, the plans I have for her, she won't be able to say what happened without blushing.

"See?! That's exactly the kind of look I don't wanna see on your face tomorrow. I don't flaunt every time I make love to my woman."

I laugh sarcastically. "That's because one can read it all over your face and in your attitude because you're as giddy and happy as a clam when you get some, instead of the nudnik you usually are. So don't worry, it's pretty evident just how often just as clear as it is when the hellcat you have for a fiancée gives you the silence treatment and doesn't give you any."

"Ella hasn't done so," Luke argues.

"Yet, but we all know that moment will come, and we'll all know when it happens as it happens."

"Jackass."

With that last revert ricocheting across the room, having me chortle, Luke smiles before he straightens his large form and walks away.

It is moments later after my best friend leaves that I also make my way toward the exit. That of course, once I have the leather jacket on, phone inside one of its pockets and fish the keys for my motorcycle off the bar top together with my helmet.

With my belongings in hands, I stride out of the bar and lock the door behind me. All throughout, all I can possibly think about is the gorgeous brunette waiting for me at home. And said gorgeous brunette is my woman.

How things have changed in the span of only a few weeks since I recovered from the coma and since I was discharged from the hospital. They have taken a turn I could have only dreamed of. That kind of life turn where the guy gets the girl although he's not worthy of her and the only thing that isn't tainted about him is the love he has for her.

Ensley is now my woman and I'll be damned if I won't fight with every cell of my body to keep her, to deserve her and to protect her.

Shaking my head to push away the thoughts so I can prevent a delay in getting home, I head for the motorcycle parked just in front of the establishment.

Just as I'm about to put on the helmet, a loud sound stabs my ears. A noise that the metal makes at the contact with the cemented ground. Almost instantly my neck snaps in the direction of where the sound came from and I realize it comes from the alley between the bar and the adjacent building.

I don't have time to brush it off, thinking it might be a stray cat, because not even a second after the noise, a piercing scream fills my ears. My alerted gaze homes in on the entrance of that very alley. Meanwhile, my long strides toward the side path turn immediately into a rapid sprint. I round the corner with such speed I'm surprised how I missed and didn't run right into the bricks.

The scream that punctured my eardrums earlier now is silenced. What I hear in lieu when I near is a whimpered cry, and my stare doesn't hesitate to halt to my left side. It then immediately drops down the length of the brick wall, and a pair of wide, timorous green eyes meet mine.

I blink in surprise and slowly lower myself as though in a squatting position.

"Hey, little man," I speak gently, eying the little boy who doesn't look to be older than seven or eight years old. One hand is around his knee, while the other rubs at his shoulder. "Are you alright, buddy?"

His little head full of dark brown, unruly hair with slight curls moves. "Y...Yes. I... I just fell," he speaks, a little timid and embarrassed.

"Did you hurt yourself there?"

My voice is still soft, mirroring the look in my eyes as I take him in. He has on a jacket that has wears and tears, a pair of jeans that have seen better days and shoes that seem a size too big. His entire appearance has me fight the impulse of narrowing my eyes.

Once again, he nods. "Just a scrape."

"Want me to have a look?" I suggest, not getting close until he allows me to.

And he doesn't right away. His green eyes analyze me unhurriedly for a moment or two, moving over my large form once, then twice, before they return and lock onto my brown ones.

It is only then that his head moves in assent again.

"Are you a doctor?" The little boy asks, his voice filled with curiosity and a fraction more of confidence.

My head shakes.

"No, I'm actually a firefighter."

"Wow, that is awesome."

His eyes beam with glee.

"Do you get to ride one of them big trucks I see driving on the street with the sirens on?"

I can't fight the smile at his excitement as he asks the question. Especially when his lips tip in a small smile of his own.

"Yes, I do."

"Coooool," the little boy speaks, rolling the "o" a little longer.

"What's your name, buddy?" I ask, coming a tad closer to have a look at his knee.

"Zane."

As I get closer, Zane removes his hand, and I note the jeans now have a hole where he injured himself. One that allows me to see the extent of how badly or not he hurt himself.

"It's nice to meet you, Zane. I'm Mason."

After I introduce myself, I drop my eyes back again to the injury on his knee. It doesn't look that bad.

"Looks like you should be a doctor when you grow up.

You're right, it only seems to be a scrape. But we should get it cleaned up, alright?"

Again, he nods his head in assent.

"What are you doing here all alone, buddy? Where are your parents?"

When the question makes its way through my lips, my eyes move once over the little boy, his rugged clothes already having me fear the answer.

A reply that doesn't delay. "I don't have a mommy anymore."

His timid voice becomes even frailer and his green eyes turn glossy. The image before me has my heart drop into the pit of my stomach.

For a moment or maybe two, his reply reverberates in my head: *"I don't have a mommy anymore"*. Six words so soulful and filled with pain.

"I'm sorry, bud. What about your daddy?"

His small shoulders lift.

Immediately, my eyes dart to the cardboard box he sits on before they zoom out on the entire scene taking place in front of me. All of a sudden, his words and his somewhat rough appearance in this scene make so much sense.

"Zane, do you sleep here, buddy?"

The question pains me as I ask it.

I don't know this kid, but it fucking hurts to know he is all alone in this world, sleeping rough.

The thought begins seeping into the forefront of my mind. Yet, before I get to ponder on it, I knock the thought away, not willing to entertain it. A thought I haven't allowed myself to have in so many years.

"Sometimes. The kids at the foster home are very mean and pick up on me all the time because I'm the new kid."

Foster home.

Worn-out clothes.

The size of the shoes that's one too big for him.

He most likely wears the clothes from the other kids in there. Maybe the children there are a little older than him.

My chest tightens and my gut churns.

"For how long have you been out here, Zane?"

"Two or maybe three…"

Please say hours. Please say two or maybe three hours, I find myself urging inly.

"…days."

Merda!

Even through the shock, I suppress the curse inside, not letting it come out.

Two or three days and nobody is looking for this kid? Two or three days and nobody realized that he's missing from that home?

"Buddy, let's get some food in you and get that wound looked at, shall we?"

Once again, his cautious eyes scrutinize me.

And I don't take offense to that at all. On the contrary, I'm glad he does it. I'm glad he is prudent and watchful. God, he should be so.

My hand extends with the palm up, giving him a clear indication that it is his choice.

After a tick, he sets his much smaller hand in mine and we both get up.

"Are you sure you can walk on that?" I check with him, gesturing with my chin to his knee.

Zane shakes his head.

"I'll pick you up then, bud, and we can get a taxi."

At that, he nods, and I bend to wrap my arm around his small legs, lifting him up to my chest and we make our way out of the alley.

"You don't drive?"

I chuckle at the shock in his voice.

"I don't own a car. I own that."

With a cock of my chin, I point toward the motorcycle just before we make our way to it to retrieve the abandoned helmet.

I watch his eyes go wide and excitement takes over his face once again, his smile growing bigger with each passing second.

"Coooool," Zane attests animatedly.

Even if I want to—not that I do—, I can't fight the chuckle from erupting out of my chest.

"Why can't we take this?"

"Because it isn't safe for a kid to be on it, bud."

A little bit of disappointment washes over his face and he sighs gently.

"But I'm sure you can wear this."

Yet again, pure glee gets plastered on his little face and I smile to myself as he takes the helmet and places it over his head. Although it is too big for him and a tad too heavy, that doesn't decrease Zane's excitement. On the contrary, he laughs at himself as he struggles to keep it on.

Waiving at a taxi, we walk to it once it pulls over and Zane removes the helmet before we make ourselves comfortable in the backseat of the cab.

Nena, I hope you don't mind if this little man joins us for dinner, I think to myself, my eyes still on him.

ENSLEY

As I wait for Mason to appear so we can go on our date, I take one last look in the mirror and smile to myself.

Not at my appearance. Although I must say I look quite hot in a wine-red bodycon midi dress with two Cami style straps and a sweetheart neckline that has a knot detail in front just a little above the breast line. I smile at the thought of why I've just spent the last couple of hours getting ready.

Because I have date with Mason.

A date with my husband—although he still doesn't know that detail, not remembering it.

It is on that thought that guilt assails once again. It has been attacking me on and off since I've made the decision not to tell him that we are married. Yet, from the moment we shared our first kiss since he's recovered from his coma, I felt guiltier and guiltier.

Culpable because I keep from him the fact that we're married. That we share a past together and memories he cannot remember. That he's been a part of my life and I've been a part of his more than he can imagine.

I sigh, passing my hands over the length of the dress to tidy a couple of non-existent creases. I know I do it because I am nervous. Nervous about the date and about what it means.

Running a hand through my hair this time, I smile when I hear the sound of an engine approaching and I rush to step inside my nude-colored heels.

My heart swiftly begins to hammer in my chest. It leaps and thrums eagerly. So powerfully that I need to rest my palm over it to make sure it doesn't simply jump out.

"Oh, be still, my heart," I urge.

The moment I register the sound better and I realize it sounds nothing like the roaring of Mason's motorcycle, a tad of disappointment washes over me. Or maybe more than a fraction because it sounds nothing like that smooth, revved-up purr of that engine when Mason pulls into the driveway. And my own engine—a.k.a. my pussy—more than purred at that sound whenever I'd hear him ride that motorcycle nearer and nearer to home. It is as though it has a sixth sense and gets very excited.

Well, truth be told, Mason Carter is a through and through Greek god on a motorcycle. He didn't come sweeping me off my feet on a white horse. He rode in on a damn motorcycle, knocked me off my feet and I fell head in first right into that spell he put me under.

Silence envelops the room, and the feeling of disappointment soon is replaced by utter zeal when I hear the familiar drop of the keys into the stainless-steel bowl by the front door. I hear it because the door to the bedroom is open and the sound travels so quickly. Just as quickly as my heart begins to thump again my chest.

Maybe because of the nerves of our date. But also because of the surprise I have prepared for him when we return. Especially when Aracely left us all on our own in the house, telling me she's having a drink with Mom. Although Mom did pick her up, I doubt the two of them will spend a whole night out—not that they haven't done so many times before to prove contrary to my statement.

"Mason, baby, is that you?" I shout, making my way to exit the bedroom. "I'm almost ready."

Saying that, I slowly head down the hall, my cheeks heated up at the thought of the little surprise Mason will get at the end of our date.

While I descend the stairs, I bring my hand up and fan my face, trying to disperse the sheer heat burning at my cheeks.

"*Joder!*"

The curse interrupts my line of thinking, and my eyes meet that brown chocolate pair of eyes that has embedded itself so deeply under my skin that nothing will ever remove it. That very set of orbs that sets my flesh alit with one single glance my way and turns me into a wildfire every time it roams over my body.

Mason waits for me at the landing of the stairs, his tattooed arms draped by his sides while the denim he's wearing hugs delectably his thick thighs and long legs. His jacket is off already, the gray t-shirt tightly stretched over his muscles.

As I make my way down, his eyes rove over me. From my discreet makeup to the bodycon dress that accentuates all my curves. From the sweetheart neckline to the width of my hips. From the narrow waist to the length of my legs. And then all the way back up.

His gaze turns darker and darker. Hungrier and more ardent. With each step that I take, his body tenses further and his stare burns me to the point that I am barely able to walk down the stairs without stumbling over my own feet.

Somehow and only by a miracle, I manage to stop on the last step from the bottom, right in front of him without falling. But if I think even for the briefest of seconds that I am safe now, I am utterly mistaken.

The proof is in the way his arm snakes around me. Possessively. With claim. Without room for argument. How he tightens his hold on my waist and brings me flush to him, needing to look up a little since the heels together with the height of the step give me a few extra inches on him.

"*Quitas o meu alento.*"

("*You take my breath away.*")

These are the words he whispers to me only a mere centimeter away from my lips. But they also transport me for a second to the first time he saw me wearing this dress on our anniversary in Paris. These are the exact words he whispered to me then after I made my way to the table that he reserved for us at the hotel's restaurant. I told him to wait for me there, knowing if his lips land on mine or his fingers even graze me, we won't make it to dinner or out of the hotel room for the remainder of our stay.

Yes, I wore it on purpose. First, because I know he likes this dress because he could barely keep his hands off me during that dinner. Secondly, because deep down I hope it could stir up a memory in his mind. Perhaps kick off that lid he put over his recollections of me, triggering something within him.

"Your red lips are so inviting."

His whisper wrenches me from the thought.

Mason's baritone is low and guttural. Smooth and sleek and so goddamn sexy.

"This dress already begs to take the night off on my bedroom floor."

Holy shit!

My body shakes.

Involuntarily and without warning, it trembles between his arms as I let his words sink in.

Throwing my own arms over his shoulders, I have them meet at the nape of his neck and smile at him.

"Hello to you too, handsome!"

Mason grins. It isn't an innocent kind of smile. No, it is one full of dirty promises. "Hello indeed, sexy!"

The tip of his tongue darts out and swipes over his lips.

"I'd kiss the living life out of you right now," he proclaims. And oh, boy, there is sheer certainty in his voice. Meanwhile, his eyes are filled with hunger and that causes my body to shudder against his.

In the name of all things holy, the effect this man of mine has on me. It is incredible how sometimes I hear couples complain that the chemistry they had has waned over the years. Fifteen years of relationship and our chemistry is still rampant. Because even when Mason asked me for the divorce, the attraction between was still unbridled. Even when he told me that he wants a divorce, behind that chocolate brown pair of eyes I could see hunger.

"Then why don't you?" I dare, a playful smile tipping the corners of my lips upward.

"Because we're not alone."

As though that has ever stopped him, I think to myself.

"If you're referring to Ary, she's out with my mom, having a drink, so we got the house all to ourselves tonight."

A groan surges out of his chest, the sound vibrating into my own body.

"*Doce Xesús, nena!* You're killin' me," he mutters under his breath. "Do you mind if we have dinner at home? I know I promised I'll take you out—"

Untangling one arm from around his neck, I bring the hand to Mason's handsome face and rest two of my fingers on his lips.

"Anywhere you are, it is fine with me."

Mason kisses the pad of my fingers gently and every part of my body begins to tingle at the sweetness of it.

"Do you mind if we have someone join us for dinner?"

My eyes narrow curiously.

"Who?"

As though on cue, after my question, a sound fills the air. The sound made of someone's shoes hitting against the hardwood floor while running.

"Mason, Mason, I think I'd like this."

Lifting my eyes from Mason's brown ones, I look over his shoulder to see a little boy racing toward us, up the few stairs that separate the foyer and stairs landing from the living room. While he runs our way, his small arm is lifted in the air, waving one of the restaurant takeout flyers we keep in the kitchen.

My gaze instantly snaps back to Mason's, who smiles at me innocently.

"This little guy," he speaks, answering the question we left hanging when we heard his rushed steps heading our way.

The little boy brings his running to a halt when he gets close to us and his small face beams with pure joy, his green eyes filled with excitement. When they land on me, however, they turn timid. So shy that he avoids my gaze for an instant.

"Hey, little man," I greet him, rounding Mason and stepping off the stair. Immediately after, I lower myself from the knees in a close-legs squat position in front of the boy who cannot be older than eight. "I'm Ensley. What's your name?"

"Zane," he answers shyly, shaking my extended hand with just as much timorousness.

His green eyes are striking and so unique in color. Although most of the iris is a rich green, around the pupil and spreading almost halfway across the irises, there are flecks of gold and blue.

"You know, that's my favorite restaurant."

With a lift of my chin, I gesture toward the flyer he holds and once again he smiles, indicating that it is enough to break the ice with him.

"Is it? The pizza here…," Zane pauses to turn the flyer over and his little finger points to the image he refers to exactly. "This pizza looks so good. Can we have that?"

His beautiful eyes gleam with plea and hopefulness, and I look up at Mason, finding him with a wide smile on his face as he watches the scene taking place before him.

A moment later, I revert my attention to Zane, and I nod with a smile. "Of course we can have it, honey."

"Yay," he says, turning to run back toward the living room. However, as though he forgets something and with more confidence this time around, he spins back on his shoes and kisses my cheek. "You look very pretty, Ensley."

My heart swells with infinite love for this little boy who I have just met. "Thank you! Such a little gentleman we've got here."

His chin tilts for him to look at Mason.

"You were right, Mason. She is very beautiful."

And when his eyes dart back to me, he winks cheekily.

He winks at me.

Then as though he did no such thing, he turns around and races to the living room.

"Look, *nena*—"

Springing to my full height and standing in front of Mason, my fingers rest on his lips for the second time tonight, interrupting him.

"Although there is an explanation that you'll need to give me as in where he comes from, he is adorable. I'll get changed in something more comfortable and then we should get him a warm bath or shower while the food is on the way."

"So, you're not mad?"

"Why would I be, Mase? This little boy is innocent and I'm sure there must have been something that got you to bring him in tonight." I press a quick peck on his lips. "And as long as we don't get arrested for the kidnapping of a minor, I'm good."

We both chuckle at my joke.

"I'll make it up to you," he promises.

My head leans in, my lips just a breath away from his. "Oh,

I'm actually counting on it, handsome." Quickly, I press my mouth to his.

With that, I turn and begin to make my way back upstairs to get changed. However, as I move to take a second step, I am stopped when a hand wraps around my wrist and I twist my body a little to look at Mason.

"You do look absolutely breathtaking, *nena*. You can put this dress back on later tonight because I sure as hell will enjoy peeling it off you."

Mason winks at me with promise in his voice.

"It will be worth the wait."

"You are worth all the wait," I revert, my heart thundering inside my chest.

He is certainly pleased with my reply because he leans in and kisses me gently, yet still with claim.

Once he withdraws, I wink and turn.

Right away, a surprised yelp tumbles out of me when his palm collides with my ass cheek, causing me to halt while the sound of his chuckle fills my ears. A sound so rich and naughty that it spurs me to look over my shoulder at him, giving him my most seductive look.

"Oh, you're gonna pay for that," I warn.

Straightening my posture, I walk up the stairs unhurriedly. With each step I take, I make sure my hips sway left and right, right and left with as much sensuality as I can master.

And the guttural groan that I hear coming from behind me is all the answer I need that I am certainly mastering quite a bit of it.

While I make my way inside the bedroom and carefully remove the dress and toss the heels aside, my mind drifts to the little boy in our home. My heart drops into my stomach at the unkempt and rough appearance. At the worn-out clothes. At the shoes that seem a little big for him when he ran our way.

Not a moment later, my heart leaps back in its place at the thought of how he rushed to Mason and how excited he was to share with him his choice of food. How swiftly the two of them bonded.

The truth is that Zane is a sweet boy and his shyness and that tad of cheekiness—considering the wink he gave me after he confirmed Mason's statement that I am beautiful—make him so precious, crawling under one's skin within moments after one meets him.

He just has that effect.

* * *

The effect Zane has on both Mason and me is even more evident as the three of us lay on the sofa, one unopen box of pizza on the coffee table while Zane has an open one atop his lap and Mason has another on top of his.

Zane digs in hungrily, and we just as starvingly eat slice after slice.

Once I changed into a pair of leggings and a hoodie, and went back downstairs, we put the order for the pizza with the restaurant and then ran a shower for Zane who now wears one of Mason's much larger t-shirt and a pair of shorts that we used the string to tie them securely around his small waist.

Now, with the pizza already here and with the three of us eating, we also have the television on. It is on the same family show it's been for the past half hour with us paying no mind to it as we savor our food.

"This is the best pizza I have ever had," Zane speaks, taking another bite out of his slice.

Watching the little boy, I cannot help but smile into my own slice while he finds joy in the smallest of things.

As I sense someone's gaze on me, I cock my head to the side a little to meet Mason's chocolate one, before it drops to the smile tipping at the corners of his lips.

"Mason," Zane begins shily and we revert our attention back to him, noting how he fidgets with the fingers of his right hand. "Are you going to take me back to that home?"

"Do you want me to, buddy?"

Quickly, Zane's head shakes from side to side.

Without delay, Mason lifts his arm and Zane nestles against him, making sure not to tip over the box of pizza while doing so.

My heart fills up to the rims with contentment and warmth at the sight. With a feeling of joy and happiness that this image my eyes land on brings me. The same sight that confirms exactly what I believed: Mason would make such a great dad—protective, caring and kind. And when Mason cocks his head to the side lightly to meet my eyes again, I see it in his stare. I see it right there behind his brown gaze that he doesn't want to let go of this instant.

With pure marvel, I sit there on the sofa, chewing on a slice of pizza that I have been nursing while the boys have gone through more than a box between the two of them. It is only the empty and the half-empty boxes that serve as an indication of how long has passed since I've sat there. Looking at the both of them nestled together. Listening to them talk about little things. Listening to Zane ask Mason about how it is like to be a firefighter and seeing his expression grow even more excited when he finds out that I'm a firefighter too. That and the image of Zane's eyelids closing and reopening, fighting to stay awake, only solidify the thought that quite a bit of time has passed since we have sat down.

Not a moment later, Zane's eyelids become too heavy, and he slowly closes them, his small head leaning further against Mason.

What has me chuckling lowly though is how he still holds a half-eaten slice in his hand, and I reach over Mason's chest to gently take it from him.

"He is out," I whisper, placing the slice in the half-empty box.

"He was behind the dumpster in the alley near the bar," Mason utters quietly, his gaze on the little boy who sleeps against his chest. "He told me he was trying to get to look inside the big dumpster. But to do that, he went up on the smaller one and fell."

I listen to every word, soaking it in while my eyes dart from Zane to Mason and back to the little boy.

"He doesn't have a mother anymore and there's no father in the picture, so he was thrown into the foster care system, but the parents he has neglected him. Can you believe he's been out there for two or three days and nobody's looking for him?"

As my body is pressed against Mason's side, I sense the anger flowing through him as his form shakes lightly. So my arm wraps around his bicep and I give him a light squeeze. A squeeze that wants to give him reassurance that we will do something for this kid.

"We'll find a solution, baby."

At my muttering, Mason presses his lips gently against mine

and then withdraws, aiming his brown gaze at Zane who now sleeps peacefully, his small form balled close, and I can't help but reach out and brush a couple of tousled dark brown locks back from his face.

"He really got to you, didn't he?"

"How can he not? You should have seen him, *nena*. The thought that he has slept on top of a cardboard angers me and pains me."

Zane's situation affects Mason.

More than he wants to let on. I can clearly see that.

"Let's take this little guy upstairs so he can sleep properly," I offer and get up. "I'll take these into the kitchen and be right back."

While I pick up the boxes of pizza, I note Mason moves slowly, making sure not to wake Zane as he gets up with him in his arms.

Once I dispose of the boxes in the kitchen quickly, I return to them. Together we make our way up the stairs and I keep stealing glances at Mason holding Zane. I walk in tempo with them, admiring the sight.

It is an image I pictured many times before when I allowed myself to think about having a kid, about being a mother. I have imagined Mason carrying our little boy's or girl's tired, asleep body into their room. I have pictured us tucking in our son or daughter.

And this thought tugs at my heartstrings. It pulls and pulls at them one by one as we enter my bedroom and Mason lays Zane down on the bed before I pull the covers over his small frame, covering him just up to his shoulder.

When I straighten my back, Mason's arm snakes around my waist and we stand there for a tick or two, watching the little boy who only just entered our lives but left an imprint already.

MASON

Ensley and I leave Zane to sleep peacefully after we both drop a kiss on his forehead, and close the door to the bedroom, careful not to make too much noise.

"This isn't how I really planned this evening for us," I attest, wrapping my hands around her waist from behind.

"And how did you plan it?"

There's that usual dare in her voice that has me teetering on the line between wanting to tear her clothes with my bare hands and fuck her hard or wanting to slowly undress her and make gentle love to her.

"Well, I wanted to take you to a really nice restaurant, have dinner and then bring you home. Kiss you on the porch in front of our house until your mind focuses on nothing but me. Get you inside the house and peel that dress off you, throw you on the floor and kiss my way down each inch of your body until I have my head between your legs, tasting that sweetness you hold there."

My cock jerks in my jeans, protesting at the images that tumble through my mind. Complaining because he isn't inside her heat already. Because after craving her the entire day, thinking about all the possibilities we have after we finish with dinner, when I saw her walking down the stairs, looking gut-wrenchingly beautiful and absolutely breathtaking in that tight red dress, I knew it will be a long night.

Doce Xesús, how good she looked in it.

Truth be told, Ensley Walker looks good in anything whether it is a nice tight dress or a pair of leggings and a baggy hoodie, she still takes my breath away.

But when I watched her walk down the stairs in that red dress, I felt the air get knocked out of my lungs. I gasped for it at the sight of her.

At that very view, flashes of red flickered behind my eyelids with each blink. They zigged and zagged from one corner of my eye to the other. Although they had me very close to squeezing my eyes shut, I tried to keep my face from contorting at the sheer speed with which those flashes assailed me. Instead, I focused on the woman before me. The vision of her, prompting out of me the words that resounded in my mind like an echo, as though demanding I say them.

"Quitas o meu alento."

And, *Xesús*, how much I meant them.

"Are you just going to tease me?"

Ensley's sweet voice powers through my thoughts, having me knock them away before I get to ponder on them for too long. Her tone isn't just sweet, though. It is also daring.

"Or are you gonna do something about that?"

Rock-fucking-hard.

This is how she gets me.

Painfully hard to the extent that when I bring her flush to my body, she can feel me pushing low against her stomach and she moans.

"I'll go and shower," I whisper. "You will go into that bedroom and take off all these clothes." This time, my baritone is filled with control and demand. "I want you bare for me, but *xuro, nena*, if you as much as flick that sweet clit of yours, I'll tie you up and smack your ass red. I'll take you so close to coming with my fingers and my mouth that you'll be able to taste your orgasm. So close that it is within reach, but it will be so far away, *nena*. Because I won't let you come if you touch yourself. I'll play with you all night long. Drive you to the brink of insanity."

She trembles between my arms.

That is her body's response to my warning.

So natural.

So goddamn familiar.

"Now, *nena*, take this tight ass into my bedroom."

With a playful, wicked smile on her face—one that reaches her eyes—, she pushes against me. So I release my hold on her and she spins on her feet, walking to my bedroom.

As fast as we can as though we both race against an unknown clock, we race in our directions—Ensley into my bedroom and I enter the bathroom. I take the fastest shower of my life. Not even when I take a shower at the firehouse whilst on duty and the alarm happens to go off, I don't shower this fast. But I needed to wash the day off before I touch Ensley. And I do, with the speed of light, I shower, pat myself dry, wrap a towel around my waist and walk out of the bathroom.

Sauntering down the hall, I go toward my bedroom and open the door.

My eyes land on her instantly.

There she is.

Naked.

Just like I've demanded.

But when I take her in, I realize I got more than I bargained for. What I get is the kind of present one unwraps on Christmas morning.

Ensley in my bed with nothing on but red lipstick.

She lays on her stomach, her upper body propped on her elbows, her legs bent from the knee, dangling in the air. She seduces me with the way she looks at me, her green eyes roving over the length of my body.

Cristo, the way they darken with unrestrained need.

"Liking what you see, *nena?*" I taunt, bringing my hand to where one side of the towel folds inside.

"I'd love the view even more if you drop that."

Before my starving gaze, she darts the tip of her tongue over her lips right before she catches her bottom one between her teeth.

My dick twitches at the sight of that.

It jerks beneath the fabric of the towel, begging to take a peek at the seductress before me. At the incredibly gorgeous brunette who is unbelievably mine as much as I am hers.

Without delay, I slide my index between the towel and unhook the material, letting it pool at my feet on the floor. My cock springs free, straight and hard as steel.

Ensley's eyes spark at the sight, but they set aflame like a wildfire when I step closer and closer to the bed. My length throbs with each stride and I fucking ache to touch her, to taste her, to worship this woman who's completely bare in front of me. To lick my way down her body until I have the taste of her juices on my tongue.

Bringing my hand to her face, cupping her cheek, my thumb traces her bottom lip back and then forth a couple of times. Then, I stop when I reach the middle of her lip and Ensley parts them, swallowing the tip of my finger inside her hot mouth.

"Tell me, *nena*, have you touched yourself?" I question, eying intently how she slowly takes my thumb deeper into her mouth.

I can't suppress the groan from surging out of me even if I try. Not that I do, though. Especially when the sound only eggs Ensley on, her stare never leaving mine as she withdraws, only to circle her tongue around the finger.

Joder!

One of the hottest things I have witnessed.

"Answer the question, *nena*."

At my urge, she smirks, her mouth removing from my thumb. Her eyes gleam with pure wickedness and I know I will soon lose the control I'm trying extremely hard to keep in check. "You'll have to check it for yourself."

Clearing my throat, I smirk at her, leaning forward until my hand is in her hair, tipping her head back so my mouth can capture hers.

I kiss her only for a moment, then I step back.

"If I touch you now, am I going to find your clit swollen and pulsing, Ley?"

Her own moan dances in the air as a response to my question.

"Have you been a good girl and listened to what I've told you, or have you been a brat who'll have her ass spanked red?"

As my question hangs between us, I watch Ensley attentively as she squirms, trying to create some friction where she aches for me. But there's something in the way her ass cheeks tighten and relax, though. There's something in how she seeks to ease down the yearning.

I don't think twice and in a few long strides, I am on the opposite side of the bed, having the perfect view of her heart-shaped ass. When she lifts her pelvis off the mattress and pushes that sweet ass in the air, my heart races in my chest and my dick throbs at the sight. Not only is Ensley's ass a fucking temptation, but now it is a goddamn invitation.

And I say that because of the jewel peeking from between her cheeks as she pushes herself further in the air.

While the guttural groan tumbles through my lips, my hand reaches out and I grab a handful of her ass cheek before my other hand does the same with its pair.

Ensley turns her head to the side, wanting to see my reaction as she looks at me over her shoulder.

Over the length of her back, my eyes journey to meet hers. The wickedness they possessed earlier hasn't ebbed. On the contrary, it only grows when her stare remains locked onto mine, knowing the kind of unbridled hunger she finds in it.

"Fucking hell, *nena*. You're tryin' to kill me. If I've ever had a doubt, now it's crystal clear."

I cannot even recognize the sound of my own voice when I speak this time. It is filled with desire. It is fueled by the carnal need to possess my woman in the filthiest and most obscene ways known to humankind. Possess her body and dictate each one of its reactions. Own her mind and rule her heart.

And this, right here, is her consent.

Her permission.

To possess *her*.

To own *her*.

"Do you like it?"

In her voice I can hear the effect. She is just as affected by this as I am. Just as consumed by this warp need that courses through our veins.

"I fucking love it," I reply, spreading her ass cheeks a little further while I use the hold to bring it closer to me.

Kneeling behind her on the bed, I lean forward and graze her skin around the red jewel with my thumb. The very thumb she sucked on only moments prior.

Ensley instantly quivers. It turns into a full-body shake when I catch it between my thumb and index finger and pull at it gently.

"Oh, fuck," she curses breathily.

Her dark hair falls down her back and to her sides when she

throws her head back with another moan while I press the buttplug back in.

"You are a fantasy turned into reality, *nena*," I whisper in her ear once I lean in over her back and my teeth dig softly into the shell of her ear. "Now, tell me, Ley, do you want my cock inside your pussy while this fills up your ass?"

"Yyyy-yes," Ensley wheezes out, arching and pushing her ass further into my touch.

"If I touch you, will I find you drenched?"

Her head nods right before it dips into her chest as though too heavy for the whirlwind of desire that I can sense flows through her form.

My hand collides with her right ass cheek and Ensley hums in return.

"Don't think this will get you off the hook for being a brat, *nena*," I warn, my dick pressing hard against her behind, eager to slide inside her and slam it home. "For not listening when I told you not to touch yourself."

"I was aching," she whispers, and I don't let her see the smirk playing on my lips knowing she doesn't just *want* me, she *needs* me.

Just like I *need* her.

More than I need to take my next breath.

More than I need yet another beat of my heart.

I need her to survive.

We both need each other.

We do, so we can survive and keep sane.

"You just wanted me to smack this tight ass, didn't you, Ensley? You like it dirty and rough," I utter, grazing the shell of her ear with my teeth only for the twisted desire to feel her shudder below me. And the expected response doesn't delay. Just the same way how the salacious noise she makes in her throat doesn't dawdle when my palm lands on her ass cheek, giving her a thwack. "A woman made after my own filthily perverted mind and heart."

"Please, Mason. I need you, baby. I need you in me," she pleads, pushing her ass against me without any restraint.

Ensley is so far gone. So far that she rubs her sweet butt into me, tipping her ass and hoping she might manage to somehow slide me inside her.

But I am too far gone too while I feel the head of my cock grazing her heat. I am so gone, but I don't forget about the promised punishment. So, I push off her altogether, grinning as I round the bed so she can see me. All of me, naked and ready to take her. Not until I have her on the brink. Just like I promised.

If I do have the strength and restraint to see it through that is. Because now, after I've seen just how desperate she is for me and how much she wants me, I begin to doubt I won't slide inside her after the taste of her desire touches my tongue.

She looks up at me, her eyes flaring with need. A need I'm about to only heighten.

Turning on my bare feet, I walk up to the dresser and retrieve a belt. When I spin back to face her, I swear I hear her breath hitching and if her eyes flared up earlier, now they are in full blaze mode.

Once I bring the tail of the belt to the buckle end and hold it with one hand, while with the other I grab the curved middle. Under Ensley's darkening gaze, I pull the ends close and then snap them apart, the leather thwacking as the two sides hit.

The beast inside of me has been unleashed and if Ensley wants to run, now would be the moment.

MASON

Nothing prepares me for her response though. Nothing that I could have ever anticipated prepares me for the sweet submission when she lifts the upper part of her body off the mattress and keep her knees bent and backs until her ass rests on the heels of her feet.

Fuck me sideways.

And after straightening her back, when she lifts her arms in front of her with her palms up and wrists close, my pulse is racing a million miles an hour. Not only that, but my cock throbs between my legs, making it difficult to walk back to her without aching.

The sight is pure marvel to witness.

She looks like a vision my mind concocts and transpires into reality right before very own eyes. She looks like a vision of unbridled submission—one that only seems to be present when we are in bed, considering that outside of it all she does is challenge and dare me, having me dance a tango with my own insanity.

"*Doce Xesús, nena,*" I mutter under my breath, my chest rising and falling while my lungs viciously strain to get another scintilla of air. There is no doubt in my mind that they just forget how to function at the sight.

Cristo, everything within me forgot how to function properly. One organ is in overdrive, thrumming inside my chest with brutal force. Another is one damn step away from collapsing.

The only part of me that evidently works is my dick, standing straight and rigid.

"I see you can be a good girl too and not only a disobedient brat."

Each word that leaves my mouth struggles to do so at how low and guttural my voice becomes with every second that ticks by, and I drink in more of the vision that Ensley is. It is as though an imaginary hand is wrapped around my throat and chokes out my every word, glazing it with unmitigated yearning.

"Now, *nena*, I believed I made myself blatantly clear when I said I'll tie you up and smack your ass senseless if you touch yourself. In fact, I don't believe the sultry minx that you are took my warning seriously."

Unhurriedly and with her flared-up gaze on me, I saunter toward the bed, letting go of one end of the belt before I begin rolling it over my hand. Her eyes follow all my movements, journeying from my own darkened gaze to my jaw that ticks as I fight the impel to rush to her and drive my cock inside her to the hilt. Then they move cursorily over my wide, tattooed chest that tenses with each move I make in rolling the belt. And when they land on what I am doing, her stare turns hungry, lust clouding the greenness of her orbs. Especially when they move lower to my throbbing cock and her teeth attack her bottom lip, digging into it mercilessly.

While she watches me with her roving eyes, I let my own ravenous peer study her. I take her in. Her lust-filled glance. Her chest that rises and falls with each heaving breath. Her small breasts with the pebbled nipple that are hard as bullets. Her tight abdomen. Her thighs spread enough for me to see the arousal dripping and note her pussy lips glistening with the proof of her need, the proof she touched herself although I told her not to.

"Such a teasing brat," I croak, my eyes remaining homed in on her pussy. "Spread those sweet thighs a little more. Let me see just how much you need me."

Ensley trembles.

Yet, she does my bidding without protest, parting her thighs more until the action also spreads her folds, her excitement dripping.

With a smirk on my face, definitely pleased with what I see, I stop right in front of her and undo the belt from around my hand.

As my eyes meet and hold hers, I thread the tail of the belt through the buckle to create a loop, then I bend it back and thread it through the top again, forming a second loop. When I bring the lopped belt up to her hands, my gaze seeks any ounce of doubt in hers. But my search comes up empty and I slide her hands through, before I tug at the belt, tightening it around her wrists.

Pulling at her hands, I note the belt handcuffs are securely in place.

"Now, *nena*, let the fun begin."

My words send a rush of excitement through her form. A surge of need that prickles her skin. A need that also bolts through me. Brutally. Unstoppably.

"Please, Mason. Touch me," she pleads, clearly too far gone to care how wantonly she sounds, begging her man to pleasure her.

Her body tells me that at this rate, she only needs a graze of my finger over her heated flesh, or a stroke of my tongue and she'll combust. She'll detonate from inside out faster than she ever did before.

"On your stomach and tip your ass up," I command, my baritone filled with desperation. Desperate to disperse some of that unmitigated need that burns us both to the bones. That need that I've tried to fight against. That attraction that instead of decreasing with each denial has turned out to be even more rampant.

Without delay, Ensley does my bidding.

Since her hands are now tied with the belt at the wrists, she lifts to her knees and pivots. I lose the sight of her beautiful face, but instead I get her back and her luscious ass. Especially when she leans on her elbows and drops to her stomach, tipping her butt up in the air just like I've asked.

Fucking hell, the vision she is.

In any position, in any circumstance and in any setting, day or night, Ensley Walker is a vision. My fantasy to have and to turn into reality.

There's no warning when my hand lands on her ass with sheer possessiveness. I don't miss the way she clenches her cheeks, tightening her inner walls around the buttplug.

That goddamn buttplug that prepares her for the girth of my cock when I'll take her ass. Which won't be tonight, though. Tonight, she gets to be punished for disobeying me.

I know she wanted to surprise me with it. She wanted to see my reaction when I notice the new accessory decorating her body. I saw that in her eyes and received the proof of it when she sought my opinion, asking if I liked it. I have also noticed she nearly came undone when she heard the groaned sound that surged out of me when I pulled at the jeweled end and pushed it back in.

"Perfection," I utter, my breath is so close to her skin that she shivers. A full-body shiver that starts at the tips of her toes right to the roots of her hairs. "Now, I'm gonna have a very long conversation with this impertinent pussy of yours. Try not to make too much noise."

As though that is possible.

The proof is right in the second my hot mouth latches on her sex, my tongue lapping at her excitement.

"God, oh, donotstop," she mumbles on a moan.

I fuck her with my lewd mouth and tongue without mercy. I drink her up and toy with her, enjoying every moment of her taste hitting my tongue. Meanwhile, her hips push back into my face, wanting more of me. Needing more of what I give her. More friction. More of everything so she can come.

Only a couple of strokes later, I know she can taste the orgasm. It is so close that she is ready to scream it out loud. That until I draw back and she loses my tongue.

"That was so close."

She can hear the satisfied devious grin in my voice before I dive right back in.

For what seems like forever, it is all I do. I work her up with my mouth, adding my fingers to the mix as well after the second time I deny her the orgasm. I fuck her with my thick digits, pumping in and out of her. I flick her clit with my tongue. I lick her. And in the end, after all the building up when her breath heaves and her lungs strain for air, when her vision turns blurry and she can see stars, when her tied hands grip the bedsheet so tightly I can only assume her knuckles turn white, and when she thrashes shamelessly under my mouth, I pull away and with-draw my fingers, refusing her that sweet taste of the climax.

"Oh, God, I can't. Please, Mason, let me come."

My lips are now on the curve of her ass, kissing my way up her spine and to the shell of her ear.

"Only if you had listened to me," I whisper, my voice filled with lust to the extent that I can barely recognize it. "I'd be inside your snug cunt by now."

My hard cock pushes into her ass cheek and she rolls her hips over me to find a little more friction.

I know I have punished her enough.

Cristo, I certainly have enough of being punished.

This is why one of my hands reaches up to her tied wrists, my lips dusting kisses over her bare shoulder.

"I'll untie you now."

And I do exactly that. I unloop the belt and loosen the hold, the belt dropping to the floor with a thud.

Her neck cranes to the side and my darkened gaze meets hers. She looks so far gone. Her half-hooded eyes are filled with lust. Unmitigated. Unrestrained.

"Reach back and line me up, *nena*."

It is that demand that sets her in action. And she doesn't delay reaching back as instructed, or to wrap her hand around my shaft.

I can swear I hear my own skin hiss at the touch.

It simply sizzles at the contact.

And further proof that I burn with need for her—not that she needs any further evidence—the same way she is alit with need for me is the way my body trembles. Especially when instead of lining me up to her entrance, she slides her hand up and down the length of my cock.

"Wanna give me a hand job, I'm more than happy to get behind that, Ley. But right now, I need to be inside you. I need your snug cunt to squeeze my cock and I need to hear those sounds you make when you come around me."

She moans in return, stopping her hand from jacking me off after one more pump. A blink later, I feel the nudge. I feel the head of my cock at her entrance and that is all I need.

There's no hesitation when I thrust my hips forward and slam it in home, the walls of her pussy clutching in a vice-like grip around me, welcoming the intrusion. With the buttplug inside her ass and my thick shaft inside her pussy, she is filled up to the brim and so fucking tight.

We both struggle to find our breath at how good that feels. How good it feels to be balls deep inside of her. How good it feels to have her wrapped around me.

"*Joder*," I groan, throwing my head back at the sensation. "*Doce Xesús, nena,* you're dripping down my thighs at how wet you are."

Her pussy—sleek, wet and so snug—wraps around my girth like a glove, notably when I draw my hips back and she wants to keep me inside of her.

Ensley whimpers as I pull out of her until only the tip is inside, and when I drive back in, she fucking catches fire, crooning her pleasure.

"Holy shit! More," she pleads on a hard slide in.

"You want more, *nena*?"

Without waiting for a response, I squeeze a handful of her butt cheeks and use the hold to tip her ass up. On her own accord, Ensley spreads her legs a little more, exposing more of her sweet ass to me that contracts around the buttplug in the same wanton manner that her pussy chokes my cock.

"I'm gonna take you rough, Ley. Are you okay with that?"

Once again, a lewd sound slips out of her mouth. A lascivious melody that spurs me on as swiftly as it does her.

And we both go wild when I drive back inside her and Ensley pushes into me, meeting me thrust for thrust. Stroke for stroke, she is right there with me. I withdraw, she rushes to swallow me right back in. I drive inside of her, she meets me halfway.

All to the extent that I don't know if I fuck her or if she fucks me. Or maybe both. All that I am aware of is just how fast her walls become even tighter.

"Oh, Mase... I'm coming."

On the interjection, it is when I feel Ensley drop her head into the mattress. When she calls out my nickname, that is when her pussy spasms around my cock. By the time she tells me she's coming, her body already shakes and rides the waves of her orgasm.

All throughout, my drives do not ebb. I continue thrusting into her through her excitement, her sweet cunt becoming snugger and wetter, more slippery and sleek.

"Mouth," I demand, leaning further over her back when the shuddering of her body wanes.

Panting, Ensley turns her head until her lips are just a breath away from mine.

"More."

It is all she whispers before her mouth charges for mine and kisses me with the very same hunger I have flowing through my veins. That starved feeling that pumps into my veins.

"Ride me."

Although my voice is low, vibrating through her when I ask her to ride me, it is no less commanding. Demanding because the need for her gets the best of me.

Ensley cries out when I pull out of her completely and whimpers when my hand collides with her ass cheek just before I land on my back.

When she turns to face me and throws a leg over me, straddling my lap, she is a vision.

A vision of desire, warp abandon and wild need while a hand covers one of her tits, playing with the nipple, and the other runs through her hair, pushing it back. Meanwhile, her hips roll over me, taunting and telling me that as much as I like to be in control in bed, right this second it is her turn. She sets the rhythm. She dictates the tempo.

And I am game.

Because I want to see her ride me.

I wanna watch her fuck herself on my cock.

"Slip me in, *nena*," I growl, my timber dark and filled with sheer yearning. A craving that has been simmering within me for too goddamn long. "Fuck me, Ensley. Take me inside you and fuck me. As slow or as fast as you want, but do it."

With a deliciously playful smile on her face, she pushes to her knees and her hand lowers from her tit to wrap around my length. The head of my cock finds her entrance almost instantly and I fight the urge to pump my hips to fill her up. Instead, I allow Ensley to lower herself on me inch by inch, driving me to the brink of insanity.

All the while, my eyes focus on all of her. On her gorgeous face, how they change with each inch that takes me further inside of her. On her eyes that catch fire right before my very own ones. On her bottom lip that falls victim to the assail of her teeth that dig in when she takes me yet another inch. On her chest that rises and falls with her futile attempt to catch her breath. On her taut abdomen that tightens harder while she tries not to slam herself down on my cock.

But when my gaze zeroes in on where we are joined and I watch how she slips me inside her pussy, that is when I cannot hold on any longer and my hips thrust upward, burying myself balls in deep within her heat.

Ensley's eyes almost roll to the back of her head and her mouth falls open in a beautiful "O" shape while a strangled, prolonged groan tumbles through her parted lips. Right away, my arms hasten around her back, cradling her to my chest as I let her accommodate to my thickness and the rough manner in which I have taken her.

Her legs encircle me and lock at my back. Her arms rush over my shoulders, holding me as tightly as I hold her.

Our bodies are so closely pressed together that there is not even the smallest of gap between us. In this instant, we are one. We are so connected. In the most intimate of ways.

"I love you," I whisper in her ear, my eyes closing as I breathe in her fragrance. That sweet jasmine smell that now is mixed with sweat and arousal and sex. Yet, it is a smell that has me intoxicated from the very first inhale I take.

"I love you too, baby," Ensley utters in response, her heart thrumming a wild rhythm against my chest.

Pulling back just a fraction, I bring my hands to her face and cradle her cheeks. My eyes lock onto hers before I peck her lips gently.

"I don't exist without you, *nena*. Although I don't remember much before the coma, I clearly recall how the past weeks have been without having you like this. I constantly felt like something was missing and right here with you between my arms, I know for a fact that it is you who's been missing."

A mixture of emotions crosses her features, and her eyes avoid mine for a split second. When they revert to mine, something coats her gaze.

"Mason, I need to tell you some—"

My thumb darts and presses against her lips.

"I need to tell you something too. But, *nena*, I need you to ride me first."

ENSLEY

I do ride him.

I fuck myself on his cock, writhing on top of his taut body, while his fingertips dig into my hips.

He lets me set the pace. As slow and as hard as I want, just like he said. And each slow glide up is followed by a hard slide back down on his length. The tempo is desperate and filled with lust. Just like his gaze as he peers down at me through half-hooded eyes. The intensity of his regard sets me aflame so effortlessly. It coats my skin with the savage flames of a wildfire. It spreads exactly like one on my flesh—fast, torching me to the bone.

Mason's groan is strangled, and I lose his eyes for an instant only when I drop hard and ground down in his lap, my walls tautening around his girth.

"*Doce Xesús, nena!* Gimme more of that."

And I do as he instructs. On each glide up I keep my inner muscle relaxed, but on each slide back down, my walls tighten around him, slowing the speed of how I take him.

"Fucking hell," he curses aloud.

His fingertips dig further into the skin of my hips at how firmly he holds me. I know they will still be there tomorrow, perhaps the skin will even bruise, but I don't care. I don't because it is my man's mark on me. His fingertips on my flesh.

"Lean back, grab my thighs and lemme see how your snug pussy takes my cock."

There is clear possession and claim in his dark timbre and I cannot help the smile from twisting the corners of my lips upward.

I smile because he might have tried to stay away, yet the pull of what we have is more powerful than anything. It is also the reason why only moments ago I was ready to admit the truth to him. Why I wanted to tell him the truth.

When I have finally garnered the courage and the guts to tell him who I really am, he had to stop me.

"*Nena.*"

This time around, his voice is dark and filled with demand. Demand for me to follow his instruction. But there is also something else that coats his tone. Necessity. A necessity to see the extent of his possession of me. An imperative to see the magnitude of his claim.

Dominance.

Claim.

Ownership.

They are three words that describe Mason Carter.

And right now, when he peers at me with his dark gaze, drinking me in as I move in his lap, he is not a man to be denied.

Forthwith, I reach with my hands back to his thighs. I delve my fingernails into his taut muscles while my chest pushes upward, and my hips create a back-and-forth rhythm now instead of an up-and-down movement.

Almost immediately, his stare follows down the length of my body, turning my already pebbled nipples into two hard rocks with the sheer intensity. It then zeroes in on where we are joined right when I bring my hips forth, taking in every single thick inch of his beautiful cock.

Mason groans at the sight, his hands removing from my hips. One instantly travels to my breast. The heel of his palm gets placed at the underside of my tit before the rest of his hand cups it. His other hand traverses to the junction between my legs, his thumb zeroing in on my clit.

My head throws back at the action, the tips of my hair brushing over his thighs.

"*Joder, nena*, you're gonna make me come," he announces and presses against my bundle of nerves, rubbing it faster. "Tighten that pussy some more and you'll make your man come."

"Yes, yes," I rant and fuck myself harder on his cock, lifting and dropping my hips.

At the same time, the crazy tempo of his strokes only eggs me on, serving as my encouragement to quicken my pace. The angle of my motion drives his cock so deep within me, touching that sweet spot that drives me wild, and I know I cannot hold it any longer. I am aware I will detonate.

Again.

My walls tighten around him as he continues to play with my clit and while I move back and forth in his lap.

"Oh, God. Ah, donotstop."

Letting go of his thighs, I throw my arms over his shoulders and press our bodies together, needing to feel him close. His naked skin is burning hot against mine, the muscles of his back straining beneath my roving hands that don't hesitate to explore his flesh. His flesh sizzles against mine and our eyes burn red-hot while we keep eye contact.

Our pleasure-filled sounds ricochet across the room, mingling with the ones of bare skin slapping against bare skin. Sounds that are so arousing, contributing some more to the pressure building in the pit of my stomach.

"Stop fighting it," Mason's voice breaks through my fog. "Come with me, *nena*. Let me feel your sweet pussy grip my cock. Let your cunt squeeze my cock dry."

Holy hell.

That filthy mouth. That dirty talk.

So erotic.

But once the pressure builds to the extent that I can barely hold up, that is when I become aware that I have indeed been fighting my release. I have been fighting it because I know what comes next. Because I cannot hide the truth from him any longer. I cannot hide that he is my husband. That we are married. I cannot do it a moment longer without feeling the guilt assailing me with tremendous force.

And I fight the climax because I'm afraid this might be our last time. Our last time together because once he finds out the truth, there might not be a next time.

"I love you, Mason," I mutter, my lips just a breath away from his mouth after I lean my forehead against his.

Mason's hands cup my face, and he uses the hold to draw me

back a little, his eyes locking onto mine. His peer turns from lust-filled into soft as he moves it over my features as though he sees something there, and the pace of my now up-and-down motion in his lap slows down.

"*Nena*, where have you gone?" The gentleness in his voice makes me cock my head to the side to avoid his gaze. Yet, he has none of that and turns my chin until my eyes are back on his. "Ley, you fight it the same way you did a couple of nights ago."

"I don't want this to be our last time."

"It won't, nena. I told you I'm done pushing you away. I'm done fighting you. What I'm not done with is fighting for you. I promise I'll—"

My fingers rest over his lips, interrupting him.

"Make it sweet," I whisper. "Make sweet love to me."

Searching something in my gaze, I note his Adam apple bob on a hard swallow and then he nods gently as though he understands.

One hand withdraws from my face and dusts over my back so softly that I cannot help but shudder against him.

"Pretty difficult to keep it slow when you've got this shoved up your tight ass," he declares, his finger circling around the jeweled end.

A moan surges out of my chest and my head throws back when his digits grasp the buttplug. His lips drop feather-light kisses on the exposed column of my neck while he pulls at the end and I feel it slowly sliding out of me, the muscles of my ass tightening. I whimper lowly at the loss, my eyes squeezing shut.

Once the buttplug is out, my inner muscle spasm. Yet, in that instance, I don't know what I can focus on first. On his lips on my neck. On his gentle caress on the skin of my back. On my ass that tries to accommodate to the loss of the metal. Or on the cock that jerks inside of me, still buried so deep.

"On your stomach," he commands in my ear in a gentle voice.

Blinking twice, I do what he asks. I lift to my knees and I instantly lose the hardness of his cock from inside of me. With a low cry, I lay on my stomach, my chest off the mattress as I prop myself on my elbows.

A mewl slips through my parted lips and my eyes close simultaneously when Mason's mouth drops low on my back before he slowly makes his way up. My head tilts back and my stomach pushes further into the mattress, while I suck my bottom lip into my mouth at his searing touch.

Mason takes his time with me. He coaxes. He gives. He also takes what he needs. He doesn't rush and that drives me crazy.

His gentle lips and hot tongue alternate between salaciously kissing up my spine and lasciviously licking the flesh as though with them he writes on my skin the most seductive, enthralling and erotic poem. One that exacerbates all my senses. One that has me floating. One that sets my entire body alit. It starts from deep within and diffuses through me until it scorches my skin. His touch is so hot, so sizzling it burns. But, God, if it is not the best kind of burning.

Soon enough but not too soon, his lips reach my left shoulder and his body hovers over mine, covering me like a blanket. A prolonged moan crawls up my throat when his teeth sink gently into my skin before his tongue darts over to calm the sting.

"Mouth," he croaks in my ear as I begin feeling more of his weight on my back. "*Dáme a túa boca, nena.* Give me your mouth."

Mason doesn't wait for me to comply with his command—because that is what it was, a feral order coated with primal need. While he props his weight on one elbow, his other hand reaches and slides up the column of my neck, using his hold as leverage to tip my head back and more to the side, his fingers pressing a little into my skin. And just like that, his mouth crashes against mine. He savagely takes. He thrusts his tongue inside my mouth, having mine capitulate before his without mercy.

His naked body moves over mine. His length is hard as steel and heavy between us, still aching and throbbing from the delayed release, and I moan into his mouth. A moan full of neediness. Full of desire. Of a hunger that is matched down to the last ounce by Mason.

"I will make slow, sweet love to you, *nena*. But make no mistake, it isn't because it is our last time. Because from the moment you took your clothes off for me the other day so I can smack your ass, you became mine."

I almost whimper when I lose the heat of his body, but I am not given enough time to because Mason flips me on my back so effortlessly and then lowers himself back on top of me so fast that I barely get to blink.

Keeping our gazes locked, his hand travels to my thigh and he grabs a hold of it, lifting it until my leg is around his waist.

"Spread," he demands an inch away from my lips.

And I part my other leg to give him room.

Immediately, I feel the head of his cock nudging my entrance and Mason doesn't hesitate to push in while his mouth drops to mine.

Slowly. He does it so slowly.

Both, gliding inside of me and kissing me.

He does that so slowly, I feel the unmitigated claim and the sheer ownership of him over my body, over my heart. I feel it in the way he begins to move inside me. In how his lips move over mine and his tongue dances with mine. In how his hands touch me everywhere and I feel as though he has ten pairs of hands instead of one, each caress igniting my skin. In the way he cups my breast and kneads it, passing his thumb over my hard nipple right before he shifts his weight on that same arm so his other hand can grab the pair of my breast.

Just as unhurriedly he takes us both to the edge. To the peak of our pleasure. And with one last hard thrust, he plunges us right over the cliff. His arms tighten the hold on my hips. His cock buried deep, spurt after spurt of his cum coating my inner walls. His body falling against mine, giving me enough of his weight to feel the veracity of what has just happened between us. Our mouths wrench away from one another. Our groans tumble past our lips. Our bodies ride the waves of the orgasm.

My libs still shake when Mason withdraws from inside me and falls beside me. Not even a blink later, he reaches out and pulls me against his chest. I lay my head against his thrumming heart, draping my leg over his thigh.

There is a silence that covers the air in the room. Only the sounds of our panting as we try to catch our breaths bounce across the bedroom. But moments later, it is a heavy sigh that joins the panting.

"I love you, Ensley," he mutters against the top of my head before he kisses it. "I've loved you for as long as I remember. So, I want you to bear that in mind for what I'm about to say."

My neck cranes to the side, tipping my chin, and I look at him. A frown mars my forehead.

"There's something I haven't told you. Something about me."

"Mason, baby, you're worrying me."

Once again, he lets out a heavy breath.

"I owe you an explanation about what made me bring Zane here tonight. What had me make this decision without giving it a second thought, without considering the consequences."

Mason stops briefly and I nestle closer to his chest, listening to his heartbeat that now thunders erratically under my ear.

"I saw myself in him," he declares on a hard swallow and my brows furrow. "I saw that I could have been him had it not been for my mom."

"What do you mean?"

This time around, Mason shifts and lifts his back off the mattress, leaning it against the headboard and pulling me up with him at the same time. In this position I only draw a little to the side and crane my neck, looking at him.

"What I mean is that my mom is not my mom. Well, she is, but she isn't my biological mother. I was given to her by my grandmother."

"Was? You mean—"

"My biological mother died when I was born. She had some complications with her heart, and she knew that bringing a child into the world could put her life at risk, but when she fell pregnant, she didn't want to get an abortion and decided to risk it."

Although he tries to keep his voice as leveled as possible, there is a shake in his baritone. A shake that is rarely there. A shake that only appears in moments of vulnerability. Instantly, my heart breaks for him and I reach out, taking hold of his hand and squeezing it.

"Mason, I'm so sorry, baby."

His head nods.

"When she found out she was pregnant, she had my grandmother promise she'd give me up if something happens to her."

I hold my breath.

"The reason I haven't told you is because of who I am. Not because I've been given up, but because of whose blood runs through my veins."

"Mase, baby, that—"

"My father and my grandfather are criminals."

As my jaw falls slack in shock, my eyes widen.

His father and grandfather? Criminals?

Is this a joke? I know I haven't met Mason's father and he only remembers him from what Aracely told him, but from what he's told me, he was one of the most stand-up men and always spoke about him with nothing but admiration.

Also, his grandfather? I had the chance to meet him multiple times before his passing. He was one of the loveliest men I've met, and he was the only father figure Mason has known.

Unless…

My brain finally catches on after the shock of the news. If Aracely isn't Mason's biological mother, this only means…

"I'm not referring to my father Dennis or my grandfather Richard. I'm referring to my biological family. To my biological mother's father and to my biological father, although his father was just as much of a criminal before his son took over the so-called family business. I'm referring to Carlos Montoya and Raul Guerrero known as the leaders of the *Os Diábolos* clan."

The Devils clan.

I don't even realize I am holding my breath until Mason's laborious one pierces my ears and his chest falls.

When I twist my body and push off his to be able to see him properly, I watch him raise a bulging, tattoos-covered arm and runs his fingers through his dark hair.

Mason? The son and grandson of clan leaders?

This gotta be a joke.

He must be pranking me.

How can it be possible?

"*Os Diábolos* is one of the most notable organized crime clans in Spain. Drug trafficking. That's what they do but murdering and witness intimidation are not far from their repertoire. Now you understand why I tried to keep you away?! Why I've fought you with everything I've got so you won't get caught up in the middle of this?"

"Do… Do they know about you?"

My heart hammers in my chest as I wait for his answer.

"I believe they know I was born, but I'm not sure they know that Mom and Dad got me out of the country. Someone from the DEA, someone who used to work with my dad, has been keeping me in the loop about their whereabouts. We've been pretty safe so far. No threats made to us, nobody coming in with guns blazing."

For the briefest of seconds, my mind shifts to the flowers I've received a couple of times and a shiver shudders my body at the wonder if this has something to do with what Mason has just told me. Yet, it is a thought I knock out of my head the moment I have it because it doesn't make sense for them to send threats to me.

It is not reasonable. Besides, Mason just said someone from the DEA keeps him in the loop. I'm just overthinking that.

"I also didn't tell you because I knew it makes me unworthy of you, Ensley. I didn't tell you for selfish reasons because I think deep down I hoped that we'll get to the point when having you in my arms would be a life we could have. I am not only tainted because of a tarnished legacy, but I am also fucking filthened by it"

Oh, this beautiful man of mine.

Is this what he's been thinking all throughout our relationship? During our marriage? Did he actually believe that he is not worthy of me? Because of this?

"Baby, listen to me, okay? This, whatever you're telling me right now about your biological family doesn't define you. Doesn't define who you are, the man you are. Because you are good, Mase. You are a good man who chooses to run into buildings on fire to save people he doesn't know, although you can easily not work and live with the hefty inheritance you've received after your grandad passed. Or you can certainly do something that doesn't endanger your life and your accident proves just how much of a risk you're taking. You could do whatever, but you chose to do this job and I don't believe you do it to wash away your family's sins. You decided to be a firefighter well before you knew about it. Because I doubt you knew your biological family was made of criminals when you were four years old."

Pushing to my knees, I swing a leg over him and sit in his lap without a care that I'm naked. My hands reach up and cup his face. While I keep one palm on his cheek, with the other I caress him softly along the length of his jawline.

"You are selfless," I utter, looking him straight in the eyes.

"Unless, of course, we are in bed." At the addition, I chuckle, and Mason's lips turn into a suggestive smile as his eyebrows wiggle at me just with as much insinuation. "You are kind, because not everyone doesn't hesitate to bring home a child who sleeps on the street. You are also generous."

"I'd say I'm pretty generous with your orgasms," he rasps, the playful smile now on his face as his eyes drop to my bare breasts.

After I let out another chortle, I nod.

"I'm not contradicting that, baby. But what I actually meant is how Ella just mentioned that she's doing the charity event to raise funds for the school in San Antonio and you didn't even doubt saying 'yes' and I already know where the anonymous donation of fifty thousand dollars she's received on the funding page came from. Baby, I could have not given my heart to a greater man."

"You really are truly mine, aren't you?"

Disbelief glazes his voice and coats his eyes.

"I've always been yours. So, believe me when I say that it is true, I am yours."

"Well, my cum slipping out of you and dripping on my thighs is pretty good evidence of that," Mason points out cockily.

My cheeks catch on fire at that.

"Ohmygod," I whisper-shout.

Mason throws his head back and laughs. Deep, rich and smooth.

"I need to clean myself up."

His head shakes as his hands hasten to my hips, holding me in place.

"No, you don't. I like to know that my cum is inside of you right now."

It is my turn to shake my head at him. Yet, I try very hard to suppress the smile from forming on my lips at his admission.

"You really don't care whose son I am?"

"No, baby. I don't care whose blood runs through your veins because I know the man you are. As far as I'm concerned, you're the son of Dennis and Aracely Carter. And you are also *my man*."

"I am your man. I've always been your man even when I haven't because all along my heart has belonged to you. And I know I've cost us so much time, but *nena*—"

The pad of my finger darts to his lips, covering them and

stopping him mid-sentence. He watches me with his brown gaze, and I look at him in return.

My mouth opens for me to speak, but no sound comes out. For a tick I contemplate, knowing I had planned to tell him the truth. To stop hiding from him that we are married and let him make the choice.

"What matters is now, baby. Only now."

And I take the coward's way out.

I don't tell him the truth.

When I have the perfect moment to tell him the truth, I choose not to.

MASON

The longest time it took me to fall asleep last night. Probably just as much as it took Ensley who kept tossing and turning between my arms until she eventually found her place. With her head on my chest, right atop my heart, her hand on my abdomen and her leg over my thigh.

Maybe my restlessness caused her to have an agitated sleep. Although I barely moved, my mind was uneasy. Unsettled by what I have just confessed to her. Troubled because telling Ensley the truth about me made it more real, made it present. Before, when only Mom and Luke knew it was easier to brush it off. But now that she knows? Now I can't help but feel uneasy.

For the most part, because my mind is all over the place. I finally came clean to Ensley about who I am. About Mom not being my biological mom but no less of a mom to me. About my biological mother who died giving birth to me. About the rest of my biological family and their ties to criminal organizations and clans.

I must admit that it did take a weight off my shoulders, especially her response to what I've told her. Her understanding. Her support. Her love.

Now the clock on the nightstand ticks just a few minutes after three in the morning and my eyes are wide open though I'm pretty sure I've only managed to get in just a couple of hours of proper sleep.

After all this, I should be more tranquil. Instead, there's a whirlwind in my mind. A storm caused by my memory loss. All night I couldn't help but wonder why does my brain block out all these memories? Moreover, why does it seem like my mind fights to remember all of it now more than before? Because otherwise, I can't explain the hurricane of thoughts assailing. The voices that attack me whenever blurry flashes of images swiftly flicker behind my closed eyelids. Too swiftly to figure them out. Too rapidly to understand them. Too uncertain if they are memories or pure fantasies that my mind concocts, fooling me into believing they might be real.

Ensley's head is still on my bare chest, the cotton t-shirt she wears not doing anything to layer the heat that emanates from her skin. After we jumped in the shower to wash off our sweat-covered bodies, I fished a pair of boxers for myself that I put on and a tee and shorts for her. And oh, man, she looks breath-taking with my clothes on. Though they're a few sizes too big for her, she pulls them off so well, inciting—once again—a feeling of possessiveness within me. Exceptionally when she looked at me with those lazy green eyes, ran a hand through her messy, just had off-the-charts hot sex hair and then we climbed into bed and went to sleep. Or tried considering that only after plenty of thoughts, I finally managed to fall asleep for a couple of hours.

A gentle noise coming from the hallway has my head twist to the side. Once I hear a soft knock against the door, it is a couple of seconds after that I see it open and a small head peeks through.

"Hey, buddy. Come on in. Are you okay?"

My voice is down, yet the worry still evident as I push one side of my body up on my elbows after I set Ensley's head down on the pillow.

"I had a bad dream."

It is impossible not to hear the faint cry in his voice and my heart shrinks at the sound of that. Although after I see the door open further, I note a slight lift of his shoulder, sign he casually brushes it off while he walks in with quiet steps. A kid his age should not just brush these off as though it is normal. A little boy his age should have nice dreams, not nightmares.

"Get in here, little bud."

Dragging my form a tad more to the side of the bed, I pat the free space that is now between Ensley and me, Zane climbing over the comforter until he gets in that exact spot, nestling himself under the covers.

"I dreamed of my mommy," he whispers, and I don't miss the gleam in his eyes when they dart my way.

"Oh, buddy. Wanna talk about it?"

His little head shakes and instead he gets further under the covers until it comes right under his chin.

"It's alright, little man. It's all gonna be alright, okay?"

When his big, hopeful eyes meet mine, it becomes even harder not to want to do whatever is in my power to keep Zane safe.

"Promise?"

A smile forms on my lips. "I promise, bud. Now go to sleep, alright? Ensley and I are right here for you."

"I like her," Zane mutters as a wide smile takes over his features.

"I'm fairly sure she likes you too, bud."

It is on that sentence that Zane cranes his neck to the other side, and I cannot help but continue smiling. Especially when Ensley turns in her sleep and rests her hand on his stomach just atop the covers. There is a protectiveness in the way she gently does it even in her sleep after she must have felt his small figure next to her.

Throwing my arm above Zane, I place my hand on Ensley's hip and we both scoot closer.

And just as I close my eyes to go to sleep again, a thought strikes me: *I'll do anything to protect them.*

* * *

When my eyes flutter open again, the morning light already seeps through the window and this time around it feels as though I slept like a baby. And the instant my eyes adjust, I see the reason why I did. The serenity of the sight my gaze lands on. Ensley peacefully asleep with Zane's back snuggled into her front while her arm is draped over his small body.

I cannot fight the smile from tipping at the corners of my lips at that view.

Ensley would make such a fine mother. Sexy as fuck—hands

down the hottest mother out there. In addition to that though, she'd be an incredible mother figure—loving, protective and caring. And it is on that thought that for the briefest of ticks, behind my closed eyelids flashes an image. An image of Ensley with a swollen belly, my hand atop it, caressing it. Touching her belly gently to feel the kick of our baby girl or baby boy that grows inside of her.

For yet another second, I also think of the number of times I spilled inside her. How I took her without a condom every time we made love. How for the same number of instances, I wonder just how effective is the pill she is on. But then I push that thought away without further contemplation. Although I do that, I still drink in the image before me for a few more moments before I toss the covers off me and throw my legs over the edge of the bed.

Pushing up to my feet, I grab a pair of sweatpants and a t-shirt from the dresser, and I pad out of the bedroom, then down the hall toward the stairs.

As I reach halfway down the stairs, I hear a click, my neck snapping toward the front door. So, I lower and sit my ass on the stairs, clearing my voice.

"Please remind me to never wake up this early so I can prevent myself from needing an urgent eye bleach from seeing my own mother doing the walk of shame."

Mom freezes mid-turn, her heels in hand.

"I still demand respect, young man. I'm your mother after all. And you should also thank me for leaving you and Ensley alone all night."

"Yeah, as if that had nothing to do with your wish for us to have a baby," I call her out as she walks closer.

"Oh, well, nothing wrong for a mother to wanna be a grand-mother, correct?"

Mom takes a seat next to me and places her shoes beside her.

"I thought about it just now, you know? How it would be if Ley and I had a baby, an actual family together."

At my confession, Mom smiles widely.

"I'd say about time."

"I wanna take a chance on us, Mom. I wanna try having a life with Ensley without looking over my shoulder. I wanna make happy the woman I am in love with. I wanna love her and give her everything and anything she asks for. I wanna give her the love she deserves."

Mom's head rests on my shoulder. "That's all I've ever wanted. For you to be happy."

"I've told Ensley the truth about me. About my biological family. How you took care of me and loved me, all these years. How although we don't have the same blood running through our veins, you are my mother."

"You'll always be my son, no matter what. DNA and blood-line, nothing matters to me. You are my baby boy and I love you with all my heart."

"I love you too, *Mamá.*"

As my lips rest atop her head, I can feel her smile.

"Soooo, you and that guy…", I search my memory for his name. "Juaquin, was it?"

She nods.

"Are you two still going out?"

This time, her head shakes.

After Zaiden had his computer wiz do a dive into the guy's background and came back with nothing shady, I tried to be more agreeable to the idea that the two of them are dating. Only that now there's no more of that.

"What happened?"

"He wanted to move too fast for my pace," she confesses.

I sigh. This is how Mom has always been, when things get serious, she steps back.

"It's weird how you tell me to fight for the one I love, while you just push away any chance to be happy."

"You being happy is all the happiness I need in my life. Although a grandchild would make me even happier."

"Mason."

The timid voice that calls my name comes from the top of the stairs has me crane my neck to the side to look back, though I know exactly who that is.

Mom, on the other hand, snaps her neck to the side and a shocked expression takes over her face when her gaze lands on Zane. Then just as puzzled, her peer moves to me.

"I've only been gone a day, and to the best of my knowledge, babies usually take time to grow this big," Mom speaks, her eyes darting back to Zane, taking in the little boy.

"Come here, buddy."

With careful steps, he descends the stairs, and Mom scoots a little more to the side, making enough room for him to sit down between us. When he does so, he timidly snuggles more into me.

"This is my mom, Ary. *Mamá*, this is Zane."

"Hi, sweetie."

While Mom greets him with a sweet, gentle voice, her confused gaze still darts back to me. But more than confused, she is surprised at the sight of an eight-year-old in our house.

"Long story," I mouth to her.

She nods. Her chocolate eyes journey to Zane, who nestles even closer into me under Mom's peer.

"Why did you get up, bud? Had a bad dream again?"

Zane moves his little head in assent. "I dreamed you took me back to that house. The kids there were very mean, laughing at me that nobody wants me."

A sniffle surges past Mom's lips and I fight the instant urge to rub at my chest.

"And when you weren't there, I thought you maybe went to get my foster parents."

My head shakes and my arm lifts over his tiny shoulders, pulling him further into my side. "No, little guy. You can stay here for as long as you want. We'll need to contact them, though, so they won't worry."

"They never worry. They don't even know when I'm gone," Zane attests with a shrug of his shoulders.

The instant my eyes fly to Mom's, it is close to impossible to miss the glossiness of them. There is no need to tell her that long story because she already knows it. Or part of it she does. Almost as much as Ensley and I know about him.

We still don't know what happened to his mom and what had him end up in the foster care system, but that is something we'll find out though.

"You don't like it there very much, do you Zane?" Mom speaks, keeping her tone gentle and soft, the kindness oozing from each word.

This time around, Zane shakes his head.

"Are you sure you don't want to sleep some more?"

He moves his head from side to side again.

"Ensley and I need to go to work at the firehouse today. Are you alright to stay with my mom?" Before either of them say something, my eyes lift to my mother. "Unless you're going to the office today?"

After grandad's passing, Mom has taken over and led the real estate business. She has previously worked alongside him, so she knows it like the back of her hand.

"I'm still on leave until the end of this week although I still attend to urgent matters remotely, so we can bake cookies together if you'd like," Mom suggests and Zane's face lights up, nodding eagerly. "We've got a deal then."

Once she lifts her hand up with her palm facing us, Zane doesn't hesitate to give her a high-five. His green eyes then pierce my brown once as he turns his head toward me.

"But promise you'll take me to the firehouse too?"

I cannot help but smile and bring my hand to his hair, ruffling it. "I promise, bud."

"I know a few people who work for the foster system," Mom mutters. "I'll make some calls."

At that, I nod, knowing we need to find out about Zane and who are the negligent—putting it nicely—sons of bitches who don't notice when a kid in their care disappears for three whole days.

Looking down at the little boy, his green eyes journey to mine once he tips his chin up, and my smile grows further when he gives me a wholesome smile of his own, followed by a curt giggle.

This little guy is something else entirely, finding joy in the smallest of things. Finding joy even when life has been rough for him from such a young age.

He needs someone to look after him. Someone who cares if he goes missing for five minutes and loses their mind when he misses for more than ten. Someone who loves him. He needs a chance at something good.

ENSLEY

"*Miña tigresa.*"

("*My tigress.*")

The whisper has my entire body tingling.

It becomes hyperaware of the fragrance of shower gel and aftershave that pierces my nostrils. Just as acutely aware as I become of the fingers tracing gently up my spine before they focus on the tigress tattoo. The fingertips caress the strokes of the ink, then hot lips press against the skin, having my form in overdrive with cognizance.

Stretching my body, I let out a moan and open my eyes, meeting Mason's chocolate orbs for a brief moment. And I say a brief moment because his gaze homes in on the tattoo on my shoulder.

"Call me that again."

"*Miña tigresa,*" he repeats and my heart thunders louder and faster in my chest.

I stretch a bit more and Mason leans in with a smile, crashing his lips over mine without delay.

"Morning, *nena,*" he whispers when he pulls away.

"Good morning, handsome," I greet him as I turn on my back, reaching my arms over his shoulders to pull him to me.

"I'm gonna get a taxi and get my bike from the bar."

My head moves in assent.

"Where's Zane?" I ask, my eyes journeying the room for the

little one, waiting to see his small tousled-haired head pop from somewhere.

Instantly, a smile splits his lips. "He's in the kitchen with Mom. She's making him breakfast."

"Stole her heart already?

He nods with a chuckle.

"You have no idea."

My gaze takes Mason in. The instant smile on his face when I asked about Zane. The cheerful chuckle. And I cannot help resting my hand on his cheek, caressing it gently while I hold his brown stare. God, just how much I can love this man.

"Is there a way we can look into his case? Find out more about him and maybe…" His brow lifts just a fraction, his eyes expectant. "We maybe could…"

"I would want that too," Mason interrupts, pressing his lips against mine briefly. "Mom knows some people with the foster care system and I'm sure so does Derek. We can look into what we can do for him."

Surprise flows through my body at his unfaltering response. Because when I suggested, I didn't anticipate him to say what he's just said.

Which is exactly what he sees on my face. Pure surprise. Mainly because I know he told me time and again he doesn't want to have kids. Above all, because I vividly recall his reaction when he found the negative pregnancy test in the trashcan in the bathroom.

"Are you sure?"

"Absolutely."

There is no fraction of hesitation in his voice when he offers me the certitude that it is what he wants. He wants us both to take care of Zane together. To give the little boy a family who can care for him—temporarily or otherwise.

"But you know what that means, right?"

My brow quirks. "What does that mean?"

And just as the last word of my question leaves my mouth, the left corner of Mason's lips turns upward in a lopsided smirk. "No sex anywhere else that isn't our bedroom or shower unless Zane is on a sleepover."

The grin on his face doesn't ebb. Not even the smallest of fragments while his dark peer turns wicked.

"I'm sure we can make do with that," I revert, a playful look setting on my face, trying to pull him in for a kiss.

Mason resists, though, tensing his form before our mouths get to even brush. "Oh, and by the way, although I love it, you'll have to hold back on screaming down the walls of this house. Just when he's around, of course."

Relaxing his body this time, his lips press against mine. Only for a moment, though, since we pull away chuckling when we hear Zane's voice calling our names, most certainly from the bottom of the stairs. Our foreheads touch and our eyes close simultaneously as we drink in the sound.

"Is this what we'll sign up for?" Mason whispers the question, his lips dusting mine as he speaks.

I draw back a little, locking my gaze to his. "I'm pretty sure it is."

At my answer, a deep, low chortle crawls up his throat. "I wouldn't have it any other way. We'll inquire into what we can find out once we're back tomorrow. Now, I need to go and get my bike."

"You don't need to drive me. Yesterday I stopped by the shop and got my car."

"Alright then. I'll just ride directly to the firehouse and see you in the morning?"

I nod. "Take care of you, baby. I need you to come home to me."

The plea in my voice is clear. Just as evident as the feelings of worry and apprehension that courses through my body while I pull him tightly to me.

"Promise me."

The moment he withdraws and looks into my eyes, he cups my face, understanding dawning on him. Comprehension that I need it. I need to hear him say those words to me.

"I promise. I'll come back to you safe and sound, *nena*. But I need you to promise me you'll do the same because now that I finally have you, I won't be able to live without you."

Again, my head moves in assent. "I promise."

"Good. Because, *nena*, although I know if I could be born a thousand times, just as many times I'd fall in love with you, love you and only you, I'd rather have you and love you in this lifetime."

My throat suddenly clogs. It clogs with my own breath and my words while my mind replays what he's just said. It echoes once and then twice. But it is on that third repeat that I can finally draw in air. Mainly because each repetition emphasizes more and more the familiarity of a part of his oration.

"I know if I could be born a thousand times, just as many times I'd fall in love with you."

No doubt in his utterance.

Just like there hasn't been when he's first spoken them to me. To me and in front of our families and friends. To me, in his vow as he slid the wedding band on my finger.

"Today I vow to love you forever and uninhibitedly. To lift you up when you are down. To never cut your wings, but instead fly with you. From today on, we are one because, nena, if I could be born a thousand times, just as many times I'd fall in love with you. I know that because you are my missing piece and with you it is when I'm whole. God knows I've tried denying that, but the truth is that I was born to love you, to worship you and to cherish you. Your body. Your heart. Your mind. You were born to be mine as much as I was born to be yours, and from here on out, you are forever mine just like I'm forever yours."

Without hesitation, Mason leans in again, his lips smashing over mine, knocking the moment away from my mind. Astonished as I am by that sentence that brings me back to the day of our wedding, I still kiss him back. With just as much potency. With the same amount of fervor. With the same rampant desire. With the same unbridled love that we have for one another.

"Ensley, Mason, grandma Ary told me to say to you to stop goofing around and come down for breakfast."

Zane's voice causes us to wrench our mouths away from each other. This time, we also snap our heads to the side because it doesn't sound as far as the first time when he called out our names. Rightfully so since the little boy is in our bedroom, standing in the doorway, his small palms covering his eyes.

"Grandma Ary, huh?" I ask, unable to restrain the giggle.

Zane nods with an eager smile, not removing the hands from his face.

"She told me I can call her that."

His tiny shoulders lift casually.

"Did she also tell you to cover your eyes when you come in?" Mason asks and, with the corner of my eye, I see him shaking his head at his mom's antics.

"Uh-huh," he swiftly agrees, adding another nod. "She said something about kissy-kissy."

"Well, I think you should remove your hands from your eyes, otherwise you won't be able to see where you're running."

"Running?" He questions Mason's statement, slowly removing his hands until his beautiful green eyes take us both in.

There is no delay in Mason's action when he charges out of bed and lounges for Zane who barely manages to turn around before my man is next to him and scoops him under his armpit like a sack of potatoes. Zane's loud squeal is immediately followed by a roar of laughter while Mason carries him out of the room. Their joined snigger pierces my ears and I close my eyes, letting that sound sync in as I take a deep breath.

* * *

My smile is wide as I park the car on the side of the road just by the firehouse. That after I enjoyed breakfast with Mason, Zane and Ary—laughing with the little guy who couldn't stop smiling and talking. Throughout, he didn't mention anything about his mother. We didn't pry, wanting him to come to us when he wants and is ready to talk. Whatever it is, it mustn't be good.

Although I fight the urge of smiling like an idiot at the thought of this morning's events as I step out of the car, the feeling of happiness that flows within me doesn't wane.

Once I walk up through the open doors of the apparatus floor, I go to make my way to the firehouse's entrance. Yet, before I do, my steps come to a halt.

"Sorry, ma'am. Got a delivery for Ensley Carter."

The voice comes from behind me. The exact voice that stops my steps and has me glued to the spot, swallowing hard.

Ensley Carter.

It has been a while since I've been called that. Just as long as Mason has been out of the coma. Though I don't think on this for too long, there's still a feeling of emptiness in my chest, realizing just how much I missed being addressed as that.

As the cold shiver runs through my body, I turn, assuming already what the delivery guy holds. When my eyes land on a bouquet of roses again, my assumption becomes a confirmation.

"Who sent these?" I ask.

My attempt at getting information is met with a shrug. "I don't know. I'm just the delivery guy, ma'am. Are you Ensley Carter?"

"I am."

I barely get a chance to affirm it and he shoves the flowers in my arms, walking away.

Without waiting any longer, I look through the roses and find the small envelope with the note. Slipping it out, I read.

"If you run someone off the road, is it really an accident? She made it just too easy."

The thrumming in my chest becomes alert as I reread the words printed on the card. The thunder of my heart just as alert as my body becomes at the mention of Aracely's accident—because it must be about her. But the implication that it wasn't an accident? That it was intentionally caused? That has my brain in a whirlwind with questions.

Questions that only one person can answer.

Aracely herself.

Racing inside the firehouse, I drop the flowers on the table in the common room so one of my fellow firefighters can put them in water. Once I shout my greetings over my shoulder to the men and women in the common room, I head for the locker. Meantime, with my right hand, I fish my phone out of the cargo pants pocket and tap on it several times until it calls Aracely's number, voice greeting me after the second ring.

"Ola, miña nena fermosa!"

(*"Hi, my beautiful girl!"*)

"Ary, I need you to answer me one question." The severity in my voice is crystal clear. So much so that I can almost see the smile dimming on her face. "Is there even the tiniest of chances that your crash wasn't an accident?"

The line remains quiet.

For approximately five seconds, I stand there, with the phone at my ear and my free hand rummaging through my locker, trying to find the other two cards.

"Ary," I urge her when I note that she doesn't answer me. "Please, Ary. I need you to tell me the truth."

The heavy breath that stabs my ear is more or less of a reply to my question.

"No, it wasn't an accident," she confirms, letting out another hefty exhale. Holding out on us like this has clearly taken a lot from her.

"Why would you tell us it is?"

"Because I knew if I had told my son the truth, he would have pulled back and pushed you away. I couldn't have that, not after all that you two have been through. Not after you two have finally found your way back together. No chance in hell."

Sheer protectiveness and vehemence coat Aracely's tone. And both tell me she would do it again without blinking.

"How do you know?"

Her question doesn't surprise me when she shoots it my way. I expected it.

"I had my doubts, but it's because you're not the only one who's been keeping secrets."

"How do you mean?"

"I keep receiving roses and notes at the firehouse. I didn't take them seriously until now when the last one I've received confirmed my suspicion that it wasn't an accident."

"Ensley." The protectiveness and vehemence turn into caution and worry as she says my name.

"Do you think it's them? Mason's biological family?" I know I don't need to clarify that last part, but I do though. Maybe because it is still something I am trying to digest. Perhaps because saying it out loud makes it real.

"I don't know, Enz. I sure hope not because help me God if they as much as touch a hair on my son's head or on yours, I will make them pay."

"How's Zane?"

The question isn't only meant to distract us. It is meant to bring us a tad of tranquility because at this moment, right now, only he can do so.

"This little guy is getting spoilt. We're going shopping in a bit."

I smile. "Give him a kiss for me, okay. I'll see you both tomorrow morning."

"Will do, *fermosa*. Stay safe out there, *vale?*"

"Always, Ary."

With that we drop our call and I close the door to the locker with a loud bang. And just as I go to open the door, it gets opened.

"Rushing somewhere, doll?" JJ asks, her brow quirked as she takes me in.

"I need to do something. It can't wait."

"Be on radio." It is all she says, understanding from my tone that there is no time for jokes. "Do you want me to come with?"

For a moment I ponder her question. Right after, however, my head shakes. "I'll be back as soon as possible."

Before I get a chance to twirl on the heel of my shoes and leave, JJ's hand wraps around my wrist, halting me.

"Be careful, a'right? I know that look you have on your face and that is the kind that gets you in trouble."

"I'll be careful, JJ," I respond.

It is on this last assurance that JJ nods her head at me and lets go of her hold. So, as swiftly as I can, I race out of there, into the gear room to grab a radio and then rush back into my car, driving off.

I drive as fast, yet as careful, as I can until I find myself parking next to a building I've wheeled Mason in when we found out that Ella got abducted from the scene of a fire—the Washington DC FBI field office.

Maybe my sister, Renée, can help me with this. With locating who keeps sending these. There should be a way to track the purchase of these flowers to someone. I hope there is because nobody gets to mess with my family and get away with it. Nobody runs my husband's mother off the road and doesn't get punished for it.

As I get out of the car, I slip my phone out and call my sister. It rings four times before she picks up and during that time, I question whether she is at the office or not. Because truth be told, it didn't strike me that she might be out in the field or even maybe at the FBI headquarters in Quantico, Virginia, where she is most of the time when she doesn't assist with a case in Washington. Well, she's pretty much everywhere considering that the BAU teams get called out wherever they're needed.

Renée has been working with the Behavioral Analysis Unit since she graduated from the academy when she was twenty-eight. She has been in the U.S. Navy for ten years which she joined right after high school. The day she finished the academy, she was approached with a case and ever since, she's been part of the team.

"Hey, Enz," she greets right away. "Is everything alright?"

"Hi, Rennie. Are you at the office today? I've just parked my car outside."

"I'll get security to bring you up."

Her voice is on alert. It is as though she feels something is wrong. As though she can hear it my voice despite the fact that I try to mask my worry. But considering she profiles people for a living, it is only logical that she does.

"Thanks, Rennie."

I know she hates being called that. In our family, with the exception of Luke—her forever defender—, everyone else calls her *Rennie*; most of the time at least. Which is something she hates with passion, unless it is Dad who calls her that. Hence why each time I call her Rennie, I can already see her eyes rolling. But since defiance is something that flows plentifully and generously through the genes of the Walker ladies, she's learned to brush it off just like I've learned to disregard her daring eye-roll.

Knocking away the thoughts, I slide my phone into the pocket of my fire department-issued windbreaker and walk inside the building. Immediately after doing so, a man in a black suit with a crisp white shirt beneath approaches me.

"Ensley Carter. I'm here to see my sister, Supervisory Special Agent Renée Walker."

"Follow me, Mrs. Carter. SSA Walker announced your visit with us."

That is all he says before he turns on the heels of his black shoes and walks in front of me toward the elevator bank. We quickly enter the steel cart once it hits our floor and he presses the button, setting it in an upward motion.

Soon enough the doors ping open, and he extends his hand in a gesture for me to exit. Which I do, my eyes instantly landing on my baby sister who waits for me by the elevators.

I don't miss the slight tiredness in my sister's green gaze. A green stare that matches mine exactly. Truth be told, we look so much alike, having inherited our features—the green eyes, the small freckles dusting our cheeks, the shape of the nose and mouth—from our mother and only our brunette hair from our dad. Although I also got more of his genes when it comes to height, standing tall at five-foot-nine, Renée is similarly as short as Mom is at five-foot-four.

"Hey, Enz," she greets me again and pulls me into a hug. "What's the matter?"

And just like I perceived over the phone, now I get the confirmation that she did sense in my voice that something is wrong. Which is what prompts her green orbs to peruse me alertly as though to search for any possible physical signs that could perhaps tell her what is happening and what the issue is.

When they find nothing, they journey back to mine.

"I need your help, Rennie."

That only substantiates her belief further. Not that there was any need for additional proof.

"Tell me how I can help," she urges with not even the smallest of doubts in her voice as she leads us both through the desks and agents until she opens a door.

We both enter a room with a couple of sofas—one across the other—and a coffee table in between. We take a seat next to each other on the same couch and her green gaze peers at me expectantly.

Promptly, I dig my hands into my pocket and slide out the three little envelopes that contain the cards.

"I've been receiving flowers and these notes."

Her eyebrows knit together, and she takes the envelopes from me, opening them.

Renée slides the first note out. The exact note I've received first and her sharp stare lifts from the words written on the card to meet my eyes.

"When did you receive this?"

"This was on the backseat of my car when I've left the bar the day Ella was rescued."

"Ensley, that's over a month ago." Her voice raises a fraction in reproach, her orbs just as scolding. "You found it on the backseat of your car... As in inside your goddamn car and didn't think to bring this to my attention until now?"

I sign. "I didn't take it seriously. I thought maybe some of the guys were playing a prank on me."

This time Renée scoffs, shaking her head as she continues with the second note. "What secret does it refer to? I gather your secret. But Mason's?"

"It's about who he is. Who his biological family is, or at least that's what I think they refer to," I confess.

"What do you mean by that?" Confusion is written all over Renée's features. A moment later, her eyes drop to the note between her fingers, reading it again.

"Aracely isn't Mason's mother. He was given to her when he was born because his biological mother suffered complications and died."

My sister's eyes widen in surprise.

"His mother was the daughter of a criminal, married to the son of another criminal who took over his father's side of the business. They are the leaders of the *Os Diábolos* clan. *The Devils* clan based in Galicia."

"Holy fucking shit," she breathes out the curse.

Yes, what the Walker ladies also share is the swearing. Oh, yes, we swear a lot, though Mom and Renée most often than not resort to it more than I do.

"I've just found out myself. This is the reason why Mason tried to keep me at arms' length before. He was trying to protect me in case they've found him."

"Have they? Are you sure this is from them?"

Running a frustrated hand through my locks, I shake my head. "I don't know for sure, but what if they have? What if they've found Mason? That would explain the last note I got today."

Without delay, Renée opens the last envelope and reads the note. "Ary's crash wasn't an accident?"

"It wasn't. I called Ary right after and she admitted it wasn't. She was run off the road by a car, but said it was an accident because she knew if she'd said otherwise, Mason would have pushed me away again."

"Not like he hasn't been doing that." The sarcasm in my sister's tone is followed by a gentle roll of her green eyes.

"That was the night he stopped pushing me away. The night he lost all his control and..." I halt my sentence, feeling that there is no need for my sister to know my husband smacked my ass senseless, and ate me out like I was his last supper right before I jacked him off. "Then when Luke called, we went together to the hospital and the entire time he held my hand. Ary saw that and told us it was an accident."

"Does he know about these?" She asks, lifting the notes between us. "What kind of question do I even ask?! Obviously, he doesn't otherwise your ass would be on a one-way flight to Alaska right now, hiding you in a cabin somewhere where nobody can find you even if they tried, not even Big Foot."

Although her words are sharp, her gaze softens while her free hand reaches for mine, giving it a light squeeze.

"I'm gonna look into it, Enz. We've got the flower shop here on the card and I'll see what I can dig. But please, if you receive any more flowers and notes, let me know. Preferably not after a month."

The dig in her last sentence is clear.

Clear as the day is long.

"I will. I promise."

"And anything out of the ordinary; you feel followed or get calls, anything at all, you call me," she insists, giving my hand another squeeze. "I can try and get an FBI squad to watch your home."

My head shakes, declining. "That would be a lot of explaining that I'll need to give Mason. I've just got my man back, Rennie, I'm not going to lose him."

"But you're taking a great risk."

"One I'm willing to take to keep the man I love. I want to keep them safe too."

She nods, understandingly. Yet, there is something I can clearly see in her stare. Determination—another trait deeply rooted in the fibers of the Walker ladies.

MASON

Two weeks have flown by since I returned to the firehouse. Since I've got back to doing the job I love—being a firefighter, helping people at times of need when they feel like their world is coming down on them.

It has also been two weeks since I've told Ensley the truth about me. Since she's found out that I am the son and grandson of criminals. Nothing has changed. She doesn't look at me differently like I thought she might. She sees me as the same man. She sees me as her man.

Ensley has never brought them up after my confession though. She has asked me about my biological mother, but never about them. Not much I could tell Ensley about her apart from what I've already told her since Mom didn't know her very well and only knew her from what her mother told her since she worked for the Montoya family. My biological grandmother knew about Mom's relationship with my Dad, which is why she chose to give me up to her, so they can take me away from the bloodthirsty, criminal legacy that would've expected me growing up in that family.

"Give my son a future without crime. Give him a chance to be good and choose his own future." It is what Mom told me that my biological mother told my grandmother when she handed me to her as a mere only minutes-old baby. She gave me up with the last strength in her body since just moments thereafter she passed away.

Which is exactly what Mom and Dad did when they took me to the States. They offered me a choice away from the crime family. They offered me the opportunity of having a family of my own without tarnishing their future.

This brings me to another thing that's been going on for just over two weeks. Zane has been staying with us since the day I found him in the alley behind the dumpster. With the help of an acquaintance of my mom who works in the foster care system, Zane can stay with us indefinitely. Firstly, because the foster care family he was in the care of has blatantly said they didn't want him to begin with. Secondly, because when she asked Zane if he wants them to find him another home, he said he wants to stay, and I quote: *"with Mason, Ensley and grandma Ary"*. Yes, he still calls mom "grandma" much to our amusement and Mom's happiness. We still need to get all the paperwork done to properly become Zane's foster parents, but because the little boy's wish warmed the heart of the social worker, he still gets to stay with us.

Although Mom has now moved back home, she helps us take care of Zane. Derek and Angie have also been introduced to the little boy and have watched him just two days ago when Ensley and I had been at the firehouse until we picked him up the next morning.

It is safe to say that our little man has just conquered the heart of everyone he's met in this short span of time.

"Hey, man. How's your little boy doing?" Rhys asks as he enters the locker room, and a broad smile tips the corners of my lips.

See what I mean by everyone?

Derek brought Zane by the firehouse the other day and my fellow firefighters got to see a side of the Deputy Commissioner of the DC Fire and EMS Department that they've never seen before. No more of the imposing, fearful Deputy Commissioner, but instead they saw a soft side of him. A side brought out by an eight-year-old boy who's got him—as much as everyone else, including me—eating from the palm of his hand.

"He's doing well."

Zane is actually doing well. Better than before and that is clear on his face. He's happier. His eyes gleam with glee and he's so full of energy, rubbing it off on all of us. He has also been sleeping better, especially during this past week.

The week before last, he had a few nightmares and we brought him into our room, sleeping between Ensley and me. This one, on the other hand, has been much quieter from this point of view. We have been giving him the care and the love a kid like him needs. We have given him a family and in return, he has given us a family too.

Although with the involvement of the social services lady that Mom knows, we have managed to find some things about Zane's mother, we didn't pry with him. All that we know from her, though, is that she died of an overdose and he doesn't have any other known family. We also found out that even then with his mom, they still used to sleep rough. Abandoned buildings, shelters for a short period of time while his mother attempted to get clean, relapsing and ending up taking Zane with her back on the streets.

Thinking back on the day I met my little boy and on the makeshift "bed" of cardboard, it makes sense. He was used to it. Something an eight-year-old should definitely not be.

"He's home with Angie. She'll take him to the park this afternoon. And to be completely honest, I don't know who is more excited about that, Angie or Zane."

Rhys smiles. A wide smile filled with meaningfulness. "You've got a good thing going on for you, Carter. Don't screw it up by being an idiot."

"I won't," I reassure him.

Although he nods, in his eyes I can distinctly see the warning. That unspoken *"you better or else…"* threat which he doesn't need to say aloud to be heard.

"Besides, if the Deputy Commissioner's daughter is happy, he is happy which in conclusion makes us all happy because I'd really hate to break your pretty boy face if he rides our asses because you broke his daughter's heart."

"Never," I vow.

Because this is what it actually is.

A vow.

A promise.

A pledge.

To never hurt Ensley.

To never break her heart.

To never push her away—more than I already have.

Because Ensley is my woman.

Always has been.

Always will be.

I don't care who has been in her life until this point. All I care about is that she is mine now.

Opening the door of my locker, I drop my duffle bag inside. When I go to close it though, my hand freezes on the metal. It is as if it gets glued to it while an overwhelming feeling floods through my body. And I say overwhelming to put it succinctly, because what overcomes my form is an amalgamation of emotions. One so strong my other hand slams against the adjacent locker and my chin drops into my chest. My eyes squeeze tightly shut as though impossible to contain the overpowering surge of feelings. But that is to no avail because they keep attacking from all sides as a voice fights to break through, assailing me with force.

Fuck me, everything hurts.

My head throbs.

My chest aches.

"Baby, it's me. How did we get here? How did we get to this point?" The voice stops briefly, and the sound of a bitter chuckle fills the air. "My intention wasn't to leave all this in a voicemail, I'm sure you might be on a call, so... Baby, I will sign the papers. If that is what you want, I will sign them. I will because my love for you isn't defined by a signature on some goddamn piece of paper. It is within me, engrained so deeply, I always felt you down to the marrow of my bones and if I sign the divorce papers, that won't change a thing. But if you need me, if you ever need someone to talk to in the middle of the night after a rough call, honey, I'll be only one phone call away. I don't care we're not together anymore, I will always be there when you need me, so call. Even if you don't say anything and it will be just the sound of your breathing at the other end, I'll quietly stay on the line and listen. I've learned to listen when you don't say a word, I've learned to love you even when you deny me, and I will always love you even when you don't anymore. File the papers and I will sign them. I love you."

The sound of the voice dies down, yet, for a second, I can hear a gentle breathing and the tremble in it.

My eyes snap open.

Every word resounds in my mind.

It resonates. Not only in my head. It reverberates through my entire body with such viciousness that the hand on the adjacent locker drops to my chest, rubbing at the ache.

Although the voice is distorted for some reason, the sentences are clear. Just as distorted as the other time this kind of feeling overwhelmed me. The voice is indiscernible, making it impossible to figure out whether it is one that I recognize or a completely unfamiliar one.

Is it a memory? Is this one of my suppressed memories? It could be. But divorce? That doesn't make any sense. Maybe it is a memory, though. Maybe it is a memory from one of the call outs. Perhaps my dissociative amnesia is expanded to more parts of my life than I thought. If that is true, it dismantles my belief that the dissociative amnesia mainly concerns Ensley.

Or maybe…

It can't be…

Can it?

No, it can't.

That would explain…

No, it wouldn't.

But what if my mind fights for me to remember? What if there's something so crucial that I forgot that now my mind urges me to recall, turning everything into more of a jumbled mess.

Knocking the thoughts away, I manage to slam shut the door to the locker and with heavy steps, I storm out of the room.

Involuntarily, my left hand lifts and my eyes zero in on my fingers. It is as though I heedlessly look for signs. They aren't there. At least what I believed would serve as proof isn't there—the tan line.

My head shakes and the stupidity of the thought hits me. But even more idiotic is when I slip my phone out of the pocket of my cargo pants and unlock it, taping on the recent calls icon right before I tap on the voicemail function, bringing it to my ear.

"Welcome to your voicemail. You have no new messages or saved messages."

Fucking hell, Carter. There is no chance in hell so stop being a goddamn idiot, I berate myself, shoving the phone back inside the pocket.

"Are you alright, brother?"

Luke's voice wrenches me out of my foolish thoughts and I heedlessly nod.

"Positive?"

I go to nod. Yet, my head remains still, while my eyes stay on his blue-grayish ones, expecting an answer from me.

"I remember Jesse's seeing a psychologist recommended by that buddy of his, Cruz, I believe?"

Luke's brows furrow. "Cruz Livingston, yes. Someone he knows underwent therapy with the doc. Ivy Melton, I think it's her name."

"She does hypnosis, doesn't she?"

My best friend's brows knit closer together. "What's going on, Mason?"

A sigh crawls up my throat just as my hand lifts, and I rake my fingers through my hair. "I have had these flashes and have heard this distorted voice. I'm trying to make sense of it. Are they my actual memories? Are they recollections or just something that my mind makes up? I'm trying to figure out what it is because I feel like I need to remember."

He nods. "What kinda flashes?"

My mouth opens to answer him, but before I get the chance to, Chief Sinclair walks our way. "Walker, in my office."

"Uh, looks like someone is in trouble with Dad," I joke.

It isn't the first time we refer to our chief as *Dad*. As the highest-ranking officer in our firehouse, Chief Sinclair looks after us and has our backs. He knows when to back us up and when to tell us off. Just like a father does. Hence why we occasionally refer to him as Dad.

"Keep that thought. I'll see what Chief wants and then we can talk about that."

Although Luke is clear, after he turns and follows our chief, I retrieve my phone once again and look for Jesse's number in my contacts, ringing him.

"Hey, bro," he answers, his voice

"Hi, brother. I have a favor to ask you."

"Course, shoot."

"Your psychologist…"

"Doctor Ivy Melton?"

"Yes. Think you can put me in contact with her?"

There is a moment of silence in our conversation.

"Are you alright, Mason?"

"I need to talk to someone, Jesse. Preferably someone who isn't linked to DC since Derek knows everyone and I rather not have him know that his daughter's boyfriend is a step away from the looney bin."

"His daughter's boyfriend? I better pray to God that I don't contract whatever bug is going around that firehouse."

"You're a little too late for that, brother. What was her name again? Elena Renaud?"

A growl fills my ear through the speaker.

He forbade us from saying her name ever since we found out about her hence the deep, guttural sound he makes to express his gripe.

Elena Renaud is Jesse's ex-fiancée. They've been together for a few good years before Jesse popped the question. They also had a date for the wedding, and everything was planned out until there was no more wedding. Hence why he gets grumpy and growly whenever the name comes up. Although I'm fairly sure there's another name—of another woman—who will have him blow a gasket. She's his version of "the one who shall not be named".

Hell, we wouldn't even know if it weren't for Jesse's younger brother, Zaiden. Well, that and an extremely drunk Jesse who spilt the beans without knowing he was doing so.

Jesse met Elena on the plane when he was traveling home to see his family after he returned from his deployment. They had seats one next to the other and they struck up a conversation. That was all it took and seven years later—the day before the wedding—his fiancée called everything off. And it wasn't wedding jitters. She didn't just get cold feet. According to Jesse, she got talked into canceling everything by her best friend—here enters the woman who can have him go berserk faster than he can shoot his gun. I've seen him shoot his gun a few times when we went to the shooting range and that man is so incredibly fast. This is why I'm tempted to mention her name now just so I can hear him lose his mind.

"I'll put you in contact with Ivy. She's in DC for a conference for the next two weeks and maybe she can schedule something with you," Jesse says, breaking through my thoughts.

"Thanks, man. You'd really do me a solid. I'll owe you one."

"Never speak her name again and we'll be square."

I smirk. He gets so easily riled up by this. For someone who *doesn't* care, he sure as hell *does* care an awful lot.

Before I get to say anything else, Jesse cuts the call.

* * *

Entering the house, the smell of freshly brewed coffee pierces my nostrils and I breathe it in. Simultaneously, a pair of laughs dance in my ear and I cannot help but smile, knowing very well that one belongs to Ensley and the other to Zane. If this isn't the best sound that one can come home to, then I don't know what it is.

I drop the keys on the high-table and leave my duffle bag at the bottom of the stairs, making my way toward the kitchen.

My eyes widen when everything is covered in a white-colored powder, but an instant smile tugs at the corners of my lips when I peruse the room.

I find Zane on the side of the kitchen island that is closest to me, hiding while his small hands gather some more white powder from a bowl on the floor.

On the other side of the island, I note Ensley getting up with two handfuls, ready for attack. One that doesn't delay when Zane springs to his feet and the white powder—which I assume is flour considering the eggs and all the other ingredients atop the island counter—flies into the air from one side to the other and vice-versa. Both of them are oblivious to my presence. The two of them are just too engrained in their flour war to acknowledge me—or maybe they just can't see properly because of the powder covering their faces.

For a moment, I drink the image in while I record the sound

of their laughs, storing them both in a drawer of my mind. The instant after that, however, I charge for the bowl of flour beside Zane and join his side in the attack.

He laughs harder and high-fives me. While I take a handful and throw it at Ensley whose eyes are playful and wicked at the same time, Zane takes advantage I have her focused on me and crawls on the other side until he gets to her, wrapping his small arms around her waist.

"Got ya," he chirps with a broad smile.

Ensley's gaze aims down at him, and I note how she cannot fight her smile.

"You did get me, didn't you?"

Zane draws back a little and nods his head, his green eyes gleaming with pride. However, when he sees the mischievous grin on Ensley's lips, he pulls back further.

"Uh-oh!"

Almost immediately and without giving him a chance to get too far, my woman's arms snake around him and she tickles his sides. There's a laugh that surges out of him as he squirms to get away from her.

"Ma...Mason, he...lp me."

Another shrieking laugh dances in the air and when Ensley stops for a moment and lets go of him, he races to me, hugging my legs.

There's no hesitation when I bend and pick him up in my arms, covering myself in more flour.

"Having fun, you two?"

Zane nods his little head eagerly, extra flour falling out of his hair at the motion.

"Hey, handsome," Ensley greets, taking a few steps toward us until she eats the distance between us.

The softness of her lips presses against mine and I cannot contain my chuckle when she pulls back, still all covered in flour.

"Hey, *nena.*"

"We're making pancakes," Zane says, gesturing toward the mixing bowl that is on the counter by the hob which I assume contains the batter.

"Oh, is this how you two are making pancakes?"

An innocent smile plays on both of their faces while they

shrug casually. At the same time, my girl extends her hand to dust off some of the flour from Zane's tousled hair and t-shirt.

"I started it when I got Ensley covered in it," Zane admits, peering down at me with his green orbs that have flecks of blue seeping through. "But only because I poured flour from the bowl to help her to the mix, and it made me sneeze."

The adorableness oozing out of him as he explains the situation to me tugs at my heart. Judging by Ensley's soft expression, it does the same to her. Because how can it not? How can it not when in such short span of time, he's crawled his way into our hearts and become like our own son? How can our hearts not overflow with joy and happiness at this?

"What do you say if you go and wash off all this flour, while I help Ensley clean up so we can make pancakes?"

Just as eagerly as before, Zane nods his head, and his eyes shine with glee.

I set him down on the floor and he rushes out of the kitchen. While he does so, my arms snake around Ensley's waist, bringing her to me.

My eyes lock onto hers and I peer down at her as she throws her arms over my shoulders. We keep our gazes connected for a tick, leaning in. My lips almost brush against hers when something hits right into us. Or someone. Zane, to be exact. He now has an arm around my knees and another around Ensley's.

When we look down at him simultaneously, he tilts his chin and smiles at us.

"Thank you for taking care of me."

Ensley and I immediately lock eyes, my heart thrumming in my chest just as hard as hers does.

"We love you, buddy," I utter, removing a hand from Ensley's back to rake it through his still flour-covered hair, tousling it some more.

"I love you both too."

It is on that last statement that escapes his lips that he turns and rushes out with a wide grin on his face. He leaves Ensley and me with an even bigger smile on ours while we stand there, my arm around her waist and both her arms snake around my torso, watching him run.

"We've got a good one here," Ensley whispers.

"We certainly do."

The smile on my face is clear as I turn to her.

Bringing Ensley flush to me again, there is no hesitation in how my lips press against hers. I use it to tell her just how much I missed her even though it's been just a little over twenty-four hours since we haven't seen each other. But the way she kisses me back with just as much fervor, I can tell she missed me just as much, the twenty-four hours feeling like days.

When her moan vibrates through me, my fingers dig into her hips and I lift her on top of the kitchen island, devouring her mouth.

Holy hell, I am a hungry man. Starving for my woman. Thirsty for her taste. And she can sense it also as my own groan reverberates through her achingly enticing body.

My hands squeeze her ass cheeks just as my tongue thrusts into her mouth, stroking hers. We continue kissing for a moment longer before we pull away.

"*Cono, nena*, I love this mouth of yours," I rasp just a mere inch away from her inviting lips.

Ensley's eyes gleam with mischief when I draw back a fraction, more to be able to lock our gazes. The playful smile on her face is there only to complete the wickedness of her intentions.

"Is it just my mouth you love?"

Tease.

This is exactly what she is—a tease.

"Fishing for compliments are we now, *nena?*"

Her shoulders casually lift, but the rascality coating her gaze and her smile doesn't ebb.

"There's plenty to love about you, teasing brat." My fingertips dig into her butt cheeks while her legs wrap around my waist. "I love you for all that you give me and for how you fought for me when I'm not sure I deserved it."

A deep frown settles on her forehead, marring her gorgeous features.

"Mas—"

"I love you, Ley, and I swear I'll spend every single day of my life proving I was worth fighting for."

Ensley's eyes soften while her arms lift to my shoulders, snake around my neck and pull me even closer than her legs do.

"After breakfast, I'll need to go for an appointment, but we can go to the zoo with Zane or to the park."

"Appointment? Is everything okay?"

Worry coats her voice, and I cannot help but cradle her face with my hands, having her eyes lock onto mine.

"It is, *nena*. I promise I'll tell you all about it after, okay?"

Her head nods gently, though she does eye me suspiciously. "Would you like me to come with? We can leave Zane with my mom."

I smile at her before my hands lift and I cup her face.

"I think I should do this on my own, Ley."

Again, her head moves in assent and this time she doesn't insist.

"Now, let's clean up this mess until our boy gets back."

"Our boy, huh?" The question leaves my mouth just as my lips quirk upward in a smile. "I really like the sound of that."

"So do I."

And as though he knows we were talking about him, his steps race down the stairs and in no time he appears in the kitchen, his green eyes filled with excitement.

"Let's make pancakes."

Chuckling, I lift Ensley off the countertop and her feet touch the floor. We first clean up the mess quickly and then begin preparing the pancakes.

Moments later, with Zane in my arms, I hold the bowl of pancake mix and he dips the ladle inside, scooping some of the mix before he pours it into the pan. That is when Ensley takes over and flattens it a little more with the bottom of the ladle.

We continue doing so until we finish all the batter and have a stack of pancakes big enough to feed the whole neighborhood. That even after Zane and I munched on a few when Ensley would turn around to get something. She'd pretend she's clueless whenever she look at it, earning a giggle from Zane each time.

Now, as we dig in after we plated them with some fresh blueberries and maple syrup, I can't help but take in the image before me. Of Zane and Ensley sitting on my right on the bar stools on one of the sides of the kitchen island. Zane sits between Ensley and me, eating. Yet, I don't miss how he tips his chin up and looks at Ensley and then at me, his green eyes filled with the joy of an eight-year-old instead of the sadness I've first seen in his gaze.

This moment right here, as I take them in, dawns on me. *This is now my family. They are now my family.* My family to protect. To love. To take care of. And if doing so weighs heavily on remembering all the memories I've forgotten, come hell or high water, I'll do it. Whatever it takes, I'll remember what I've forgotten.

MASON

"Tell me, Mason, why do you want to remember?"

The question comes from Dr. Ivy Melton.

Luckily, and although with quite the short notice, after Jesse contacted her yesterday, she's agreed to see me today. She typically works with veterans and soldiers in Killeen, coming highly recommended mainly because, to determine the source of somebody's PTSD, she uses hypnosis. And as much as I don't like to admit it, my mind blocking out memories is caused by my trauma because hell, I came close to death many times before in my fifteen years as a firefighter, but never this close.

"I would like you to first close your eyes and don't ponder too much on your answer. Just tell me why."

Clearing my throat, I do as instructed and close my eyes. Instantly, the bright smile on Ensley's lips plays behind my eyelids. Just as immediately, it is followed by the image of Zane all covered in flour, fighting his war with my woman. An image that swiftly transpires into one of my mother, then into my best friend and my family of firefighters, before it reverts to Ensley.

"Because I feel that I am missing a crucial part of my life, doc. Because I feel that whatever I am suppressing will lead me to the answers to the questions I've been asking myself."

"What kind of questions?"

Her voice is soft and soothing as she begins digging for more information.

"Does my dissociative amnesia only relate to Ensley? If so,

why? And why the past week my mind fought to make me remember? What is so important that I've forgotten that has me torturing myself over so badly?"

She doesn't say anything to that as though waiting for me to continue.

"I want to remember because whatever it is that my mind suppresses is essential in keeping my family safe. I want to remember because it feels as if my subconscious tries to warn me about something. Something I know, but I don't remember."

"Why do you think that?"

My shoulders lift because I don't have a concrete answer to that. "I don't actually know. I can't explain it but there's this feeling that nags and jabs at my gut. Just the same feeling I had the day of the accident."

"What do you remember from that day, Mason?"

"With the exception of the last moments leading up to the explosion, nothing else. I remember walking into that building. I vividly recall the flames and the roar of the fire. I can remember everything from the moment I stepped into the building up to when I pushed my lieutenant and best friend out of the way before the explosion. But for the life of me I cannot recall what happened before it, even the truck ride to the location of the fire is a blur.

"I've laid in bed for so many days and nights trying to will myself to remember, but nothing came to me. Nothing except for a voice and some fast flashes. But I don't know if they're from that day or not. Hell, doc, I don't even know if they're memories related to me or to someone else."

"Do you recognize the voice?"

"I don't know. It is distorted."

Although my eyes are still closed, I hear the sound the pen makes as she scribbles something on a notebook that she has atop her thigh since the beginning of our session.

"Earlier you mentioned someone by the name of Ensley. Who is Ensley? Who is she to you?"

"The love of my life and one of the reasons I want to remember. She is the woman I've loved since I was fifteen. She is the one who fought for us even when I didn't deserve it."

"Why do you think she did it?"

"It is beyond me. I can't explain why this woman fights for

me with all her might. But, I'd be damned, doc, I really want to fight for her too. Fight with her for what we have. And that is why I'm here. That's why I want to fight to get my memories back."

"I would like to make one thing clear, Mason. It is all up to you if you remember or not. It is only you who can unblock the memories your mind has built a barrier around for one reason or the next, preventing you from remembering them."

Nodding my head, I take in a deep breath.

"Tell me about the flashes you've had," Doctor Melton encourages. "When did you have the first one?"

I lean back in my seat a little.

"I've had the first one a month after I came to. I was riding my bike, trying to get distracted, but I ended up on the Waterfront. I stood there for what seemed like an eternity, looking at the water. I didn't know why I was there or how the hell I've ended up there. All I wanted to do was ride until I find a bar where I can hook up with someone only so I can forget, even for a while, that the woman I want and crave can never be mine again.

"So I stood there, losing track of time, but it wasn't until I turned and looked at one of the office buildings that an image flashed. An image that felt like an out-of-body experience to me. It felt like it because it was as though I could see myself from afar, fighting to get free."

"Free from what?"

"I was cuffed to the door of a police car. I was desperate to free myself and with just as much helplessness I watched the flames engulfing the building." I pause momentarily, letting out a heavy breath. "The images flashed so fast before my eyes that I had to replay them again and again. But nothing explained the wretchedness and forlornness I felt at that moment. Or why it felt as though my heart was being ripped out of my chest."

"You can open your eyes now," the doctor urges.

I do exactly that, meeting her stare.

"I believe we're ready to see if I can get you under."

"Alright, doc."

"You can either lie on the sofa or just sit. However way you think you'll feel more comfortable."

At that, I remain put in my seat and the doctor takes that as my choice.

"Great. Now, I'll want you to close your eyes again. Close your eyes and relax as much as possible. I want you to concentrate on nothing else but the sound of my voice and on taking deep breaths."

With a curt nod from my part, Ivy takes it as her cue to proceed.

"Imagine you're in your home, in front of the TV."

Breathing in and out slowly, I will myself to focus on her voice and to picture the setting.

"Now, reach for the remote that's by your side on the sofa. Pick it up and turn on the TV."

Next to me on the cushion, I see the remote. I take it and press the button to switch on. Soon enough, the screen is brought to life.

"I want you to bear in mind that whatever happens on the screen, it is in your past, Mason. Whenever it gets too intense, just remember that all this happened and you're safe now. You are not in danger."

"Okay," I reply.

"Picture yourself on the screen of that TV. Paint the picture from that day with your fellow firefighters when you get out of the truck."

I begin an out-of-body experience. I sit on the sofa and right before my eyes, there's an image forming. One of me in full firefighter gear while I fiddle with my gloves right before I put them on. My eyes take in the building in front of me.

"Tell me, what do you see, Mason?"

"Flames. I see the fire engulfing the building."

"That's good. What else do you see?"

"My teammates. I see them in my purview, and I hear my lieutenant organize the team for the search. I see Rhys, Nolan on my right, fastening the breathing apparatus around their waists, and Luke slipping his gloves on."

"Now, take yourself back. Before you and your team exit. Picture yourself back inside the truck. Where are you, Mason?"

"I'm on the back bench, right behind Luke."

"Who is next to you?"

"Nolan. Rhys drives and Luke is in front with him."

"Tell me more. How are you feeling? Breathing in and then out, try to focus on your emotions."

I follow her suggestion and slowly inhale, before I exhale. I concentrate on what I feel, the heaviness in my chest hitting me right away.

"Wretched. Angered. Like I'm losing something I don't want to let go of."

"What are you doing?"

For a moment, I don't answer, trying to clear my blurred vision.

"I have something between my fingers. It's a picture."

"Can you describe it for me?"

My head shakes. "I can't see it properly. It is faint and unclear. Like a layer of fog covers it."

"Pay close attention only to what you can see. Anything striking? Colors?"

Once again, I focus on the image.

"Red," I reply as the tint becomes clearer and clearer. "It's a red dress."

"Can you try and see who's the one wearing it?"

The harder I try, the vaguer becomes the face.

"No."

"That's alright, Mason. On the remote, press the rewind button. Go back to the start of that day. Imagine yourself in bed, just slowly waking up."

The morning light seeping through the large windows of the bedroom has me squeeze my eyes shut for a tick. I then attempt to reopen the heavy lids and fight to keep them that way.

"Now, let yourself feel the emotions of that morning."

In my chest, there's an onerous feeling. A burdensomeness that only appears to sink me further into the mattress.

"Are you alone?"

I let out a sigh, turning away from the light and on my back. My eyes glue to the ceiling for several moments before my head cocks to the side. They take in the back facing me. The ink black hair falling down the length of the bare skin.

"No, I'm not. There's someone next to me."

"Does it feel like they are a stranger or like you know them?"

My hand lifts and drapes across my chest, ready to brush off the strands of hair. It stops mid-air though. With the most ridiculous amount of energy that I can garner, I halt myself. I restrain myself from feeling that familiar flesh beneath my palm. From reaching out and pulling her to me.

"Like I know her. There's familiarity about her."

"Can you describe her?"

"She sleeps with her back to me, but she has long, dark hair."

"Tell me, what do you smell?"

The gentle floral scent that permeates my nostrils is floral. A perfume that is a combination of sweetness and wildness. A scent intense and intoxicating. An aroma so sensual.

"I smell something sweet and rich, maybe a little bit musky even. It is floral. It's jasmine."

My heart thunders a million miles an hour now as the scent continues to tease my olfactory senses. It surrounds me and grips me, inebriating me with that sweet aroma more than ever before. Testing my limits. Pushing me to send everything to fucking hell only so I can still wake up to that scent.

"Skip forward. What do you hear?"

The sound of the water running in the shower pierces my ears while the mist in the air hits my nostrils. The humidity blocks the sweet fragrance to an extent.

I couldn't be more grateful because I can finally breathe. Not because the smell is strong, but because of its effect on me. Of how badly it overpowers me and tests my will and determination. Which I don't have much of, but enough to put an end to this.

"The shower's running."

"Press the button and skip forward again."

At the instruction, I press the button on the remote and jump sequences. The images move with the speed of light before my eyes. They skip and jump, unable to focus on any of them.

"Stop."

The pad of my thumb lifts off the forward button.

"I picked up an extra shift this Saturday, so I won't be able to make it to dinner at your parents."

It is the sound of my voice that feels the air in the bathroom now. A sound deadpan. So stony and emotionless. One even I question if it even belongs to me. But one I know is necessary. Because I need to put an end to this.

She pivots toward me and my heart falters before it thrums. The traitor that beats inside my chest does what it has always been best at:

betraying me in her presence, reminding me that I am weak when it comes to her. That I'll give her as much as she wants to take from me.

"Mase, what is happening to us, baby?"

The frailness of the words nearly has me stumble over my feet as I fight the urge to eat the distance between us. I also battle that goddamn impel to waver just like she always gets me to.

But I cannot. I cannot do it this time around regardless of how badly I want to. I can't because...

"What is it, Mason?"

"I can...can't." The stammered mumble leaves my lips, and my head moves from side to side sporadically.

"It's okay, Mason. It is all in the past and you're safe. Try and remember."

"It wants to take me back."

"It? Who wants to take you back?"

"My mind."

"Let it, Mason. Let it take you where it wants."

"I don't want to," I refuse.

"And why is that, Mason?"

"Because I'll lose her."

"Who are you going to lose?"

A sigh crawls up my throat and I keep quiet momentarily, my eyes fixated on the TV screen.

My left hand lifts to rake through my dark locks and my gaze homes in on the gold band. My fingers freeze before they get to push through my hair and my heart sinks into the pit of my stomach. Meanwhile, my stare doesn't vacillate. It remains on that ring that thrones my finger.

I answer Ivy's question. "My wife."

My wife.

My wife.

My wife.

The two words resound in my mind.

They tumble and assail me, making my head spin with the velocity. It is only moments later that it starts hurting like a motherfucking bitch when my brain gets attacked as an amalgamation of flashes move on the screen and words that don't make any sense get thrown at me. I groan, squeezing my eyes shut, gritting my teeth, and balling my fists atop the cushions of the sofa.

"Fuck," I grunt, the pain of it excruciating.

"Mason, focus on my voice. Take deep breaths and focus on my voice again."

With all the might I can garner, I do that. I concentrate on the sound of her gentle voice and on leveling my breathing, inhaling and exhaling.

"That's it, Mason. Breathe in and out. In and out."

As I continue doing so, the fibrillation of my heart ebbs one breath in and breath out at a time. Simultaneously, my haywire mind arrests the thoughts one by one, throwing them back in the cage. Yet, before all of them cease, an image plays on the TV screen, wrenching me along.

The very picture I've left the earlier memory on.

I stand there, watching the hurt overtake her features. At the sight, the impel to rub at my chest isn't just ridiculous, it is gut-wrenching. Just as harrowing as it is for me not to extend my hand and reach up to her. To grab hold of her and bring her flush to me.

It is on that itch that I am taken back.

"Cutter, there's someone asking for you," Emilian Trevino informs me. "He's on the apparatus floor."

His voice has my eyes peeling from the beef stew dinner I'm cooking for everyone in the firehouse.

My gaze narrows just a fraction before I turn my head to the side until my stare lands on the clock. It just ticks after seven-thirty.

"Thanks, man. Luke, brother, you got this?" I ask my best friend who also has been acting as my assistant in the kitchen this evening.

"Of course. Go," he replies, taking over at the stove to stir in the stew.

"Don't let it stick."

At my warning, he laughs, dismissing me with a hand motion and I make swift work of wiping my hands on the towel.

Sauntering my way out of the common room, into the hall, I go through the doors that split the firehouse from the apparatus floor.

When I walk around one of the trucks, I see the back of a man facing me. His hands are deep in the pockets of his pants and his form is not at all relaxed.

The instant he senses me approaching, he turns. Amber eyes connect to my brown ones, before they take me in. Meanwhile, I do the same. I analyze the man standing in front of me. From his salt and pepper hair. To the stubble dusting his cheeks. To his average height. Although he looks to be in his late fifties, he is still in good shape.

"Mason Carter?" He asks, a ring of familiarity in his voice.

"That's correct. What can I do for you?"

It is not unknown for us firefighters to receive visits to the fire stations. Victims pulled out of wrecked cars or carried out of the burning building. So I try to search my mind for any previous instances where we could have met.

"I'm Patrick Carver."

At that, the air nearly gets knocked out of my lungs, already fore-seeing what he'll tell me and what it means for everyone around me.

"We've established we'll only see each other face to face when I've got news."

Patrick Carver is the man who's been keeping tabs on my biological family. He is the DEA agent who has been working with my dad and the one I'd call, every once in a while, to ask for updates.

After I found a picture of him and Dad a few years ago, I had to find out who he was. I did and I called him. Ever since, he's been keeping me in the loop. Something he has done, with us only meeting face to face under a singular circumstance.

"Montoya is in town. According to my sources, the first thing he's done when he landed was to visit a private investigations company that has been on retainer for Raul Guerrero for a long time."

"Fuck," I breathe out, nearly stumbling over my feet.

"I don't believe it is a coincidence that Guerrero just happens to employ a PI company in DC all the way from Spain."

"Goddamn it."

Anger seeps out of me when I punch the side of the truck. Fury takes over me further when I kick my boots and bunker gear pants.

"Fucking Christ, why now?!"

Both hands rake through my hair in despair, before the palms rest against the nape of my neck, my fingers lacing together. Garnered from deep within my chest, a heavy, protesting grunt escapes me.

"I'm sorry we had to meet this way, Mason."

My eyes drop lower to him.

"I wish they were better circumstances too."

At my admittance, he nods his head. "I gotta go now, but whatever you need, I'm here to help."

"Thanks, Patrick. You did more than enough all these years."

Extending my hand, he clasps it and gives it a shake before he pulls me in for a hug, patting my back. "Dennis would be so proud of the man you've become, Mason. From the moment he held you for the first time, he has loved you."

As he pulls back, an appreciative smile curls my lips at the mention of my father. "I wish he'd be here now too."

"Take care of yourself and that beautiful wife of yours, Mason. Take care of your mama too."

"I will do that, Patrick."

With that, the man walks out of the apparatus floor through the still-opened doors of the firehouse. I take a few steps until I reach the pillar where the button to close the doors is, and I press it. Meanwhile, my eyes take in as the man gets swallowed by the night. Once he disappears from my line of vision, I let my gaze roam the street.

If he's in town and knows who I am, everyone is in danger. My wife. My mother.

My form becomes agitated, and flashes assail again. Image after image. Face after face. All the while, different voices attack me also.

"Mason, that is enough. Press the stop button on the remote," the doctor instructs calmly. "Push the button, Mason."

With my eyes snapping open, they connect with Ivy's ones.

"It's okay, Mason. It's all over now."

My head shakes. "No, doc, this is just the beginning."

Simultaneously, I attempt to wrap my mind around what I've just seen on that screen. My memories. Part of them at least.

The ugly.

The hurt.

The pain.

It is what I've seen in those memories.

But now I know.

I know why I had to remember. I had to because I need to protect my family.

My wife.

I've got a wife.

One whose face was still blurred in those memories and no matter how hard I tried, the image of her remained fuzzy. Yet, the emotions awakened within me were clear.

I have a wife.

I am a married man.

Meanwhile, he is out there somewhere, looking for me, and every moment that ticks by, puts my *wife*, my *son,* and my *mother* in danger.

Springing to my feet, I grab my belongings and bolt out the door.

I got to get to them.

ENSLEY

It's been almost two hours since Mason left for his appointment, while Zane and I have played with the new Legos we've gotten him just the other day.

Right now, we're both sitting on the floor. I sit with my legs crossed as Zane lays on his stomach, his legs flinging in the air every so often, constructing a building out of Legos.

Truthfully, he is the one who has made this amazing block that towers in front of me with the pieces of plastic toys. I, on the other hand, all I've been doing apart from occasionally placing a Lego here and there is looking at him. Taking him in and enjoying the glee in his green eyes. Those green orbs that have been shining with utter happiness. The same happiness he fills our lives with.

"Ensley, can I ask you something?" The question escapes him with a fraction of timidness that is now mirrored by his gaze as he gently tilts his head a tad to look at me.

"Of course, honey," I encourage, placing a Lego atop the building. My eyes don't peel off him.

Unhurriedly, he pushes back a few strands of tousled hair as though biding his time.

"Sweetie, you know you can tell me anything, right?"

A heavy sigh crawls up his throat and dances in the air. "If you and Mason will have a baby, will you take me back to the foster home?"

My heart squeezes so tightly that I even forget how to

breathe for a moment. And when I note how he now avoids my gaze, it breaks, and I swear pieces of it clog in my throat.

"Come here, honey," I speak, opening my arms.

His eyes return to me for an instance before he stands up and walks to me. My arms wrap around his small frame and his tiny arms wrap around me, sitting on my lap.

My lips press against his forehead, and I hold him close.

"You'll never go back there again, Zane. I promise you this, honey," I whisper against his temple. "If Mason and I will ever have a baby, he or she will be extremely lucky to have an older brother like you."

"I didn't want to leave." His arms snake around my neck and he nestles closer. "I want you to be my mommy if you want, too."

Hot tears brim my eyes at his words.

"I'd be honored to be your mommy, sweetie."

At that, we hold each other tighter for a moment longer. We then pull apart, his green gaze locking to my own.

"My mommy was good to me. She took care of me, but not the way you do."

"I promise I'll be to you the best mom I can be."

I am unaware of the tear that rolls down my cheek until Zane's small hand wipes at it.

"You are the best mom already."

Holy. Shit. Fuck.

The curses in my head reverberate with emotion.

"Do you think Mason will want to be my daddy?"

Just as earlier, the timidity appears again in his voice.

"He would love that."

"You think so?"

"Absolutely," I reassure him, my lips kissing his forehead gently.

While I hold *my son* to my chest for another tick, the sound of the doorbell fills the air.

"Mason should be home soon, why don't you go upstairs and get ready?"

At that, he nods with excitement and springs to his feet. Getting up, I chuckle while I watch him race toward the stairs with speed.

"Honey, careful."

"I am," he throws excitedly over his shoulder.

With a shake of my head, but with a wide smile on my face, I move toward the front door.

Opening it, the smile wanes, and my eyes narrow when they land on two men. They both have their hands inside the pockets of their black pants.

The one on the left—who stands farther from me—is tall with a leaner figure, dark brown eyes and hair as dark as the t-shirt he wears.

The man closest to me, on the other hand, is shorter and bald, his eyes stony and jaw tight.

My skin crawls.

"May I help you?"

"Ensley Carter?"

This time, the frown on my forehead deepens, a strong foreign accent in his voice as he speaks my name.

Both men look at each other and share a smile.

Alarms begin blaring in my head and I go to push the door shut. Immediately, a wince gets wrenched out of me when one of the men blocks the door from closing with his own massive frame while his hand snatches a hold of my hair.

He pushes his way in while he uses the tight grasp on my hair to force me backwards. Behind him, the other man follows, closing the door as though they aren't just barging into my home.

Please, please, don't have Zane come down. Don't have Zane come down, I pray to myself.

"Who are you?" I gripe the question, my hands covering his big one in an attempt to release some of that hold.

My attempts are futile, of course. On the contrary, actually, since the man tightens his grip until he shoves me, and I land on the hardwood floor.

"We've tried to warn you, bitch."

A prolonged yelp surges out of my chest when he kicks me in the stomach with force. I fold in two on the floor, my arms flying to wrap around the exact spot he hit.

Oh, shit!

I cough when he kicks me again, my eyes squeezing shut for a brief moment while I attempt to drag my own body away from him.

When I lift my eyelids, his stare is darker now, filled with malice and pure venom. Meanwhile, the other just stands there, hands deep in his pockets, his gawk browsing the space as though waiting for his partner to be done with me.

Dragging myself next to the stairs landing, I prop my back against the wall and my arm on the bottom stair. I look at them, trying to figure out who they are.

"We've tried to warn you, bitch."

The sentence reverberates in my head.

Are they the ones who've been sending me those notes and flowers?

"Debería matarla agora," the one who kicked me tells the other in a perfect Galician accent that they should kill me.

Galician accent.

The last two words of my inner observation repeat themselves in my head.

One piece of my mental puzzle now fits the other. The notes, Aracely's accident, Mason's biological family. It all adds up together. Amounts to one conclusion.

"Where… is he?" I ask them, a silent groan making its way out of me as I squeeze my eyes shut. "Where is the man you're working for?"

As though on cue, the tall man walks to the door and opens it, letting in another man. The sound of the sole of the shoes hitting the hardwood floor travels across the foyer and hits my ears. It is sharp and rather slow. Yet, there's something more to it. There's an additional sound of something else hitting the floor. Something pointier. And when the man stops before me, I see what it is. The cane that helps him keeps steady on his feet.

Because the man who now halts his steps in front of me is one who appears to be in his seventies, to say the least. Although from where I sit on the floor, he looks tall, he doesn't seem to be taller than five-foot-ten.

"Ola, Ensley," he greets with a superior smirk.

I puff at him because, of course, who doesn't do that in front of a criminal.

"Why are you doing this?"

This time around, he snickers. "For family," he replies, his Galician accent just as strong as the other man's. "He has a legacy to continue, and he must do so."

"What legacy?" I wonder with a mocking snigger. "One made of bloodshed and crimes?"

"And this is the... *Como dis?*" He pauses briefly as he wonders how to say something. "Reason. *Impides que o meu neto abrace o seu verdadeiro potencial.*"

(*"You hold back my grandson from embracing his true potential."*)

"What true potential are you talking about?"

"*Tráelle unha cadeira,*" the man orders the tall one, instructing him to bring me a chair. "*Tráeme unha tamén.*"

Following the man with my gaze, I watch him disappear down the stairs into the living room and couple of moments later, he returns with two chairs from the dining room.

He drops one next to the man who I have the certainty is Carlos Montoya, and he takes a seat. Once sat, he gestures with his hand toward the other man. A gesture which I can only assume is to put me in the other seat. Something the bald guy doesn't hesitate to do as he leans forward and digs his fingers in my arms, lifting me up and dumping me into the chair.

I know I could kick him at how close he is, but I don't want to cause a scuffle that will bring Zane downstairs. I want to keep *my son* away from this for as long as possible.

"Now, where were we?" Carlos asks, while his bald goon tapes my hands and ankles to the chair after the tall one brings him the duct tape. "*O verdadeiro potencial do meu neto.*"

(*"The true potential of my grandson."*)

With a wistful sigh, he leans forward in his seat, placing his elbows atop his thighs.

"You are the good that keeps him good. Through his veins runs the blood of a Montoya and we are the devil."

"Bloodline and genes don't matter. He is a good man, and you will never taint that," I speak through grit teeth.

Carlos scorns sardonically. "When a man loses the love of his life, there's nothing else he has anymore, and he loses himself. And my grandson is no different."

"Because you don't know the kind of man he is. You only waltzed in here, expecting to just take over his life, but you don't know shit about him. You don't know how good of a man he is and whether your blood runs through his veins or not, that's just irrelevant. He'll never be like you," I spit, struggling a little bit in my seat to lean forward so I can stare him right in the eyes.

This time, he smirks. *"Tes razón. Nunca será coma min. Será moito peor."*

("You are right. He will never be like me. He'll be so much worse.")

"Bullshit."

"I don't believe so. *Ver á muller que queres morrer diante de ti faralle iso a un home."*

("Watching the woman you love die right in front of you will do that to a man.")

My skin crawls at his words.

Cold shivers run down my spine.

My heart begins thrumming in my chest faster than it did before.

"Also, finding out you've lied to him. Finding out that you two are married and didn't tell him, that will be a blow too." A demonic smile takes over his features. "Nothing personal, Ensley. You're just standing in the way of his legacy."

With that said, he looks over his shoulder toward the front door and that is when I understand. When I see the stratagem of having me tied to a chair in the hallway. It is because the instant the door will open and Mason walks in, his eyes will land right on me.

"Agora, onde está o meu neto?"

("Now, where is my grandson?")

I believe the question is more to himself and rhetorical or for me even. Only for a brief instance until the bald goon picks up his phone, presses a couple of times on buttons and lifts it to his ear.

"Onde está?" The man spews.

Though my ears are focusing on what he speaks on the phone, my eyes are still glued to Carlos' light brown ones as I take him in from up close.

This will be the man who will dictate the remaining minutes of my life. The one who will order the exact moment I will take my last breath.

Do I want to go out like this?

Hell no.

As a firefighter, running toward the danger and into the fire, one can only be aware that there is a possibility this instant will come. The ticks that click by with the expectancy of drawing your last scintilla of air.

"Está a dúas cuadras de distancia."

(*"He's two blocks away."*)

It is on that piece of information that I realize. He's had us followed. He has someone following Mason right now.

"You're a piece of shit," I blurt out with spite. "Do you really think you're gonna win this?"

"Xa estou gañando," Carlos proclaims with a smile.

(*"I'm already winning."*)

It is my turn to let out a sardonic laugh. *"Teña coidado co que desexa,"* I say, warning him in a butchered Galician to be careful what he wishes for. "If he'd ever become the man you're saying he will turn into, it's gonna be your head he'll come after first."

"No, *cariño*. We will become a team. With him at my side, we will be true *diaños*."

"You're an absolute nutcase if you believe this," I rebut with utter certainty in my voice. Because he is a fruitcake if he truly believes Mason will side with him.

"Rage can drive us to do things we've never thought we'll do," he says as though that is an actual explanation.

I snicker with disdain. "You are more out of your mind than I thought."

"Está a piques de chegar," the bald man informs.

My heart stills for a moment when I hear and translate the words in my head: *"He's about to arrive"*.

Is this it?

It can't.

It cannot be it.

Not after all that we went through to get to where we are now.

To the point where we were this morning.

Happy and with an entire future ahead of us.

With a family to love.

With a son.

"You know what? Fuck you!" I spit out. "And if you didn't understand that then *vaia a merda!*"

Once again, a diabolic smirk curls at the corners of his lips. *"Valiente. Agora entendo por que tes o meu neto tolo por ti."*

(*"Spunky. Now I understand why you got my grandson crazy about you."*)

My jaw clicks tight when his hand shoots and grasps hold of it, his fingers digging into my cheeks.

"We wanted to take our time. Mess with you a little more, but then your bitch sister started looking into us. She got too close for my liking."

My eyes widen. "Leave my sister alone."

"I did. But I know someone who's been looking for her."

On that threat, anger courses through me. My teeth charge for the skin between the thumb and the index finger. He groans loudly and it immediately blends with my own when his other hand connects with my cheek.

Fuck!

The skin burns and my eyes squeeze, while my teeth let go.

"*Cadela!*"

("*Bitch!*")

Another strike comes on the other cheek, feeling now that my entire face is on fire. When I turn my head to look straight ahead, but Carlos isn't there anymore. Instead, now he walks down the stairs to the living room.

Shit, the toys.

He'll see Zane's Legos.

Taking into consideration he seems to have us under surveillance, he most likely already knows about Zane. What I don't want is for him to get his hands on my son.

Or on Mason.

Fuck, baby! Is this it?

"It will be my pleasure killing you," the bald man grins, his jaw clicking shut.

The ice-cold shiver that runs through me shakes me to the bone. I need to get out of this mess now.

I need to fucking do something.

MASON

Drops of cold sweat travel down my spine when I pull in front of the house as an unsettling feeling overpowers my body.

Perhaps it is all that my mind has had to put up with since Doctor Melton hypnotized me. All that my brain had and has still to wrap itself around. The splinters of memories. The heavy information. All that I didn't want to see. All that was right there in front of me all along, but I refused to see it.

But it all now fits in perfectly.

The pieces to that mental puzzle I've been trying to resolve have now aligned and amounted to that big picture that I didn't want to see. Not because I didn't *want* it, because God, I did. I do. I fucking do.

I know that the reason I kept refusing myself to see it is because I was afraid of what it meant. I subconsciously tried to negate the possibility because that means the danger she will be put in is even greater.

Although I don't remember how we've gotten there, how we got to be married, we are. She is my wife. It doesn't make sense for anyone else to be, right?

I am aware it is just a theory, but it is the only one that adds up to me in this instance.

She's been at my side in the hospital.

She lives with me in this house.

She's spent every single day doing physiotherapy with me during the three months that I've been in a coma.

Her voice is all I've heard during that time.

She hasn't been waiting for me all this time. She's been mine all along. She has been by my side all throughout and I have no recollection of her. Not beyond her twenty-first birthday. I have snips and instances that don't make sense because my mind has blocked the rest of them in a futile attempt to perhaps keep her at arm's length.

Just like before, I couldn't fight her.

I tried and lost because a battle against Ensley is one I was always meant to lose.

She is my wife.

Ensley Walker is Ensley Carter.

Has she taken my name?

I chuckle to myself and shake my head before my eyes land on the front door of the house.

If she has taken my last name or not, that doesn't matter. All that matter is that she was mine, she is mine and will forever be mine.

The thought reverberates in my head with sheer incredulity.

Mine.

She is mine.

She's been mine all these years.

She belonged to me and there's this twisted feeling of greediness that overwhelms me at that realization.

Joder, nena, why didn't you tell me?

Why did she not tell me she is my wife when I came to? Why did she hide it from me?

Pushing the questions away before yet another wave attacks, I unmount my bike and hang the helmet on the throttle. I do it because thinking back the past few days about how Ensley has parked her car, there won't be any room for my bike. Again.

I chuckle to myself, coming to the conclusion that I wouldn't have it any other way. Even if that means leaving my bike out front, getting inside the house to grab her keys and walking to the garage to move her car.

Keeping the smile on my face, I make my way toward the front door. Once I insert the key and unlock it, I go to open the door.

"*Nena*, I'm gonna move—"

My words get occluded in my throat when after I step inside

the house, and my eyes land on Ensley's figure. Tied to a chair. Her face swollen. Her eyes red.

"Ensley," I call out her name, setting the pace of my feet into a sprint.

"Behind you," she yells.

Before I get to do anything, a discharge of electricity jolts my body.

* * *

My eyes open while a groan surges out of my chest. A pained sound as though I have just been hit by a goddamn truck. My entire body aches.

Joder!

What the fuck happened?

Ensley, my brain reminds me.

Tilting my head, I shut my eyelids for a tick before I reopen them as if that would somehow disperse some of that pain. Instantly after, they home in on the light that comes through the window.

As I try to get up from the seat, I become aware that I cannot. It is on that realization that my head cocks to the side and my line of vision drops to roam the space around me. Right away, I note the rope that keeps my ankles tied to the chair's legs. Immediately after, my eyes move to the rope around my wrists that keeps them bound together in my lap and another around my chest, keeping me pinned.

What also grabs my attention is the unique, pungent scent that stabs my nostrils. One I know all too well from all the fires that have been started using it, including the fire I nearly lost my life in—gasoline.

Where does the smell come from?

"Por fin cara a cara, meu querido neto."

(*"Finally face to face, my beloved grandson."*)

My eyes widen and I swallow hard as the voice fills my ears, each word hitting me right in the throat.

Vigorously, I pull at the binds that dig right into my skin. A series of grunts crawl out of my throat with each struggle. My teeth grit, and my jaw clicks tight.

As the steps get closer and closer, I also hear an extra sound hitting the floor. When the man gets in front of me, I can't help but drop my gaze first to the cane that's just in front of his feet, both of his hands resting against the top.

"Where is Ensley? Where is Zane?"

The questions flow out of me with an angered growl as I lift my hard stare and look at the man before me. I instantly take him in. The light brown eyes. The white hair. The pressed pants he wears. The crisp white shirt. The average height.

For the first time in thirty-five years, I'm face to face with my biological grandfather. The reason my biological mother and grandmother had to give me up. The man Mom and I had to hide away from. The man Mom and I have been looking over my shoulder for. Mom since she took me in her care and I since I've found out who I am.

"*Por fin te teño diante.*"

("*I have you in front of me at last.*")

"*Déixame ir, fillo de puta,*" I roar, my voice hard.

("*Let me go, son of a bitch.*")

"*Este non é o xeito de falar co teu avó,*" he scolds as though he has any right as he tells me that it isn't a way to speak to my *grandfather*.

"*Polo que me importa, podes ir ao carallo inferno.*"

("*You can go to fucking hell for all I care.*")

He lets out a chuckle, tilting his head back.

While he does that, I try to pull at the binds once again. No luck this time either just like the last. Something that doesn't ease the cold chill that runs down my spine.

"Where is Ensley?"

Just like before, he ignored the question, the rage simmering inside me.

"What do you want?" I spit out angrily.

"*Estou aquí para levarte a casa.*"

("*I'm here to take you home.*")

This time, I let out a sardonic laugh. "I am home. I don't know in what kind of twisted world you're living in, but I am home. Here is my home."

"You have a legacy to take over," he states.

"I have nothing to take over."

At my unequivocal rebuff, his head shakes.

"I've got a life here. I'm not just going to—"

"Non tes nada aquí."

(*"You don't have anything here."*)

His shout is angry.

"Xa non terás nada aquí. Non despois de que remate con ela."

(*"You won't have anything here anymore. Not after I'll be done with her."*)

"What the fuck did you say?" I struggle in my seat, the binds digging deeper. So much that they sting my flesh as they bite into it.

When he sees the fury that emanates from me, the one I feel building inside me and flowing through my veins, a fiendish smile gets plastered on his face.

"This is exactly the man I knew you will turn into being given the right incentive."

"Where is Ensley? Where's Zane? Where are my wife and son?" I shoot the questions again one after the other, my fingers fiddling with the rope in a trial to set myself free.

"Wife? So you know she's your wife."

I ignore the question, pinning him to the spot with a hard glare.

"Where are they? I swear to God, if you touch either of them, I will kill you with my bare hands."

His head moves as though in a silent command and the sound of a pair of footsteps fills the air.

"Ela está ben polo momento."

(*"She's fine for now."*)

For now.

The way he accentuates the last two words has me fear for the worst. Whatever plan he has, he's planning on bringing an end to it.

And soon.

"I wanna see her."

A cruel smile tips the corners of his mouth and the footsteps I heard earlier now come to a halt.

"Desatarlle os pés."

(*"Untie his feet."*)

The order Carlos Montoya gives to the man—whom I assume could only be his goon—is clear and absolute. Something he does without hesitation.

There is no doubt in my action either when I kick him in the face after he unties the bindings around my ankles and his head is close enough for me to do it.

Blood trickles out of his nose when he gets up, ready to charge for me.

"Tócao e matareino."

("Touch him and I kill you.")

Sheer warning and vow are present in his words when he makes the threat. The goon doesn't seem pleased in the least, his eyes sending daggers into my skull.

"Your wife is there," Carlos informs, his chin lifting in a signal somewhere behind me.

Springing to my feet with the speed of light once they undo the rope around my chest, I turn and my eyes meet hers. They are terrified this time around. Duct tape covers her mouth. Her ankles are bound to the legs of the chair and her hands are tied behind her back.

I go to run for her. Yet, before I get to take a step, a gun gets shoved in my face while I hear another cocked at Ensley's temple.

The bald man beside her has a crazy look on his face as that very sound slashes the air inside the room.

At this moment, I don't care about the gun I have pointing at me. All I care about is the one that points at Ensley.

The realization also strikes me that Zane is nowhere to be seen and because of it I let out a half-relieved breath.

"En lugar de perder o tempo, suxíroche que te despidas," Carlos speaks, standing right next to me while my eyes are locked on the woman I love. On my wife.

He has just told me not to waste my time and say my good-byes to her.

For the briefest of moments, my gaze removes from Ensley, taking in all the armed men in the room. One next to me and one next to Ensley.

The bald one who holds the gun to my woman's head looks too trigger-happy for my liking. While the one who has his gun almost shoves in my face, appears as though he cannot wait to get back at me for getting kicked in the face.

"Let her go," I ask Carlos as my eyes revert to Ensley. "This is between you and me."

"She's the reason you still have a heart. *Di adeus.*"

"I'm so sorry, *nena*. I'm so sorry I couldn't protect you from this."

My eyes never leave hers as I speak, and I feel my chest aching with powerlessness.

"I've been selfish. I should've let you go this time around when I was given the chance to. I should've, but I couldn't because memory loss or not, my heart knew it belonged to you and yours belonged to me. My heart recognized yours. My body recognized yours."

Even from afar—since I am in the living room of our house and she's right at the bottom of the stairs, now facing me—I can see the tears rolling down her cheeks. I can see their glister on her skin. I see the glossy eyes.

When Carlos gives a signal, the man who stands next to her pulls at the duct tape that covers her mouth.

"I love you, baby," she whispers, a tremble in her voice. "I'm so sorry I didn't tell you."

"It doesn't matter, *nena*. You always fought for me, and I promised you I will fight for you this time. You are the best thing that's ever happened to me. I love you."

"*Non sexas tan cursi.*"

("*Don't be so cheesy.*")

My gaze stays on Ensley's. They're pleading and filled to the brim with so much love. The kind of love only she can give me. The kind that one needs to fight tooth and nail to keep.

The sound of sirens resounds across the house, and I take advantage of the moment of distraction. Without a second thought, I shift my attention from Ensley—after I give her a look filled with promise and vow—and bring my elbow into the stomach of the man next to me, hitting him so hard, he folds in two. As I then bring my bound arms around his neck, I lift my knee simultaneously, hitting his face. He drops with a thud to the floor, and I launch for his gun.

Before I make it, a piercing sound punctures the air followed by another, just as loud as the previous one. I don't need to look to know which direction it came from. It was from somewhere on my left.

My heart thunders in my chest a gazillion of miles an hour. The strong feeling of fear that surges through my body over-powers me when instead of looking at the source, my neck instantaneously snaps to the side in Ensley's direction and my eye land on her.

"Nooo," I shout with despair. "Noooooo."

With my vision blurred, I stumble over my own two feet as I run as fast as they can carry me up the stairs of the living room and drop to my knees in the foyer.

Nothing else matters.

Nothing but the woman in front of me as I make swift work of the tape that keeps her hands bound. Wrapping my tied hands around her, I bring her to my chest to gently lay the chair down.

Between tears, I see her beautiful green eyes glimmer as she holds my brown ones. When my gaze drops to her face, there's a small smile on her lips. I focus on her the whole time I unhook my arms from around her and press them against her chest.

"I'm sorry," she whispers, her voice frail while tears roll down her face. "I was planning on telling you today."

"Don't talk, *nena*." Contrary to my plea, her lips part as though for her to speak again. "No, baby, please, don't talk," I plead with her again and press down. "Call an ambulance, you son of a bitch."

My desperate yell is only met by the sound of sirens getting closer. But that doesn't ebb even a fraction the wretchedness that takes over me. Not when her blood covers my hands. Not when her eyes seem to be heavier and heavier with each moment that ticks by.

But the sound made by the blaring sirens isn't the only one that punctures my ears. There is also the crackling noise and the roar I am accustomed to. The flames that engulf the living room and some of the objects in the hallway.

"Lembre, isto é só porque decidiu escollela."

("Remember, this is only because you decided to choose her.")

At that, steps mingle with the sound of the burning flames.

"Stay with me, *nena*."

Tears roll down my cheeks as helplessness downs on me. I cannot remove my binds because that means taking my hands from the wound I press on.

When I feel her soft touch on my skin, I nearly hit rock bottom. Especially when with weak, trembling hands, she works to untie my binds.

"I can't undo them," she whispers, a hot tear slipping down

her cheek. And then another. And another. "Get Zane and leave, baby. Save our son."

"I'm not leaving you," I vehemently respond, my forehead touching hers.

"You have to, baby."

Not a moment later, I begin losing her touch on my skin and my eyes jump to the spot. I witness with despair how her arm turns limp, dropping to the floor. It happens as though in slow motion and my gaze begs for it to lift back up.

"No, *nena*. Nooooo."

The sudden commotion, the blaring sirens, the burning flames. They all disappear and only Ensley is my focus. Not even when my form is ripped away from her, I don't acknowledge any of it as everything begins spinning around me. Everything is blurry and as I try to reach back for her, I am met with resistance.

"Mason, let the paramedics do their job," a familiar voice breaks through, my eyes connecting to a pair of green ones.

Jesse.

How did he get here?

"My son," I utter, knocking away any questions and not bothering to make sense of it all now.

"I got Ensley. You go get him. Firefighters are still three minutes out."

MASON

Adrenaline takes over my body and I race up the stairs with all the force that I have. While my arms swing at my sides, I realize Jesse must have cut the rope after he took me off Ensley to give room to the paramedics to work.

"Zane," I call out when I reach the second floor. "Zane!"

Charging for the bedroom that has been his ever since I've brought him here that evening, I open the door and my eyes search the room. They rapidly scan it, until I run in, drop to my knees and look under the bed.

He's not there.

"Zane!"

For the third time, I shout his name and spring back to my feet, sprinting the short distance to the dresser. That only to open and just find clothes.

"Zane!"

Where are you, buddy?

As the question ponders, the answer hits me in the form of Ensley's sweet voice.

"This is the best hiding spot in a game of hide and seek. If there is anything that scares you very much, get in here. Only Mason and I will know, and when this lid comes off, you will know you're safe."

Without delay, I rush for the master bedroom and, once inside, aim for the ottoman sofa by the window. Immediately, my hands reach for the lid, and I try to ignore—for now, at least —the blood covering my hands.

423

Ensley's blood.

Two to the chest.

She fucking took two gunshots to the chest.

She took them because of me.

The series of thoughts and all the blame that assail me get forced away when a pair of terrified green eyes meet mine. They are not only scared, but they are also filled with tears. Tears that roll down his small face.

"Hey, buddy," I whisper, as calmly as I can. "It's okay to come out now."

A couple of sobs escape him when he lifts his arms and wraps them around my neck. I pick him up and hold him tight.

"I…I saw…the sca…scary…men," he mutters between sobs.

"It's alright, bud. They cannot do anything to you."

His small head moves in a nod, and I carry us both out of the bedroom. He is still in my arms with his much smaller ones wrapped tightly around my neck when I grab a jacket from the dresser, covering him with it. Without wasting any more time, I rush down the hallway until I make it to the stairs.

"Daddy, there's a fire."

His green eyes widen while his tiny finger points at the flames that roar viciously.

Although I try, I can't ignore the way my heart skips a beat and fills to the brim with a feeling of joy and contentment when he calls me "*daddy*". My hold on him gets tighter.

"It's okay, buddy."

"I'm not scared because you are a firefighter."

Goddamn, that I am.

Think, Mason. Fucking think, I urge myself, trying to stay focused, though it is the first time—hopefully the last too—that I pull *my son* out of a fire.

Foster parents?

Adoptive parents sounds more like it.

Because I'll be damned if those foster parents' papers won't turn into adoption papers.

Focus now, Cutter. You need to take your son out of here safe and sound.

With Zane in my arms, I bolt for the stairs, walking down with cautious steps. I pull him further into my chest and cover his face with my palm to protect him from the heat.

The flames lick at the walls in the foyer and below the stairs. They are strong to pass and engulfed most of the downstairs level. A couple of the flames even charge for us to bite us, causing me to retreat our forms a little.

I try to take as least breaths in as possible, the smoke thick in the air.

"I got you, buddy," I tell Zane reassuringly.

Not a moment later, the fire jumps behind us, trapping us between at the landing of the stairs. Zane lets out a staggered breath and I pull him closer as the fire now surrounds us from each side, the heat burning at the skin while the flames ferociously attack us.

I look around, trying to find the best way out.

The living room and kitchen are a no-go. The flames have engulfed the ceiling, hissing and screeching their hunger. Hunger for more.

With as much force as I can garner and as much speed as I can get my body to muster, I speed and make a beeline for the front door that remained open after paramedics carried Ensley out.

Zane's hands hold tight to me all throughout and when we finally make it, releasing a bit the tightness of my hold, I drop my eyes to him, noting they are squeezed shut.

I stumble over my own feet, plunging to my knees as the power of the events overwhelms me.

"It's alright, buddy. We're out now," I whisper, bringing him to my chest once again as the breath I held until now slips out of my mouth with relief, right before I have the first intake of fresh air.

"We got him, Cutter."

Blinking several times, I begin acknowledging. I become aware of the firefighters rushing past me and inside the house. Of the two paramedics who are next to me, one has their hand on my shoulder to get my attention and the other tries to take Zane.

My eyes move in the distance, noting Jesse as he runs to us.

"We need to make sure his lungs are clear of any smoke inhalation, Mason," the paramedic informs.

Zane's eyes meet mine. They are filled with solace and comfort. Instead of it being me who offers him reassurance and calm, it is him who does that for me. And he does it only with those green eyes of his.

I nod at the paramedic, and he takes Zane in his arms, placing him on the stretcher.

"We need to check you too," the other paramedic says, but my head shakes.

Springing to my feet, I turn to Jesse. "Ensley."

Her name is all that I mutter before my hands rake through my hair with despair. The breath I took earlier, now clogs my throat, making it impossible to take another inhale.

"They took her to the hospital. Derek's with her. He was in the car and the call come in on the scanner."

"I gotta go to the hospital."

"Go, I'll stay with Zane."

Without delay, I head for the ambulance where my son gets checked up by the paramedics, needing to reassure myself that he is fine before I leave. He has a small oxygen mask on and when he sees me, he goes to remove it.

"Leave it on, buddy," I whisper to him gently, giving him the only smile I can muster. "How's my son?"

"There's no smoke inhalation. Nothing to worry about. We have him for a few on oxygen, but other than that, this brave little man of yours is all fine."

A sigh of relief pushes up my throat. "Daddy needs to check on mommy, okay bud?" He nods his head, his eyes glistering. "Uncle Jesse will stay with you, alright?"

Once again, his head moves in assent, and I press my lips on his temple.

"I love you, buddy."

With that, I rush for my motorcycle, throw my leg over its body as I put my helmet on and turn the key, riding away with speed.

Fuck!

Joder!

Cono!

Merda!

Goddamn it!

Every curse I know races through my head as I twist the throttle to speed up further. The needle on the small dashboard is way past the speed limit, but I still twist as my own mind races a million miles an hour.

You gotta be strong for me, nena. You gotta be strong for our son. You gotta fight for us.

Two shots to the chest.

Fuuuuuuck!

Inside me there's a battle.

A raging fight.

I should have shot that delirious son of a bitch when I had the chance.

Now Ensley suffers the consequences.

She is the one who took two shots to the chest, not me. She is the one who now fights for her life, not me.

How on fucking hell is this fair?

Why do our relationship and marriage need to be tried this way? First, my accident and my dissociative amnesia that had me forget that she is my wife. Now Ensley gets shot and gotta fight with all her might to stay alive for us because otherwise I'd be fucking lost without her?

Why does everything gotta wager against us, against our love and against that happily ever after we promised to each other? Why does this vow feel so close that's within reach, but so dangerously far all the same? Why does this love that has my heart beating fast in my chest feel so pure, but concurrently so tainted?

For a moment, I can't help but wonder if loving Ensley is my fortune or my penance. If loving her as strongly and as fiercely as I do is somehow forbidden on some invisible scale of love. If burning with need for her is to some extent illicit.

Pushing away the ponders, I bring the motorcycle to a stop in the hospital's parking lot, and I climb off, sprinting for the entrance. Immediately, fear settles in the pit of my stomach as I run into the hospital like a madman, and I don't stop until my hands covered in blood and soot land on the counter of the reception.

"Ensley Walker," I speak, a tremble in my voice.

"Sir, you're injured."

My head shakes.

"Ensley Walker."

At my repetition of the name, she moves her wide eyes from me to the screen, beginning to type on the keyboard.

"I'm sorry, Sir. There's nobody here by that name."

"She was brought in with two GSWs to the chest."

Goddamn it, did I get the wrong hospital?

As I draw two breaths of air one after the other, I then let a prolonged one out. "Try Ensley Carter, please."

Eying me suspiciously, she types again on the keyboard. "Are you family?"

"I'm her husband," I reply.

This time around, her eyes narrow at me as though saying *"yeah, sure"*. Under normal circumstances, I wouldn't take offense to the fact that she is protecting her patients. But these are not regular instances and I need to know how my wife is doing.

Yet, before I open my mouth to say anything, an older nurse comes next to her. She first takes me in, before she looks over her colleague's shoulder. I am unable to shake the pity in her gaze as though she somehow knows me.

"She's in surgery, Sir. We don't have any updates, unfortunately. You can go to the waiting room and the doctor will be with you once they have any news."

With a nod of my head, I turn, feeling how my knees almost give way. I still need to stop for a tick while I garner whatever amount of energy that I have left in me.

"He is the patient who was in a coma here not long ago. I know his wife; she's been by his side for the whole three months he's been under. I recognized her when they brought her in with the GSWs. Poor thing, she flatlined once in the ambo and once when they were prepping her for surgery. The paramedic and the doctor shocked her back to life both times."

My feet only carry me until I reach the side wall and I drop down with my back against it and my knees do what I knew they eventually will—give up on me. Because there might not be many things that can bring me to my knees, but Ensley is certainly one of them.

With my face in my palms, I let my entire body shudder as a wave of emotions takes over me.

The hand that rests on my shoulder and squeezes lightly has me lift my gaze only to meet Derek's blue-grayish one.

"It's alright, son. She's a fighter," he whispers, his voice trembling and his look completely disheveled.

I nod, unable to say anything because if I do, I will break. My chest aches so badly, I have to bring my shaking hand up to press against it. The action is futile because the ache is still there. The pain is so excruciating, I feel as though I'm being ripped apart.

Is this the pain she's been going through?

Is this what Ensley felt when I was brought in?

Is this the ache she had to endure during the three months that I spent in a coma?

Fight, nena. Please, don't give up, baby.

"She...flat...lined twice," I whisper, my voice breaking just like I expected.

"You have to believe she's strong, son. She will fight through this just like you did."

"I can't lose her, Derek. I can't lose my wife."

There's an instance of silence and regret takes over his features.

"She's asked us not to say anything. She wanted you to remember on your own."

"I want us to get a divorce, Ensley."

The words pierce through my ears and the image from the bathroom gets pictured right before my eyes. The scene I've remembered while hypnotized.

"I asked her for the divorce," I utter, causing a frown to form on Derek's forehead and his eyes to look at me with utter disbelief. "The day of the accident, I asked her for a divorce because I was afraid this will happen. They've located me through a PI company in Washington and I was afraid someone from my biological family will find me and punish me through her.

The heaviness in my chest feels heftier.

"God, you must hate me. The son and grandson of criminals has married your daughter." The scoff that escapes me is filled with cynicism and snicker at my own person.

The puff that Derek lets out, on the other hand, is amused to some extent and mocking. "And do you actually think I didn't know all along who you are, Mason?"

My eyes widen.

"Aracely told me and my wife just a few months after we've

met her. I've known all along just as I also knew you're the best man my daughter could have ever chosen to have as husband."

"One hell of a husband. She has two bullets in her chest because of me."

His head shakes. "No, don't blame yourself for it. Don't blame yourself for what he's done. There's nothing in this world that will make it your fault. Nothing, do you hear me? And don't you dare give up on my daughter."

I don't get a chance to tell him anything because a wave of people come in: Mom, Angie, Luke, Ella, Jace, Jesse, Zane, JJ and all her crew from the firehouse together with Rhys and Nolan.

"We've heard what happened."

Zane rushes to me and I catch him between my arms, holding him tight while over his shoulder I meet Derek's eyes. It is a look that makes as much as a thousand words. He doesn't need me to tell him that I won't give up on Ensley, he already knows that.

"Are you okay, buddy?"

He nods against my chest and doesn't say anything else. He only wraps his arms around my neck firmer and gets close.

Seconds tick by.

Then seconds turn into minutes.

Minutes turn into over an hour.

Time during which Mom, and Angie take Zane—who has stayed in my arms until then—to the cafeteria. JJ and Ella pace up and down the room. Rhys and Nolan are just quiet—something that doesn't happen often for them.

The only moment I moved from my spot during this hour was to go to the bathroom and wash my hands. Instance I nearly drove my fist through the mirror. I would've done it, had it not been for Luke who recognized the tempest simmering inside of me and followed me.

Now Luke and Derek sit on my right while Jesse sits to my left, and we all simultaneously let out a heavy breath while we wait for news.

"Were you able to find them?" I let the question out, anger building inside of me. Even more at the thought that they have gotten away.

"We've arrested them all, brother. Raul Guerrero gave up his father-in-law and the Organized Crime unit were just getting ready to go to his hotel to arrest Carlos when Zane called 911."

My head snaps to the side. "Zane called 911?"

"He did. He told the operator that his mommy taught him how to."

I cannot help the small smile that forms on my lips at how natural it sounds for Zane to call me "daddy" and call Ensley "mommy".

"They definitely underestimated your kid," adds Jesse with a sincere smile.

"This young and saves lives already," Derek utters with a proud smile of his own. "I can only see a bright future for my grandson."

"You've got a brave one, Carter," Luke attests.

I nod.

It is true.

Zane is a brave kid.

We wouldn't be here now had it not been for him.

I would've not been able to take my phone out from the pocket of my jeans to dial 911. I wouldn't've been able to release the press on her chest otherwise Ensley had bled to death.

"Raul gave him up for you, Mason. He knew Carlos was set on doing anything to get you."

"Is this why he had a PI company look into me because he wanted to protect me?"

"He's been keeping tabs on you for thirty years, Mason. If your father wanted to hurt you, he would've done it by now. But he told Renée that the decision to give you up hasn't only been your mom's, it has been his too. They both wanted to keep you away from the world they were living in."

"Renée? My daughter?" Derek asks, snapping his head forward to shoot Jesse a glare.

"She's been looking into them after Ensley brought her some cards."

"Ensley? What are you talking about?"

"I don't know the details, I only know this much from Renée."

Too much.

This is too fucking much.

All I want to know is that my wife is alright. That is all I want to focus on right now.

And as though God finally has pity on me, a doctor walks through the doors and I spring to my feet.

"Ensley Carter's family?" He asks as he approaches.

"I'm her husband," I swiftly say with hope in my voice.

"Ensley lost a lot of blood. One of the bullets didn't touch any major organs and it was through and through, but the other... Had it not been for this to ricochet the bullet the two centimeters, it would've pierced her heart."

The doctor takes something from his pocket and hands it to me. It is a necklace. One that has a wedding band looped on. One that is too large for her finger. But not too large for mine. Because it is mine. It is my wedding ring. With a part of one side chipped off by the bullet.

"I was planning on telling you today."

Her words from earlier make sense now.

She wanted to tell me today that we are married. That she is my wife. She wanted to tell me and show me the wedding band as proof. Not that I needed one piece of evidence. Not when everything inside me has been shouting at me all along that she's mine.

Two centimeters from her heart.

"She's stable now and still under the effects of anesthesia."

"Can I see my wife, doc?"

"She's sedated, but you can."

Looking back at the rest of *my family*, they nod, while Luke and Derek pat my shoulders encouragingly.

Without another word, I follow the doctor, breathing in and out. Everything within me trembles and my heart beats so fast I'm afraid it might jump out.

And the instant the doctor opens the door, I rush to her side, my lips pressing on her forehead, while my hand takes hold of her much smaller one. On the other hand, I hold the necklace with the band on it. The one that saved my wife's life.

"Hey, *nena*."

"I'll give you a few moments."

I nod heedlessly at what the doctor says and kiss her forehead again.

"You are quite the fighter, you know that? And I'm so

goddamn relieved that you are because, *nena*, we have a lifetime ahead of us to love each other and to fight for each other."

With my head leaning against hers, I inhale deeply while I close my eyes.

"I love you, *nena*! I'll be here when you wake up, I promise you. You've been by my side every single day for three months. I'll be by your side and wait for you to come back to me."

Pulling the chair next to her bed, I take a seat and hold her hand between both of mine. My lips press on her knuckles before my forehead leans atop them.

Briefly, I remove one hand to take out my phone from my pocket. As though my fingers have a mind of their own, they type on the screen until a sound fills the air.

"Who knows what tomorrow brings. In a world few hearts survive. All I know is the way I feel. When it's real, I keep it alive."

The lyrics course out of me in a mumble as I lay my head on my bent arm while I hold her hand with my left one, and close my eyes again.

ENSLEY

Time and time again, the music fills my ears and my eyes open. With a bad headache that thrums my brain and with the pain in my body, they cause a groan to surge out of my chest.

Yet, when my gaze lands on a head filled with dark locks, I cannot help the smile from forming on my face. Especially when I let the melody and the lyrics dance in my ear, realizing that it is our song that's playing on repeat from his phone.

Our song.

Does he remember it?

Is it a coincidence that it now plays?

With a wince, I lift my hand and grab the phone, stopping the music. Right away after, I reach for him to thread my fingers through his hair. I do it so slowly and gently, careful not to wake him up.

The events that happened must have taken a toll on him. I know that is exactly what it did to me the day he had his accident, the emotions got me so tired. The roller coaster of feelings he must have endured this time.

"My handsome man," I whisper under my breath, caressing his cheek with the back of my fingers before they trace his jawline.

"Mommy."

Zane's voice gets my attention, and my head turns to the side to look at my little man walking in followed by Aracely.

He runs to my side and jumps on the bed on the other side, wrapping his arms around me.

"Zane, *bebé*, careful not to hurt her," Ary tells him, her tone soft and kind just like it usually is.

"It's alright," I utter, kissing his temple while I rest my hand around him. "How is my little handsome man? Why are you awake at this time?"

With my finger, I point toward the clock in the room that ticks just a little past seven in the morning.

"I wanted to see if you were awake. I wanted to see you, mommy."

"He woke me up at six o'clock and told me he had to see his mommy."

I cannot fight the smile from forming on my face at Aracely's words.

"I can definitely say that I feel better now after seeing you," I speak, tapping the tip of his nose.

"How are you feeling, sweetie?" Softness takes over Aracely's brown gaze as she looks at me. "Can I get you anything?"

"Can I get a little bit of water?"

Ary rushes to pour me water into a glass and brings it to my lips to take a few sips.

"I'm better now. I feel like my chest was cut open, but I'll be alright."

While I say that, my eyes move to the little man who nestles closer to me, then it moves to the one who sleeps in the chair next to the bed, his head atop the mattress.

"I'll be alright," I repeat, trying to push all the unwelcome memories aside before they attack me.

"Better be prepared to have a lot of people in and out of this room today. They all want to make sure you're okay."

I nod, knowing exactly how my family and friends are. Growing up in a family of firefighters and being a firefighter makes one aware that at times like this, they will always be by your side.

"How did you get in here anyway? It isn't time for visits."

Ary opens her mouth to reply, however Zane rushes and impedes her reply: "Jace let us come in and see you for a little bit."

"He did?"

To be honest, I am not surprised he did since he's always sneaked my brother in when Mason was in a coma.

Zane nods with a smile while his green orbs turn to me with glee. "He also told grandma that she looks beautiful."

"Oh, did he now?"

At that piece of information, my brow quirks up with interest and a teasing smile gets plastered on my face while I take Ary in. I don't miss the blush that creeps at her cheeks.

Quickly, she brushes me off with a hand gesture and lucky for her, Zane begins talking again, telling me all about how his daddy is the coolest firefighter and how he saved him from the fire.

The fire...

Once again, I don't allow myself to think about what happened and about the what ifs. I only focus on the present.

* * *

It is about twenty minutes later that Zane and Ary leave. Alone with my husband, I crane my neck to the side and look at him. He looks so handsome and my heart feels so wholesome that he is here.

My fingers begin to gently rake through his hair again and not long after, his head moves then tips back until my eyes get to meet his beautiful brown gaze.

"*Nena*," he whispers, springing to his feet and leaning over me to smash his lips with mine.

"Hello, handsome," I mutter, a small smile playing at the corners of my mouth when he draws back to meet my eyes again.

"How long have you been awake for? How are you feeling?"

"Not long," I reply with a gentle shrug that has me wince a little at the movement. "I'm fine, my handsome man."

Although I've been trying to push away everything that has to do with what happened, there is something that I cannot shake: *"We wanted to take our time. Mess with you a little more, but then your bitch sister started looking into us. She got too close for my liking."*

"Where is Renée?" I ask agitated.

"She's fine, Ley. She's on her way back from a case. What happened?"

"He told me someone was looking for my sister. He—"

"It's alright. She's alright. She's coming here. We'll talk to Jesse and see if he can get more information. It's gonna be alright."

My hand grasps his shoulder while he pulls me into a calming, reassuring hug.

"I'm so sorry, *nena*."

At the utterance, my head shakes. "No, baby. No more self-blame. No more denial. No more pushing away. No more lies."

"I promise, *nena*." His lips press against mine briefly. Too briefly for my liking considering I pull him back in for another kiss. "*Miña fermosa muller.*"

(*"My beautiful wife."*)

"You remember."

"I got hypnotized. That's what my appointment was about. I kept having those flashes and I had to get to the bottom of them. It was like my mind was trying to force me to remember all that's been blocked out. Subconsciously, I knew you were in danger." His forehead leans against mine. "You flatlined twice, *nena*. I thought I'm going to lose my mind while I waited for them to operate on you."

"Seems like we're square now," I try to joke, my body hurting when I chuckle. "So, no more scares, okay?"

"Deal, *nena*. Because without you, I am nothing, and with you, I'm whole."

"Don't you just know how to get to my heart?!"

Withdrawing, Mason grins for a tick. An instant later, his lips capture mine with a fierceness filled with hunger, relief and love.

Because why should one want a happy bubble when they can have messy as fuck? The kind of love that when you actually live it, you realize that it was worth the ache and all the fighting that has been done for it.

The instant Mason pulls away, I want to take his lips into another kiss, but before I get to protest, he lifts something to my eye level. He can immediately read the recognition on my face. The cognizance at the sight of the necklace to which I attached Mason's wedding band.

It was an impulse to put it on. A whim I hoped will give me the courage I needed to tell him the truth. To finally admit to him that we are married.

"The second bullet could have touched your heart," he speaks. "The edge of the ring caused the bullet to miss."

"I could say you saved my life."

My hand lifts, gingerly caressing his cheek until he leans into my touch further and further.

"You saved mine first, *nena*. You've been saving me from the day I've realized I'm in love with you."

"I love you."

"I love you too, *nena*. So fucking much."

His eyes close as he enjoys my gentle caress.

"And for the record, I've never wanted to divorce you."

"I know," I revert with a smile.

"That obvious?"

"Oh, no. You had me fooled for a little while, but then it only took for me to look once at you and realize that you love me just as much as I love you."

"And I guess I'll have to pay for that little while I had you fooled, right?" His brow quirks and he just looks so goddamn sexy.

"You just wait until I get out of the hospital, Mr. Carter."

"I can't wait, Mrs. Carter."

My eyes close and I let the moment sink in. "Call me that again."

"Mrs. Carter."

"You're lucky I can't move, otherwise I'd jump you right here."

Once again, I wince as I chuckle, stopping me abruptly.

"I'd rather have you healed and well, then I will let you do anything you want to me, *nena*."

"Anything?" My brow arches with challenge.

"Anything," he replies, no doubt in his mind.

Just as there isn't any when he smashes his lips to mine again. Of course, that happens before we hear a knock on the door and need to pull away. Especially when immediately after the entire room gets filled with people: family and friends. Everyone we care about.

MASON

A month later

Four weeks have passed since Ensley got shot.

A month since I've found out the truth about who she really is—my wife. Although my memories are fuzzy and nothing else has come back to me, I am happy the way it is. Even if there are recollections I'd die to know and to remember, what we have now is more important. We have the now and we have the future to make new memories that I will remember.

It's been a month also since my biological grandfather and his goons set our home on fire forcing us to now rent a flat. But truth be told, we are not going back into that house. Not after what happened. Not after I nearly lost the woman I love there.

Although there was mainly the first floor that fell casualty to the roaring flames, most of the second floor was saved and everything in the attic was still in pretty good condition. The contents inside the boxes in the attic were the proof of all our memories. The ones Ensley put away so I wouldn't see them and discover we are married before I pulled my head out of my ass the second time around.

This time, I did do it for good. This time around, there is no more denying. Only fighting. For us. For each other. For our son. Because we have already put the papers in for us to adopt Zane officially. It will be a long process and we're aware of it, however, as long as he gets to stay with us, we're all happy.

With the bar up and running, Luke and Ella have taken point on it for now while I look after Ensley. More like making sure she doesn't overdo something since this has become her specialty recently.

During this month, Ensley has been recuperating and healing after the surgery. She is still in recovery, but the scars already formed where the bullets pierced through her flesh. It is our reminder of what has happened. A reminder of just how fleeting life could be. But my woman is strong. She's been recovering like a champion. Hence why the past week, she has also been trying to jump me more often than not, tempting me to break my inner promise that I will only touch her when I know she's properly healed. It is safe to say that I did touch her, with my fingers and mouth.

"I'm so fucking lucky to have you, *nena*," I whisper in her ear, my arm draped around her waist to bring her flush to my bare chest.

"Prove it," she drawls, her hips rolling over my cock that twitches happily at the morning awakening.

She is such a tease.

Begging me to take her.

Daring me to have her.

Oh, *joder*, I'm losing my mind with need and unbridled desire for her. To touch her. To claim her.

"It's been so long, Mase."

Her hips circle, her body shakes while she moves over me.

"Please, baby," she begs and the affect in the sound of her voice is my near undoing. "I want you to tie my hands up and drive your cock inside me so deep and hard. I want your lips on mine while you make me come around you. Please, baby, I need you to touch me."

Fucking hell.

How can I refuse her when she begs me for my cock this beautifully?

Especially when she awakes the beast within me that has been raging for the last month with an incessant craving for her.

With Ensley laying now on her back, I lift my weight and

prop myself on top of her. Her green eyes gleam with mischief and her lips twitch with a winning grin.

She might feel like she won, but it certainly feels like winning to me too.

The smirk disappears a moment later when her gaze focuses on mine, noting the unmitigated necessity for her. She can feel the potency of my need for her especially when I don't waste even a fraction of a second before I claim her delicious lips with mine.

She moans in my mouth as though it has been decades since she felt the taste of my lips. To be completely honest, I know that to me if feels as if centuries have passed since I last tasted her lips, although I've kissed her mouth just earlier when I stepped behind her in the shower. After we had our morning routine, we decided to take advantage that Zane isn't roaming around the house just yet and have a lay-in. Or more concisely that I made the decision, only so Ensley could continue having her rest.

Our tongues tangle and duel, and Ensley's beautiful submission comes like it usually does and my mouth takes over hers, deepening the kiss further.

Her hot palms trace up the skin of my back, my muscle tensing and straining beneath that roving touch that burns me.

It is my turn to groan when her fingers dig into my ass cheeks. A sound so primal as it reverberates through her too.

Her hands are not the only ones that rove, though. Mine seem to be in an undeclared contest with hers, touching and skimming every inch of skin they can find. Especially when my hand slips beneath her large t-shirt to find her hot flesh.

"Are you sure, *nena?*" I ask after I rip my mouth from hers.

My hand continues to touch her skin while my eyes lock onto hers. And, *ai joder*, what I see in her gorgeous darkened green gaze is sheer, unmitigated need.

If I thought even for a second that I will find doubt in her eyes, now I am proven wrong. There is not even the smallest scintilla of doubt in her orbs.

Not a splinter.

Above all, they don't only tell me she wants me. They tell me she fucking needs me. Just like I need her. More than I need to take my next breath.

"Please, baby."

Ensley vocalizes the exact thing I see in her eyes. Her voice filled with craving and a passion that courses through me instantly at hearing the affect in her tone.

But it runs through me with an unrestrained feeling of possession and greed. Something only she wakes in me.

"I want you on top of me, *nena*. I want to see your hungry eyes get even hungrier when you're so close to coming around my cock. I want you to move nice and slow, got it?"

"I'm not gonna break, Mase," she insists.

Chuckling, I cup her cheek and brush my lips over hers. "I know, *nena*, but I will. I'll come faster than a schoolboy and that doesn't speak well for my reputation."

This time around, Ensley is the one to giggle. "What reputation?"

Ai, Deus, the tease in her voice.

My brow quirks at her challengingly. "Don't dare me to punish you, *nena*, because instead of slippin' inside that pussy, I'll be slippin' in your ass and fuck it until you're so close to the edge, you're crazy for it."

The response to my warning comes in the form of a shudder. One so beautiful that I feel it right through me too.

"Or is this what you want, *nena*? Have I fucked your ass before?"

Her head moves in assent.

"My dirty, sultry brat. You like it when I claim you there, don't you?"

Once again, her nod comes. Yet, that is not sufficient answer for me.

"Word, *nena*. Give me words."

"I love it because I feel completely claimed and possessed by you."

Holy hell!

What have I gotten myself into with this wife of mine?

"You want me to give that to you? You want me to completely claim and possess this tight body of yours right now?"

"Mason," she gripes, another tremble quaking her form beneath mine. "Yes."

"On your hands and knees then, *miña muller sensual*," I

demand, pushing back on my knees to give her room to do my bidding.

With my gaze fixated on hers, I wait a tick.

I don't know what has her eyes sparkle more, my command or that I called her "*my sultry wife*" in Galician. Maybe both. Whatever it is, it ignites her gaze. And when it moves over my bare, tattooed chest, there's something that flickers in her orbs.

Without hesitation, Ensley pushes her back up and her scorching palms roam from the waistband of my black boxer briefs, up my abdomen that tightens beneath her touch. Then they move further up while her lips press softly just below the waistband.

"*Nena*," I caution, my voice deep and guttural.

Her sparkling green eyes lift to meet mine and my hand moves to her face, my thumb tracing her lower lip. There is no uncertainty when Ensley catches my thumb between her lips and sucks on it as though it is my cock she has in her mouth—fact that has my dick twitching beneath the confinement. There is also no faltering in her gaze as she holds mine as though to see how crazy she drives me with need. But when her lips let go, they travel up my abdomen and get to my chest. She kisses just above my heart, the muscle jerking, before she moves to my other pec, her tongue rolling over the silver barbell piercing.

As though she's done it so many times before—which she probably has—, her tongue gets replaced by her lips that dust over my nipple, only to then alternate between circling it and the piercing with her tongue and kissing around it.

"*Joder*," I curse under my breath.

Unable to take the torture any longer, I hook my hand in her hair, pulling at it gently but enough to wrench her lips from my skin.

"On your hands and knees," I command again, getting an all-knowing smirk from her.

Oh, yes, I have no doubt now that she's done this many times before. She knows the effect it has on me and how crazy it drives me. Because she knows the response of my body to her touch just as well as I know how her own body croons beneath my caresses.

As she turns on her knees with that proud grin still plastered on her gorgeous face, my hand collides with her ass cheek, drawing a salacious sound from her. One that is half-yelp of surprise and half-moan of pleasure. But it is a sound that has me groaning.

Without hesitation and with delicious submission, Ensley drops to her elbows and pushes her ass shamelessly into my dick after I yank the underwear down her legs and the t-shirt off her body.

"Come on, Carter, are you going to satisfy your wife, or will she need to take matters into her own hands?"

Again, my hand smacks her butt cheek, causing her to launch forward a little. Only for a second though, because on the next tick, I have her back on my length and she rubs her delectably luscious ass against me.

I let her have it for a moment or two, until I know an instance longer would be enough to have me come in my underwear. Hence, I draw back and throw my leg over the edge of the bed, then the other to push to my full height before I go to the nightstand. Pulling the drawer open, I retrieve what I need and return to bed, knowing damn well she follows all my moves.

Retrieving my previous spot behind her, I lock eyes with her over the length of her back and pop the cap of the bottle open with a smirk. One that doesn't ebb when hunger coats her gaze. It gets wider when a sigh of anticipation escapes her, dancing in the air and into my ears.

With the bottle upside-down, I squeeze it just above and between the crack of her ass cheeks, a tremble coursing through her body while her eyes close for the briefest of instances. When there is enough lube on her flesh, I snap the cap back on and throw the bottle on the tangled sheets.

My eyes remain connected to hers while I rub in the slippery liquid over her ass. I then proceed to tease her tight hole with the pad of my thumb as I slowly lean over her back to capture her mouth. I feel her moan reverberating into my throat, egging me to continue with my ministrations.

Still with my mouth on hers while our lips feast on each other's taste, I feel her shift and one of her hands reaches between her legs just the moment my index finger slips inside of her. I tease and prepare her to take me there, first with one, then with my middle finger joining in.

"Make yourself come, *nena*. Rub that sweet pussy for your

man."

Xesucristo!

(Jesus Christ!)

And how she listens to that demand.

She rubs her clit while I finger-fuck her ass and kiss her mouth as though our lives depend on it. My cock throbs in my boxer briefs and fuck if I can wait any longer until I'm inside her. But I do until I feel her body ripple under mine and hear her moan pierce my ears.

So fucking beautiful as she trembles beneath me.

Pulling her body against mine, I hold her close, her head leaning against my shoulder as she catches her breath. My lips take advantage of the exposed skin on the column of her neck and dust kisses over the heated flesh.

Ensley's eyes close and her hands rest on my thighs while she rubs her naked ass on my cock. But they rest there only for a tick because in the next, her fingers dig into the fabric of my boxers and pull at it until she frees my aching cock. I lose the heat of her hips for an instant while she drags my underwear down to my knees.

Her hand wraps around my shaft and Ensley gives me a couple of pumps.

"I need you, Mase," she breathes out.

She doesn't need to tell me twice. I pull away from her hot body and pull my boxer briefs the rest of the way down my legs until I kick them to the floor, then I drop with my back against the pillows.

Her eyes catch fire when I reach for the bottle of lube and pour some in my hand before she watches me wrap it around my cock, pumping several times to cover myself with the liquid.

"Come here, *nena.*"

And I don't need to repeat myself. I don't because she is eager to do as I tell her. She's even more enthusiastic when she comes closer and throws her leg over my thighs straddling me.

My eyes take advantage of the beautiful view and drink in the sight of her on top of me. Her gorgeous green eyes aflame. Her skin hot. Her tits perky with the nipples hard. Her taut abdomen. Her sweet folds parted to fit my cock in between while her wetness drips on my flesh. She has my heart skip a beat.

Yet, what has my heart lurch to the pit of my stomach are the scars on the left side of her chest. One higher—the bullet that went straight through. The other one is lower—the bullet that could have claimed her life. The one that could have taken her away from me.

With my back knifing upward, I wrap my arms around her, resting them on her back to feel the skin beneath my palms.

Unconsciously, the pad of my index traces the tattoo while my gaze remains locked on hers.

"It's because of you I got this tattoo. You always called me your tigress in Galician when I'd get feisty."

My heart fills up to the brim with possession at the thought that she marked her skin permanently with me.

But when my gaze drops again to the scars, she immediately understands what my eyes are saying.

"I'm fine, baby. I'm here with you."

"I thought I'll lose you," I admit. "I was so fucking scared, *nena*. I was because I don't know how to do life without you."

Her hands cup my face.

"And you don't need to learn to because I'm here." She moves her hips in my lap, her body pressing further into mine. "Feel me?"

I nod.

Oh, yeah, I do.

Reaching back, she removes my hand and places it on her breast, tightening her fingers atop mine in a sign to squeeze. I do and her eyes roll in the back of her head while a moan escapes her.

Without any scintilla of doubt, Ensley pushes me back to the mattress and lifts to her knees. Her hand reaches behind and wraps around my dick that is hard as a steel rod. She rears a little before she leans forward a fraction more to give herself room, then she slowly eases the head of my cock inside her tight hole.

A carnal groan tumbles out of my chest and her teeth assault her bottom lip while she gently adjusts to the intrusion and lets my length push through the ring of muscles and then takes more of me.

"*Joder*," I cuss aloud, feeling how tightly her walls squeeze me.

"Oh, fuck," she joins in when I rest my hands on her ass and spread her cheeks, driving myself deeper.

I see stars when she stops only to lift her hips up and just as gently to drop them down. She fucks herself on my cock, using him at the pace she sets, while I'm a mere spectator, too captivated by her beauty on top of me and by all the sensations.

"Kiss me."

It is a demand.

Because I need her.

And she sees it, leaning forward even more until her chest presses against mine and her lips capture mine.

Just like that, she continues claiming me just as much as I claim her. Especially when I begin pumping my hips from beneath and she meets me thrust for thrust, and slips a hand between our joined bodies so she can rub at her empty pussy.

"Oh, god, more," she demands when I thrust deep.

I give her more. I do until we're both sweating and panting. Until we both reach our peak together and fall over the edge. I come inside her, and her own release drips down my thighs while her ass spasms around my girth.

"Holy cow," Ensley breathes out with a chuckle.

She can say that again.

"How are you feeling, *nena?*"

"Absolutely, completely and utterly claimed," she replies, resting her head on my chest.

I cannot help the chuckle from rocking my body before I kiss her head. "As much as my ego is pleased with your answer, I meant—"

"Yeah, I know." Her neck straightens and her eyes meet mine. "I feel fully recovered. Your dick has healing powers."

This time, I let out a loud laugh. "Glad you think so."

"You shoulda given it to me a while ago." She winks. "Simmer down now, you're gonna wake Zane up."

Seriousness takes over my features. "I love you, *nena.*"

"I love you too, baby."

Her lips drop to mine for a short yet passionate kiss before we pull away and jump again in the shower to clean ourselves up, and get a start on the day.

Of course, we can barely keep our hands off each other in the shower too. Even when we finish and pat ourselves dry, then put clothes on, my hands still touch everything they can.

"Mommy? Daddy?" The sweet, gentle voice pulls us apart, and our eyes turn to Zane who now stands in the doorway.

"Morning, buddy."

"Good morning, my beautiful little man."

We both greet him, and I rush to pick him up, dropping a kiss on his cheek as I ruffle his tousled hair before he leans in for Ensley to give him one too.

"Are you hungry, sweetie?"

He nods eagerly at Ensley's question.

"Great, let's make you some breakfast then."

At that, Ensley spins on her feet and pads out of the room, while I turn to follow her with Zane still in my arms.

"What's that?" My son's curious question has me just as inquisitively wondering what he means.

Once I look over my shoulder and see what he's looking at, I regret doing so. His finger points at the abandoned bottle of lube on the bed.

"Mommy needed a massage," I lie swiftly.

His eyes narrow, nose scrunches up and then he lifts his shoulders.

I cannot fight the chuckle from thundering out of me at how sweet and adorable he is. Our son. He may not be our flesh and blood, but he is ours. If there's someone who knows a thing or two about being raised and loved unconditionally by a mother who does not share any bloodline, that someone is me. And bloodline or not, Zane is now our son.

Ensley turns and her smile widens at the sight of Zane and I padding down behind her.

And this woman, she is mine.

She has always been mine and mine alone. When I denied her, she fought for us. When I did not deserve her, she still chose to love me. When I was not worthy of her, she gave me hope that one day maybe I will. When I didn't deserve her love, she still gave it to me. When I was lost, she helped me find my way back —to her, to us.

Ensley is the love of my life.

She makes me complete.

And for the rest of my life, I will prove to her that I was worth fighting for.

JESSE

My heavy steps stomp up the hall toward the office and throw the door open once I get there.

After the director of the FBI stormed into my office, dropped a folder on my desk, and told me to get my ass to my brother's urgently, I did exactly that.

"Something crawled up your arse?"

Zaiden Lewis is such a cocky, sarcastic asshole. As much as he is my younger brother by two years, he's a goddamn dickhead sometimes.

"Hi to you too, prick."

"Wanker," he reverts, his British vocabulary clearer than his accent, although it is still quite strong even after over twenty years in the States.

He and I are half-brothers.

We share the same motherfucker of a father. We also share the same abhor for the man. The man who played with the feelings of two beautiful women, pushing them both toward self-destruction.

"What's your deal with the Director? I know how you work, bro. Usually, Mr. President has you on speed dial."

"This isn't my usual gig because this isn't a usual case to me. Or just a case for that matter. You'll get all the information once IT comes in," he explains, his blue eyes sharp and jaw tight.

What is the whole secrecy about?

National Security?

"Where is Coop?"

Cooper is the guy in charge of IT for Hellhound Corps. If there is even the smallest piece of information, he finds it. That guy is a treasure finder because more than once the information he dug out ended up saving the lives of many people.

"Found love and shit like that, and abandoned us."

"So who's your new IT guy?"

"*He* is a *she* and *she* stands right behind you."

It is on his statement that I turn, an intrigued smile on my face.

Right away, I see red, and the smile disappears.

"What the fuck is she doing here?"

There she is.

The bane of my whole fucking existence. The person I hate with every fiber in my being. And it says a hell of a lot since until five years ago, my father was top of that list. Because in this world, there's only one person I hate more than I hate him. She now stands in front of me, chocolate brown eyes and smile filled with pride, just as unapologetic as she's always been.

Fuck, I hate her.

I loathe her.

Her and all that she reminds me of. That I'm just like *him*. That I'm never good enough for good things.

She's the reason why I've been left at the altar by my fiancée. She's the reason why now I only have women for a night. She's the reason why I don't trust them. I thought we were friends— yes, she was my fiancée's friend first, but we became friends regardless. Foolish of me to believe so. Especially when her words from over five years ago still resound in my head as though it was yesterday: *"What do you want me to say? Do you want me to tell you he's not good enough for you? He's not good enough for you."*

She is the fucking shrew who turned my fiancée against me and my life upside-down.

She's Alexandra Ivan.

The woman with the look of an angel, but with the soul of the devil. I was once fooled by that sweet voice and bewitching appearance. That ain't happening again and I won't anyone be deceived by her because now I know her true colors. Now I know how rotten her soul is.

* * *

When FBI Supervisory Special Agent Jesse Lewis hates somebody, he abhors them with every fiber of his being.

IT Specialist Alexandra Ivan is that person for him. The one he hates with all he has for what she did to him five years ago.

Find out if she'll make him change his mind in the next installment of *Badges of the Capital*, **Ace**.

ACKNOWLEDGMENTS

To you—*the reader*: I thank you.

Appreciation does not even begin to sum up how I feel toward all of you. Thank you from the bottom of my heart and with all the sincerity in this world for picking up Mason's and Ensley's story. For rooting for them ever since you've heard about them in Luke's and Ella's story. For waiting patiently—or impatiently—for their turn to get their beautiful happily ever after.

OTHER BOOKS BY MISHA BLAKE

Badges of the Capital Series
Flash

Cutter

The Rayton Brothers Series
Unraveling Shaylee (Book 1)

Unraveled (Book 1.5—to be read after Book 2)

Denying Red (Book 2)

Denied (Book 2.5)

Protecting Shannon (Book 3)

Protected (Book 3.5)

Sinners of the City
The Sinner's Deceit (Book 1)

The Sinner's Deceit Special Edition Cover

ABOUT THE AUTHOR

Misha Blake is a Contemporary Romance author, who after a long postponement, now follows one of her dreams—being a writer.

She invites you to embark on a journey of scorching deep romance with Alpha heroes who know how to treat the women they dare falling for, and heroines who are no damsels in distress but stubbornly crawling their way into the heroes' hearts.

Her favorite genre to write is romance with a dash—or maybe more than just an iota—of suspense.

Join her newsletter for details on future releases.
Stalk her on Instagram and Facebook.

There are many more books in this fan fiction world than listed here,
for an up-to-date list go to www.AcesPress.com

You can also visit our Amazon page at:
http://www.amazon.com/author/operationalpha

Special Forces: Operation Alpha World
Christie Adams: Charity's Heart
Linzi Baxter: Unlocking Dreams
Misha Blake: Flash
Anna Blakely: Rescuing Gracelynn
Julia Bright: Saving Lorelei
Cara Carnes: Protecting Mari
Kendra Mei Chailyn: Beast
Melissa Kay Clarke: Rescuing Annabeth
Samantha A. Cole: Handling Haven
Lorelei Confer: Protecting Sara
KaLyn Cooper: Spring Unveiled
Janie Crouch: Storm
Jordan Dane: Redemption for Avery
Tarina Deaton: Found in the Lost
Riley Edwards: Protecting Olivia
Dorothy Ewels: Knight's Queen
Lila Ferrari: Protecting Joy
Nicole Flockton: Protecting Maria
Hope Ford: Rescuing Karina
Michele Gwynn: Rescuing Emma
Desiree Holt: Protecting Maddie
Kris Jacen, Be With Me
Jesse Jacobson: Protecting Honor
Rayne Lewis: Justice for Mary
Callie Love & Ann Omasta: Hawaii Hottie
JM Madden: Rescuing Olivia
A.M. Mahler: Griffin
Ellie Masters: Sybil's Protector
Trish McCallan: Hero Under Fire
Rachel McNeely: The SEAL's Surprise Baby
KD Michaels: Saving Laura
Olivia Michaels: Protecting Harper

Annie Miller: Securing Willow
Keira Montclair: Wolf and the Wild Scots
MJ Nightingale: Protecting Beauty
Melinda Owens: Betraying Katie
Victoria Paige: Reclaiming Izabel
Danielle Pays: Defending Sarina
Lainey Reese: Protecting New York
KeKe Renée: Protecting Bria
TL Reeve and Michele Ryan: Extracting Mateo
Deanna L. Rowley: Saving Veronica
Angela Rush: Charlotte
Rose Smith: Saving Satin
Lynne St. James: SEAL's Spitfire
Sarah Stone: Shielding Grace
Jen Talty: Burning Desire
Reina Torres, Rescuing Hi'ilani
LJ Vickery: Circus Comes to Town
R. C. Wynne: Shadows Renewed

Delta Team Three Series
Lori Ryan: Nori's Delta
Becca Jameson: Destiny's Delta
Lynne St James, Gwen's Delta
Elle James: Ivy's Delta
Riley Edwards: Hope's Delta

Police and Fire: Operation Alpha World
Freya Barker: Burning for Autumn
B.P. Beth: Scott
Jane Blythe: Salvaging Marigold
Julia Bright, Justice for Amber
Hadley Finn: Exton
Emily Gray: Shelter for Allegra
Alexa Gregory: Backdraft
Deanndra Hall: Shelter for Sharla
Jenna Harte: Dead But Not Forgotten
India Kells: Shadow Killer
Amber Kuhlman: Protecting Paisley
Reina Torres: Justice for Sloane
Aubree Valentine, Justice for Danielle

Maddie Wade: Finding English
Laine Vess: Justice for Lauren

Tarpley VFD Series
Silver James, Fighting for Elena
Deanndra Hall, Fighting for Carly
Haven Rose, Fighting for Calliope
MJ Nightingale, Fighting for Jemma
TL Reeve, Fighting for Brittney
Nicole Flockton, Fighting for Nadia

As you know, this book included at least one character from Susan Stoker's books. To check out more, see below.

SEAL Team Hawaii Series
Finding Elodie
Finding Lexie
Finding Kenna
Finding Monica
Finding Carly (Oct 2022)
Finding Ashlyn (Feb 2023)
Finding Jodelle (July 2023)

Eagle Point Search & Rescue
Searching for Lilly
Searching for Elsie
Searching for Bristol (Nov 2022)
Searching for Caryn (April 2023)
Searching for Finley (TBA)
Searching for Heather (TBA)
Searching for Khloe (TBA)

The Refuge Series
Deserving Alaska (Aug 2022)
Deserving Henley (Jan 2023)
Deserving Reese (May 2023)
Deserving Cora (TBA)
Deserving Lara (TBA)
Deserving Maisy (TBA)
Deserving Ryleigh (TBA)

Delta Team Two Series
Shielding Gillian
Shielding Kinley
Shielding Aspen
Shielding Jayme (novella)
Shielding Riley
Shielding Devyn
Shielding Ember
Shielding Sierra

SEAL of Protection: Legacy Series

Securing Caite (FREE!)
Securing Brenae (novella)
Securing Sidney
Securing Piper
Securing Zoey
Securing Avery
Securing Kalee
Securing Jane

Delta Force Heroes Series

Rescuing Rayne (FREE!)
Rescuing Aimee (novella)
Rescuing Emily
Rescuing Harley
Marrying Emily (novella)
Rescuing Kassie
Rescuing Bryn
Rescuing Casey
Rescuing Sadie (novella)
Rescuing Wendy
Rescuing Mary
Rescuing Macie (novella)
Rescuing Annie

Badge of Honor: Texas Heroes Series

Justice for Mackenzie (FREE!)
Justice for Mickie
Justice for Corrie
Justice for Laine (novella)
Shelter for Elizabeth
Justice for Boone
Shelter for Adeline
Shelter for Sophie
Justice for Erin
Justice for Milena
Shelter for Blythe
Justice for Hope
Shelter for Quinn
Shelter for Koren

Shelter for Penelope

SEAL of Protection Series

Protecting Caroline (FREE!)
Protecting Alabama
Protecting Fiona
Marrying Caroline (novella)
Protecting Summer
Protecting Cheyenne
Protecting Jessyka
Protecting Julie (novella)
Protecting Melody
Protecting the Future
Protecting Kiera (novella)
Protecting Alabama's Kids (novella)
Protecting Dakota

New York Times, *USA Today* and *Wall Street Journal* Bestselling Author Susan Stoker has a heart as big as the state of Tennessee where she lives, but this all American girl has also spent the last fourteen years living in Missouri, California, Colorado, Indiana, and Texas. She's married to a retired Army man who now gets to follow *her* around the country.

www.stokeraces.com
www.AcesPress.com
susan@stokeraces.com

Made in the USA
Coppell, TX
21 July 2022